Then at last Amanda

against his chest, but sh

Figuring that the late hour and the fatigue were doing strange things to her mind, she dismissed it as her imagination. But in the silence between them, away from the city and the noise, the only breathing she heard was her own.

I must be losing it. But as she stared up into the sky, too many things fell into her mind, persistent in their logic. Amanda had never seen Jesse during the daylight, had never seen him more than perhaps taste food, didn't know what he did for a living other than "freelance computer work", and now she couldn't hear a heartbeat nor him breathing.

"Jesse?" she queried, her hesitancy showing in her voice.

Feeling him freeze behind her, she wondered if he knew what was on her mind, and thought to phrase her next words with caution.

"You're not a normal guy, are you? I mean," she continued, trying not to rush through her words, let alone sound nervous, "not that I'm...all that normal myself, and all, but...." Her voice trailed off. Amanda did not know what to say, or how to say it.

Many moments passed without a response. With great deliberateness, he ran his hands through her hair, and she delighted in the feel of his fingertips as they coursed through the strands, brushing against her neck as soft as silk.

In that moment she remembered their first dinner outing, when Jesse showed her the Latin magickal text, which referred to strange allegories, symbols and various arcana. She recalled that the text kept referencing "blood" in some mystical context.

"Jesse?" Her voice was quieter, and she was no longer so certain that she was crazy.

Your time has come.

What others say about this book:

"Adrianne Brennan spins a tale that enthralls and delights..."
~ 5 Dark Divas by Kissa, Dark Diva Reviews

"Adrianne Brennan wove a fascinating and imaginative story..."
~ 4 Tombstones by Megan, Bitten by Books Reviews

"Blood of the Dark Moon is as engaging as it is well researched."
~ 4 Halos from Andrew, In Pure Spirit

"If you are looking for a good vampire read, you have found it!"
~ Missy Brown, PNR Reviews

Other books by this Adrianne Brennan:

Blood and Mint Chocolates
The Longest Night
A Memory on Record
The Oath: a chapter book series

Blood of the Dark Moon

by

Adrianne Brennan

Freya's Bower.com ©2008

Culver City, CA

Blood of the Dark Moon

For information on the cover illustration and design, contact
Valerie Tibbs.

Editor: M. E. Ellis

ISBN: 978-1-935013-51-8 – ebook
978-1-936222-07-0 - paperback

Freya's Bower.com
P.O. Box 4897
Culver City, CA 90231-4897

Printed in The United States of America

Dedication

To Robin, Mark and Mary for being my faithful editors—thank you SO much for your encouragement, support, and everlasting friendship. To Eric and so many of my other friends who kept pushing me to succeed no matter what—thank you for keeping the lamp lit. A special thank you to the staff of Freya's Bower—especially Emmy!—for being awesome. To those who knew me back in the days of science fiction fan writing and pushed me to go as far as my Muse would travel—thanks for standing by me! Last but not least I dedicate this novel and those that come after it to Apollo, the Muses, my Holy Guardian Angel and All Those Who Shalt Not Be Named: I give you warm hugs, offerings, and tribute. PROS TON THEON! I could not have done this without you all.

Legal Citations

Various quotes from *Liber Al vel Legis* ("The Book of the Law"), Aleister Crowley.

Blood of the Dark Moon

Sing to me, O Muse, of a time outside time and a place outside place,
Where creatures not living and not dead walk the earth,
Where those who can see, aspire for rebirth,
And nighttime is neither time nor place for mirth.
Sing to me of sorrow, sing to me of hope, sing to me of pain,
Sing to me of ecstasy, sing to me of love and passion's sting,
And, when hence I have written all that I can bear and heard all you can sing,
I pray to you, O dear Muse, that you might sing it all to me again.

Chapter One

"The Moirai have their hands in this...."

I once dreamt of a storm.

The dark gray sky hovered threateningly; the wind blew over the landscape, picking up speed. The trees stood vividly against the spectacle, defiant bright green wooden giants holding their own against the weather, bending but not breaking. I stood next to a nondescript building, gazing at the heavens above as the wind blew the leaves and dust along the ground. The sky stretched on forever into oblivion, and the world contained nothing but shadows. Thunder rang in my ears.

The land before me screamed with its terrible beauty. It embodied life at its most dangerous yet seductive, the epitome of nature at its most powerful, which forced me to gaze upon my own mortality. It struck me deeply that this world imprisoned us, forcing us to become completely a part of this wondrous chaos. The wild storm continued to grow, its presence beautiful yet mercilessly devouring all into the void. Such divine madness.

It left me standing in awe.

Lightning illuminated the window. Amanda glanced up from the computer monitor and watched the jagged bolt tear across the sky. It made her think of Zeus and his thunderbolts. Inwardly, she wondered why the lightning appeared, and another part of her answered: *The game, it's all about the game—the divine play.*

She kept thinking about the dream from the previous night. Its vividness stuck out in her mind, and she couldn't shake it.

A woman stood in front of her with curly blonde hair. Try as she might, Amanda could no longer remember what her eyes looked like or what color they were except that they seemed both incredibly bright and dark at the same time. The blonde woman's clothing appeared non-conspicuous enough: short black leather jacket, blue jeans, and a white t-shirt. Very normal. Almost too normal.

Amanda glanced up at the woman's face and instantly regretted it. The blonde's intense gaze smacked her with a nearly physical blow. In spite of the shock, her feet weighed heavily on the ground, rooted to the spot. A sense of calm swept over her. Her surroundings, as she recalled them, were quite commonplace.

They shared a table in a coffeehouse where they drank tea,

discussing something about Graeco-Roman witchcraft. Graeco-Roman magick played a huge role in her thesis, so this was an apt topic for her to discuss. Hence she dove in eagerly, mentioning all of her source texts and the correlations that she'd discovered. She delighted in discussing the evidence that cultures had borrowed much from each other, more than what the popular *Greek Magical Papyri in Translation* indicated, and so on.

Then the conversation abruptly changed.

"I'm Persephone."

She could only nod. Of course Persephone dwelled in the woman now seated beside her. Here she sat, drinking her tea with Persephone in a coffeehouse, chatting with her about esoteric concepts and philosophy. The goddess acted friendly and approachable—even human. Her affable nature caused all apprehension about those strange eyes to depart.

The more she drank her tea, the more she forgot the goddess's eyes.

Amanda pondered the rest of the dream, the events of which played out less comprehensibly than the rest. Something about performing a ritual, a pit opening in the middle of the room, and a hideous, three-headed monster that she feared would devour her. She perceived that Persephone wished for her to jump into the pit, yet she couldn't bring herself to do it. The goddess just nodded as if this was expected, and disappointment appeared to be absent in her reaction. Amanda couldn't handle the result, at least not yet. All in due time.

That beast terrified her. And there was no way, she decided fervently, she would jump in unless she possessed a greater certainty that the goddess or some other deity waited on the other side.

"During the winter, I miss my mother," Persephone told her absently. *"But right now, I miss my husband."*

* * * *

A crash of thunder brought Amanda back to her work. *Gotta finish this before it gets late,* she mused. *I can't afford to be late.* With a few quick keystrokes, she rewrote a sentence that dissatisfied her. After relentless typing and retyping, she checked her watch. Making her meeting meant saving her work now and getting the hell out of her apartment. Besides, the weather outside didn't look very cooperative.

She quickly strolled through the city streets, dodging through the crowds. The coffeehouse that served as the meeting place resided some blocks away, and at this point seven minutes remained before the mutually arranged time. And she hated being late. Being late never looked good, especially for a first time introduction. It lacked both professionalism and etiquette.

I'm sure he'll forgive me, she reassured herself. *But at least it's not—*

A sprinkle of water hit her face. She looked up. It started to pour.

Raining....

Amanda ran down the street, taking advantage of the crowd already going through the crosswalk in spite of the oncoming traffic. She made it to the coffeehouse with two minutes to spare, ordered herself a mug of mocha, and sat down at one of the tables in the corner. The too-hot mocha burnt her tongue, but it gave her something to put in her system before she met some guy whose first name and email address were all she knew—that and an apparent mutual interest in ancient studies. The magazine from one of the tables and the mocha distracted her from her nervousness, and after a time, the rest of the coffeehouse.

She thought she heard someone calling her name. She lifted her head from her magazine to see a young man who appeared to be in his late twenties, perhaps early thirties. He looked at her with intense, dark brown eyes.

"Amanda? You are Amanda, right?"

She smiled. "Yes, that's me. You must be Jesse. Here, have a seat." She gestured towards the chair on the opposite end of the coffee table. He took it with a grateful grin. She noted that his chosen attire included a leather jacket, a dress shirt, and a pair of slacks—all in black. A silver chain hung from his neck, but she couldn't see the bottom of it, for the rest lay concealed under his shirt. His short, slightly wavy dark brown hair was neatly combed. One thought leapt to her mind: *Business goth, perhaps? I wonder if he's Italian?* She figured probably Italian but of mixed heritage, for his skin was paler than average, especially against his attire and dark hair and eyes. His smooth features reminded her of a Roman sculpture.

Jesse smiled, and she realized that his features appeared quite striking to her, even by her particular standards. His email initially brought all of the academic stereotypes to mind; Jesse sounded very intelligent and thoughtful. It made her anticipate meeting a very prim-and-proper looking gentleman. J Crew with a side of geek, perhaps.

"Do you come here often?" he asked. "I hear their vanilla chai is pretty good."

She blinked, realizing that she had been staring at him. "Vanilla chai? No, I've never tried it. I've come here maybe once or twice. I typically don't have time outside of my studies," she added in an almost apologetic tone.

He chuckled. "Yeah, so I figured." His face got serious, and he rubbed his hands together. "So," he said, "I hear you're an expert on Ancient Greece. What got you into the subject?"

Amanda sipped her mocha before answering. "My religion."

His eyebrows went up slightly. "Your religion?"

"Yes. My beliefs are based on Ancient Greek religion." She gave him a shy smile. "I'm actually a devotee of Apollo."

He blinked hard, clearly taken aback. "Really?"

"Yup." She took another swallow from her mug. Of course, his response would satisfy the litmus test of how well he could stand being in the same room as her, let alone engage in a conversation....

"Great." He grinned. "I'm actually a Kemetic myself."

She nearly choked on her drink. He laughed quietly as she sputtered and coughed. "I take it that I don't look the part?" he asked with a fairly amused tone, taking in her reaction.

"I, um," she managed to choke out, "wasn't expecting that. I typically run into either atheists or Christians who think that my soul needs saving, or something. And don't even ask about the academics." She coughed some more, feeling her cheeks grow warm—and not due to swallowing her mocha the wrong way, either. She tried not to cringe in her embarrassment.

"You okay?"

"Yeah, just went down the wrong pipe." She gave him a quick smile of reassurance. "Looks like we have some things in common. But, I gotta ask, why is a Kemetic like you interested in my, um, research about Ancient Greek religion and Apollo?"

He looked at her questioningly before glancing in the direction of the counter where people were ordering coffee, then turned his attention to her again. "Actually, my interest is somewhat on the, well, unusual side. I'm fascinated more by the mystical elements in common between both religions." He gave her a lopsided grin, his friendly demeanor giving way suddenly to a shy awkwardness. "I'm sure that you know of the *Greek Magical Papyri*?"

"That mishmash of Greek, Egyptian, and Hebrew spells? Yes, along with several other books on ancient Greek magick on my shelf." She leaned back in her chair, completely intrigued by this guy. What exactly was he about? Curiosity struck her, and she dared to ask, "So, do you study, practice, or both?"

His mouth fell open slightly, but he closed it fast. "Since you ask...both, actually. I have an interest in magick and mysticism." He shrugged. "One of my many hobbies." He smiled.

"Ah." She half-smiled in return. She had no clue what to make of this individual whatsoever and wondered if he were completely out of his mind, or just easily impressed by women who attempted to earn an academic degree in unusual fields of study.

He leaned forward slightly and looked into her cup. "What are you drinking?"

"Mocha."

He nodded thoughtfully. "Mocha. Okay. I think I'll grab some and then I'll be right back."

"Gotcha. I'll be here." She watched him go to the counter and order the beverage and began wondering just who Jesse truly was. He didn't look like your standard occultist; aside from the all-black attire, he looked like someone who had just stepped out of a law office or some other professional building. Jesse also handled himself in a very assured, graceful manner—not to mention so far sounding reasonably intelligent and well spoken.

The fact that he was good-looking as hell also disturbed her slightly. Perhaps more than slightly, she admitted. She continued to sip her mocha thoughtfully, maintaining a casual expression on her face as she continued to watch him order at the counter.

Amanda hadn't dated anyone for a while; her studies kept her from socializing very often. She realized that she hadn't had much time to meet any potential significant others since high school. This side of things made what she had hoped would be a nice, professional meeting with an interesting conversation or two into a not-too-welcome distraction in the least. Amanda originally envisioned the potential of helping someone with their own research into the classics, particularly in her fields of study. She sighed, praying that this wouldn't keep her from finishing her thesis.

She frowned slightly, remembering his earlier words. Amanda also possessed a strong interest in theurgical practice. Being a devotee of a Greek deity renowned for oracles and divination, she frequently received dreams and visions from Him that later proved themselves accurate. Nothing about this man or her meeting with him came from Apollo in earlier dreams or visions—not a peep. This struck her as strange and seemed to imply that either this guy would prove unimportant in the long run and would fade from her life quickly, or...perhaps the oracular god had reasons for not telling her.

Either way, Jesse piqued her curiosity, and she wished to know more about him.

He returned with mocha in hand and sat back down in the chair. "Okay," he stated, "Now where were we?"

"Ancient Greek magick, I believe." She gave him an inquiring look. After all, this face-to-face meeting came about due to *his* email.

"Right. Ancient Greek magick." Jesse put down the drink and began to talk about the reasons for his interest in her thesis.

It struck Amanda that he seemed to know a bit more about her than she'd initially thought. After an extensive conversation on folk magick versus religious magick, the discussion somehow got into modern magickal practices. Apparently Jesse's studies spanned a number of subjects, including Golden Dawn and Thelemic work. She knew of the Golden Dawn and worked on her own as a solitary practitioner via her studies in books by Israel Regardie and the Ciceros, but he had her beat on knowledge of Thelema. He chattered enthusiastically about some ritual he referred to as "Reguli", which she had never heard of, and also referred to texts that he claimed resembled Thelema in some ways, but contained more ancient practices and beliefs.

Amanda tried to press him for more information, but he kept changing the subject. Her thesis work fascinated him, particularly in regards to personal religious practice in Ancient Greece, and thus he had assumed that she might know something of the more esoteric religious practices that also took place. Referring to himself as an "occult geek", he stated in the same breath that he wanted to learn more about Greece. He'd studied some of the Greek influences that made up Egyptian practice—and more in reverse—and wished to learn more from her. Rambling some more, he talked about how he "sorta stumbled into hearing about her work," and about his intense interest in the subjects she studied.

Curious, she thought skeptically, wondering if he belonged to one of those "trad Wiccans" who claimed to have witches in their family dating back to year 30,000 BC. Propriety kept her from chuckling out loud at the thought.

Glancing at the clock on the wall, he announced that it was getting late and would she like to continue the conversation at another time? She nodded, amazed to see that the clock indicated a time of eleven p.m. They had been talking for the past three hours. As she grabbed her bag, she observed that his mocha was hardly touched, if at all.

They started to walk out of the coffeehouse, and she noted appreciatively his opening the door for her. "So where did you grow up?" he asked. "I've been talking to you this whole time about ancient languages and cultures and have completely forgotten to ask you about your present." He smiled at her as if in apology.

"I grew up in Westchester County, but moved here after I graduated from high school. I've lived here in the city ever since."

The rain had finally stopped, and the streets held that damp smell mixed with the scent of city grime and street corner hot dogs.

"Do you like it here in the city?"

She nodded. "I like the pace."

"You must live off-campus, I presume?"

"Y-yes, I do."

"I can walk you to your building, if you like. How far away is it?"

She hesitated. She barely knew this guy, and giving him information about where she lived before she got to know him better didn't seem like a safe idea.

"I take the subway," she said. "But it's not far."

He nodded, looking at her facial expression, which she hoped appeared blank. Then he smiled. "I'll walk you to the subway, then."

She nearly sighed with relief. Jesse seemed like a nice guy, but certain habits were drilled into her that she couldn't get rid of, and being paranoid of new people—especially strange men—was one of them.

"Would you mind if I called you sometime? I had a great time tonight and, well, I'd like to speak with you again, if you don't mind."

Amanda glanced up at him. It occurred to her that he seemed shy beneath the surface. *Maybe he's interested in me romantically or something?* It was then that she realized that he wasn't that tall for a guy—probably wasn't more than 5'11" in comparison with her 5'6". *He seems to carry himself as if he were taller.*

She smiled at him brightly and gave him her cell phone number. He took it with a grateful nod, mumbling something about how he really enjoyed talking with her and he didn't know many people who shared his interests. A strong electric shock struck her deep at the core of her being as his fingers touched hers, accompanied by a heaviness in her chest.

The Moirai have their hands in this, she suddenly thought. She wondered if she would dream of him that night, and if so, what she would dream.

* * * *

Jesse watched her get onto the subway with a strange weight in his heart. Something about her demeanor convinced him that he had known her before, but he didn't know from where. Sadness seeped into him at the thought of parting from her so soon.

I'll have to give her a call sometime. Just not too quickly, in case she thinks I'm stalking her or something. He smiled, remembering her elfish face, her long, near-black hair which she had worn pulled back. He wished that she would wear it loose. She would look even prettier with her hair falling around her shoulders and back.

Amanda, in his eyes, embodied the perfect woman for him. Only.... He began kicking himself, realizing the potential consequences of his impetuous actions. He shouldn't have met her under such circumstances, even if after sundown. Undoubtedly people from his Clan were looking for him right now, and he would have to tell them that he had been performing research in a college library somewhere.

Research, he thought wryly, *which comes attached to a very lovely, young woman, a woman who is terribly, terribly mortal. And innocent....* Within Amanda's personality dwelled a crisp demeanor that often came with people who spent long hours in a library or a computer lab doing research, but she also gave off the vibe of being sheltered from the outside world, buried in her books and notes and not much else. He wondered briefly if she was even a virgin. Jesse hoped such inexperience wouldn't add to his list of potential woes—it would add one more complication if he decided to pursue her. He instantly regretted the thought, which made him feel hypocritical; after all, ages had passed since he had been with his long deceased Sire, who once blessed him with her presence as both his mentor and his lover.

Cringing, he berated himself for even thinking about chasing after a mortal woman—especially one so devoted to a sun god. Amanda, with her vivacious brightness, didn't belong with someone who couldn't go out in daylight hours without long sleeves, sunglasses, and certain types of magick.

He remembered the mocha that he'd ordered but hadn't drunk. Did she notice? Jesse shrugged off his paranoia. It wasn't like not drinking a cup of mocha marked you as a vampire.

With the piece of paper with her number on it still clenched in his hand, he made up his mind to call her. He would regret it later, no doubt, once she discovered his attentions towards her. Then again, his meeting with her marked him as a doomed man regardless. One more damning offense wouldn't be noticed, right?

Jesse walked off into the night, remembering her eyes.

Chapter Two

"Amanda, be careful."

In spite of the rather intriguing encounter with Jesse, chaotic and disturbing dreams filled Amanda's head that night. A particularly clear, vivid one haunted her during her classes the following day.

Within the dream echoed sounds of chanting and visions of people in dark, hooded robes. She could hardly hear the words they recited, and none of it sounded like any recognizable language: *Ah-ay-lan-nar, ay-lay-oh-lan-dran-nah.* The speech struck her as terribly strange, and none of the hand gestures or rituals that she recalled from the dream reminded her of any recognizable magickal tradition or ancient language. Shadows covered the area of her dream, obscuring the forms that moved to perform an elaborate, dark ritual.

She found herself moving towards the circle of hooded robes, and someone from the crowd walked up to her. A face, an elderly woman's face, appeared in front of her. She could've been her grandmother, but her energy seemed far older and reeked of something metallic.

"You, you who come here, the Dark Moon will claim you. The Dark Moon will have you as its own." Her bright eyes flashed. *Gray-eyed Athena,* Amanda thought involuntarily as she awoke with a start. Sweat drenched her body, beading down her skin and soaking her pajamas. Amanda turned to the window for a sign of familiar light and heard the street traffic that was ever present in the city.

After repeatedly praying to Apollo and meditating on him for an hour or two, she finally fell into a formless, dreamless sleep.

* * * *

She came back from her classes that day, refreshed but weary, and finally checked her cell phone messages. One from her mother, and one from Jesse. Her mother's she barely passed over, but Jesse's she knew by heart already.

"Hello, Amanda, this is Jesse."

She had forgotten what his voice sounded like. The tone sent pleasant shivers down her spine.

"I was wondering if you were available tonight, or perhaps

tomorrow night? I found one of my books in my library that I had mentioned and I figured you would like to take a look at it."

She smiled, remembering the references to Thelema and older magick. This should be interesting.

"Anyhow, no rush or anything, just remembered that you were very interested in researching different forms of magick, and this is one of the more uncommonly found texts that I happen to have. My place, yours, another coffeehouse—I'm pretty open. Just let me know. Ciao!"

Ciao. She could've laughed, remembering her previous thoughts on whether or not he was Italian. He certainly had the build, but the "ciao" in addition to her suspicions amused her.

I bet he has a large family and an overly doting set of female relatives, composed of his mother and grandmother, who yell at him to eat, eat. She snickered to herself, thinking of her own relatives. Her family hailed from England, and she was a first generation American. She had no siblings and only kept in touch with her parents in Westchester County. Sometimes she called her funny, offbeat aunt—her father's sister—whom she adored, with a prepaid calling card. She resided in Banbury, which she only knew as some town in England. Her grandparents—those who were still alive—never contacted her often, save for holidays and birthdays.

The trail of thought led her back to her original game plan. Part of her hopes included someday moving back to England and attending school at the University of London. Maybe even teach. She made the Dean's List every semester and stood an excellent chance of being accepted. Once she finished writing her damned thesis, that is.

Beethoven's *Fur Elise* cut into her concentration, and it took her a few seconds to realize that it was her cell phone going off. She picked it up. The caller ID too easily revealed the source of the call; she took a deep breath before answering.

"Hello?"

"Hey, Amanda, this is Jesse."

She cringed, her insides jumping like a nervous schoolgirl's at the sound of his voice. "Jesse, good to hear from you," she replied, keeping her tone even and professional. "I just got your voice message."

"Excellent. What do you think? I have the book right here, and ooh...can you read Latin?"

Can I read Latin! came the indignant thought. She cleared her throat, attempting to speak coherently. She was, after all, a student in the Classics. Of course she could read Latin! "Yes, as a matter of fact—"

"Great!" He almost sounded like a schoolboy himself in his excitement. "When can I see you next?"

He so doesn't beat around the bush, she thought with amusement. "How about around eight or nine tonight?" came the unthinking suggestion from Amanda. She blinked. Where did those words come from? *Oh, Apollo,* she thought, chuckling ruefully. *What the hell is happening to me?*

"How about eight-thirty?" he replied, not missing a beat. "And where would you like to meet this time?"

Oi theoi.... "Anywhere is fine by me. Do you have a preference?"

Laughter. "There's this wonderful restaurant near my place. Do you like Italian?"

"Of course."

"Great!" He gave her the name and address of the restaurant. She did a quick mental calculation in her head. It was already around five-thirty; she would have to be out of her apartment by eight. *Not a problem.*

It wasn't until after she hung up that she realized that he'd named a relatively expensive restaurant and she had no clue as to what to wear.

* * * *

Jesse hung up with a considerable amount of relief. That had gone far easier than anticipated. He hoped that she didn't think he was stalking her or something, but instead displayed an eager interest in someone who shared uncommon interests with him.

Right.

Who was he kidding? As if trying to escape the notice of his fellow Clan members wasn't bad enough, chasing after a mortal woman just because she had an interest in the Classics?

And was pretty, jeered the voice inside his head, the one that never failed to mock him at a moment like this.

"Shut up," he hissed at it, almost baring his fangs. This was intolerable. What could he to say to the guard keeper when he left that evening?

Jesse strolled through the narrow corridors of the Clan's

Sanctuary. The enormous place, which had been built sometime after the turn of the century, reveled in luxury and the feel of an era long gone. Dark wooden paneling lined the walls of the corridor, and covering the floor trailed a long, scarlet rug with golden tassels on its sides. Rarely did someone walk down the lengths of these corridors and not smell polished wood; the Clan would not tolerate letting their Sanctuary become unkempt. The Order had a considerable amount of money, as a number of vampires among them possessed independent wealth or had connections. His Clan in particular, after acquiring a major hotel in the West Village that served as their income base, managed to buy an entire building nearby for themselves and renovate it to include everything that they needed: a library, ritual space, offices for the higher ranking vampires—even housing. Enough fortune fell into their laps to purchase it before anyone else could have done so with the intention of making it into a hotel or a series of apartments—or worse yet, tearing it down to make newer buildings. After all, Washington Square made the list of prime real estate territories, especially given the proximity of NYU.

When seven-thirty came, Jesse noticed Amaltheia making the rounds, clucking as she went. *Wasn't she supposed to be in the library*? he wondered irritably.

"Ah, Turel," she called out, half distracted. "Going somewhere this eve?"

Jesse stopped and looked at her, hoping his expression revealed nothing out of the ordinary.

"Hunting, Amaltheia. I'll be back late."

She nodded and went on her way. He left quickly and with as little fanfare as possible. Blood only knew just how many others might see him leave....

Jesse arrived at the restaurant early—approximately ten minutes before Amanda did. It gave him the time to take the place in and watch the people come and go. The restaurant fit as the quaint, but classy establishment where he wanted to treat Amanda to a wonderful meal. He observed its various patrons come and go, all of whom appeared to be having a wonderful time enjoying both food and ambiance. Centerpieces of flowers and lit candles decorated small tables lined up in rows, and the scent of freshly made Italian sauce filled the air.

Then Amanda showed. Taken aback by her beauty, he could only stare stupidly and hope she didn't notice. Up until now, he had only seen her, either in person or in passing, dressed in her khakis, dresses, or long skirts. Tonight, a black top and a short, red skirt—which he figured she must've had stashed in the back of her closet—adorned her small but curvy frame. Not her typical clothing as a Classics grad student, and he appreciated the care she took with how she looked. He noted with glee that her long hair fell loosely down her back. As he suspected, her hair looked gorgeous and sensual.

In his eyes, it suited her.

He hadn't even begun to think about the basics of ordering, or his efforts to attempt to feign the desire to eat. The sight of her long, shapely legs in the short skirt engrossed him far more than the menu. Obviously she recognized this as a date and dressed to impress him—and if his heart could beat, it would've leapt at the thought. She was interested in him! This outfit would not have been worn by someone to simply read some dusty Latin over casual drinks and a meal.

Jesse ordered the wine. He insisted upon it—after all, how could you enjoy good Italian food without a nice red to go with it? Amanda was all protests, but she seemed to enjoy the vintage and sipped very slowly. He chose Chianti and in spite of his misgivings he relished a few sips at odd intervals. Being a vampire forced caution upon him not to take too much and simply taste. He thankfully remembered to wear the special ring for use on such occasions when he either needed or desired to ingest food and drink. Normally he wore it for religious ritual, but tonight was...special.

He took out the book he'd mentioned earlier over the phone. In mere moments she held in her hands both her notepad and dictionary, furiously translating with great glee in order to understand its contents. Obviously she possessed more than a rudimentary knowledge of Latin, even if she did prefer ancient Greek.

"Jesse, where did you get a hold of this? There are words in here I've never even seen before!"

"Old family secret," he replied, laughing as if it were a joke. It was no joke; the volume had been in the Order's possession for millennia, but he wasn't about to tell her that, nor about the Order.

He couldn't. He'd be executed.

It became rather apparent within the next twenty minutes or so that the more she translated, the less she became concerned about how much wine she drank. Finally, she glanced up at a waiter coming through, carrying a tray filled with dishes as he walked past, trying to make his way to the kitchen as fast as he could on a busy Thursday night.

She held out her hand and caught a plate as it fell off of the tray. Jesse's eyes grew big as she handed the waiter the plate without preamble.

"No trouble at all," she stated with a smile, obviously talking to the waiter. He blinked and grabbed the plate with a nod and several muttered thank yous, continuing his way to the kitchen.

How did you know it was about to fall? Jesse was about to ask, when she turned to him and replied before he spoke, "I, um, tend to be more observant when I'm a little buzzed." She smiled and waved her hand as if to distract from the topic at present and continued to translate the text. Her brow furrowed.

"Jesse, this is most puzzling. There are a lot of references to *blood* in here, and it's clear that they're not necessarily talking about some form of sacrifice. Do you have any light to shed on this?"

He blinked but kept his expression steady. "Well, I, um—"

She laughed. "It's okay; I don't think that this text is talking about ancient vampires or whatever. I'm in fact wondering if it's a symbolic allusion to some kind of ancient Eucharist. But still, it's quite strange. Any chance that I could borrow this from you?" Amanda looked up at him hopefully. She was clearly both enthralled and intrigued with the book.

Jesse found it difficult to refuse her—in spite of the little voice in his head reminding him that if the Clan elders discovered the text missing and in the hands of a mortal, he'd most likely be staked. "I—perhaps, yes. Was there something you wanted to look into further?" As he gazed into her liquid, dark brown eyes, he tried desperately to remember why he gave her the text to begin with. Ah, yes, to impress her. And certainly she was impressed—and perhaps was also more observant and skilled in Latin than he had originally anticipated. Her translation proceeded at a rate even Amaltheia would've found proficient.

Finally, she stopped scribbling and took an additional sip from her glass. "Hold on one moment," she requested, grabbing her purse, "I'll be right back." She smiled at him and ran to the women's restroom.

He started to speak but thought better of it, gazing at her half-finished wine. *What a lightweight she is,* he mused. *And how incredibly competent at Latin. Not to mention,* he thought with a frown, *very…intuitive…when intoxicated.*

Idly, Jesse wondered how a few drops of blood mixed with her drink might aid her psychic skills. *You idiot. You do that and there's no turning back.* Having her ingest his blood as a mortal would give him a light psychic connection to her, enough to know her location, or perhaps read her thoughts. That connection also would be very difficult to get rid of if he later desired to do so.

Glancing out of the corner of his eye, he watched Amanda standing by the women's restroom, engaged in what looked to be friendly banter with another male patron. Perhaps a little…too friendly for his tastes.

Eyes narrowing, he quickly stuck his finger into his mouth, nicked it with his teeth, and deposited a few drops of his blood into her wine.

She'll never notice, he thought smugly.

She returned some moments later to find him sitting calmly, sipping his wine. "Hi, I'm back," she declared with a grin. "Now, where was I? Ah, yes…how old did you say this text was? And where did it come from?"

"I'm…not certain," he admitted. "At least a thousand years or so ago it was written, I am guessing." More like two thousand, but he didn't want to admit to that. Not just yet.

He watched her carefully as she took a sip of her wine, slowly placed the glass back on the table, and made scribbles in her notebook. At one point she stopped reading and looked up, her finger on her mouth. Jesse couldn't tell if she was confused or deep in thought—or both.

"Is there something wrong?" he asked her, inwardly cringing with anxiety. Did she taste the blood? Did she perhaps sense something wrong with the wine?

"Oh, um, no, no, nothing at all." She shook her head as if dispelling something. Then she shrugged and laughed. "Was just wondering something."

Amanda put her head back down in the book and took notes while Jesse observed her, fascinated. While her focus was still on the Latin writings, she reached out her left hand to the wine glass, which slid, of its own accord, a few inches closer to her hand.

It took Jesse a few moments to register what he had seen. *By the*

Blood, she's a natural. Dazed, he kept watching her, but she gave no appearance of having noticed what she had apparently done while under the influence of a glass or two of wine. It occurred to him that perhaps she had always been telekinetic and didn't think much of using it while intoxicated. Either that or the blood he had slipped into her drink had temporarily—or perhaps permanently—increased her abilities. He suspected, given her keen interest in occult Latin texts, that he would be seeing much of this young woman in the days to come.

Not that I would mind, he figured, observing the way the folds of her sweater fell over her breasts and hips.

Some minutes later, she finally put down her pen. An animated dialogue ensued about various other occult texts that she had read while working on her thesis, mostly medieval and modern derivations of Ancient Greek and Roman magick. Amanda spoke of how they related and were also altogether, unlike this work, part of which she had translated. While she conversed with him, he couldn't help but wonder whether or not she guessed his real purpose in showing her this text and taking her out for dinner. Perhaps she might realize that maybe he was interested in her?

* * * *

Hours later, he walked Amanda to the subway station, smiling and nodding along as she rambled about various Greek and Latin texts, responding when he could to some of her statements and answering vaguely to others.

Amanda, be careful, she heard in that small but clear male voice which sometimes spoke in her mind.

Apollo? she thought back, but heard nothing afterwards. *Maybe it was my Agathos Daimon.* Her guardian spirit.

They stopped at the entranceway, and she turned to thank him for the wonderful evening and for tolerating her rather fanatical interest on some subjects and for a lovely dinner, but was interrupted by Jesse leaning in so fast she almost didn't see him move. Before she could utter another word his lips were on hers. Everything at that moment stopped except for her heart, which she heard in her ears. Upon finally pulling apart, she realized that she wasn't breathing and an electric current ran through her skin. Amanda was on fire, and she was alive, so alive, in that moment.

He left shortly after that. Amanda stared after him, agape. She turned to look up at the sky, but all she saw was light, endless light from the buildings, the faint traces of stars in the moonless sky, and all of it swirling around her.

Chapter Three

"In advance."

The next morning, Amanda groggily looked at the alarm clock that sat next to her computer, unable to believe the time displayed. Strangely enough, after the odd dreams of the past few nights, she barely remembered having any from last night. She stumbled out of bed, tripping over her feet. Showering and dressing for the day produced fumbling efforts at best.

More than once she cursed how small and cluttered her place was, but there was no way that she could afford anything larger than a studio—especially one so close to NYU. Her place consisted of wall-to-wall bookshelves, her twin-sized bed, the computer desk, a small kitchen space, and a tiny bathroom. She didn't own a television set and had no interest in one. Decoration was sparse, save some Greek art and statuary. A marble bust of Apollo sat on top of her computer and kept her inspired during her long hours of work.

In her classes that day, Amanda sat half listening, half dazed. *He kissed me, he kissed me,* she kept thinking incredulously, her mind playing over last night's events and remembering the feel of his lips upon hers. Analyzing Iamblichus's work, *On the Mysteries,* lacked its usual appeal as she wondered instead when she would see Jesse again.

And yet, she pondered how this could happen to her. Jesse had demonstrated himself to be intelligent and attractive, along with sharing common interests—not to mention the fact that he had even been, so far, a perfect gentleman. Up to the present, she hadn't experienced much luck with men, and while she had dated a few, they'd never understood her, nor her interests in the Classics, let alone her religious beliefs. It made for painfully awkward conversations, particularly with one secular Catholic turned agnostic who couldn't comprehend that while she believed in a singular divinity, she worshipped the gods and the gods alone. Then there were those who exhibited jealousy of her love for her god Apollo and made dating difficult until she wound up breaking up with them.

But Jesse was a Kemetic! He worshipped Egyptian gods. *Osiris in some circles was considered to be the Egyptian Dionysus. This could work.* Finally, she could be involved with someone of similar religious beliefs, someone whose mind and body attracted hers, whose eyes made her melt and whose voice caused her to shake and did strange things to her insides. Finally, both her brain and her body could be fully engaged at the same time. She wondered what sorts of conversations she could have with him and whether or not he would comprehend her mystical leanings and unusual perspective on reality.

Amanda wasn't just walking on air, she was dancing on it.

When would she see him again?

* * * *

A tall, terribly thin young man walked down the corridor towards Jesse. He recognized the man on sight, if not by the smell of his blood and the aura of his energy. It was his Clan's Magister, Janius, who sat on the council for the Order itself. Jesse tried not to squirm. He had an extreme dislike of the magister's adherence to rules, structure, and ordinance.

Sometimes, Jesse wondered if the man ever had a moment of fun in his entire unlife.

"Hello, Turel," Janius greeted him cordially. "Where have you been lately?"

Jesse fought back a smirk. "Oh, hi, Janius. I've been quite well, actually. Just been going on walks and errands for Amaltheia."

Janius quirked an eyebrow. "Errands for Amaltheia? Since when have you been so attentive to our Clan's favorite librarian?"

Jesse thought quickly. "Since I've discovered some amazing reading material," he explained. "I've been reading up on ancient Greek magick."

"Ah, I see." Janius paused thoughtfully. "Does this mean that you won't be finishing that assignment I gave you?"

Jesse cringed. Right. He was supposed to make this spell for the Order that would assist in guarding their Sanctuary. He originally based the idea on a relatively new esoteric order's way of dealing with magick—specifically, the Hermetic Order of the Golden Dawn. New in relation to their own Order, at least, as the Golden Dawn had come into existence in the late nineteenth century. He had figured that the order's concepts of the Anubis of the East and the Anubis of the West in its initiations would make excellent guardians. They could watch both the inside and outside for intruders who might discover their existence. But ah, it had fled his mind. He had been preoccupied with the vision of a lovely young but innocent woman, well versed in the classics and with the aura of a natural mage.

"Actually, I thought that it might help," he replied rapidly, but tried not to look nervous or stutter. This wasn't his night. Thankfully, he was still in a good mood after having met with Amanda the night before.

"But you work so much better with Egyptian gods." Janius's tone was almost scolding. "It would be like me working with the Celts."

Jesse shrugged. "Romans invaded Britain, Greeks learned magick from the Egyptians...I guess in the end it all makes sense."

"Riiiiight." Janius drew out the word almost as if he were singing it. "No more ideas on using newfangled magickal technology? You do know," he continued sternly, "that there is way too much interest in the occult and vampires among today's youth, and adding additional protection is the only way that we can protect our way of life?"

"But of course," Jesse responded, half on the defensive and half apologetic, "obviously I realize the importance of this assignment. Hence I am looking into as many avenues as possible."

A slow smile spread across the magister's face, to the point where his fangs grew and actually showed. Turel tried not to grimace. *Oh shit, he Saw something.*

"Give my regards to that wonderful brunette," Janius told him smoothly, a sardonic tone underlying his words, "whatever her name is, and I hope that she is helping you in your research and not distracting you from it."

Jesse stared agape. Janius's skills of Sight had done it to him again.

The magister just chuckled at him, and only barely refrained from rolling his eyes. "Just please don't reveal yourself to this mortal, all right? Remember your blood." Shaking his head, he continued to chuckle as he walked off.

"Oh, and by the way, Turel?"

"Yes?" Jesse answered hesitantly.

"If she's Order material, please let me know." Implied in the magister's tone were the words: *in advance.*

"Certainly, Janius." Jesse didn't remember the last time he'd walked so fast out of the building. He needed both to feed and to clear his head. Blood was he in trouble.

* * * *

Meanwhile, Janius paused in his steps and frowned, wondering if he should've spelled out the words *"in advance"* or not and contemplated whether Turel would truly prove to be that thoughtless and stupid. He concluded that it would be best to speak to the young vampire at some point and assess his level of interest in this mortal woman. In the meantime, he had important business to attend to, which involved neither Turel nor his latest mishaps.

Janius regarded the other vampire calmly. Headstrong, stubborn, and reckless—and lastly, he was a bullshit artist whose vampiric name ought to have been "Loki-el" and not "Tur-el", or rather, "Tyr-el" as it had originally been spelleod in the documents written after he had been Turned. But no matter. In spite of these flaws, his impressive talents in both magecraft and the vampiric magickal arts would make him an excellent candidate for magister someday—that is, if he didn't have the continuous tendency to disregard protocol and responsibility. But, Turel was still young, and youth would go away in time. He had high hopes for the young vampire yet.

He remembered looking at Turel and catching a brief but vivid image of a woman with long, streaming black hair and deep brown eyes that were reflective and serious, young yet wise, and studious. She wore red.

I suspect she'll make a good initiate—there's something about her that I like. But I am afraid for her because of who will be her Sire. Damn that boy....

* * * *

Amanda was just finishing up her homework at her computer when her cell phone rang. At this point, she knew who it was, and her heart did a spirited dance. Jesse.

"Hello?" she answered in what she hoped was a nonchalant way.

"Hi, Amanda, it's Jesse." His warm tones filled her ears, and something about them made her lower stomach clench in anticipation.

"Hello, Jesse, how are you?"

"Good. What are you doing tonight?" Amanda heard the smile in his tone, and she tried not to giggle.

She glanced at her homework, which was now done. She ought to study some more, but....

Amanda answered automatically. "Nothing."

"Would you like to get together again?"

"Of course."

Later, as Amanda made her way out the door, she was practically skipping.

I am twenty-five going on fifteen, she thought ruefully as she made her way to the entrance of the restaurant. This place doubled as an upscale pub and was thankfully not too crowded.

Amanda saw him standing there in the foyer, dressed in his leather jacket, hands in pockets, once again in dress slacks—all in black—his dark hair carefully brushed back, and his dark eyes twinkling when they met hers. In the middle of her rapid race towards him, somehow his arms were around her and his hands holding her tight as he picked her up, and in that sublime, radiant moment, he kissed her again. When she came to, she found her own arms wrapped behind his neck. Her lipstick was probably gone, but she didn't care.

She was content.

The nearby clock signified that it was nearly quarter after eleven. She realized that she needed to start her journey back home. An early class awaited her the next morning—eight a.m.—and she knew that she had to leave and get some sleep.

But oh, she enjoyed talking with him far too much.

"When will I see you again?" he asked her, and in his voice and eyes she heard and saw the expectant longing. Amanda thought of her schedule in dismay. She had papers due and that thesis to work on—and her study group was meeting that week too.

"I'll be free this Friday or Saturday night," she answered, her tone bright.

Jesse frowned. "It's Tuesday," he told her. He sounded disappointed, and she was too.

"I know," she stated, not able to keep the sadness out of her voice. "I have this crazy paper or two that I'm working on, and...." She gestured with a helpless air.

He smiled. "I understand."

* * * *

Although he kept a happy façade for Amanda's sake, inside he screamed. Four more days until he could see her again? Jesse could hardly picture it, and in spite of his best efforts he was having difficulty picturing himself without her. Had he really only known her for a short time? He was growing entirely too fond of her chatter, her intense and curious mind, the way she brushed back her hair as she spoke, and the light in her eyes when she looked at him.

Sometime when her back was turned, he'd once again nicked his finger with his teeth and let a few more droplets of blood into her glass. Leaning back with a smile, he'd watched her drink the last of her wine. Recently, he had felt her thinking of him and wondered what her second drink of his blood would bring. She was shielded in a fashion which told him of her familiarity with either psychic talents or magick. Would a second drink allow him to peek through the shield?

He wanted to be with her and hoped that her studies would not take her from him for too long.

* * * *

Amanda fought off a wave of nausea as she stood in front of the mirror. It was far too early in the morning, the sunlight was unusually bright—she must have a hangover. Why she would have a hangover after one glass of wine, she didn't know.

After talking herself out of the idea—such a silly idea, and she would be laughed at besides—she grabbed her sunglasses before heading out the door. Her head throbbed, and she wished it would stop.

After her third class that day, one of her professors caught her before she left.

"Mandy," he called, and she winced. She liked him and hence let him get away with the nickname.

"Yes, Professor Korbin?"

"Are you feeling well? I can't help but notice that you've gotten... distracted as of late."

She laughed it off. "No, I'm fine. I've just had a lot on my mind lately."

He nodded. "You know, one of these days you could be teaching at Harvard. Or Columbia University. I want to see you excel. Don't let yourself lose track of the goal, okay?"

Amanda smiled, but it hurt her face to do so. "Okay."

"Good. I'll see you in class on Friday."

As she walked out of class, she could've kicked herself. She maintained high goals for herself and desired very strongly to reach them. Somehow, she needed to strike a balance between her newfound love interest and her efforts towards getting into graduate school for her Ph.D. Only a short while awaited this event, and she didn't want to disappoint herself or her god. She had a promise to keep.

* * * *

For the next few nights, Amanda's dreams were odd. She kept dreaming of Jesse and being inside big, strange buildings, and every time she woke up she tasted something odd and metallic. Maybe she was accidentally biting her lip and tasting blood as she slept.

In response to her feelings about missing Jesse, the strange dreams, and the overbearing sense of responsibility towards her workload at school, she buried herself in her work for the remainder of the week with an intense zeal. Once she got some rest, she slept deeply but kept seeing Jesse in her mind—Jesse talking to people, Jesse going places, Jesse doing things she couldn't quite see clearly—and upon waking, she did her best to try and block it out of her mind.

She couldn't afford the distraction.

She came back to her apartment late Friday night. The week was finally over, and she breathed a huge sigh of relief. As soon as she managed to get into bed, she slept as if she hadn't slept in years.

* * * *

"Lynne, I am concerned about Turel. Have you spoken with him lately?"

She frowned. James was the one of the few vampires in the Order who not only remembered her real name but actually called her by it.

"No, I haven't. Why, you think he's up to something?"

Now it was his turn to frown. "I'm really not certain, but I suspect his head is getting caught up with some woman. A mortal. I wondered if you had any insights or if he had said or done something in your presence?"

Asherael snorted. "The only things he says and does in my presence, James, are the things that I actually allow him to do."

James laughed, but she continued, "He thinks he's the James Dean of this Clan or something. I'm amazed that no one has yet disciplined him outright, and it's a wonder he's still alive."

"Hold that thought, Lynne," the magister interrupted. "He's coming."

"Right," she replied.

Sure enough, Jesse's familiar features were visible down the hall, and in a matter of moments they caught up to him.

"So, Turel, what are you up to?" Lynne asked him casually.

He just glared at her, and she saw in Janius's face that he was quietly refraining himself from strangling either one of them.

"Nothing, just heading over to the library. I need to talk to Amaltheia."

"Why, you need a love spell or something?"

"Asherael," James spoke quietly, his tones conveying a message of warning. But she didn't care.

Jesse's only response was to glare and hiss at her and continue walking. She continued to watch him as he walked away.

"Yup, still the same ol' Turel. What were you so bugged out about, exactly?"

"Sometimes, Lynne," the magister drawled, no longer bothering to stop himself from rolling his eyes, "I wonder if you don't enjoy provoking him as much as he provokes you."

"And sometimes, James," she responded sweetly, "I think you just enjoy *watching*."

He looked at her mischievous green eyes and decided wisely not to reply.

Chapter Four

"Jesse James"

Jesse called Saturday evening, and Amanda managed to reach her cell phone before it went to voice mail. He wanted to meet her again; he knew of this perfect little restaurant that she would love. She found herself saying yes and yes again, and her heart pounded so loudly that she wondered if he could hear it on the other end.

As she changed into a floral skirt and black blouse, Amanda shook, partly in anticipation and partly from the realization that things were moving fast, very fast. Her feelings never ran this strong for anyone so quickly, and she wondered if she was entirely in her right mind. She still had a ton of work to do for her thesis and she couldn't help but feel a little afraid that Jesse was taking over just a little too much of her life. The voice mail he had left Friday night was full of passionate longing and affection, and she heard the slight tone of impatience. When would he see her again?

Following on the heels of those thoughts were concerns about her health due to her nausea and constant headaches. *I hope I'm not coming down with something.* But at the moment she didn't experience any discomfort. Perhaps she needed to get out more often and quit spending too much time in front of the computer doing her work. *Maybe Jesse is just what I need, in spite of it all.* She thought about it some more. They were already on their third—fourth outing? She couldn't remember—and he hadn't once pushed her any further intimately than passionate kissing. Most guys she had been romantically involved with had been far more impatient, and some had even tried to get her to sleep with them on the first date.

When they finally met at the restaurant, all of her doubts were chased from her mind. Their eyes locked, and the couple embraced immediately. Amanda heard roaring in her ears. Her lips encountered his, and the world swirled around her and melted away, their bodies pressed together. His arms tightened around her waist, and she throbbed. *His kisses,* she thought to herself dazedly, *just get better and better.*

Over the course of the evening, Jesse mentioned a friend he wanted her to meet.

"He's extremely interested in your thesis and, well, he's like a brother to me." He grinned boyishly.

Amanda laughed. "Ah, you're having your friends check me out, now?" she teased.

He laughed in return. "No, no, nothing like that, honest. It just would mean a lot to me for you to meet him, is all."

She smiled. "Sure, no problem."

Jesse and Amanda settled on Monday night and spent the rest of their evening discussing philosophy, classical literature, and religion. The more they talked, the more Amanda was compelled to be with him, unable to resist the allure of someone who could converse with her and make her think more about concepts she hadn't had a chance to express to anyone.

It grew late, much later than she had wanted to stay out, and this time Jesse insisted upon making sure she got back to her apartment safely. She decided that it would be okay at this point, and they went together on the subway back to her place. As they talked, the dialogue that she had with herself started again: Would he try to talk her into letting him stay the night? Was she doing the right thing? Were they moving too fast as a new couple? Her heart and her thoughts were a chaotic whirlwind, and she desperately sought the calm eye of the storm, the part of her that knew what she consciously didn't.

They stood on the steps of her apartment building, and she gazed into his eyes. All her previous thoughts abandoned her once their lips met. The touch of his lips sent a slow fire raging through her veins, and Amanda found herself pressed against the door to the building; his lips and tongue did wondrous magic to her mouth and neck that made the moisture between her legs grow. His hands smoothly slid under her blouse and caressed her bare back, and she gasped aloud. His hands were cool to the touch but left a burning trail across her skin.

The moment they spent intertwined seemed to last for minutes, perhaps even an hour. With great reluctance, he gently broke free and with a surprisingly gentle kiss to her mouth, bid her goodnight. He walked to the street and turned the corner in the direction of the subway, and before she knew what was happening, he was gone.

Amanda stared after him for a while, then slowly made her way into the building and up to her floor. She didn't know whether to be more stunned at the fact that he had let her go back to her apartment without asking to be invited in, or the knowledge inside of her that if he had asked, she would've let him in, all too eagerly and without reservation.

Once again, fear and uncertainty struck her heart.

* * * *

James sat at his desk, quietly reading through various papers and manuscripts. Jesse walked in with a flourish, interrupting his train of thought.

"Yes, Turel, can I help you?" The magister's voice sounded both distracted and impatient.

Jesse replied without hesitation. "Yes, Magister, I would like you to review a potential candidate for our Order."

James blinked at the formal address, then realized the nature of Jesse's request. "Ah, the brunette, I assume?"

"Yes, the same. I believe she would be a valuable asset to our Order, and with your permission," he paused briefly, "I would like to be the one to Turn her myself."

Janius looked up with a start. Turel, a Sire to a vampire Childe? "Turel, do you think that you can handle such a responsibility?" he inquired severely.

"I do."

The magister looked at him solemnly, noting the intense fire in his eyes. *He is extremely set on this. Best to approach this cautiously.* He nodded. "When can I meet her?"

"I've arranged for the three of us to meet this Monday night. Would that be acceptable?"

James glanced down at his hands, which folded in front of him as his elbows rested on the desk, as if he might find something in them to determine the correct course of action. He looked back up at Jesse and nodded thoughtfully. "It will do."

"Wonderful," Jesse exclaimed enthusiastically. "You pick the meeting place, and I'll bring her there."

The magister graced him with the briefest of shrugs. "I do not care. Do you have a preference?"

Jesse thought about it before responding. "Yes, someplace where they serve alcohol." A broad grin spread across his face. "You must see her after a glass of wine. Janius, she is a natural. I've seen her move a wine glass without touching it. Once, I watched her reach out her hand—and a waiter dropped a plate onto it! She is remarkably intuitive."

Eyebrows lifting, James simply replied, "Fascinating. Does she practice magick?"

"Yes, she does."

James rubbed his hands together. "Well, I'm looking forward to meeting her. We can establish then whether or not she fits the criteria."

"Oh, she will, I assure you. She will."

* * * *

Amanda met Jesse at the back table of a relatively crowded restaurant. The place was upscale and very popular. Photos of famous people and areas of the city decorated the dark, stained wooden walls.

With Jesse was a very tall, thin, and pale man whose light blue eyes struck her as being older than the rest of his features. Like Jesse, he looked to be in his late twenties to early thirties. He wore khakis, a black top, and a long brown trench-coat. He came across as very professional, every bit the J Crew personality she had originally anticipated Jesse would be when she had first met him. He also struck her as being extremely polite and formal in his introduction.

"Hello, Amanda, I am pleased to meet you. My name is James." He extended his hand in greeting. A momentary feeling of oddness swept over her. They shook hands, and an unusual sort of energy caught her off guard. It made her uncomfortable. Amanda filed away the data in the back of her mind. Perhaps she would have an insight on it later.

"Jesse...and James," she stated and began to laugh.

Janius looked at her strangely, but after a few moments he seemed to get the humor. "Oh, yes," he chuckled. "Believe it or not, you're the first to make that joke."

"'Jesse James'? I'm rather surprised. No one else has seen that little bit of humor but me?"

"No, believe it, you are the first," Jesse told her with a smirk.

Once they were all seated and had ordered drinks and appetizers, James began conversing with Amanda. It didn't go unnoticed by her that as he spoke, Jesse moved closer to where she sat and put his arm around her. The gesture seemed affectionate, yet protective.

"Jesse here has told me a lot about you, Amanda. All good

things, I might add. I hear you are working on a thesis in Classical Studies?"

"Yes," she answered, "on Greek and Roman magick."

James's eyebrows went up slightly, and he nodded at her. He then rattled off a list of a dozen or so scholars to see if she had heard of any of their names, and he appeared to be surprised when she knew nearly all of them.

They began discussing Greek philosophers and writers, but it was when he mentioned Iamblichus that Amanda squealed with delight. She couldn't prevent herself from babbling, running for the topic like a delighted child towards a pile of candy. She observed Jesse stifle what appeared to be a chuckle and wondered if she'd said something wrong.

* * * *

Meanwhile, Jesse quietly observed the magister more taken aback than he had seen him in recent memory. James listened to her for a while with eyebrows slightly quirked; then he nodded at Jesse.

At this point, the topic shifted, and Amanda babbled about Iamblichus and Orpheus. After a lengthy conversation on theurgy, the Osirian and Dionysian Mysteries, and Pythagorean philosophy, it became more than obvious to him—and hopefully James as well, he thought—that her tastes ran decidedly to the more mystical subjects within Classical Studies.

Amanda had finished most of her glass of wine at that point and turned to James to ask him a question. Moving quickly yet unnoticed, Jesse moved her glass a little out of reach. It was when she unthinkingly reached for it—and the glass slid in a slight and causal way into her hand without physical aid—that the magister's interest was piqued.

Yes, Turel, you're right—this woman has much potential.

Jesse caught the telepathic message and merely smiled in return.

After a few hours of philosophizing, James politely thanked her for meeting with him and wished the two well. He had business to attend to, and didn't want to interrupt what time Amanda and Jesse had to spend together.

"And Jesse," he added nonchalantly, "if you don't mind, I need to speak with you about a professional matter. Would you mind excusing us, Amanda? It won't take long."

She smiled. "No, not at all."

"Now, what did I tell you?" stated Jesse matter-of-factly. "I did say that she has potential."

James nodded. "Yes, yes, she does. Enormous potential, and definitely someone whose skills I would like to see flourish in our Order."

Grinning like a madman, Jesse turned to go back into the restaurant.

"Just one thing, Jesse," the magister interjected.

"Yes?" he asked, his tone expectant.

"Take your time with this one. Give it about a month before you Turn her. At the very least. That's my advice."

Solemn, Jesse nodded. He saw the reasons for his advice, even if his heart screamed to do otherwise.

"Just remember," James admonished, "once you Turn her, you're stuck with her for a long time—even if you two do not work out."

Jesse frowned at this. "I'm sure it will work out," he stated, his tone flat. "One way or another."

"I'm sure too—but to be doubly certain, if nothing else, to gauge what her reactions will be to all of this. Please, Jesse, take your time. For what it's worth, she does have my approval. I will discuss this matter with the other Clan elders, and if any others want to meet her before you decide to take the next steps, I would recommend that they do so and that you let them."

Jesse shoved his hands into his pockets and looked away. Clan elders. Approval. And scrying sessions to see if any of the clairvoyants among them would psychically pick up anything about her, either good or bad. Probably some paperwork too.

The magister looked at him pointedly. "Turel, if you want this woman so badly, you know that this has to be done right. Both for her and for you."

"Yes, yes, I know," he replied. But Jesse's voice carried an undertone of frustration.

The magister's gaze grew sharper. "I could always say no, you know. But I'm not. I recognize her potential as well, and I think she'll be a very suitable mate for you."

At that remark, Jesse's mouth turned upwards—albeit reluctantly. He didn't like being reminded of Janius's power over the Clan, let alone his own life.

James's voice grew gentler as he continued, but it didn't lose its sternness. "Remember, our Clan has a reputation to uphold in the Order. We can't just decide overnight to Turn someone and accept them into our fold. Not even for you, Jesse."

Jesse nodded. "I understand."

"Good. Now, go back and entertain your date. I'll be around if you have any questions or have need of my assistance."

With that last remark, James vanished into the night, disappearing into the crowds so quickly that even with Jesse's excellent eyesight, he didn't see the magister depart.

Jesse smiled, fought back the urge to light a cigarette, and went into the restaurant towards a particular table in the back of the room where a dark-haired young woman waited for him with a smile in her eyes and a kiss on her lips.

Tonight, he wanted to claim that kiss and make it all his.

* * * *

When the two men exited the restaurant and stood out front by the street, Amanda watched them both from behind. With James in his long brown trench-coat and Jesse with his black leather jacket, Amanda reflected that when combined, the two of them really could make Jesse James. She giggled to herself in amusement.

They were not gone for long. Jesse returned to the table, and Amanda greeted him with an eager smile. "Welcome back," she told him warmly.

He seated himself next to her, then slid over to put his arm around her and kiss her softly on the lips. The embrace was so sweet that it seemed like a musical note reverberating within her, and Amanda reveled in it.

"My apologies for leaving like that, but James had some private business that he wanted to share."

"No, that's quite all right." She took another sip of her wine. "Are you two business partners?"

Jesse nodded. "I suppose you could call it that. We do some—I guess you could say—freelance work together."

"Interesting." With a wicked grin, she asked, "So, did he approve of me or what?"

He laughed. "Most certainly, he did. I believe his words were something to the effect of 'I think Amanda would be really good for you.'"

"Really now?" Her grin grew wider, and Jesse smiled back at her.

"Yes, truthfully."

Amanda said nothing in return, but continued to beam.

Chapter Five

"Just a dream, eh?"

Jesse looked into those eyes—Amanda's eyes—and something stung him deep inside his heart. It couldn't be real, it couldn't be true. She was ideal for him, stunningly so, and he admired everything about her: her intelligence, quirks, and passions. But he knew there was no way he could truly share anything of himself with her.

It wasn't just that he was a vampire; he held membership in the Order. *Ordo Draconis et Rosae*, better known as the Order of the Dragon and the Rose. Based on the vows he had made upon the partaking of the blood of his Sire, nothing could pass from his lips to a mortal about who and what he was. The only way for someone to join his Order was to be Turned by another already initiated into it.

Because of this truth which pressed itself upon his very soul, when Jesse watched her lean back unknowingly and ask with such innocence, "So where did you grow up? Did you know James from your childhood?" something inside was dying. He both adored and despised her purity in that moment. An aspect of him wanted to drink deep and cherish her naïveté while another part wanted to rip it to shreds with his hands, his teeth—his fangs. This was her nature that prevented her from seeing that whenever they got together, he rarely actually ate or drank. That they only met when the sun had gone down. That same innocence would prevent her from ever realizing she would never, ever see him in broad daylight. Ever.

Blood, she has no idea. None.

She couldn't have known how much that line of questioning would make him wince. Jesse shoved his feelings of desperate rage deep inside where she couldn't see and graciously replied, "No, we met later on, when we were adults."

What more could he say to her? He thought with a grimace of what the truth would sound like: *Actually, Amanda, I was born in 1932 and was Turned when I was twenty-five. I'm old enough to be your grandfather. I'm also not allowed to tell you any of this or I'll be executed—and probably you with me. Which means that I'll be forced to Turn you right now in order to save us both from certain death. Hope you enjoyed your wine.*

Even though his thoughts grew cynical, he remembered with

a degree of nostalgia what the process was like for him and what it might mean—would mean—for her. Even courting a potential initiate had its rules, regulations, and traditions, and they could only learn what was to be their fate once they had passed the point of no return. The theory was that even if mortals who came to them didn't consciously choose the path of the vampire, it was an unconscious choice determined by their individual alchemy and true will. The very process that would transform them from mortal to vampire was likened to that of the transformation of lead into gold.

He stared into her eyes and was reminded of gold, gold like the sun that he couldn't see anymore, except through numerous vampiric spells, tinted windows, and dark sunglasses.

* * * *

The next thing Amanda knew, she was pressed against Jesse in a bone-crunching passionate embrace, his lips devouring hers, his hands tightly wound in her hair. The only thing gentle about his kiss was his tongue, which slid in her mouth with sensuous, snake-like movements, driving her mad with desire. The kiss was over far too soon for her tastes, and when they pulled apart she found herself unable to breathe or speak with any degree of coherency.

"It's time for me to go," he stated, his tone strangely abrupt. "I'll walk you home."

Amanda blinked, confused. But she nodded.

As they made their way for the door she thought to ask him, "Jesse—the bill—was it—"

"James took care of it earlier," he replied with a slight smile.

"Ah, okay." She added, "Please thank him for me. It was very kind of him."

They didn't speak too much to each other on the way to her apartment. Amanda sensed something inside him that she couldn't quite identify, but that something made her timid and hesitant to speak. She didn't know how to act around him and didn't know what to say. It didn't help that between her legs, she ached due to their earlier kiss, and was extremely thankful that, once again, she had chosen a skirt over jeans. She didn't need the additional friction one bit.

Amanda fought to put a word or phrase to the feeling she was getting from him as she once again stood in front of the door to the apartment building with Jesse's arms around her.

"You have an early day tomorrow, I know," he told her. "Get some rest. I will call you tomorrow evening, and we can make plans then." A note of firmness tinged his voice, and she wondered if he was telling her this matter-of-factly or instructing her.

Before she could respond, his lips once again found hers. But this time, it was a gentle touch, as light as silk. Jesse pulled back slowly and looked into her eyes for a long moment before saying good night and walking off into the streets of the city.

Dangerous, her mind whispered. That was it, the word she kept trying to conjure to describe what she had sensed from him.

* * * *

It was all Jesse could do to prevent himself from staring at the throbbing pulse in her neck and the delicately exposed cleavage that peeked from her blouse as he walked away from her.

He knew that she wouldn't have minded if he had asked to spend the night—except that he couldn't wake in the daylight with her, and it was too soon besides. And yet, the longer he waited, the more he tested his resolve. He had to find a workaround soon before he lost his sanity and did something that he would regret later.

Contrary to what the magister believed, he *did* have some measure of discipline. If he hadn't, he would've slept with Amanda on the first date—hells, more than that, he would've Turned her already. But Jesse kept what Janius said to him firmly in mind, agreeing with the spirit if not the letter of his law. He wanted things to go right between him and Amanda. He just didn't know how.

Turning down an alleyway, he spotted a homeless man sleeping upright, his back propped against a convenient building, his head tilted to the side. It was almost too perfect. With practiced efficiency and speed, he knelt down and sank his teeth into the man's neck. The warm blood flowed down his throat like bittersweet silk and filled his veins. Turel was careful not to take too much, as the last thing the Order needed was dead bodies littering their trail.

Not that one dead body would be noticed in this city. He watched the man stir and moan in his sleep. But he didn't wake.

While the blood kept down his physical thirst, he found himself still hungry for Amanda. But that was a different hunger, one that couldn't be solved through obtaining food. Jesse still felt her skin beneath his fingertips and tasted her in his mouth, and all of the blood pouring from the veins of every New Yorker couldn't wash that away.

Dammit.

* * * *

Blood. It stained her underwear.

Ah, I started my period.

The underwear had to go while she went looking in her medicine cabinet for tampons. She figured that she could wash it later. The tampon was more important right now.

Dammit, they're all gone.

With a sigh, Amanda shut the door and left the bathroom to look for some in her purse. She didn't get very far.

There he stood, right in front of her, dressed in black, his eyes as dark as his clothing. There was a moment of silence, both comprehending and not understanding.

"Jesse."

"Amanda."

Growling. She heard growling, but she wasn't sure where it was coming from.

Jesse?

Next, she was lifted off of her feet and somehow she was in her bedroom, lying down on her bed. Her clothing was gone. Had she been wearing any? She couldn't even remember. Jesse knelt on the bed, bending over the lower half of her body while she couldn't do more than stare. She was frozen in place, unable to move.

With a grace that could only remind her of some of the yoga practices she had done in the past, he simultaneously slid down onto his stomach and parted her legs.

She realized again that she had her period, and a brief moment of embarrassment ensued. Maybe she should probably say something....

That moment was instantly followed by mindless, searing bliss when his tongue penetrated her. The world around her went bright white, and she clutched the bed sheets, gasping. With sharp teeth pressed against her now oversensitive folds, Jesse's tongue continued to lap inside of her. A vision of him accidentally piercing her flesh with his teeth filled her with terror, and that terror mingled with the ecstasy until she rode wave upon wave of emotion and sensation.

He's sucking me dry. She no longer had any control over her thoughts or body, just feeling and sensual awareness without end. Amanda was as terrified as she was enraptured in sharp bliss. She heard herself crying out but didn't recognize the sounds she made. His tongue probed inside of her, his hands seemed to be everywhere, and his teeth, his sharp teeth pressed against tender parts of her. Finally, it grew to be too much, and the torture just kept going on without end. Would the end be pain, pleasure, or both?

"It's just a dream," she gasped, now fully lucid. "It's only a dream."

A chuckle came from between her legs.

"Just a dream, eh?" Jesse asked in a roguish tone.

Once again she froze on the spot, unable to move.

He lifted his head and looked her dead in the eyes. It jolted her.

"Come for me."

The waves of mindless pleasure instantly became a crescendo that ripped through, shook her senseless, and turned her inside out. Amanda screamed.

She awoke, her heart pounding and the orgasm still pulsating through her. She stayed there, lying on the bed, wondering what had just happened to her and if it was really a dream or not.

She decided that she was too afraid to truly know. Amanda couldn't deny that she wanted Jesse, wanted him very much. But all of this was too intense, far more emotion than she could possibly handle. And if this had truly not been a dream...the implications of that line of thought weren't anything she wished to either deal with or explore.

Was she right in continuing this relationship? Would it be wise to pull back and let things cool off a bit before either one of them did something regrettable? She still had her college degree to complete and a focus to maintain and she was afraid to lose it. Not only that, but she wondered how all of this excessive passion would fit in with being a devotee of a god of moderation and balance.

Apollo, help me. What do I do?

No reply came, at least none discernable to her in her current state.

Gods help me, I am an idiot.

Her mind was too disturbed to rest, and it was a long while before she was able to go back to sleep.

Chapter Six

"The storm will pass soon enough."

Slowly, Jesse emerged from his deep trance state. Astral travel had proved to be useful on more than one occasion, and the results of tonight's expedition pleased him immensely. He could still taste Amanda on his tongue, and her scent seemed to be everywhere. Somehow, this particular astral trip had been more vivid than the others, and he speculated that the blood he had slipped into her drinks earlier was to blame.

His blood had provided a light psychic connection with her, allowing him to know her whereabouts and sense her emotions. Sometimes he even felt her as he slept during daylight hours, and it gave his sleep a measure of comfort that wasn't there before.

And yet, he still couldn't know her exact thoughts, no matter how much he tried. Amanda was well and truly shielded. It made him curious about where she had learned to shield and what thoughts lay past the veil that separated him from her. He would think upon it at moments during his nights out hunting for blood. Was she thinking of her thesis right now? The gods? Magick? Him? Someone else, perhaps? The momentary thought of her possibly being attracted to anyone else in her classes made him burn with resentment.

She can't be, he reasoned. *She has her head in her books all of the time. Amanda wouldn't notice anyone, or care.*

Of course, this feeling provided him with little comfort given his conversation with Amanda later. She had her thesis to finish and was getting anxious that her time spent with him would prevent her from meeting her deadline.

"I'll make it up to you when I'm done," she had told him.

Amanda, Amanda...a week without you? Two weeks? How will I do it? How? he had thought grimly. He had forced a smile and replied, "Not to worry. How would you like me to take you on a weekend getaway when you're done?"

Jesse vividly remembered the delighted squeak she had made on the phone. Clearly, she would miss him as well. No worries, right?

But still, he couldn't bring himself to focus on the task Janius had given him. Creating that new magickal defense structure for the Clan's Sanctuary was the furthest thing from his mind.

Ah, screw it, he thought with annoyance and left the building to take a walk in the city, lighting a cigarette on his way.

* * * *

Feeling conflicted, Amanda hung up the phone. She missed Jesse incredibly but wanted to disconnect for a while and come back to herself. Elements of the dream about him—while incredibly arousing—were also quite disturbing, and she feared that if she didn't keep focused on finishing her thesis, she might never get the chance to do so. Visions of being forced to take her classes again and losing her financial aid filled her mind. She couldn't let any of these things happen.

Therefore, she made a quick prayer and a small offering to Apollo that evening: help her finish, help her to graduate. It was a simple, yet heartfelt request. A sense of ease filled her afterwards, and she and dove into her work that night with great vigor.

* * * *

Not even a week later, she received a buzz on her intercom. A delivery had arrived for her. Curious, she went downstairs to the main door. The delivery man stood there, holding a bouquet of red roses. The note attached read: *Thinking of you and missing you. Good luck with your thesis. With love, Jesse.*

Amanda grinned and cheerfully made her way back to her apartment to put the flowers in water.

How sweet of him. It made her feel better about abandoning plans with him for a while; obviously he wasn't taking it to heart.

For what seemed like the one millionth time, she settled down in front of her computer. Excitedly she typed away, secure in the knowledge that her work was nearly done and soon she would see Jesse again—and maybe the time apart from each other would help to ease her fears about them as a couple.

Jesse wasn't Amanda's only concern these days. Somewhere in the back of her mind, she wondered if it might be a good idea to give her parents a call. She hadn't spoken to them for at least a week, and while they were well aware of how busy her life was towards the end of semester, she wanted them to be sure she did all right. It had been an exceptionally long career for her so far in school, between the internship abroad in Athens and the class load that she had chosen for herself.

But soon, Amanda would have her Master's degree in the Classics. All of her hard work would pay off. Then she could study for her Ph.D.—which she already knew she could do automatically with the program she was enrolled in at her current graduate school. She could always continue at NYU and transfer later to the University of London. She hated the idea of being away from Jesse, but she yearned to study abroad. It was one more conflict out of many with which to contend, and one she refused to deal with until her college work was done.

Her degree would be earned soon. Just a few weeks more....

* * * *

"And you're letting him?" Lynne queried incredulously, her voice almost an octave higher than usual. She stood in front of the magister's desk, staring him down with her arms crossed over her chest, a perfect picture of disgust and disbelief. He couldn't be serious. He just couldn't.

"Asherael, I met Amanda myself," James replied patiently, holding his hands behind his back. "She's quite bright and has enormous potential, not just as a scholar, but as a magician."

Am I hearing this correctly? she thought in amazement. She knew the magister favored Turel and frequently gave him an immense amount of leverage, but this was bordering on sheer lunacy. "'Bright'? 'Potential'?" Lynne wasn't in the least bit convinced.

"James, this is Turel we're dealing with here. *Turel*! A Sire? *Him*? Do you honestly think he can handle something like that?" She shook her head, filled with increasing fury. *Of all of the ridiculous things....*

Sighing at her reaction, James pressed on, obviously doing his best to keep his voice calm. "He deserves a shot, and I will be keeping a close eye on him. At the very least, perhaps caring for a Childe will teach him responsibility. Perhaps his judgment may be sound in this. She really does have potential."

She snorted. There was that word again: potential. Turel supposedly had "potential" too. "So, Turel bangs a mortal, now he gets to Turn her?" she asked derisively. "I doubt he is expressing sound judgment, and I am beginning to have my doubts about yours as well."

James's ice blue eyes became remote glaciers. "Amanda may be just what this Order needs—let alone our Clan. Should Turel fail in his responsibilities as a Sire, I will dutifully take over her training myself."

Throwing her hands in the air, she declared, "So be it. If he fucks up, it's in *your* hands." With the word "your", she pointed at James for emphasis.

"And so is Turel. That I can assure you," the magister responded, his voice deliberate and measured.

Lynne turned her back on him and left his office abruptly, afraid to do or say anything that would further compromise her standing with the magister. *Best left unspoken.* She gritted her teeth.

But the words filled her mind nonetheless. *Men are idiots,* she seethed. *Turel gets a hard-on for some woman, and Janius has to fulfill his ludicrous request to have her Turned.*

She stomped down the hall to her own office, which at this point was in its usual state of disarray. "Ordered chaos" she liked to call it. It was in direct contrast to James's rather spartan office that contained only his desk made of dark oak and an office chair similar to her own. The papers on his desk were always neatly contained in wooden trays that matched his desk, or filed away carefully in drawers.

Lynne couldn't care less.

And who is this tramp? she angrily continued to think. *Some hot chick in college. "Potential", my ass.*

Lynne threw herself down into her black leather office chair with a loud thud, her sudden weight forcing the chair to smack into the wall behind her. Forget about voicing these concerns to the Clan's magister—and especially the Order's Council. She knew it would fall on deaf ears.

However, should Turel screw up—which I'm sure he will—I'll be only too happy to voice them.

Happily picturing their normally detached, stuck-up faces melting into complete horror and fury at what she would ultimately tell them—once, of course, Turel had succeeded in making a total ass of himself—she leaned back in her chair with a big smile.

The Order can suck me, she thought gleefully. If Lynne could have the privilege of witnessing Turel's ass handed to him by the Council, it would be worth it. It would be worth whatever punishment they dished out to her for telling them exactly how it was—that Turel had been a big, fat waste of time and energy from day one of his Turning.

And James would have no choice but to admit that she had indeed been right about the young vampire.

* * * *

James propped his feet up on his desk—an unusual thing for him to do on such a nicely polished piece of furniture—and folded his hands over his chest in contemplation. He knew that Lynne had her reasons for disliking Turel, and while he often thought that some of her criticism of the rebellious, headstrong young vampire was valid, much more of it was due to her own personal issues.

Never mind that, he reasoned. *The storm will pass soon enough—especially after she meets Amanda.*

There was no doubt in his mind that Lynne would appreciate both Amanda's intelligence and her studies in Greek and Roman magick. In fact, the magister was extremely certain the two women would get along very well. He suspected that beneath Amanda's scholarly exterior was a very passionate, dedicated young woman with her own opinions about things—much like Lynne. Time and fates willing, they might even become good friends.

Once, of course, he thought irritably, *Lynne gets through her hang-ups about Turel.*

If she ever did. The magister sighed. His colleague's flare-ups in regards to the young vampire were rapidly getting on his nerves. Why didn't she trust his judgment? Didn't Lynne realize there were very good reasons for giving him moderate treatment, even if she didn't completely agree? This was no small matter, and nothing of which she wasn't already aware; Turel had been James's personal responsibility for many decades. How precisely he came to that responsibility was even more of a justification—the young vampire's Sire had met her final death not very long after he was Turned.

It was too soon for her to cross the abyss, he reflected sadly. *And they were Bonded besides.*

He rubbed his temples, remembering how much Turel went through after Minervia's passing. It took some of the Order's best healers to repair the psychic damage left by the brutally broken Bond. The recollections of what had occurred overwhelmed Janius;

he had no desire to take the trip in his mind to wherever ghosts of people and emotions might haunt him. He could only conclude to himself, *It is a miracle that he is reasonably sane.*

Beyond excusing him due to the trauma of his past, giving Turel a chance was something that he believed he owed to Minervia. After all, she hadn't been just Turel's Sire. A stunningly brilliant woman, who advanced in the Order to the rank of 4th degree "Servant of the Blood", as Lynne had, Minervia had been an amazing vampire deeply in touch with her blood. Besides, he assumed partial responsibility for her final death—not just as the Magister of the Clan, but as someone who had been a close friend of hers.

Even now when James looked at Turel, he still saw echoes of Minervia's blood coursing through him. In his eyes, the magister caught a glimpse of something which gave him hope that the young vampire still had a heart to give, even if it couldn't beat.

The magister thought about everything he knew in regards to the situation, and in the end, he nodded his head with certainty, knowing that he was making the right choice in allowing Turel to Turn Amanda. What occurred happened decades ago, and the young vampire's interest in Amanda was, in his eyes, a good sign. This could be a great opportunity for the young vampire, one which Janius could never find it in himself to deny him.

* * * *

Letting her head drop into her hands, Amanda laughed. It was a laugh of relief, exhilaration—and delight.

Her thesis—it was finally done. Finished!

"Oh, thank you, Apollo, thank you!" she cried aloud, blowing a kiss in the direction of the bust on her computer.

Typing so fast that she could barely proofread as she went, she submitted her paper via email to her professor. Afterwards, she fired up her printer without a moment's hesitation to produce a copy on paper. Amanda was taking no chances. Her professor would have this on time, no matter what. It took a few minutes to print but when it was done, she stared at it for a few moments with a huge grin on her face. Giddiness filled her at the realization that her long, hard work was finished.

Never one to let grass grow under her feet, she produced a folder and stuck the thesis inside, grabbed her purse and keys, and left her apartment to head for her professor's office.

A subway ride and a stroll through the campus later, she was there. The crowning moment was slipping the folder underneath the professor's door. The finality of the act satisfied her. Her work was complete.

Now all Amanda had to focus on was finishing her semester and then graduating. At this point, she had no doubt she would succeed. She thought about the rest of the requirements, running through them as if she were composing a shopping list. The Greek and Latin translation exams she had already finished—and she had done extremely well in them. As for her thesis, it was a carefully crafted work—one that she had no doubt would be the basis for further work in the Ph.D. program. In order to get her doctorate, it was required to do two separate papers, one in Greek and one in Roman studies. Her paper analyzed both and provided the foundation for the dissertation she would write later.

Everything was set. Everything was perfect.

She couldn't wait to call Jesse with the good news.

A few hours later, Amanda hummed with delight. They would be going on a trip outside of the city, he told her. He had a car and would come pick her up for a weekend getaway. She had pressed him for details, but he refused, only saying to pack lightly and bring whatever necessities she required along with clothing she would feel comfortable wearing.

A cabin in the woods, perhaps? No, he didn't seem like the rustic sort. Perhaps a nice hotel somewhere. Or better yet, a bed and breakfast.

Rummaging through her things, Amanda was glad that she'd remembered to pack her birth control medication. She had gone off of it a while ago, but had gone back on the moment they had started dating. The thought of being able to spend some time alone with Jesse filled her with delicious excitement.

Everything was ideal, and her entire being from her skin down to her bones vibrated to some unknown yet beautiful music.

Chapter Seven

"Your time has come."

When Amanda stepped out of her apartment building, she found Jesse standing beside a black Honda—and he was double parked.

Definitely a New York driver, she thought, amused.

It didn't take him long to dash through the spaces between the cars to the sidewalk where Amanda stood—and literally sweep her off her feet. She relished the feeling of his strong arms wrapped around her, his firm hands clasping her back. Despite her anxieties about their relationship, she had missed him a great deal. She blamed the stress for her jitters; that and having gone for so long without being in a serious relationship.

"It is *so* good to see you," he murmured in her ear.

Closing her eyes, she delighted in the sound of his voice. Then he pulled back just enough to meet her lips with his own. Her thoughts gone, the rest of the world crumbled away and vanished in the heat of that kiss. Her world burned, and she felt herself melting from the heat as he took her breath away.

Pulling back ever so slowly, Jesse looked her in the eyes and smiled. "Let's go."

"Yes," she replied with a cheerful tone, picking up the bag that she had dropped in her excitement. "Let's."

He put her bag in the trunk and opened the passenger door for her as she leapt in with grace. As he drove away, she watched her apartment building in the side mirror fade off into the distance.

For the next several blocks, they talked about her thesis, how she had done on her exams, and her plans for the summer. She hoped to dive right into an internship or some other study program that would aid her in getting her Ph.D., but would settle for just getting a part time job in the city that would help to pay bills and give her a little bit of extra money.

Jesse laughed at her. "Have you considered...you know...taking time off? Relaxing?"

With good humor she replied, "Yeah, I don't get to do that very often, I confess."

"No kidding." He flashed a quick grin in her direction as he continued to maneuver his way through the streets of Manhattan.

"Which reminds me," he added some moments later, "I don't

think I've ever gotten the opportunity to ask you what got you here. Why a Classics degree? Tell me the details. What inspired you?"

Amanda smiled in recollection. "I would have to say it was Apollo," she replied. "I promised him that I would go forth and get a degree in the Classics and use that to educate myself and others about Greek religion."

"Wow." He glanced at her before turning his eyes back to the road. "That's—that's really something. I mean it."

Not knowing what else to say, she smiled in return.

Jesse smiled back before asking, "What brought you to Greek religion? Worshipping Apollo?"

"Apollo has always been there for me, even in my childhood," she told him. "When I got older, I knew who it was—who he was, I mean—that small voice in my head, guiding me."

Pausing for a moment, she did her best to choose her next words with care. "He's just always been there, in everything I do, wherever I am. It's a little like...I dunno, being in love. Not really sure how else to describe it." Amanda gave a nervous laugh. She wasn't used to discussing it, and the times she had brought it up in, the reaction was negative to say the least.

However, she was quite surprised to see Jesse nodding and smiling. "Yes, I can tell. He's definitely been a positive influence in your life and has made you into the wonderful woman you are. And for that," he added with a great amount of warmth, "I should give him a few offerings myself."

Blinking, she sat upright in her seat, stunned. She considered the possibility that she had either misheard him or he was being insincere—but she sensed neither. Could it be? Could it be that he not only meant it but accepted her beliefs?

She decided to keep her response simple. "Thanks." A moment later, she inquired, "So where are we headed?"

Jesse removed his hand from the wheel and squeezed her own with an expressive twinkle in his eye. "Still not telling you. It's a surprise." He winked.

With a little frown she answered, "Okay, but please tell me that you haven't done anything crazy."

All she got from him was laughter as he continued driving them towards their destination. Amanda shook her head ruefully, not knowing how such surprises would affect her, but figured her best bet was to trust him, pray, and hope for the best.

* * * *

At some point on their journey, Jesse took her to a charming little diner in what she knew to be Astoria. Astoria was the "Little Greece" of Queens, and she delighted in the opportunity to be able to enjoy some delicious Greek food.

"The food here is quite good," he stated. "Believe me."

And indeed it was. She chose the chicken souvlaki and wasn't in the least bit disappointed.

She was amused to discover that he had once again ordered a small meal with a drink. "Don't you ever really eat?" she questioned him in a teasing tone of voice, but she was genuinely curious, as most of the men she had dated had much larger appetites than Jesse apparently possessed.

Jesse tensed slightly. "I have a sensitive stomach," he explained, "and so I eat vegan whenever possible."

"Oh!" she exclaimed. "I had no idea." She decided not to ask him for the specifics.

He smiled, looking a little embarrassed, and she was glad she hadn't pressed the issue.

"Don't worry about it. I don't discuss it too much." Jesse reached across the table and held her hand. "I hope that you are enjoying your food?"

"Oh yes." She smiled. "Their tzatziki is delicious. I could eat it all by itself."

"The way it was designed," he replied, chuckling.

Sometime during her meal, Jesse insisted upon ordering a bottle of Retsina. "Have you ever tried this stuff?"

She shook her head.

"You should," he informed her. "It's wine, but don't expect it to taste like the wine you're used to. It's actually quite good."

With a small swallow, she tried to discern the flavor but couldn't quite describe it. The wine tasted like fermented pine needles with small amounts of grapes.

"Have you ever heard of Retsina, Amanda?"

"I have, but I never had the guts to try it." She took another thoughtful sip. "When I was in Greece, I had Ouzo but not Retsina. I've tried many other Greek wines back home since my trip."

They spent the remainder of the meal discussing their travels and experiences that they had partaken of on their respective journeys. She expressed amazement to hear that not only did Jesse visit Greece, but he had also traveled to Italy, Japan, and the United Kingdom.

"Whenever you feel like visiting England we should go together," he suggested. That suggestion made her adore him even more.

* * * *

Some time after they had left the diner, Amanda could only guess that they were venturing further into Queens and would soon, perhaps, be in Long Island. She kept scrutinizing the roads and the signs, looking for places she recognized. Unfortunately, she hadn't traveled very much out of Manhattan during her stay at NYU and so nothing looked familiar to her. She settled for chatting with Jesse and enjoying the view from her window.

It was almost midnight when Jesse finally pulled off a major road and stopped at a nearby rest stop. He parked the car off to the side and gestured towards the sky.

"You can't see this in Manhattan. Damn, it's beautiful."

She stared up at the sky and saw all of the individual stars that had been obscured by the pollution from the city. Amanda leaned back against the car, finding herself awed by the majesty of the sky combined with the gentle, clean breezes that swept through her hair. Away from the highway and the noises of the city to distract her, she experienced the outdoors at its fullest. She was spinning away in the galaxy towards the stars.

With a flourish, Jesse opened up the back door of the car.

"Here, sit down with me." He sat on the seat and pulled her onto his lap. Wrapping his arms around her, they gazed up together at the night sky.

"Gods, it's beautiful," she breathed.

As he brushed her hair away from her face he merely commented, "And so are you."

She turned to smile at him before resting her head onto his chest. They stayed that way for a few moments until Amanda began to feel that something was odd. She racked her brain to figure it out, still bedazzled by the night sky and the feeling of being in his arms, but couldn't think of it.

Then at last she realized what it was: her ear was up against his chest, but she couldn't feel nor hear a heartbeat.

Puzzled, Amanda wondered if it was just because his leather jacket muffled the sound, but that couldn't have been it. At their close proximity, she should still be able to hear or feel something.

Figuring that the late hour and the fatigue were doing strange things to her mind, she dismissed it as her imagination. But in the silence between them, away from the city and the noise, the only breathing she heard was her own.

I must be losing it. But as she stared up into the sky, too many things fell into her mind, persistent in their logic. Amanda had never seen Jesse during the daylight, had never seen him more than perhaps taste food, didn't know what he did for a living other than "freelance computer work", and now she couldn't hear a heartbeat nor him breathing.

"Jesse?" she queried, her hesitancy showing in her voice.

Feeling him freeze behind her, she wondered if he knew what was on her mind, and thought to phrase her next words with caution.

"You're not a normal guy, are you? I mean," she continued, trying not to rush through her words, let alone sound nervous, "not that I'm...all that normal myself, and all, but...." Her voice trailed off. Amanda did not know what to say, or how to say it.

Many moments passed without a response. With great deliberateness, he ran his hands through her hair, and she delighted in the feel of his fingertips as they coursed through the strands, brushing against her neck as soft as silk.

In that moment she remembered their first dinner outing, when Jesse showed her the Latin magickal text, which referred to strange allegories, symbols and various arcana. She recalled that the text kept referencing "blood" in some mystical context.

"Jesse?" Her voice was quieter, and she was no longer so certain that she was crazy.

YOUR TIME HAS COME.

She couldn't tell if he spoke out loud or if she imagined him saying it in her head. The words rang clear and strong, but she *didn't* hear the words with her ears. It struck her as not unlike the rare moments when Apollo spoke to her directly.

Time froze in that moment as she continued to stare up at the sky, finding herself unable to move or utter a sound—not even to ask Jesse what was going on. Amanda felt the Retsina swimming through her bloodstream. She sank into the sensation of intoxication, lightheaded and dizzy.

She could do nothing but remain in that state as she relished the sensual feel of Jesse brushing her hair away from her neck, moving it over her left shoulder. The gentle winds blew on her neck, but she could neither feel his breath nor his lips.

Perhaps this lack of expected sensations made what happened next all the more startling.

Quick sharpness came down on her skin where her right shoulder met her neck. This action, filled with such surprising violence, made her scream. That scream was the only sound that filled her ears, and that scream matched the sharpness of the teeth that now pierced her flesh. It echoed as if it would go on forever, that primal scream.

Terror. Terror beyond terror, beyond mere words, filled Amanda, leaving her unable to think. This particular type of fear could drive one mad, to do unthinkable things, if only to flee the source of the horror. Would she die, or would she lose her mind? Had she the capacity of thought, she would've prayed. Prayed to her god, any god, for her to be saved from whatever was happening to her. But she couldn't. She didn't know why; her typical first instinct would've been to call upon her god. Power to think and act in a rational fashion was stripped from her, leaving her to merely absorb the moment. Her willful nature had been sapped from her as fear held her spellbound and hopeless.

Jesse's arms gripped her body and held her close to him as he drank. He was warm to the touch to her earlier, but now she was up against a small furnace. Amanda heard no breathing from him, no intake of air. If he was swallowing she couldn't hear it—yet she knew that her blood flowed into him. While he held her tight, he was completely rigid—and alien. Would he drain her dry? Would he kill her?

At the same time that fear flooded her, a sharp ecstasy cut through, rippling into her core, splitting her world apart. Her breath couldn't fill her lungs fast enough as strange noises came from the back of her throat. This mindless ecstasy terrified her more than the fear and pain itself, producing not just a physical sensation but an energetic one, not unlike some of her past mystical experiences with Apollo. It reverberated in her and all around her, completely drowning out the sharp pain of Jesse's teeth buried in her shoulder. A strange energy gushed out of him into her. It invaded her veins, her body—her mind. This energy, however, was vastly different from Apollo's:

heavier, richer—darker. It contained darkness beyond darkness, darker than the night sky above her, darker than the shadows that lived between the trees off in the distance.

Chthonic, her mind whispered. Earthy. Of the underworld. Like Persephone's eyes.

Intense, unearthly pleasure filled her. Losing complete control of her body's reactions, she threw back her head. She didn't know if it was of her own accord or by Jesse's hand. Somewhere in the back of her still-thinking mind she remembered the art of Ancient Greece, the depictions of the crazed women worshippers of Dionysus, their heads thrust back as they danced the night away for the god in a state of divine bliss.

Sharp piercing filled her everywhere, not just her flesh, but her insides. Dread, rapture—pain—it all saturated her until she couldn't bear it.

The stars brightened, and the world went from black to white. And as if she was witnessing the Big Bang, the very birth of the universe, that whiteness exploded in a burst of noiseless sound—and then all went dark.

Chapter Eight

"I never had a choice...."

When Amanda came to, she sat on the ground, propped up halfway against something warm and strong. It took her a few moments to realize that it was Jesse whom she leaned against and that his arms held her.

The taste of coppery sweetness coated her tongue. With this realization images both vague and sharp flooded her mind. Jesse pressing his wrist, dripping with blood, against her open mouth. A glint of silver. The feeling of something sharp piercing the palm of her left hand. Bizarre incantations, Jesse saying odd things she couldn't understand. A vivid flash of Jesse holding his still cut wrist to her palm.

Some of the memories made sense while others didn't. Confusion set in when Amanda looked down at her unmarred left hand. *Strange.* Maybe she had been hallucinating.

"No, it wasn't your imagination," Jesse said from behind.

Amanda blinked. He could hear her thoughts?

"I'll explain everything," he reassured her. "But first, let me help you stand."

The world spun as she tried to get up, her mind reeling at how dizzyingly clear and sharp everything around her now seemed. With a firm grip, Jesse steadied her and got her on her feet.

"Are you okay to walk?"

Unable to speak, Amanda could only nod and with caution began to move. After a few moments, the world stabilized around her.

I'm sea-sick, she thought, and a mad mirth filled her.

"I'm glad that you find this amusing," Jesse told her with a smile.

They walked side by side, and as the moments passed, Amanda began to realize that something was off, something was wrong. She sensed an uncomfortable, almost overwhelming feeling of intimacy with Jesse.

"You lied to me about being vegan," she abruptly declared. Her world was moving again, and she tried to will it to stop. Amanda took small, slow steps.

"You wouldn't have believed me if I told you," he replied quietly.

"I've never believed in vampires. I mean, that's what you are, right? They're supposed to be myth and legend. Then again," she added, "my gods are too, according to some people. So maybe I should be rethinking this mythical stuff."

Jesse just nodded, watching her with an attentive gaze as they strolled along the side of the road. His car was still parked a few hundred feet away in the opposite direction of where they were headed.

"I used to read vampire novels when I was younger. I loved Anne Rice. Bram Stoker's Dracula was a good movie, wasn't it? I didn't care for the book too much, but I enjoyed the movie. I guess I'm a sucker for romantic plots." At this point, Amanda realized that she was babbling, but kept rambling anyway. "Actually, that was a really bad pun, wasn't it? 'Sucker'?"

The silence from Jesse was almost as deafening as the strange feeling of closeness between them. Many painful minutes passed before he finally spoke.

"You're not done yet. The changes are still happening. We need to head back to the car."

"Changes? What changes?" Her voice sounded higher than normal.

"Follow me."

Without another word, she turned on her heel and walked with him back towards the car.

Jesse opened the passenger door. "Get in."

Soon he sat in the driver's seat again. In a matter of moments, they headed back towards the city.

With a brief touch of his hand to her shoulder, his only words were: "Hang on."

She nodded mutely. A strange, unsettling calm came over her. She embraced the numbness, but her thoughts kept racing.

"If you start...not feeling well, I'll pull over. Just let me know sooner than later, okay?"

An eerie, icy grip seized her chest. Staring at him with wide eyes, she asked with a trembling voice, "What have you done to me?"

"You'll be fine, Amanda." His tone was calm and soothing and it made her head spin even further. "I promise."

"That's not an answer to my question!" Now she was both angry and panic-stricken. *What the hell is going on?*

Then it hit her, all at once, the truth of the situation slamming into her like a runaway car.

"Gods, no. You didn't. Tell me that you didn't." Her face went into her hands. *No. Please, for the love of the gods, no….*

A moment of silence lingered. "Amanda." Jesse stated her name quietly, yet firmly.

"You—you made me into what you are, didn't you?" She could still taste the blood in her mouth. Would she ever be able to taste anything else ever again? Briefly, she wondered if she was losing her mind.

"Yes," he replied simply.

A desperate, fierce rage filled her. "Why?" she demanded.

Jesse winced at the sharpness of her tone, but tried not to show it. She watched him with growing irritation. Her annoyance drove her mad as it dawned on her that she *knew* his emotions, sensed him cringing as she spoke, knew he tried to hide it in his facial expression and body posture. She didn't want to feel or know any of these things so intimately.

Never before had she been this connected to him—or anyone else—and she hated it, utterly hated it. The sensation of unnatural familiarity kept pressing upon her, smothering her with its insistence.

"I wanted to show you my world," he answered at last. "And besides, had you found out, even if by accident, I—and you—would've gotten into trouble. Or worse."

Bitter laughter emerged from her. She stared down at her hands, then out her window. If only she could jump from the car and run. Where, she didn't know—nor did she care. "But you gave me no choice."

It only added to her anger and frustration that she could feel no pity or remorse from him, only unbending resolve.

"It was never yours to begin with."

"That's not true, and you know it."

Jesse frowned at her. "Amanda, I had to. I had to do it."

"But *why*?"

Fixing his gaze on the road, he only replied, "You're safe now. Don't worry, everything will be fine. I will help you."

"Help me?" Her harsh tone hurt her throat. "Help me with what?"

"I know that you are angry right now, Amanda," he said, his voice gentle and compassionate.

"You have no idea." In contrast, her voice was stone cold.

"In time, however," he paused briefly to change lanes, "you'll realize what I've done and why I did it."

"I keep asking you why! And you keep not telling me!"

Out of the blue a powerful wave of drowsiness hit her.

"Get some rest. I will talk with you later."

Amanda tried to fight him, but the feeling of sleep overcame her. In spite of herself, she couldn't help but be grateful and sank into unconsciousness.

Shivering and sweating, she awoke with a start. Jesse bent over her, holding a damp cloth to her forehead. She felt something soft underneath her and realized that she lay on a bed. How long had she been asleep? When did they stop driving? Where were they?

"I'm right here. I promise you that this will be over soon."

A wave of nausea hit as she tried to sit up. "Where am I?"

"It's not important right now. Just take it easy."

The fury that she experienced earlier swept over her, and she snarled back, "Why won't you tell me anything?"

As Amanda spoke, her upper jaw came forward. Then she realized that it wasn't her jaw, but a strange sensation of something moving through her gums over each of her incisors. *Teeth,* she thought hazily, *I'm growing teeth. Like I'm a child again.* Indeed, it was the same sensation she had when new teeth were coming in—except that this growth was much faster. The teeth emerged in a matter of moments, and oddly enough, the experience completely lacked pain.

She stared in confusion as Jesse simply looked on her with an expression she could only describe as "beaming."

"You'll do just fine," he assured her. "And I will tell you everything later, I promise. Just relax. One step at a time."

"Later when?" She ran her tongue over her incredibly sharp teeth before they retreated safely back into her gums.

"After you're done with the Turning process."

Her sole reaction was to turn her head and throw up.

Hours dragged on before the nausea subsided and Amanda was able to think coherently again. She still had no idea where she was, or what was happening to her. Her only certainty was that she was clearly transforming into a something else—a something which, had she been asked twelve hours ago if it had existed, her response would've been to laugh in the person's face.

Apollo, why? Why is this happening to me?

There was no response, but she was too caught up in her emotions to perceive one. *I never had a choice,* she thought with impotent rage. *If only he could've given me one.*

Something rumbled in her gut, and she thankfully noted that the room had an adjacent bathroom. And the door stood conveniently open.

When this is over, Jesse has a lot *of explaining to do.*

A painful cramp seized her, and she doubled over. One thing was certain—she definitely didn't choose to be in this much agony.

As a matter of fact, he can't begin to explain enough. Or to even begin to make up for this.

Oddly enough, she remembered her mother telling her the story of how she was born. According to her, she had practically bit her father's head off while she was in labor, yelling at him, *"See what you've done to me?"*

When she first heard the story she had laughed. However, the memory brought her little amusement, if any.

Somehow, she thought with chagrin, *I think that this is a little different....*

* * * *

"How is she?" James asked Jesse, who had been summoned to the magister's office with due haste upon learning of Amanda's Turning.

He gave a slight pause before he responded. "As well as can be expected. She's currently in her room resting."

"Good, let her rest. She'll need it."

Jesse thought of her reaction when she had learned what he had done and grimaced. "Yes, she will." Never before had he seen her so incensed—and he didn't like the thought of her being so angry at him. *She'll forgive me after this is over. I hope.* Surely, once she realized that he had added countless centuries to her life as well as extraordinary gifts that would aid her in her Classical Studies, she would no longer be irritated.

"Once she's ready, we'll bring her in and explain everything. You remember the procedure. I've already arranged the hall for her initiation."

"Wonderful," Jesse breathed. "I'm sure that it will be perfect."

After all, we'd both be dead if she had discovered the truth and I let her remain mortal. He had saved her life, let alone the future of their relationship. Amanda needed to understand that—and she would in time.

The magister glanced at the calendar pinned on the wall. "Ah, her Turning occurred on the new moon. How fortuitous."

"Quite," replied Jesse.

"I will say, however, that as fortuitous as this may be, I wish that you had taken my advice." James sighed. "I told you to wait at least a month or two. If this does not go well, you have only yourself to blame. But I am willing to do my best to see that this Turning does not hurt you, or her."

Jesse's mouth thinned. "I had no choice. She is a very...observant woman. While we were out on a romantic trip together, she discovered that I am not human. It was either Turn her or kill her. I had to abide by my oath to the Order—you know this."

"And I'm sure that this 'discovery' of hers wasn't aided by you in some way, hmm?"

Jesse met Janius's words with a poignant silence.

"She'll need a Clan name," he added abruptly. "Amaltheia is working on scrying one as we speak."

Jesse nodded, slightly distracted from the conversation. Even through the shields he had put up, he still could perceive Amanda's pain mingled with continued rage directed towards him. His jaw tightened. Hopefully the worst would soon be over, for her sake.

In spite of it all, he was convinced everything would work out in the end. They had a strong connection—made much stronger by him being her Sire and by their Bond.

The Blood Bond is strong. Perhaps the initial sharing of blood in her drinks or the natural connection we share has made it stronger.

Either way, Jesse was thankful to have her in his life and to know that he would be permanently in hers. He couldn't bear the thought of her being ripped away from him.

It will never happen, he thought determinedly. *Never.*

Chapter Nine

"What's the catch?"

Amanda didn't know how long she had been in the bathroom, seated on the toilet. She only knew that she hoped to never undergo this wretched experience—or anything like it—ever again.

Given that I don't even know if vampires eat, she thought wryly, *I may never have to.*

Walking back out into the room, she realized with a start that it was the same size as her apartment, except that it was a single bedroom. A full size bed with beautiful wrought iron head and footboard sat at the far end against the wall, next to a small, cherry-stained nightstand and lamp. A matching desk stood beside the entrance to the bathroom, in front of it a carved wooden chair with a beautiful cushion that reminded her of a medieval tapestry in an art show.

She spotted two other doors to the room but didn't know to where either of them led. Opening one experimentally, she uncovered a modest sized closet. Checking carefully, she found nothing else inside other than a bar to hang clothing on and a shelf above it.

Ah, I see. This door must be the way out of here.

With a quick flick of her wrist, she turned the knob.

It wouldn't budge.

Frowning, she wondered if it was stuck somehow. She tried again. No luck.

Then it dawned on her—she was locked inside the room.

Banging her fists on the door, she yelled, "Jesse, are you there? Let me out!"

No response.

Gods, I am going to kill him. Cross, she clenched her fists. *Now what?*

There was nothing for her to do except be increasingly aware that she was in a little room with nothing but a bed and a bathroom and she was unable to get out. She had no idea where she was and very little idea of what was happening—and would happen—to her.

Pacing the room, she thought about her options. Perhaps Jesse would come for her.

He's probably the one who locked me in here in the first place. But why?

Trapped. Amanda was trapped. In some bizarre place, alone, with no contact with the outside world and no real way of knowing what was to be her fate. Would she see any of her friends again? Her family? She now regretted even more not having had the chance to have more than a brief conversation with her mother over the phone during the past few weeks. Those may have been the last words she would ever get to say to her.

The eerie, icy fear that had gripped her chest earlier now shook the very roots of her being.

Apollo? What do I do?

No reply.

Apollo?

Silence.

So, this is what it's like to be abandoned by my god.

Collapsing to the floor where she had been standing, she drew her knees to her chest and sat there, unable to do much else.

* * * *

It was during a lengthy, in-depth conversation between Jesse and James on the details of Amanda's future in the Order that Lynne barged into the magister's office, banging the door behind her.

Whirling around to see who caused the disruption, Jesse wasn't the slightest bit surprised. *She's the only one around here who can get away with such dramatics.* He tried not to sneer.

Not one to mince words, she cut to the chase. "Magister, I need your help at once."

"What is it, Asherael?" James questioned, his tone even.

"There appears to be some sort of...disturbance in the living quarters. Near where...," she paused to glare at Jesse, "Turel's Childe is being kept."

James frowned. "Disturbance?"

"Pictures falling off of walls, chairs being knocked over—"

"Who is doing this?" he demanded.

Throwing her hands up in the air, Lynne replied with an air of desperation, "I don't know. If I didn't know better I'd say we had a pretty angry poltergeist."

"'Poltergeist'?" repeated James, who gave Jesse a pointed look.

A lull filled the room.

Finally, the magister spoke. "I'll look into it. Show me the way to where this happened. Turel, follow me."

Jesse gritted his teeth and quickly followed the magister out into the hallway.

Much to Jesse's chagrin, Lynne's concise but anxious report was anything but exaggeration.

The entire area within a couple of hundred feet away from Amanda's room was in an amazing state of disarray.

"Has she left her room since she got here?"

Jesse answered James curtly, "No, I locked the door." Out of his peripheral vision, he caught Lynne rolling her eyes.

With great restraint, the magister turned to look at him. "I see. Given the circumstances, you probably did the right thing. No telling what she would've done in her state." He walked to the door but turned towards Jesse. "You have the key?"

"Right here." Jesse fished in the pockets of his pants, retrieved the key to the room, and handed it to the magister.

James put the key into the knob and turned it. With little fanfare he pushed open the door. The three of them were greeted by the sight of a bed that had been moved from its original position to the middle of the room, a lamp turned over on the desk, and a chair that had been knocked to the floor. In the middle of the chaos was Amanda, huddled on the floor with her knees to her chest, unmoving. The sandals that she had been wearing were strewn on the floor beside her.

Before Jesse could open up his mouth to speak, one of the shoes was airborne. It struck him in the face with a loud smack. He stared at Amanda, then the shoe on the floor, stunned.

The magister watched the scene with a blank expression as Jesse made his way gradually towards where Amanda sat.

"Amanda? Amanda, are you okay?"

Silence.

"Amanda...?"

Without warning, the chair slid across the floor towards Jesse, nearly knocking him off his feet. He stumbled awkwardly. Tittering quietly behind him, Asherael was greatly amused to witness the sight of Jesse being humiliated.

With clenched teeth, the magister could only bring himself to utter a few taut words: "Turel, control your Childe."

Jesse heard the magister's British accent showing. Not a good sign.

Sure enough, upon leaving the room, James only paused to turn around and give Jesse a look he would never forget. He watched the magister leave as Lynne followed, smirking as she went. Never had he wanted to slap that woman so badly.

Bitch.

Then he turned towards Amanda with a sigh. It was obvious that she wasn't in a good mental or emotional state and it had gone far beyond what would've been expected due to her being Turned. *I shouldn't have shielded myself so well from her thoughts and emotions. I could've seen this coming and prevented it.*

He surveyed the room objectively. *Although, I must admit, I am impressed with how strong her powers got....*

What should he do? Jesse decided to settle with an apology.

"Amanda, I didn't realize that you would recover so quickly from the Turning. I'm sorry that I locked the door, but I was thinking only of your safety."

I WANT TO GO HOME. The words hit him with a jolt.

"I didn't realize you knew how to telepath," he acknowledged lamely. *YOU SHOULD'VE CALLED FOR ME,* he told her, his mental voice gentle and chiding.

Her voice was small and quiet. "I don't." She mentally added, *I WOULD HAVE IF I HAD REALIZED I KNEW HOW.*

"Then how—"

"Apollo. It's how I normally talk to Apollo." She hugged her knees more tightly to her chest. To Jesse's sight, Amanda looked about five years younger with the way she sat, curled up in a ball. Her looking like that made him want to put his arms around her and cradle her. But the look in her eyes was something that he wanted to wipe away. She shouldn't have eyes like that. Not ever.

Then he realized what she had just said and blinked. "Talk? You mean pray, right?"

"No," she answered him sharply. "I mean talk."

"Oh."

An uncomfortable silence fell between them.

"You're not letting me go home, are you?" she asked quietly.

Jesse sighed. "No, at least...not yet. We can get your things for you later. But you can't go back, not permanently. No."

She stared down at the floor. "Why not?"

"Because you're new to this world, and we need to protect you," he stated simply.

"'We'?" she echoed. "'We'? Who's this 'we'?"

"Myself and the rest of the Clan here—as well as the entire Order." He looked into her uncomprehending face and added, "If you follow me, I can have everything explained to you. Like I promised."

"Why did you do this to me?" Something in her voice ripped into Jesse's heart. He didn't know how to respond and realized that words alone wouldn't do. Instead, he sent a wave of emotion to her through their Bond. Love, warm affection—and passion.

"I do not want to hurt you," he tenderly assured her. "Not ever."

She sighed, and a glint of crimson tainted her face.

Blood tears. *Dammit.*

"I want to believe that."

"But?" he prompted.

Amanda wiped at her face quickly and slowly brought herself to a standing position. It was then that she glanced at the mess in the room, her eyes widening.

"What happened?"

He smiled. "You did it."

Amanda's eyes grew wider. "I did *what*?" As she continued to stutter in protest, Jesse walked over and put his hands on her shoulders. Looking at him blankly, she stopped.

With a light kiss to her forehead, he informed her, "You do it when you're drunk too."

"I never get drunk." She frowned at him. "Well, okay, I can get a little tipsy on wine, but I have never genuinely gotten drunk. Not in a long time. And especially not around you."

"Pity. Come, James is waiting. We have a lot to talk to you about."

* * * *

James's office consisted of a few large bookshelves and a desk made of dark wood—*Mahogany,* Amanda figured. She noted the tidiness of the place with approval. It reminded her a little bit of one of her professor's offices.

The magister gestured to the leather chair in the room, and Amanda sat down in it gratefully. It was a very soft, luxurious black leather chair—the sort of furniture she had expected to see in a mansion. Then again, much of this place looked extremely well kept to her—as much as she had seen of it thus far.

"First of all, I want to apologize for the...boldness of my brother. He adores you—which is as plain as day, if you'll pardon the ironic phrase—and I can see why he made the choice that he did."

Amanda didn't know what to say in response. Choosing the wiser option, she held her tongue and waited for him to speak further.

"While you were...ill, I took the liberty of getting a few things for you from your apartment. I hope that you do not mind the intrusion, but I figured that you would want them here."

She nodded calmly. "What did you take?"

"Your computer, the statue of Apollo that was on top, and a copy of your thesis paper that you had on your desk." He added as if in apology, "I didn't think it would be wise to go through your personals. Jesse can help you with that if you wish."

She smiled. He must've known enough about her from talking with Jesse to bring the statue.

"I had the opportunity to take a look at your thesis paper and I could see that he wasn't exaggerating in the least. You are a very intelligent young woman and with great talent in the magickal arts."

She wished that he would get to the point. "Why am I here?"

"Amanda, what do you enjoy doing the most?"

Blinking rapidly, she responded, "I-I love studying the Classics. Doing research. I-I like writing and I enjoy occult study. And practice. But...."

James stood up from behind his desk and slowly paced around the room. "Amanda, imagine having access to libraries of books. Vast libraries. Books and research material, most of which are not accessible to modern academia—some of which aren't even supposed to exist."

Her head spun. "Are you serious?"

"Yes, entirely serious. In fact, there are books the Vatican believes it has the only surviving copies of—and we have them, right here."

Amanda sat there in shock for a moment. When she came to, she realized that she gaped rather idiotically at him.

"But...my degree," she stuttered. "I wanted to teach—"

"Amanda, your skills are wasted in the classroom and even more so on the scholastic community at large. Imagine working side by side with colleagues who not only have similar religious beliefs as you do, but also share your occult interests."

It boggled her mind. She had kept her religious beliefs under lock and key while she attended school for fear that it would affect her relationships with her professors and hence, her grades. Many of them were Christians who believed that no one today worshipped the gods, and they often had a fairly disparaging tone towards the ancients. She could differ with them on a number of issues, but only if she managed to achieve the same academic standing that they had obtained, would she stand a chance at being heard.

Besides, that wasn't the purpose of getting the degree, anyway. It was a promise to Apollo. It looked as if her promise to him would still be kept on some level, albeit with a twist. The gods seemed to have other plans for her.

"As for formal training in the occult, you would receive that as well—and from people who wouldn't mock you for your religious beliefs or expect you to conform to a different standard. And if you were able to pursue your Ph.D. without going out during the day, we would be fine with that, as long as we kept an eye on you to make sure that you didn't get yourself into trouble, or even hurt."

"What's the catch?"

James laughed. "The catch? The catch is that you are now like us, a vampire. You will have to take great care to avoid sunlight. In time you will perhaps be able to be outside in the day, but only while wearing a good deal of clothing and some spellwork. And yes," he continued, "you will need to drink blood in order to survive. The good news about all of this, however, is your increased psychic skills—not to mention your lifespan has been indefinitely extended."

Eternal life. Occult knowledge. Classical studies. The chance to hone her psychic skills. The opportunity to practice her spirituality without restraint—perhaps increase her connection to the god and thus her ability to serve him better.

Of course, she'd be the only Apollonian not able to ever endure the sun, and she had to drink blood. There were definitely drawbacks here.

"Are you familiar with esoteric orders such as the Golden Dawn, Freemasonry, Ordo Templi Orientis?" he asked.

She nodded.

"Good. Our structure is similar to that of the Freemasons. We have three degrees of initiation—technically four, as we have an entry level apprentice degree. There's an inner order after that, if you make it through third degree."

In spite of herself, she was intrigued. "Do you work with

alchemy?"

"Are you referring to the literal changes of lead into gold, or are you referring to the spiritual, symbolic alchemy?"

"The spiritual, but I'm familiar with using physical rituals to obtain the spiritual results."

Janius looked at her quizzically.

"Sympathetic magick," she explained.

"Ah! Yes. Hermetic philosophy, as above, so below—we study that here too, as well as other spiritual disciplines."

She couldn't believe her ears. Maybe she was still trapped in that room, delirious with fever and pain and hallucinating all of this. It certainly made more sense than what she was being told right now.

"So, Amanda, would you like to join us?"

"Yes." The word slipped out before she had a chance to think it over, intuit what would be the best option, consult Apollo....

Yet she sensed that it was the right choice.

Some time later, Jesse walked with Amanda, carrying some of her belongings into her new room.

"So, are you still mad at me?"

She glared at him. The stifling sense of intimacy was still present, but it wasn't strangling her nearly as much as it had before. She hoped it was just in her head and that in time it would just go away. "By all rights and purposes, I should be. All of that would've been so much simpler if you had just told me!"

Jesse chuckled. "Yes, but in the state you were in, you not only wouldn't have wanted to hear it, you wouldn't have comprehended, either." He sighed. "I am really sorry about locking you in the room. Honest."

"You better be."

She held the door open as Jesse placed the computer on the desk.

"I'll get the monitor next." He rubbed his hands together. "You think you'll be ready for your initiation in a few hours?"

"I think so."

"Good." He put his arm around her and kissed her gently on the cheek. "I have a surprise for you afterwards."

"A surprise?"

"Yes, I think you'll like it." With a grin, he made his way out the door.

She watched him go for a moment, then placed her bust of Apollo on top of the computer, where it had been before.

Apollo, I really hope that this is your doing, or some other god's, and I really do belong here. Because it doesn't look like I have much of a choice in the matter.

Chapter Ten

"Welcome, Lyrael!"

"Have you ever undergone an initiation, Amanda?"

She answered James with as much truth as she could. "No, only self-initiations. Through books and alchemy."

"Ah." He smiled, wistful, as if recalling a childhood memory. "This will be...rather different."

"I did work through the Golden Dawn grades, though."

"To what grade?"

"Portal."

At this, he laughed, loud and hearty. "Well, after this, you can call yourself an honorary Adeptus Minor. You've already undergone the death and rebirth in your Turning."

Go figure. Odd that she hadn't realized the connection.

"Besides," he added in a nonchalant voice, "you've already fulfilled part of the oath."

"Wh-what?" Confused, Amanda gave him a look, but he only raised an eyebrow in response.

"Tiphareth," he told her.

Tiphareth, Tiphareth.... She racked her brain for a moment, then it hit her: *"I further promise and swear that...I may at length attain to be more than human...."*

She swallowed hard. Janius noted her reaction with a nod and something akin to a reassuring smile.

Blindfolded and with hands bound, Amanda was taken into a room for the ceremony by someone who gripped her by her left arm. A strong woman's voice cried out to her right.

"Who dares to enter our Sanctuary?"

"A woman named Amanda Riverson." The words came from the man who gripped her arm. She recognized the voice as Jesse's. "She has shed the bonds of mortality and seeks initiation into our sacred Order."

Interesting that Jesse should be the one to bring me in here. But it made sense, literally and symbolically.

"Then bring her before me."

Half pushed, half dragged, she made her way with tentative steps in the direction of the woman's voice.

"Do you, Amanda, pledge yourself to studying the mysteries of this Order?"

She cleared her throat. "I do."

"Then repeat after me, stating your name. I...." There was a brief pause.

"I, Amanda Riverson...."

The woman continued, "Swear to guard the secrets of this Order...."

"Swear to guard the secrets of this Order...."

"And the identities of its members...."

"And the identities of its members."

"As well as the knowledge of the existence of our kind." The woman emphasized the words 'our kind', and in that moment, Amanda knew what she had become and that there was truly no turning back.

"As well as the knowledge of the existence of our kind."

"And should I break this oath...."

"And should I break this oath."

"May I be staked and left out in the sun for the fires to claim me."

Nervous, she swallowed and repeated, "May I be staked and left out in the sun for the fires to claim me."

A long moment of silence seemed to drag out longer than it should have. A trickle of sweat ran down Amanda's back.

"Very well then. Amanda, I welcome you as an apprentice degree initiate into *Ordo Draconis et Rosae*, otherwise known as the Order of the Dragon and the Rose, and into its clan, Clan Gladius. We are so named as the bearers of the double-edged sword. We are protectors and fighters, eagles and serpents, merciful and severe.

"Amanda, from this moment onwards, you will be known to us as Lyrael, she who is the servant of the lyre—the lyre being a symbol of your god. You may now be unbound and the blindfold removed!"

Suddenly, her vision went from pitch black to the direct view of a tall woman's face. She appeared to be in her mid to late twenties, and her long, white-blonde hair came down the back of her red robe trimmed with black ribbon. Her bright and friendly green eyes peered into her own calmly.

"Welcome, Lyrael. My name is Asherael, and it is an honor to have you here." She reached out to clasp Amanda's hand and shook it firmly. Beside her stood James, dressed in the exact reverse colors as the robe Asherael wore, black with red trim.

"And I am Janius, the Magister of Clan Gladius. I bid you welcome." His ordinarily somber face broke into a boyish grin.

"And this," the magister gestured, "is your Sire, Turel."

Jesse looked deeply into her eyes and smiled. At that moment, she didn't have to see the sun—it was already shining on her. In those few moments, she forgot her fear and discomfort in her newfound situation. She would be able to continue her research and be with Jesse. Surely everything would be all right.

"It is customary on this occasion to have your first drink." James presented Amanda with a chalice. At first she hesitated, but glanced at Jesse. Something in his eyes took away her apprehension, and she gulped down the sweet, metallic fluid.

As she drank, James crossed his arms into an X shape over his chest and continued to speak. "'He who eats My flesh and drinks My blood has eternal life, and I will raise him up on the last day. For My flesh is true food, and My blood is true drink. He who eats My flesh and drinks My blood abides in Me, and I in him.'" He paused, letting the words from the Bible sink in.

Blood—I just drank blood. And yet, all she felt was calm.

"Many religions throughout the ages have understood the Eucharist between the ingestion of wine as symbolic blood—or blood itself. Devotees of Dionysus ate raw animal flesh and drank wine, Jews drink wine on the Shabbos to commemorate the union of Shekhinah with Adonai, Christians partake of wine as part of their Eucharist in the Mass, and we drink blood that we may too have eternal life—and the Holy Grail.

"May you find your Grail, Lyrael. Even more importantly," the magister smiled, "may you become it."

* * * *

The rest of the ceremony was simple—in fact, it was Amanda's feeling that it was deceptively so—but fascinating, and she begged one of the officers for the script afterwards to study. She was laughed at, told that would be part of her studies, and she was more than welcome to the copy.

Jesse escorted her back to her room, discussing with her the intricate parts of the ceremony and some of the symbolism behind it.

"I assume that you comprehended the part about Clan Gladius?

The double-edged sword?"

She nodded. "Yes, the concept of moderation in duality. Very cool."

He grinned. "Glad you like it." He reached into his shirt and pulled out the rest of the silver necklace she had seen him wear on many occasions. Two charms hung from the chain: a tiny silver sword pointing downwards, and what she recognized as an Eye of Horus.

"The sword I wear on behalf of my Clan," Jesse informed her.

"And the other for your faith?"

"Yes."

"I just had one other question, though. Clans? Are they like covens or something?"

"Yes, they are. They are local 'covens', if you will, of the Order. They go by bloodline as well as location."

"Interesting."

"Just wait until you attend a gathering. That's even more interesting. The stories I could tell you...but I'll wait until later."

"Okay." She smiled.

They had just reached the door of her room when Jesse announced, "By the way, your initiation isn't over."

"What?"

He opened the door and pushed her in. But it was a gentle push. "You heard me."

Oh, that she did. Amanda laughed. Deep and throaty, it was unlike her usual laughter. She hadn't been with a man in years. Maybe not since she was a freshman or sophomore in undergrad.

She could stand to ignore the new vibe between the two of them for an hour or so, if it meant the chance to recover from her ordeal—perhaps even relieve some long held tension. It was either that or several drinks. Could she drink again? She had no idea.

"When they brought you in, you were both bound and blindfolded, remember?"

Smirking, she nodded. She saw where this was headed.

"Since you've already undergone the necessary component to your initiation," he continued, his voice smooth, "you don't need to be blindfolded."

"Okay then...."

With a great strength that took her by surprise, he grabbed her and put her on the bed.

"But...you will need to be bound."

From his pockets he produced the same cords with which she was bound during the ceremony. Amanda fought to keep herself from laughing. She had a feeling that she was going to like this.

Apparently, there had been four cords wrapped around her wrist—with all sorts of meaning attached in regards to the number, how they were bound, when they were bound—and he laid them all on the night table.

She was still dressed in a simple black robe with nothing else on but her undergarments. Jesse lifted her and swept the robe over her head and onto the floor. She marveled at the exquisite sensation of the robe and his hands on her bare skin. Every nerve in her body had been intensified, and each tiny sensation was another wave of bliss.

With an amazing amount of ease, he slid his hands under the strap and undid her bra. She sensed him debating as to whether or not to use it as an additional restraint, but the sensations of his fingers on her body were sending her into orbit around some other world, and she didn't care.

I could get to like that odd connection during moments like these, she thought fuzzily.

I'M GLAD FOR THAT.

Grabbing her wrists with one hand, he reached for one of the cords with the other. First, he bound her right wrist to the bedpost, then her left.

Amanda was both amused and delighted. One of her boyfriends had liked to play with scarves in bed, and she had enjoyed it. She wondered what other tricks Jesse had up his sleeve.

Unhurried, Jesse moved his hands over her body towards her breasts and bent his head to kiss her with such force and passion that she melted in his arms. His fingertips did wondrous things to her nipples, and at the height of their embrace, he sharply squeezed one of them.

She removed her lips from his long enough to gasp aloud at the unexpected sensation. He recaptured them for a moment before releasing her lips and moving his mouth to her nipple. His fangs grazed her breast, and his other hand slid down over her stomach to her panties. Amanda moaned as his hand dove underneath her panties, then leisurely pushed them down, his fingertips brushing over sensitive folds of her skin and the inside of her thigh. With a lifting of each leg, the underwear was soon removed.

Jesse reached for the third cord and bound her left ankle to the bedpost, then her right. Blinking, she realized that she was bound to the bed, unable to move.

This should be interesting.... Amanda couldn't help but ponder how much more creative Jesse was versus her past boyfriends.

She soon found out.

With a great flourish, he whipped out a small knife from the belt of his pants. Her eyes got a little wide.

"Um...."

"Shh."

That one sound he made was enough to relax her. With an ease that she could only describe as practiced, he scraped the knife over her body with careful strokes, which made unnerving, rippling sensations within her. Little red lines began appearing all over her stomach, chest, arms....

Then he ran his tongue down her chest to her belly. Eager, Amanda waited for him to continue, but Jesse stopped.

With the knife in his right hand, he moved his left hand to rest over the curly hairs between her legs, his tongue teasing her navel, lower abdomen.... The intensity of the waves of pleasure running through her was almost too much to bear.

Swiftly, he inserted two fingers into her, and as she flinched, he brought down the knife to the area between her breasts and made a small cut. With his fingers stroking her innermost moist softness, his lips wandered to where her blood trickled down her chest. Both his tongue and his lips were maddening upon her skin, and she didn't know which produced the most pleasure: him sucking away at the incision he had made on her skin, or the fingers penetrating her. Sometime during the dual ecstasy he was imposing upon her, she realized that he was still clothed in the robe he had been wearing for the ritual.

Realizing her thoughts, Jesse stopped, bringing his head up to look into her eyes. He smiled and removed his fingers—much to her dismay—but his hands were now able to remove his ritual garment. Amanda looked him over. He wore no undergarments, and his pale and sleek body reminded her somewhat of a wild cat. Perhaps a leopard.

The analogy was apt, as he dove—fangs extended—for her neck. She moaned, half in pain and half in pleasure, remembering the night he had Turned her. Was it only a day or so ago? Maybe a week, or a month. The feeling of drunken bliss overwhelmed her, and her hands sought to grip something, anything—but the restraints were tight over her wrists.

After a few moments, he lifted himself up and began to trace another pattern of lines and blood across her midsection, her stomach—lapping it up with his tongue. The juxtaposition of the sting of the blade and the sensual roughness of his tongue made her eyes roll back in her head.

Welcome to Clan Gladius.

Before she knew it, his head was between her legs, his teeth scraping over her sensitive folds. The noises at the back of her throat sounded to her like they came from someone else. His fingers reinserted themselves, reminding her of that intense dream that she had a while back about him—and she realized with a start how much it had tried to tell her in advance.

That was no dream.

The constant stream of telepathic messages would've unnerved her at any other time or place, but she was drowning in a sea of euphoria and incapable of caring. His tongue moved over her most sensitive spot. He touched her tiny but swollen bud which nearly made her scream. Then he began to gently suck on it, his fingers continuing to do their snakelike dance in and out of her slick entrance.

Before she could be pushed over the edge, he removed both his fingers and his mouth abruptly and dragged his tongue up and over her body. By the time he had passed her breasts and made his way to her neck, she was incapable of thought.

It was then that he impaled himself inside of her, and with the same motion, drove his fangs into her neck. The room went white as the waves crashed over her again and again.

Encouraged by a mental nudge from him, she sunk her own fangs into his neck. The two joined in a state of unnatural bliss. Jesse slowly moved in and out of her, relishing every moment that the two were joined. The strange connection that Amanda had sensed earlier between them coalesced in her chest. Surely her heart and body would both explode.

Mine, she thought she heard. It barely registered, drowned out by the tempo of their movements and the waves of delight which continued to wash over her.

Jesse thrust harder. The act came to a climax for them both, and in that moment, Amanda experienced ecstatic fusion between her and him that she could only compare to union with a god.

Chapter Eleven

"I can't seem to think clearly around him."

After their fervent union, Jesse untied Amanda and cradled her. Being worn out to the point of extreme exhaustion, it didn't take her long to fall into a deep yet peaceful sleep in his arms.

When she awoke, dazed, she looked around her room. The ceiling light was still on, but Jesse was nowhere to be found. Much to her chagrin, he had tied her right wrist to the bedpost while she slept.

Amanda was less than amused. Being tied up was far more enjoyable in the heat of passion versus her actually wanting to leave the bed. It wasn't long before once again she simmered in resentment.

Does he think that this is cute? Or is he deliberately trying to hold me prisoner for some reason?

In the midst of her stewing over Jesse's latest behavior, Amanda paused. Did he know that she was now awake? Could he sense her anger?

She reached out for him with her mind. His presence lingered, still much closer to her than she would've preferred. But he seemed preoccupied and unaware of her thoughts and feelings. He must've shielded from her. Again.

Fuck. I would so love an explanation from him when he gets back.

Tugging at the rope with her left hand, she was unable to do much more than loosen the binding by a meager amount.

Impatient, she exhaled. She realized it was the first time she had exhaled in a while, and the tiny but mounting feeling of resentment grew stronger and gave way to shock. Longer than she was capable of remembering. A day ago? Two?

Amanda was no longer breathing.

Feeling her chest, she realized it too was still. No heartbeat. She checked her pulse on her neck to be certain, but there was nothing there, just the feeling of her skin. It was oddly normal to no longer take in air, as normal as breathing had been when she was human.

I'm no longer human. Closing her eyes, she leaned back into the pillows and began to reflect. It was too late now to do anything about her state, and she had been trapped in this from the moment she'd met Jesse. *Turel,* she corrected herself. His name was also

Turel. She wondered when she would be expected to call him by his Order name versus his real one.

If it even was his real name.

Her uncertainty over his identity was one of many causes for the alarm she experienced. Joining this vampire Order, being with Jesse...none of it seemed to have the clarity of purpose that it did before. Or did it? The idea of doing research still appealed to her, but what was the catch? Did she really want this life, or had she merely been swept up in the excitement of the opportunity to be with Jesse—let alone the temptation of having access to all of those books, all of that knowledge which she couldn't find anywhere, in any university or library? And Jesse...she didn't know what to think of his having locked her in her room earlier and now having left her while she was sleeping—tied to her bed, no less—she began to wonder if being in this strange place was such a good idea.

And yet it seemed perfectly fine before. What was happening to her?

I can't seem to think clearly around him.

Amanda frowned at this realization, rubbing her head. Confusion and frustration filled her. She no longer knew what she wanted. The only thing she knew that she desired for certain was her wish to get out of bed and out of the damned room.

After spending a few moments with her eyes closed trying to will herself to calm down, Amanda looked around the room. A set of keys lay on the nightstand beside the bed. She strained and pulled, but they remained out of reach.

"Fuck," she hissed, her temper flaring. She reached out again.

Much to her astonishment, the keys slid across the surface in her direction. They didn't move much, and she still couldn't reach them.

Gritting her teeth, she reached out again and willed with all of her might to make the keys move. Whatever she did apparently worked, for the keys shot across the nightstand and almost hit her in the face as they landed on the bed beside her.

"Beautiful, just beautiful," she mumbled, irritated once more. Picking up the keys with her left hand, she began to saw away at the rope around her wrist and the bedpost. The rough edge of the key did the trick, but it was a grueling process. When a mere couple of threads held her wrists, she yanked herself free and got out of bed.

Amanda badly wanted to shower, but she spent time locating

clothing instead. There would be plenty of time to shower later. Right now, she wanted to get out of this room. Fast.

Thinking they might be useful later, she pocketed the keys in her jeans and made her way to the door.

I wonder if it's locked? Her mouth thinned. She was beginning to have the feeling of déjà vu. If Jesse had the audacity to leave the door locked as well as tying her up....

She gave the knob an experimental turn. It moved.

A smile slowly spread across her face. At least one thing worked in her favor.

For a long moment, she stared at the door, deep in thought. If she truly had this ability to move things with her mind—as she had previously demonstrated—it might be a good idea for her to consciously practice and hone this talent. Who knew when it might come in handy?

She reached out her hand, but didn't touch the doorknob. Instead, she focused on turning the knob in her mind.

It turned. Just like that. It was so simple. All she had to do was put the object in her mind and use her will. She wondered why she hadn't done it before, and it made her realize how often odd things happened to her when she drank. It was why she so rarely did drink and dismissed it as her low alcohol tolerance causing her to think and see odd things. Was this ability something that had been a part of her to begin with, now strengthened by her being a vampire? Or was it something that she now could do only *because* she was a vampire?

Ideas flowed through her mind, followed by numerous questions. Questions about herself, why she was in this room, feeling fangs coming in over her teeth as she contemplated what was happening to her.

How long have I been so unaware of myself and what I am capable of? Have I relied too often on the god, or was I too wrapped up in my studies?

It would be a lie to say that what had happened to her was entirely bad; in fact, there were elements for which she was thankful. She supposed that she owed it to Jesse to finally take her out of her sheltered existence and make her realize how important having passion in her life was to her—and what it meant to be in love.

In love. Was she truly? With him? She hardly even knew him, and yet her feelings were so strong—in ways both good and bad. His presence made her heart jump and her world shine, even as it was completely destroying her way of life and so many things that she treasured. She had gained much as a result of meeting him, but was the price worth it? She didn't know. And now it was too late, one way or another. Amanda was permanently altered and continued to undergo some odd transformation. She felt it, sensed it—it affected everything she did and thought. The changes that she experienced were totally alien to her, and she had no comprehension as to what all of them were about.

In her mind, she held the knob turned—and door ready to be opened—as she quietly reflected upon her emotions. All of these strong reactions were not like her. She was normally even tempered and slow to feel strongly about anything. Now it seemed that she was perpetually filled with rage, senseless rage.

But the rage wasn't totally senseless; she knew why she teetered on the verge of a meltdown. Amanda had every reason in the world to be angry.

Who wouldn't be? she thought bitterly.

Her mind tightened on the knob as if it were a muscle squeezing it. Somehow the anger made her focus sharper, stronger. Somewhere in the depths of her rage was a sense of calm—the eye of the storm, regarding everything with a cool passion.

In that clear state, she recognized how aggravated she was with Jesse for making her into a vampire, removing her from her home and everything that she knew and held dear, bringing her here without so much as a warning of what might happen to her. Would she be able to finish her degree? Or be able to speak to her parents ever again? And what about his treatment of her after the fact? It made her even more incensed as she went over the details: first he had left her in a locked room, then he left her tied to a bed while he went to gods only knew where.

Left her there alone, in a strange place, without knowing why he disappeared, nor what he thought when he did so. At one point she had trusted Jesse—almost blindly. Now she wasn't so certain about him or his intentions, especially after having woken up to him having departed from her bed, without as much as a good morning or a note or anything—and her wrist tied to the bedpost, trapped in that room, alone.

After the first time they had slept together, no less.

Fury burst through her as the door of the room violently thrust itself open.

* * * *

James strolled in the direction of Amanda's room when he heard a loud banging noise.

In his mind's eye, he suddenly saw the young woman surrounded by a whirlwind of dark scarlet energy as she walked out of her room. *Red, anger.*

Despite his concern, he chuckled. *Oh, to be a young Childe.* Then he forced himself to remember his responsibilities. That young Childe, Amanda—Lyrael—was most likely extremely irate at something or someone—and was also demonstrating a good degree of psychic talent for someone so newly Turned. Before, the tornado of destruction that had been caused by her was unintentional.

Now, not so much.

The magister frowned. Where was Turel? He froze as he attempted to retrace the evening's events in his mind. There was that conversation with Amaltheia, and she had mentioned something about Turel. What was it?

Hunting, he had wanted to go out for food before he could take Amanda on her first hunt.

But did he tell this to Amanda?

Judging from the furious energy in her direction, he surmised that the young vampire hadn't communicated this to his Childe. This may have something to do with her ire.

And they are lovers besides. He grimaced. Young love. This wasn't going to be a fun Turning to witness. Amanda's awakening would involve many harsh realities, including the nature of relationships and emotions among vampires.

James shook his head sadly. It wasn't his place to get involved in such matters, but if Amanda did worse things than banging doors open, he would be forced to do so.

* * * *

Lynne was busy reading a rather lengthy, yet concise paper on Greco-Roman esoterica belonging to a certain young graduate student of NYU. The paper was so impressive that she had been completely absorbed in reading it. She had even missed an appointment to talk with one of her first degree students about his research project.

I'll have to reschedule with Theodotos later, she thought, her attentions focused elsewhere. A Clan emergency. She could make something up and spend extra time with him as an apology.

Finally done reading Amanda's thesis, she stared at the sheets of paper on her desk in disbelief, stunned to the core.

This was no college floozy; no bimbo could've penned this. There was much knowledge evident in her work, and such amazingly sharp intelligence that went way beyond book learning. And through it all, she saw how passionate Amanda was on her chosen topic. The words were lively and enthusiastic. She truly enjoyed her subject matter in a way that Lynne so rarely saw in the academic communities.

How in the world did Turel find this woman? She gritted her teeth, fighting the urge to bare her fangs. Of all of the unfairness...!

How I would love to pick her brain on so many things. I bet I could even steer her towards a few projects that we have available. Amanda's insights would be valuable indeed—far more so than Asherael had ever desired to believe, not to mention admit.

Lynne desperately wanted to sit down and have a conversation with her. Why had she chosen this topic? Why a comparison with Greece and Rome? Why Classical Studies to begin with? Was she Pagan, or did she merely have an interest in ancient esoteric works? Or both?

Groaning in frustration, Lynne ground her elbows into the desk and slammed her face down into her hands. She didn't want to like Amanda, due to her association with Jesse, but she was forced to admit that the young woman had a fascinating mind and most likely also possessed quite an intriguing personality. She wished that she'd met her sooner, before Jesse had the chance to meet and Turn her. How would that have gone? What would have changed as a result? What had Amanda been like as a mortal?

Lynne was surprised to discover that she wasn't in the least bit angry at this point, only deeply saddened.

She should've been my Childe, not his.

The thought was wistful and filled with regret. She resolved to get to know the young woman on her own terms and see if there was a chance for her yet.

If I had a god to pray to, I'd pray that Turel not ruin her. Maybe, just maybe, I can help.

With that thought, she jumped from her chair and left her office with the intention of finding Amanda.

I completely misjudged her. After all, it's probably not her fault that she got mixed up with Turel. He's charming, often has a clue about magick, and probably swept her off her feet.

As Lynne turned down the corridor, she decided that maybe what Lyrael needed was a good influence or two in her unlife. Get her to think for herself and not become a mindless slave to her Sire.

She deserves better than him, she thought grimly.

The sight of Amanda walking down the corridor halted Lynne's rapid walking pace. She opened her mouth to speak but stopped when the young Childe looked directly at her.

Amanda's aura glowed redder than the carpet beneath her feet, and the fury Lynne saw in those eyes hit her very core. And she could only guess at why.

Weary, Lynne sighed. *I came just in time.*

Chapter Twelve

"Welcome to the Blue Moon.*"*

"Hello, Asherael," Amanda's quiet, measured voice greeted the blonde vampire.

Lynne stared at her for a few moments before replying. The new vampire reminded her of someone or something, but she couldn't quite place who—or what. *It'll come to me.*

Lynne jerked her head slightly, her long blonde braid reminding Amanda of a cat's twitching tail.

"Lyrael—Amanda—I just finished reading your thesis and I wanted to let you know that I was...extremely impressed by it."

Amanda blinked at her, but Asherael continued, "It's not just the content or the research—you obviously put a lot of heart into your subject matter. I loved it. Very much. How long did you work on it?"

"I...." She clenched and unclenched her fists. "Seven months, but the research I had been doing for years. You're—you're right, it's something I enjoy."

"Maybe, if you have a moment, I would love to talk to you about your thoughts on the influence of Greek philosophy and mysticism on modern theurgy. I had some ideas, and—"

"Asherael, I would love to talk with you sometime, but right now I need to go for...a walk, or something." Her voice was harsh, but at that moment she looked beyond caring.

The blonde vampire frowned. *Egads, apprentices.* Newly made vampires were known for being temperamental, rather like adolescents in the midst of hormonal changes. Amanda, as an apprentice, demonstrated not only that transitional period, but the alchemy of the newly initiated. Before long, the alchemy of the Blood would influence her and bring her away from human inclination. That time wasn't now, however—not till after her time spent in the Apprentice degree.

"That's fine," Asherael replied calmly. "But before you go running off, there's a pub not that far from here. I hear their wine selection is excellent, and they make a great martini."

"W-what?" she sputtered.

"My treat. Besides, it beats being cooped up in your room, right?"

"But...I—"

"Yes?"

"I thought that vampires couldn't eat or drink—I mean—other than—"

Asherael laughed. "Oh, we can—given certain magicks and such. It's just that it accelerates our alchemical progression as vampires to avoid human food. It violates a certain...purity."

"And you don't mind—violating this purity?"

Lynne lifted one shoulder in the semblance of a shrug. "Purity be damned. You look like you need a drink, and I'm offering." She held her hands up. "No strings attached."

"Okay." Amanda nodded slowly. "I'm game."

Asherael grinned broadly. "Good. Come with me. Oh, and by the way," she added, "call me Lynne while we're here. We really shouldn't be using our Order names in public."

"Sure, not a problem."

* * * *

The pub was a small but stylish bar that had a live jazz band playing. Above the stage where the band played shone a large, bright blue neon sign with a crescent moon and the name of the pub: *Blue Moon*. Amanda found it strangely fitting.

Amanda watched, trying not to feel self-conscious as the elder vampire studied her for a moment before heading inside the pub. *Déjà vu. I feel like I've done this before, somehow.*

"Here, put this on," Lynne ordered.

Amanda started to ask what it was she wanted her to wear, but Asherael pressed a small silver ring into her hands. She looked at it. It had an amethyst stone, but she could discern nothing else about it that was special.

As if in answer to her unspoken question, Asherael informed her, "The amethyst has special magickal properties. Wearing it will enable you to drink alcoholic beverages."

"Oh, yes. Of course. It's sacred to Dionysus."

Asherael smiled. "Yes, exactly. Plus," she added, "the ring itself is enchanted. Enjoy, it's yours."

Slipping it onto the ring finger on her right hand, she found it fit perfectly. "Thank you. I—I promise not to abuse it."

Asherael chuckled. "Just enjoy it. It's okay to take a break every now and again. I just don't want to see you trashed all of the time, okay?"

Amanda nodded. As pissed as she still was at Jesse, it wasn't likely. Tempting, but not her style. Besides, she was robbed of much of her wits around him as it was. Why make it worse by being drunk all of the time?

"Good." Asherael walked up to the bartender behind the counter. "Hi, I'll have a martini. What would you like, Amanda?"

"Cabernet, please. House would be fine."

Asherael made a noise that sounded like a cross between a snort and a sigh. "Screw house selection. Whatever you recommend as a really good cabernet, sir, would be fine with us."

The bartender nodded at them both. "Right, then. One martini for you, and for you, miss," he looked at Amanda, "I have just the thing."

Lyrael gingerly sat down at the bar. When she managed to speak to Asherael, the words stumbled out awkwardly.

"You really didn't have to—I mean—this is nice and all, but—"

"Amanda, the beginnings are always uncomfortable. And difficult. Mine were pretty harsh as well—harsher than yours, if you can believe it. But that's a tale for another time. I just want you to have the chance to unwind and...I don't know...forget about it for a while."

The bartender brought them their drinks, and Asherael took a sip of her martini before continuing.

"Whatever's going on with you, I can't solve it. I can maybe guess at the problem—or problems—perhaps even sympathize, but...." She shook her head. "It's been a long time for me since I was an apprentice. Say, do you like jazz?"

"I—yes, I do."

A nostalgic smile spread across Asherael's face. "I used to sing in a blues band many years ago. In pubs like this, actually."

Amanda looked at her, stunned. Asherael, in a jazz band? "When?" she asked.

"1920s, shortly before the Depression started. Down in New Orleans."

Asherael pronounced the city's name differently than Amanda was used to hearing it. To her ears, it sounded like "Naw-lins". Then she did a small double take. 1920s. How old was Asherael, exactly?

And another disturbing thought came to her—just how old was

Jesse, anyhow?

"But that was a long time ago," Asherael stated in a dismissive tone. "Anyway, I didn't come here to ramble about myself. Other than Turel, not many of us have had the chance to really talk to you. While some of us can be terribly stuck up and with our noses in the books, it's still no excuse. And especially after reading your essay. I would've loved to have had the chance to meet you before this. I just wanted you to know that. I'm really...grateful...to have the opportunity to meet you. Seriously."

Amanda regarded her. The blonde vampire spoke very plainly, with few frills or preamble. While she had the feeling Asherael held back certain thoughts, she didn't get the feeling of bullshit from her—and she rather liked that lack of bullshit.

Not knowing what else to say, she smiled back at the older vampire and sipped her wine. As she tasted the beverage, she marveled at the way it glided down her tongue like silk. It was neither bitter nor overpowering and had an aftertaste that reminded her of berries.

"Now, I'm not sure about that bass player, but the guy on the sax definitely knows what he's doing. He handles that instrument like he's made love to it a thousand times. Now, that's how you play a sax."

Amanda grinned. "What a great description."

"I'm serious. You can't play an instrument like that on the stage and not love it, and I mean, really love it. Heart and soul. Seriously."

The younger vampire nodded in return. "So you used to sing jazz?"

"Oh, yeah." Asherael sipped her martini. "I still miss it. Sometimes when James is locked away in his office, I dream of sneaking down to a karaoke bar and singing my lungs out."

"Why don't you?"

"Too much work to do. Too many students to look after, papers to read...I need to make more time for myself. Speaking of relaxing," she added in a self-deprecating tone.

"I've always loved singing," Amanda confessed. "I sing for the god if nothing else. Apollo, I mean. But I rarely sing for others."

Asherael gazed at her for a long moment. "We should head to this *Noraebang* nearby here one of these nights. You'd love it."

"A what?"

"*Noraebang*. It's the Korean version of Karaoke. The videos alone would have you in stitches. You rent a room for a period of time—very reasonable price—and you get to sing to all of these crazy Korean music videos."

Amanda was puzzled. "But if they're Korean...."

"Oh, the videos are all Korean, but it's done to American music. With subtitles and a bouncing ball so you know when to sing a word. It's also quite fun to do when utterly smashed. You need to try it."

"Sounds like fun," she replied with a laugh.

The band stopped playing their song at that moment, and as the lead player strolled up to the front of the stage, microphone in hand, the people in the club were applauding. Asherael joined in, then Amanda.

"Thank you, thank you, folks. For all y'all who's new here tonight, welcome to the *Blue Moon*. Here's another special tune that we'd like to play for y'all...."

A more lively song played next, and Amanda soon found herself tapping her foot against the barstool. When she noticed her movement, she almost stopped—but saw that Asherael's foot against her own seat and fingers on the surface of the bar behaved similarly, so she figured that she was in good company. The wine coursed through her veins, pulling her under into that stage beyond tipsy and into drunk. She sensed that Asherael was also considerably under the influence at this point—and an equal feeling that the older vampire didn't care in the least.

"I wonder if they have any CDs out?"

"Oh, if they do, I'm getting a copy. Trust me. Hey, bartender," Asherael called out to the man behind the bar, "what's the name of this band?"

"The Original Sin," he yelled out over the music and talking patrons.

"Thanks," she called back and laughed. "What an amazing name for a band. I rather like it." Lynne continued to sip her martini, her green eyes twinkling as she spoke.

"I have an odd question for you, if you don't mind."

"No such thing as an odd question. Well, maybe. I dunno. Go right ahead, Amanda. Ask."

"How—how old are you exactly? I mean, if you don't mind my asking...."

Asherael nearly choked on her drink, and for a moment Amanda wondered if she'd offended her. But she realized that she choked due to laughter, not anger.

Turning to Amanda with a smile and a quirk of her brow, she replied, "I was born in 1908, Turned in the year 1927."

"NINETEEN?"

"Hush, you," Asherael admonished with a swish of her finger. "No, I am not nineteen. I was nineteen. Don't make this nice bartender panic on us, okay?"

"I mean...you were—"

"Yes, most of us were initiated in our late teens, a few of us in our early twenties. Remember, different times back then. Different times."

"Wow. I mean....you...you...," Amanda stuttered, trying to explain her reaction, "you don't look a day over twenty."

For some reason, Asherael found this outrageously funny. She put down her drink on the counter as carefully as she could manage in her drunken state and roared with laughter. The elder vampire quickly wiped at her eyes. *Pink,* she thought curiously. *Her tears are pink.* She realized it was because they were tinged with blood. She wondered if this was a natural vampire trait and if all of their bodily fluids contained blood. This got her thinking about other bodily fluids and consequently her previous night spent with Jesse. She flushed, both with the pleasant memory of their lovemaking and the nasty recollection of how she woke up that evening.

As if she sensed her sudden change of mood, Asherael abruptly snapped her fingers. "Hey, mister, do us sweet gals a favor and give us another round, please?"

The bartender winked at her. "Certainly, miss."

Amanda tried to protest. "Ash—Lynne...."

"Hey, you're out with me. No worries, all right? Good music, good drink—and you gotta admit that it's a good night to just hang out and shoot the breeze. And another thing besides—"

"Yeah?"

"We do not get hangovers." She gave Amanda a toothy grin.

Hours later, Asherael and Amanda walked back to the Sanctuary.

"If you need anything," Asherael stated, "just let me know. Don't assume that we're total mind readers or have a clue in our heads. Most of us don't. Some of us are completely oblivious to anything outside of our occult research. It doesn't mean that we don't care, it's just...well, we're scholars. Old habits die hard, don't you know?"

"Sure, of course."

They got to the corridor before Amanda's room, and she heard a beeping sound. It came from Asherael's purse.

"Shit, I hate these stupid things." She made a disgusted sound. "That's probably James. Listen, I had a lot of fun tonight. I just want you to know that. Anytime you want to hang out, just let me know."

Amanda smiled. "Sure, definitely. I had a good time too. Thanks, Asherael."

The blonde vampire blurted out, "Lynne. Call me Lynne."

"Okay. Lynne."

The older vampire's face lit up. "Great, Amanda. I'll be seeing you later."

* * * *

Lynne hurried down the hallway to James's office, wondering what possessed her to allow Amanda to call her by her real name. She hadn't gone by her real name to anyone but the magister and others in the Inner Circle of their Order in...well, decades. But she sensed a certain kinship with the new apprentice that she couldn't quite describe. She wondered if there might not be something karmic behind it.

Shaking her head to clear her thoughts, she made her way to visit James. He stood there with a somewhat concerned expression on his face.

"Lynne, where have you been?"

She laughed. "Ah, James, if only you knew...."

Later on, when she went to sleep that morning, Lynne's dreams painted vivid images across her mental landscape.

She was someone else, somewhere else, somewhen else. Hastily making her way to meet someone at the docking bay.

"She's been waiting here since 21:00," an officer informed her. "And I gotta tell you, she's got quite the mouth on her."

A young woman stood there. Thick, wild, dark burgundy hair, cut way too short and spiked at the ends, as if in rage that it ended only there. Dark flashing eyes, fair skin, and facial features that portrayed her as being half Elorian. *Half Elorian?* Lynne's sleeping self wondered, not comprehending the reference.

"About time you got here," the woman snarled. "And let me

tell you, when I get my hands on Lieutenant Kilbourne, he's going to wish that I left him last week with his hand still stuck in that replicator."

"I believe he's *Commander* Kilbourne now," she heard herself responding carefully, "and while I don't know what argument you two shared, I do apologize for my delay. There was an unexpected detour that I had to make on my way towards this space sector and—"

"'Commander'? Please tell me you're joking, no." The woman put her face in her hands. "That man is disaster walking. Whatever space cruiser he's been assigned to, he'll crash it. I can guarantee it. I can even see it in my mind's eye right now. Some poor fuck of a captain will let him have the helm, just once—and down it goes. Alas, the poor fucking ship."

"Commander McKensey—Patricia—can I speak frankly?"

"Sure, sure—you're Tzian, like me. I'm not human, you don't need my permission. To do otherwise is an insult."

"Patricia, as your new captain, I can promise you that I won't let that man crash any ships, if I can help it—I'm good friends with the captain he's stationed with. And whatever he's done to you, I'm sure the Goddess will pay him back."

Dark eyes twinkled as she laughed. "Gods be praised. That bastard snuck into my quarters and left vanilla pudding all over my clothing. Undergarments too. I will never be able to smell vanilla again without retching. Thank you for your kindness."

"You're welcome," Lynne replied. She was about to say something else, but the scene in front of her blurred into non-recognition, and she found herself lying in her bed, in her room once more.

Slowly sitting up, she blinked and puzzled over the dream. *Patricia. Patricia was Amanda. Or is Amanda. Or something.*

She had no idea what the dream meant. Past life? Future life? She didn't know. Obviously there was something to it, and she would have to meditate on it if she desired any further understanding of its meaning—and her relationship with Lyrael.

Or, she figured, maybe she watched far too much modern television.

Chapter Thirteen

"You will learn self control."

Humming part of one of the jazz tunes that she'd heard at the *Blue Moon*, Amanda made her way down the hallway. Her mind still buzzed from the wine she'd had, and it made her happy that Lynne had given her that amethyst ring. She didn't want to come down from the high of the music, the wine, the joy of the evening out, and the feeling of freedom the evening gave her.

Walking back into her bedroom, she almost skipped, feeling as if nothing could possibly go wrong....

Jesse stood in the center of the room, staring her down with a dark glint in his eyes. She felt his tension and anger like a blast of heat rushing over her, as if she had opened the door to a sauna instead

His gaze continued to bore into her while she stood in the doorway, stunned. Something about the way he looked at her viscerally punched her in the gut—and not in an unpleasant way either. Deep inside, her muscles clenched with yearning, and her face suddenly warmed.

"Where the hell were you?" Jesse's soft voice sent chills into her spine and moisture running between her thighs.

Fuck, I'm supposed to be mad at him, not reacting like this! she thought desperately, frustrated to the core. *This is wrong, so utterly wrong. What the fuck is wrong with me? Fuck!*

His voice, previously gentle, now turned hard. "And why are you supposed to be mad at *me*? I left you here where you would be safe and sound. You are a Vampire Childe; you haven't even gone on your first hunt yet, and you don't even know how!"

"Why don't you start with where the hell you were?" she snapped in return, trying to regain her senses. What the hell was wrong with her? She was supposed to be angry with him, not getting all hot and bothered at him while he stood there giving her a lecture as if she were a teenager who got caught past her curfew. "I woke up, and you weren't there!" *AND YOU'RE READING MY MIND AGAIN, YOU BASTARD.*

"Yes, I can read your mind," he stated, his tone half amused, half patronizing. "And I had to go out and feed. You don't remember, but you took quite a bit of my blood when we were...together." He smiled at her, his face beaming with wicked delight.

Aloud, Amanda sputtered, "But you left—you left me tied to the bed!" In her head she retorted, *AND WHY THE HELL WEREN'T YOU READING MY MIND WHEN I WOKE UP AND WAS PISSED AS HELL AT YOU FOR LEAVING ME TRAPPED IN MY ROOM LIKE THAT?*

In less time than it took her to blink, Jesse stood directly in front of her. "I had to make sure you were okay while I was gone. Besides, I didn't think you would wake up so soon."

"But—"

"And you still haven't answered my question." His voice lowered dangerously. "Where were you?"

Jesse stood close to her, close enough for her to feel the heat and energy from his blood radiating and calling to her own blood. The energy dance played on her nerves and made her think of images, concepts and emotions that she didn't quite understand, nor know how to deal with. It didn't help one bit that she knew that he could hear her thoughts. It was an Olympic struggle to speak coherently. "I went. Out. With—with Asherael." *Gods, I almost said Lynne.*

A strange frown marred his forehead. "Asherael? You went out with Asherael? And how do you know her real name? Did she tell you?"

"Yeah. Yeah, she did. We went to a pub, we talked. I...." Her arms flailed; she didn't know why his discomforting gaze troubled her greatly, nor why she didn't want to look so closely into his eyes.

He sighed and reached out to gently seize her wrists. It surprised Amanda that she let him, but she gave in to the need for his touch. The firm but gentle grip calmed her in some alien, mysterious way. As if by magick, the intense rage she had towards him crumbled into dust and vanished. She tried to hold onto it but found herself unable to do so.

"I am not going to let you do this again," he told her severely.

"What?" she blurted out. "Do what?"

"This was my fault, I admit to that. And I'm sorry." His eyes pleaded with hers, but were still filled with that oddness she had seen when she walked into the room, and she couldn't quite meet them.

"Sorry for what? Leaving me, or leaving me tied up?"

"I had made the mistake of blocking you out, blocking our connection out. No more. I had no idea that you would react the way you did to being bound to the bed, or that you would manage to escape and run off."

"And how—how did you think I would react, exactly?"

He didn't answer her question. "I'm glad that you were with one of the elders, at least. I may not like Asherael or always get along with her," he conceded with an obvious measure of reluctance, "but I also know that she wouldn't hurt you. You are now her sister in the Blood, and she would respect that. And," he added, pulling her closer to him, "you are mine too."

"Your—I'm your...what? I'm your sister?" Dazed and mystified, she barely got out the words. Somehow the feel of his hands on her wrists, the close proximity to his body—it made her dizzy and her senses swim. The room spun around her, and everything about Jesse and his body so terribly close to her own called to her senses and screamed at them to react.

The pale, smooth skin connecting his neck and shoulder kept drawing her attention. She smelled him—smelled his skin to the point where she almost tasted him in her mouth. Amanda ached to strike at it with her lips, tongue, teeth—all of it was madness, some strange poison in her blood. She wondered if the alcohol she'd drank earlier had something to do with the emotions she experienced, or at the very least had affected her reactions towards him. Nonetheless, the sensations he provoked sparked primal emotions within her she didn't know she possessed; intense enough to the point where they began to terrify her. She wanted to run away from the room, from him, but something made her freeze in place. Maybe his hands which held her wrists also held her prisoner, or perhaps the shadowy, wild depths of his eyes prevented her from leaving. Either way, she was as stone, rooted to the spot and unable to move unless he so willed it.

Unless he willed it. This realization disturbed her also. What was he doing to her? Was it on purpose, or was it her own intense feelings, made even more intense by becoming a vampire? Maybe it was something to do with him being her Sire? Regardless, she figured nothing good could come from continuing to be in the room with him. She needed to get away from him, go for a walk, try to think clearly—anything that would aid her to come back to herself.

Amanda couldn't figure out what stopped her from bolting out the door, as she was positive she wanted to do—wasn't she?—for the sensation of his lips upon hers drowned out her thoughts. Possessive hands continued to clench her wrists as his ardent kiss sucked away the remaining vestiges of anger and pulled her under into a vast crimson tide of passionate longing.

Crimson. Amanda thirsted for something sweeter and silkier than the excellent wine she'd drank at the *Blue Moon*.

A GOOD THING I FED ENOUGH TONIGHT FOR THE BOTH OF US.

Hearing Jesse's words inside her mind triggered something deep within her, and her fangs protracted. She burned to sink them into his neck and make him scream for her....

With a quick motion, Jesse positioned her on her back on the floor. His hands pinned her wrists at the sides of her head, and his piercing gaze held hers.

"You will learn self control."

He shoved her hands over her head, and in doing so, managed to grab both of her wrists with one hand. His other hand slid down the front of her body and carefully undid the button at the waistband of her jeans. If she'd had a breath in her to hold in anticipation she would have.

At that moment, he kissed her again—hard. His tongue pulsed in and out between her lips, sensuously stroking the inside of her mouth and stealing away whatever words and thoughts she had left.

His hand dove under the front of her jeans and slipped between her legs, and human habit made her gasp aloud. The cloth of the jeans tightly held his hand against the responsive folds which throbbed between her legs, and he massaged the now oversensitive bud with his thumb.

Instinctively her hips lifted, and her legs parted to allow him wider access. Jesse continued to rub her clit gently, his other fingers lightly teasing the rest of her. The sensations were so pleasurable that it brought her pain. Amanda squirmed under his unrelenting caresses, but it only brought about a greater ecstasy. In the thrill of his touch on her most responsive parts, she ached. Her insides desired him so much that they were sore and begging to be released from their agony.

She wanted him to take her—badly. To rip off her jeans and fuck her senseless until she screamed, to feel and smell the blood-sweat of their bodies mingling, the two of them becoming one. The thought of experiencing his hard, strong member plunging into and filling her depths drove her to the brink of madness.

In response to her thoughts, Jesse slowly inserted a finger into her wet entrance. The thrill of it made her moan deep in her throat.

He partially covered her body with his, completely pinning her to the floor. Both his inserted finger and the thumb on her clit were suddenly motionless. Amanda tried to thrust her hips upwards, squirm—anything to produce additional sensation that might grant her release, but he held her completely immobile from the waist down.

If you had fed tonight, you would be strong enough to fight me.

Her eyes rolled backward, half in pleasure and half in aggravation. He was lecturing her again, or at least trying to. She didn't care. Her insides raged on fire, and the unbearable torture of his fingers made her sore and throbbing between her legs like nothing she had ever experienced before. She would do anything to end it, if she could.

Languidly, he began moving his finger in and out of her. She felt how wet she was and the moisture that trickled out of her once he removed his finger. Amanda was ready to utter a complaining moan, but he plunged it back in and with an agonizing stroke ran the tip of his finger along her slick and inviting walls. Her back arched, all of her thoughts and sensations focused on that one intolerably intense sensation. The finger continued to move down until it made its way outside of her body, whereupon it gently flicked at her soaking folds and stroked her clit. The fluids on his finger provided another sensuality that left her senselessly crying out loud with alien sounds emanating from her throat.

With his finger now removed, she realized this had become an endless cycle: him driving her to the brink of madness by touching her, him making her even more insane by no longer touching her. The more he teased her, the more she wanted him, and with his presence no longer there, she was in unceasing torment.

She wondered if half of her anger at him having left her in her room wasn't due to his physically leaving her, but having also left her mentally. He had, after all, blocked her out earlier and left her more distant from him. Had she been reacting to that also?

Amanda's eyes suddenly focused, and she realized he was smiling at her.

His thumb once again began its gentle massage over her clit, and in response her hips jerked beneath his body. Waves of pleasure pulled her under and back again. It wasn't long before the room went white and she could no longer think.

As if he knew she was close to the brink—*Damn him, of course he does*—he stopped the movement of his thumb and withdrew his hand from her pants. With great deliberateness, he put his finger into his mouth and sucked her juices off of his finger, watching her as he did so.

She waited for him to do something, anything—take off her clothes, take off his—but instead he stood up and made his way to her door.

I ONLY WANT YOU TO REMEMBER THIS.

Jesse walked out, leaving her lying on the floor, still dripping wet and aching for him. And that ache turned into almost heart wrenching agony at the lack of his presence, both within her mind and physically.

Thinking it over, she didn't know what was stronger at that point: her yearning for him, or her hatred of how he treated her and how she was reacting to it. Both emotions were already far too strong for her liking. But did she hate him, or hate what he did to her, or both?

The soreness between her thighs momentarily distracted her from her thoughts, and she contemplated using her own hands to end the torture long enough to be able to think again.

AND IF I CATCH YOU MASTURBATING, YOU WON'T LIKE WHAT I'LL DO NEXT.

She grimaced. Hatred, perhaps. It was definitely a toss up.

* * * *

With a small start, James emerged from his brief but vivid vision.

Please, Blood, no.

He sighed. It was such a human expression, this expelling of air from the lungs, but it was so expressive. The younger vampires couldn't refrain from it, and admittedly, neither could he. And it rather fit how what he saw had affected him.

The magister could still see the dark scarlet strands tightly woven together, connecting Amanda and Jesse, and knew what they were and what they meant.

A Blood Bond. He Bonded to her after her awakening. And she's still undergoing her Turning. The fool.

Groaning, he sank down into his chair and began to go over the logistics in his head. The connection was permanent until final death for either one or both of them; neither he nor the Council could alter it, let alone break it. Further blood exchanges would only enhance the connection.

And such blood exchanges, of course, were only natural for mating vampires to perform in the act of making love. Such exchanges were very intimate; an act which went way beyond normal intercourse in both intensity and potential pleasure.

He's in love. Or in lust. Or both. I can't judge him, to be sure. And I can only blame myself for not having realized it sooner.

The answer as to why was obvious: Jesse had been Bonded to his Sire, Minervia. Either he knew of no other way to Turn someone other than to Bond them, or he sought to replace that close connection he had lost so many decades ago.

Regardless, the magister now had an even more pressing motive for keeping a close eye on Jesse and his new Childe.

At the very least, her magickal progression will be affected. They will share alchemy, and he's already further along than she is. It'll affect her development and further advancements in the Order—that is for certain—and not always positively, either.

His jaw tightened.

To potentially take on more than she can handle…she has already been through a lot. She will probably suffer much as a result, far more than she could possibly conceive of right now.

James knew intuitively that she was strong, but strong enough? He didn't know.

"Lynne," he blurted aloud. "I must talk to Lynne." As much as she hated Jesse, she possessed remarkable intuition when it came to spiritual advancement and the occult sciences and may have some insights in regards to assisting the poor Childe during what was certain to be a very tumultuous process.

She might have some advice on this matter that could prevent the worst from occurring….

Chapter Fourteen

"Underwater"

It's too early to say "I told you so," Lynne thought and gritted her teeth. But she figured the time would come soon enough. She was glad that the magister had decided to meet her in her office instead of his own. Her office chair allowed her the comfort of sitting down, and she had more than enough pencils that she could start snapping in half in order to relieve her tension. Lynne rather preferred destroying her office supplies to James's. After all, she had nothing against the magister and didn't want to be held responsible for the financial burden of replacing his office supplies.

James cleared his throat. "The Bond will no doubt affect her development. It's obvious that he's smitten; he's not thinking clearly...."

She fought to keep herself from rolling her eyes. *And this is news, how?* And how would this affect Amanda? Certainly not in any way that was good. Lynne remembered the time she had spent with the young vampire in the pub and how much fun they had together. The young apprentice struck her as being a very strong, determined woman—in fact, she rarely met people with such spirit and she admired that greatly. She didn't want to see that spirit broken by anyone, or anything.

Blood help me—to help her.

"I know you have been developing a rapport with her," he continued, "and I was wondering if I could have your advice on the matter, seeing as you may know her a bit better at present than I do."

Lynne stared at James for a while before answering him. It was obvious from his readily emerging British accent that he was greatly distressed, and this fact disturbed her further. "Yes...yes. I think I can help."

"What can you do?"

Taking a deep breath, Lynne made the plunge before she could change her mind. "Magister, with your permission, I'd like to take her on as one of my students."

James looked like he didn't know what to be more stunned at: her formal address or the request itself. "You—you *what*? Lynne, you have a full load as it is. How could you possibly take her on as a student? She's an apprentice and needs a lot of hand holding right now—especially since she is still Turning."

Shrugging her shoulders, she replied casually, "Angelus is transferring over to Junio, and Theodotos is almost done with his third degree. Besides, if I don't, who will? We're all swamped with work around here. Anyway, I'm more than certain that I can handle this challenge. Has she gone on her first hunt yet?"

He blinked. "I-I don't think so. Turel wanted to wait until things 'stabilized' a bit more with her, as he put it. He plans to take her soon, not certain precisely when, however. But definitely before her Turning is over, he assured me of that."

Lynne nodded. "And she's feeding how for the time being?"

"Not certain. You'll have to ask Lyrael herself, or Turel."

"I see," was her noncommittal response. She suspected that Amanda was feeding directly off of her Sire—and her fragile stage of development could be in turn feeding the Blood Bond further. But she wisely held her tongue. No sense in accusing Jesse without proof; it would only make her look bad.

"In any event, if you truly wish to be her teacher, I can arrange that with minimal fuss. Originally I thought that Amaltheia might be a suitable choice for her, but...." He frowned, momentarily deep in thought.

"James, with all due respect, Amaltheia would be great for her if you wanted her to keep her nose in books and not much else. She's a great teacher, very knowledgeable, and a total sweetheart—don't get me wrong—but Lyrael needs balance."

He smiled. "Ah, Lynne, a good observation. I knew that I could count on you. You are most certainly right, and I think that you could provide that balance. Just one thing...."

"Yes, what?"

"Don't make every night a pub crawling night, okay?" He lifted his eyebrows and gave her one of his most serious expressions, but she knew him well enough to catch the twinkle in his eye.

Lynne kept her face composed. "You got it, James. I think every other night, or even three times a week would be just fine."

The magister laughed. "I'm serious, Lynne."

"So am I," she retorted, indignant. Then her voice and face softened with concern. "I'm deeply afraid for her with that Blood Bond, James. If her entire unlife is caught up in her Sire, it'll be extremely unhealthy for her."

"I don't disagree with you," he stated, his voice flat, a slight frown creasing his forehead. "But I want to make sure she excels and that the two of them are capable of working together in the Order—let alone our Clan." Shaking his head, he added in sad but wistful tones, "After all, young love only lasts so long in this world. I can only hope that Turel does not regret his rather...impetuous decision."

* * * *

Get up.

Amanda thought she heard Jesse speak to her. But she was barely coming out of a deep sleep.

"Amanda...."

Her eyes flew open. The first thing she saw was his face, blurred in the haze of sleepiness.

"Get up, Amanda."

She tried to mumble something to the effect of, "Go away", and rolled over.

Leaning towards her, he put his hand on her back. "I know that you're tired, but I need for you to get up."

His touch sent liquid fire searing through her system. *Great, just what I need,* she thought with annoyance. Now she was irritated at being woken up *and* she was horny. *What a fantastic combination.* When she was human, Amanda didn't deal with mornings very well. She supposed since her body clock had done a one-eighty upon becoming a vampire, she wasn't going to do evenings gracefully either.

With great reluctance, she turned to face him. "What?" she asked groggily, her voice not much above a whisper.

"Get up and get ready to leave." His voice did odd things to her stomach and made her thoughts fuzzier.

"Leave?"

"Yes, I'm taking you out. Do what you need to do in order to get ready." Jesse gestured towards the rest of the room.

"Out where?" After a brief struggle, she sat up and looked around the room, dazed. Out, like to a restaurant? Something fancy? Was she supposed to dress up?

"Just dress in normal clothing. What you would normally wear every day. Nothing fancy."

Amanda merely gave him a look. She hated it when he answered her thoughts like that.

Staring at her in return, he inquired, "Well, are you going to get up?"

Dear gods, what a pain in the ass. OH, BITE ME. She hadn't intended her retort to come out quite like that, but it did anyhow. A split second later, it occurred to her that this wasn't exactly the appropriate thing to say to a vampire. Well, another vampire.

"I mean—oh, whatever." She made a noise that was between a groan and a remark and dismissed him with a "Meh" before plopping back down on the bed, pulling her pillow over her head as she did so.

Jesse calmly sat down on the bed beside her. "Am I going to have to drag you out of bed?"

She fought the urge to give Jesse the middle finger. After all, it probably wouldn't get her anywhere, and besides, she was too tired to move. What time was it, half past sunset? Maybe if she lay still he would give up and go away.

Suddenly, a strange, discomforting sensation birthed in the center of her chest, as if something had reached inside of her and squeezed. The grip was so strong that if she still had the need to breathe, she would've gasped. As she lay there, attempting to analyze the feeling, the grip became a tug.

Amanda bolted upright, clutching her chest. *What the fuck...?* She glanced at him. His expression was completely blank, and she couldn't read him at all. *Oh, he can block me out but still read* me*? Hardly fair.*

"Good, you're properly awake. Now get up."

Her jaw tightened. If this was going to be a regular routine as part of her new vampire life, she missed being human already.

I HAVEN'T DECIDED ON YOUR REGULAR ROUTINE YET. WHY DON'T YOU TAKE A SHOWER WHILE I THINK ABOUT IT?

A shower sounded superb to her, but his "deciding" on her "regular routine" most certainly didn't. She glared at him, angrily walking towards the bathroom. On her way there she gave in to her earlier urge, sending him a strong image of her giving him the middle finger.

Amanda thought she heard a chuckle just before she slammed the door shut behind her.

After going through a few cupboards, she found a towel and set it aside. She tossed her clothing off in mere seconds and turned on the faucet in the shower.

The hot water pouring down her body was ecstasy on her back, and she closed her eyes. She savored the delight of the long sought-after shower; every inch of her skin was alive and dancing. She didn't remember when she had last bathed and figured that it had been far too long for her comfort. Fortunately, whoever saw fit to place her in this room had also stocked the bathroom with soap, shampoo, and even conditioner.

Amanda took the soap in her hands and began to scrub at her body, relishing in the sensual feeling of clean water and suds washing away the grime and sweat from her skin. She couldn't recall the last time taking a shower resembled a religious experience. It was as if she were bathing in the sacred springs of Delphi, where the god Apollo had blessed the land and its oracle as hallowed ground. Who would've thought that purification would be such bliss? Only those who didn't comprehend the god, she decided.

She was in the process of applying soap to her legs when familiar, gentle hands slid across her back. Amanda yelped in surprise.

"Oh, hush," Jesse said.

How did he get into the room? She hadn't even heard him enter. Didn't she lock the door? She couldn't remember. The power of thought was rapidly being stripped from her, washed away with the suds that went down the shower drain.

"I'm not going to hurt you," he told her.

His hands made their way onto her head, and he gently kneaded through her long hair. *Soap,* she noted. No, it was shampoo. He gave her hair a gentle cleansing and scalp massage, and she closed her eyes, enjoying his touch. Involuntarily, she leaned back—and promptly backed directly into Jesse, who stood behind her in the shower, as nude as she was.

"I haven't exactly been fair," he murmured into her ear, "so I'm going to make it up to you."

"'Fair'?" she echoed, laughing. What an understatement.

With exquisite care, he rinsed her hair, his hands stroking her head, neck, and back, guiding the water to remove the last of the shampoo from her scalp. Amanda fought with desperation against closing her eyes or leaning back, but found it difficult to do so. The presence of his naked body behind her, his hands on her bare skin, and the water streaming down was too sensual for her to withstand without reacting. In spite of herself, the back of her head came to rest on his chest, gentle and relaxed, the water from the shower head continuing to pour over them.

Something quite slippery and soft caressed her breasts...Jesse's hands, lathered in soap. He kneaded her skin, teasing her nipples, and drove her out of her mind with the touch of his hands stroking her breasts. The soap ran down over her body from his hands, his slow, sensual torture making its way over her stomach and hips. A moan escaped from her lips.

His fingers danced between her inner thighs, stroking the sensitive skin with his soap-filled hands. The briefest of caresses touched her most sensitive folds from the tips of his fingers before he bent over and with unhurried movements continued his way down the insides of her legs. It was torturous song and delight, filling her with mindless, radiant joy. The constant feeling and sensation reverberated all over every inch of her skin, and before long moisture seeped between her legs that she knew wasn't from the shower. It mingled with the soap, the water; everything blended together in a warm, liquid haze. The pleasure pulled her underwater, and without hesitation she surrendered to the tide.

Jesse massaged her thighs, her calves, then made his way back up to knead her back and buttocks. She melted, becoming one with the water and the sensations threatening to drown her. His hands worked their way over her shoulders, her arms, and over every part of her body. When his fingers went over the back of her neck, she cried aloud in ecstasy. He rubbed her neck, the sides of her face, and her head before gradually making his way down the strands of her hair to her lower back.

One of his hands glided down to slip between her upper thighs. One finger entered her, then another. The sounds coming from the back of her throat sounded part joyous—and part agony. Amanda leaned forward on the shower wall in front of her, his fingers slowly pumping in and out of her. In the experience of the intense pleasure her mind opened, and she felt his desire towards her and his enjoyment of how wet she was inside—as wet as she was on the outside—as well as the feeling of the inside of her delicate skin.

His left arm snaked around her neck, and his wrist pressed against her mouth. It was wet, but not with water.

Drink, he commanded.

Lyrael didn't hesitate, but sucked away at the wound he had made on his wrist, his fingers moving in and out of her slick entrance with rapid thrusts. Before long, her sucking matched the tempo of his hand penetrating her body without mercy. She was beyond thinking; her mind as fluid as the water that poured down over them and the blood that flowed down her throat.

When the tidal wave came, it crashed over her and filled her with its piercing glow. Her knees buckled, and only the wall in front of her plus Jesse's strong arms kept her from falling into the tub in which they stood. His lips pressed against her back, showering her in passionate kisses like she had been rained upon by the water which gushed out of the shower head.

We should get out before we run out of hot water.

Amanda agreed with him, but could neither think nor vocalize it. The delicious haze still ran through her while with leisurely movements he helped her out of the shower, his efforts to dry her off with the nearby towel gentle and affectionate. They sat on the floor for a long time, her lying against him, her eyes closed in dreamy bliss.

Chapter Fifteen

"Now it's your turn."

"Where are we going?" Amanda's voice sounded drowsy to her ears, but it wasn't due to being abruptly woken up earlier. She was clean, refreshed, and still glowing from the attention that Jesse had given her in the shower.

"It's time I show you something." Jesse put his arm around her, and they walked out of her room. The warmth of his skin—made warmer by the blood he drank earlier—excited her and she remembered how good it had been to be dried off by him and helped to dress. So sensual, so intimate.

They strolled down the corridor and past James. Noticing the magister immediately, Jesse halted.

"Ah, Janius," Jesse smiled at him. "I'm taking Lyrael out. It's time."

The magister's face looked confused for a few moments before he replied, "Time? Oh, terrific! I'm glad to hear it. Her first hunt, how wonderful." He stared down the corridor past them, as if gazing at something fascinating yet poignant. "I remember my first hunt like it was yesterday." He smiled at them. "Good luck to you both."

All Amanda could do was blurt out, "Hunt?" Turel merely squeezed her shoulder. "Jesse, he doesn't mean—James—I mean Janius—"

"Come on, Amanda." Jesse took her arm firmly and walked her down towards the stairs to the exit.

"What's this about a 'hunt'? Jesse?"

The magister left the two of them to head down the corridor, away from the conversation taking place.

Once James was out of earshot, Jesse finally responded, "Amanda, our kind needs to take blood from humans. You know that. We can't go to food banks all of the time, and donors who are willing *and* trustworthy are hard to find."

"No." She swallowed before asking in a hoarse voice, "Are you telling me I'm going to have to kill people?"

"Nothing like that, I promise you."

"But how—"

"I'll show you. Just trust me, okay?"

She bit her lip. "I do, but...."

"Then you have nothing to worry about."

They walked down the streets, Amanda growing increasingly agitated. "Asherael said that we can actually eat and drink things," she stammered out. "But I never saw you eat...?"

Jesse sighed. "It's usually best for your personal alchemy that you don't. However, I do eat the offerings that I leave for Anpu."

She didn't recognize the name. "Anpu?"

"You probably know him better as Anubis. He's my patron deity." He explained, "It's a Kemetic tradition. You always eat the offerings that you leave for the gods."

"Oh." She paused. "Greek priests did that in ancient times—at least, they had the first taste of the food being offered. Animal sacrifices were the equivalent of huge banquets for the ancients."

"Yup. Not too dissimilar from us. I must warn you, though," he added quickly, "that eating and drinking has no real nutritional value—only blood can sustain us. Besides, it's best to maintain a degree of vampiric purity by subsisting on blood alone. I make an exception for the offerings I place before the gods and no more."

Despite herself, she chuckled. Vampires *pure*?

He rolled his eyes at her reaction. "Yes, in case you haven't noticed, we're just as capable of being spiritual as humans are. And no, crosses don't work on us. At least, not unless they're being wielded as a magickal weapon. Then we might have to worry, but not much."

"I see." She followed him once he turned down a small alleyway. Ahead of them stood a very unkempt man, clothing disheveled and stained. He staggered back and forth, mumbling to himself things which even Amanda's highly sensitive vampiric ears couldn't pick up, let alone understand.

Jesse smiled triumphantly. *One lone guy standing in the middle of a small back alleyway. A perfect set up for your first hunt.*

With a slight wave of his hand and the extension of Jesse's magickal Will, the man slumped to the ground. Amanda blinked. How in the world did he do that? She watched him pick up the man and carry him over to where she stood, both stunned and fascinated by this odd turn of events.

"You're a vampire," he informed her. "Now it's your turn. You have to take his blood."

Her eyes widened, and a ripple of fear ran through her. The idea of taking blood from some stranger in an alleyway was abhorrent to her. Wasn't there some other way to deal with her needs as a vampire?

"Don't give me that look. You don't have to kill him, just take only what you need."

"How do I know whether or not I've taken too much?"

"After a time, you'll have an intuitive sense of it, based on experience and your psychic senses. In the meantime, I'm here to supervise."

She just stared at him mutely. What should she do? Should she take from his neck? His wrist? How did she drink from him? Wasn't Jesse going to provide her with more instructions? Her thoughts swam in a sea of indecision and confusion, and she found herself rooted to the spot, unable to even speak.

"Go on, don't just stand there, do it," he ordered. "I've put him to sleep, and he could wake up soon." He bent the guy's head to one side, exposing his neck. The veins that throbbed and pulsed under his skin held her under a strange sway. She stared, fascinated.

"Come on," he told her, gesturing with his head to the man's neck. "Someone could walk by and see this. We need to be fast."

She got closer, smelling the blood and sweat on the man's body. The merest hint of the metallic substance in her nose and tongue made her fangs grow. As if hypnotized, unable to stop herself but seemingly watching from a distance, she lowered her face to his neck.

Apollo, if this is wrong, forgive me, she prayed. *Please let this man not suffer on my behalf.*

Her fangs pierced his neck. The blood covered her lips and filled her mouth, and a primordial ecstasy ripped through her, quick and sharp, followed by a violent orgasm that threatened to knock her onto her knees. Wind rushed through her ears, the tempest surging within her. She fought to keep from crying aloud, not wanting to remove her mouth from his neck that was the sacred source of the exquisitely sweet, silky blood that poured down her throat. Only the strength of the Blood Bond between her and Jesse allowed her to perceive that he stood nearby, gazing upon her with pride while she drank.

How could she have thought this to be wrong when it seemed so right? With fervent glee she fed, the waves of rapture continuing to wash over her, all too willing to be caught up in the storm. Moments of endless, sweet bliss went by while she drank, only to be interrupted by Jesse roughly pulling the man out of her tight grip.

"You must learn to moderate your passions, Amanda." His voice was low and sounded breathless. She gazed dumbly at him until it hit her that he had experienced the same emotions and sensations she had through their mutual psychic connection.

Before she could reply, Jesse let down his shields, allowing her to feel the sexual heat in his thoughts and loins. He slammed his body into hers, pinning her to the wall of the building behind her, and kissed her fiercely. Some of the blood she had drank still remained in her mouth, and he sucked it down greedily, his tongue licking the blood.

In spite of the mutual lust coursing between them, Amanda couldn't help teasing him. *And I'm the one who has to moderate my passions?*

Shut up, he hissed, lightly biting her lower lip.

Still unbearably aroused from taking the man's blood, Jesse's obvious intentions only heightened her frustration. Amanda didn't hesitate to move her hands to his waist, undoing the belt and buckle from his pants. Her own jeans were already down at her ankles, and he picked her up and lowered her onto his eager, erect member. With one motion, he ripped her shirt open and sank his fangs into her right breast. She came within a few moments, clawing at his back and fighting not to scream aloud. Only after she collapsed into his arms did he thrust himself deeper into her, allowing himself his release. She experienced the same sensations he did when he came, and an answering crescendo flooded her body. At that moment, she was so overwhelmed by the sensations that she could only cling to him and ride the storm.

Amanda still floated in a state of bliss, Jesse's lips pressing against her cheek.

We have to go, he whispered.

She could only nod in agreement, and he hastily helped her redress.

* * * *

Using the birth data that Jesse had managed to collect for him, James was busy in his office analyzing Amanda's astrological chart. *Sun in Virgo, Scorpio ascendant, Scorpio moon...no wonder she's an excellent match for Turel.* Jesse was also a double Scorpio—

Scorpio sun and Scorpio ascendant, but Leo moon.

Fascinating, he thought absently and continued to look through the chart. The chart reflected aspects for her inclination towards intense academic studies, the occult, and even elements of her relationship with Jesse. Nothing was there that he didn't expect to see, and some planets were very well aspected indeed. The magister had a strong feeling that she would wind up in a leadership position within the Clan or even the Order itself someday. He would have to compare this data with the chart he had drawn for her initiation; he suspected that more clues to the Clan's newest initiate would be found within it.

But a nagging feeling gripped him as he gazed upon the astrological data before him. Something about the chart seemed familiar somehow, tantalizingly familiar. Where had he seen some of these aspects before?

He sighed. Too many long hours in the office, and too much worrying over Jesse's new Childe. He needed to get out and stretch, perhaps even take a walk to Amaltheia's office and ask her about the progress of a few of her students.

The chart, the eerie feeling he got from it—all of this could wait. Even he admitted to himself that he needed a break.

Sometimes a chart is just a chart, after all. The odd tickle in the back of his mind persisted in spite of his reasoning.

He sipped the beverage from his mug, which contained a mixture of spices, herbs, and warm blood. With it and the chart in hand, he made his way to Amaltheia's office. Maybe she had some answers for him, ideas that he hadn't yet thought of.

Odd flashes suddenly went through his mind. Lightning storms, a figure in black, red hair wildly streaming behind her—his last memories of Minervia before she crossed the Abyss and left Jesse and the rest of Clan Gladius behind to mourn and pick up the scattered pieces that she had left behind.

He owed it to Jesse to make sure that all went well between him and his new love, even if it meant bothering his colleagues with half-assed astrological data and the crazy flashes of intuition that told him that there was something more to this pairing than met the eye.

Or, perhaps he was losing his mind. Either way, he wasn't going to rest until he had exhausted all of his options for research.

Chapter Sixteen

"There are two kinds of feeding...."

"James, have you seen Lyrael around at all?"

The magister looked up from the astrological chart he was still analyzing. Lynne stood in the corridor and saw that his forehead creased in that manner which she could only describe as his "tired and concerned" look.

"No, I haven't. I think she's still out on her first hunt with Turel. Why, is there something wrong?"

"No...no, nothing wrong. I wanted to see how she was making out on her Apprentice assignment." *And I suspect she's being distracted by her Sire,* she added ruefully in her head.

James smiled. "Don't worry about her. I'm sure that she's doing just fine. Is Amaltheia in her office? Would you happen to know? I have something I want to ask her about."

"Last time I checked, she was busy cataloguing some of the books that just arrived." She started to walk away but paused and added, "If you run into Lyrael, please tell her I'm looking for her and that it's important."

He nodded. "Of course."

* * * *

Still high from the blood she had taken from the man in the alleyway and the passion she had shared with Jesse, Amanda twirled through the streets. Jesse watched her with both affection and amusement.

"Have you ever gone hunting like that before?" she asked him, a twinkle in her eye reminding him of times past.

He smiled wistfully. "A few times, a long time ago." In his mind, he saw laughing, light blue eyes—magickally tinted blue. He was one of the few who had known they were actually brown. Blue eyes, clear as the day sky—the sky he could no longer see, except through her eyes.

Sarah. Jesse hadn't thought of her in a long time—had done his best not to think about her, in fact. The Clan knew her as Minervia, but to him she had always been Sarah, the fiery, free-spirited woman who had freed him from a life of mortality—and broken his heart when she crossed over.

Amanda wrapped her arm around his waist and placed a soft kiss on his neck. *Penny for your thoughts?* she asked lightly.

Jesse's eyes gazed into hers; drawing her close, he kissed her. The kiss was intoxicatingly sweet, and he sensed her thoughts spiraling into bliss.

"Just glad to have you, is all," he answered aloud.

He held her close, smothering her in a fierce embrace. She smiled happily at him. A few moments passed before he lightly kissed her forehead.

"I should feed too," he stated matter-of-factly.

It appeared she didn't know what to say in response; Amanda simply nodded. Jesse felt her thoughts. She wondered what it'd be like to watch him feed and if it would be in any way similar to what had happened to him when he had watched her. Their psychic bond grew stronger by the day, and while she didn't entirely understand what was happening to them, she supposed that this was the natural way of all vampires and their Sires—especially since they were in such a close relationship.

Jesse allowed himself a slight smile. He knew fully well that they were Blood Bonded, but figured that it would be best to teach her of such things after her initiation into the first degree of the Order. After all, there was no need to overwhelm her with such intricate details of high vampiric esoterica. Amanda had enough to deal with as a newly Turned Childe.

They wandered into a small, slightly seedy looking bar a few blocks up the street.

"Here," Jesse told her, gesturing towards the counter. "Get yourself something to drink."

Amanda's brow furrowed, and he heard her thoughts about Lynne's gift to her—the amethyst ring that allowed her to digest alcohol.

"When you're older, you won't need the ring," he informed her quietly, keeping his voice below that of the bar's patrons. "But for now, it's a good thing to have. Your stomach is still very sensitive from the change and will be for some time. It's best that you avoid human food and drink whenever you can."

"Okay," she replied.

He gave her a soft kiss on the lips. "Wait here. I'll be right back."

Amanda nodded and sat down at the counter to order a glass of wine.

* * * *

Their house cabernet sauvignon was a little on the bitter side, but otherwise palatable. It didn't take her long to get tipsy. As she finished the glass, a sudden empathic surge of emotion through her bond with Jesse blossomed—lust, ecstasy, and primal thirst.

He must be feeding, she thought drowsily, wandering towards wherever he was. She was curious enough after the day's events and still feeling the aftereffects from the bliss they had shared.

She went to the back of the bar and paused, trying to sense his location. Closing her eyes, she did her best to focus in the only way she knew how—by calming her mind and praying to Apollo.

Flashes of brick and stone, cement and pebbles. Metallic fluid. Crimson everywhere.

He's in the back of the bar.

A door led to the back of the building, and she chose to take advantage of the convenience and head outside. The night air had grown crisp and cool, the weight of the autumn season approaching hanging in it.

She looked around, but Jesse wasn't in sight. *Where is he?* she thought, irritated. Something tickled the top of her head, and she looked up. A balcony.

Ah, so that's where he had gone. Amanda strolled over to the bottom of the stairwell and climbed up, marveling at how strong she had become. She flung herself over the rail with little effort and walked into what appeared to be a run-down, abandoned apartment building. The room she stood in had broken in walls in places, a ceiling that was falling apart.

He must be feeding off of some homeless person hiding out in here. The slight energy sensation passed over her once more, and she moved towards the source of the sensation.

In a small room with a cracked window stood Jesse in the center, in his arms a tall, long-haired blonde in black leather pants and a tight tube top. She appeared to be in her mid to upper twenties and didn't look as if she had been put to sleep as the homeless man in the alleyway had been. On the contrary, her head was tilted back; a rapturous expression claimed her face while he drank the blood out of her neck.

Amanda burned from the inside out, not with passion but with rage, and the room suddenly turned scarlet. Jesse was jolted out of his trance by the piercing empathic resonance that coursed through him, but she turned on her heel and rapidly made her way out of the derelict apartment, not wanting to see any more.

* * * *

The magister stepped into Merideth's office only to find Theodotos there, bent over study materials.

"Ah, Theodotos, have you seen Amaltheia?" Amaltheia was Merideth's Order name, and it was only polite to refer to her as such to someone not in the Inner Circle.

"No, Magister, I haven't," he answered politely. "She let me study in here while she left to go do some errands. I don't know when she'll be back."

"I see. Well then, if you see her, could you please tell her that I was looking for her?"

The young man nodded. "Certainly, Magister. I will."

"Thank you." James sighed and left the room, hearing the young vampire call out, "Good luck!" He didn't know why this astrological chart bugged him and he was annoyed that his Sight remained quiet on the matter. What sort of strange, bizarre circumstance did Jesse get himself into this time?

He was wandering back to his office when he caught Amaltheia down the hallway, chatting with a second degree vampire. At top speed, the magister ran over to her and would've been breathless when he finally stood in front of her had he any breath in his body.

Amaltheia blinked at him in a mixture of surprise and gentle amusement. "Ah, Janius, is there something I can help you with?" To the student, she smiled and said, "Go to my office and I'll catch up with you later." He smiled, and with an understanding nod left both vampires to talk alone.

"Hi, Merideth. I've been looking all over for you." Merideth smiled. Like Lynne, the magister often addressed Amaltheia by her real name in private. "There is something that you can indeed help me with. I have this chart here from the new apprentice."

She chuckled heartily. "Ah, you must mean Lyrael! Chart, you say?" Her eyebrows shot up into her hair.

"Yes, astrological chart. I've been looking this over for every possible correspondence that I can think of, but something in it eludes me."

"Eludes you? Like what? Are you looking for something in it?"

"There seems to be something familiar about it, but I can't quite place it. I was hoping maybe you might have some leads or suggestions on what to look for."

"Did you try to scry it, by any chance?" she asked gently.

"Scrying!" he cried with excitement. "No, no...I didn't. What an excellent idea. Thank you, Merideth."

"No problem at all, Magister," she replied. Was that a giggle he had heard from her as he walked away? Oh well.

* * * *

The magister ran into his office, turned off the ceiling light, and lit a few candles on his desk.

"Scrying, why didn't I think of that before?" he asked the air around him crossly. No matter. He would get to the root of the problem soon enough.

After tracing a brilliant white cross over himself, then flaming blue pentagrams in all four directions, he invoked the guardians of the elements to purify the room and his personal space before setting the astrological chart in between the candles on his desk in the center of the ritual. *Theoretically speaking, this should be a simple operation.*

James chanted various words of power before gazing into the chart printed on the paper, allowing his outer sight to drift out of focus as his inner Sight took over. The images came to him slowly and faintly at first, and after a time crystallized into lucidity. He watched the parade of symbols and movie-like imagery as it washed over and through him until the end of the web of visions was revealed.

Then it hit him.

"Blood," he blurted out, "this can't be!"

The magister ran to his file cabinet and pulled out an old sheet of paper and, with a shaking hand, placed it beside Amanda's. By the time he was done processing the information that lay before him in all of its stark reality, he found himself on the floor staring off into space.

"Well, no wonder," he mumbled. "No wonder at all."

His head fell into his hands. He had to tell Lynne as soon as he was able. She deserved to know.

And what was he going to tell Jesse?

"I can't tell him," he declared. "Not yet. And certainly not now."

* * * *

She had no idea how he had managed to catch up, but somehow there he was, right behind her. She whirled around with her fist snapping out, but he managed to dodge it by grabbing her wrist.

"Amanda, look at me."

She responded with an angry glare. A whirlwind of anger and pain still swirled inside her heart, and she could barely look at him. Jesse sighed.

"Amanda, there are two kinds of feeding," he explained to her calmly. "There is the kind you need to do in order to obtain food, and there is the kind that passes for sex among our kind. What I just did, I did to survive."

She sensed the angry look in her eyes falter and grow calmer. Witnessing the resentment she knew still lurked within them, he went on.

"You will need to do the same thing that I did, and in time you will know the difference. What I do with you is magickal, better than sex and anything in the world. In fact, *you* mean the world to me, and I would never cheat on you. You know that."

He gently took both of her wrists as he continued, "Amanda, we share a very strong, very powerful connection. It's more than just a vampire and his Childe; I'm sure that you've guessed this. And through that bond, you should know whether or not I'm telling you the truth."

Jesse paused, and she sighed. Amanda knew that he was right and that she was being foolish. But she couldn't help the part of her that was jealous and hurt over what she had seen.

WHY DON'T YOU TRUST ME?

Amanda wanted to pull away, away from his voice, his hands around her wrists, and everything inside of her. "I know—I know it's stupid," she admitted. "But I couldn't help it. And," she added in an accusing tone, "if I had some hot young stud in my arms, you would've reacted the same way."

His lips quirked in amusement. "Okay, I'm not going to fight you there. Would you feel better if I just stuck to hunting the homeless men instead?"

"I'd be lying to you if I said no."

"And I would be lying to if I said that I would be comfortable with such a restriction. Not every person wandering the streets will be male, Amanda, and sooner or later, I may reach a point where I will have to feed off of someone, male or female, attractive or unattractive, because they are there and I need to feed. And I hope someday you will understand the difference between my food and what I share with you."

Amanda squirmed. She knew she was being an insecure idiot and all of her concerns seemed dumber by the moment. At the same time, she still couldn't help but feel a tight twinge in her stomach just thinking about him having fed on that woman. It made her angry that she experienced such jealousy even though she wanted desperately to trust him.

"I-I do understand," she answered slowly, "and I'm sorry for doubting you." Looking up into his eyes, she gazed into their depths and saw nothing but a well of fathomless love and passion, and in that moment, she wanted nothing more than to drown in it forever.

Chapter Seventeen

"There is no choice for you now but to...revolutionize the world."

James spent the next few days avoiding both Lynne and Jesse, the results of his scrying session still weighing heavily on his mind. Twice he had run into Lynne and twice he had completely lost his nerve, unable to communicate what he knew he ought to tell her.

This is foolish, he admonished himself. *She needs to know. I can't keep this a secret.*

He paced in his office, wrestling with the knowledge he possessed and his instincts.

Perhaps I should say nothing. After all, it would only open up old wounds.

Then guilt set in. Lynne was his friend. He owed it to her.

"Fine," he stated. "I'll do it."

The magister bolted out of the room, determined to do what he needed to do. He turned in the direction of Lynne's office and purposefully marched to her door. It was closed, which meant that either she was working or someone was in her office. He couldn't tell which it was, as it was made magickally soundproof as were the offices of all of the professors in the Inner Circle of Fifth Degree and higher. It was the only way to conduct business in private and allow their students the privacy of one-on-one lessons.

Taking a few deep breaths, he reached out to knock on the door, then drew his hand back. He tried again but found himself once more faltering before the task.

Fear is failure and the forerunner of failure, he reminded himself sternly. Then he knocked—loudly.

There was a pause before the door opened. There stood Lynne, and behind her seated in one of the office chairs was Amanda, who clutched a notebook and pencil in her lap. Clearly they were in the middle of either a lesson or a research project, and James was interrupting.

"Hi, Janius. Can I help you?" Asherael asked briskly.

"Um...."

Amanda was in the room, and there was no way to deliver this information in private.

Lynne quirked a blonde eyebrow at him.

"Um, yes. I need to tell you something, um, in private. It's rather, well, important. Not life threatening, of course, but—"

"Janius, your accent is slipping," she chided him. "If this isn't life threatening, can it wait? I've been trying to corner this rather... busy...apprentice of ours for days." She shot a half teasing, half serious look in Amanda's direction.

He nodded stupidly. "Yes, yes, just come by and see me when you can. Please."

"All right, Magister." She smiled at him. "Thanks for your patience."

"And thank you, Asherael." The door closed in his face, and he stood there for a bit, blinking before heading back to his office. He was simultaneously frustrated and relieved. A curious sensation.

* * * *

Amanda shook her head. "That was...interesting."

"Yes," stated Lynne offhandedly. "But, ah well. Do you think that you have a handle on this project now? I mean, this is right up your alley. I'm surprised you haven't started it sooner."

Amanda blushed. *Well, she's obviously being fed well,* observed Lynne. Not that she ever thought that Jesse would starve his Childe, she reasoned, but that he often had a knack of bending rules and neglecting responsibility. And where was the magickal shield he'd promised to deliver to the magister anyway, hmmm?

Asherael sighed, running her hand through her hair with great impatience.

"Is there something wrong?" inquired Amanda.

The blonde vampire shook her head. "No, no, just...it's Janius. I don't know what gets into him sometimes." It was a partial truth, not entirely a lie.

Amanda nodded, tapping her pen to her lips before she spoke. "How did he become a vampire anyway? Or is that classified information?"

Sitting down on her desk with her arms folded, Lynne pursed her lips in thought. "No, no...not classified. But it's definitely an interesting story. James may kill me if I tell it to you, though."

"Oh," replied Amanda lamely, her disappointment obvious.

"But that won't stop me, however."

Amanda blinked. Lynne grinned wickedly.

* * * *

London, 1897

In a shamefully small study within his home just outside of London—far too small to really perform much in the way of useful ritual—James used his paint brush to painstakingly trace Hebrew letters across the yellow handle of a small dagger: *Raphael, YHVH, Chassan.* He added various magickal sigils beside them with care and intent.

He smiled as he admired his handiwork. Once it was dry, he would have to paint his magickal motto on the back of the handle: *Veritas Gladius Mea Est*, or as translated from the Latin, "Truth is my sword."

It wasn't without anxiety that he eyed his creation, as he wanted to be done with this dagger sooner so he could perform the rituals he was learning in his newly acquired grade of study. *Patience,* he reminded himself, *patience.* One didn't go through the subgrades of the Adeptus Minor overnight, after all.

Perhaps taking a walk would help him focus. Yes, a walk—this was the right course of action. A leisurely, meditative stroll to help calm his nerves. It was night out, but he didn't care. He removed his hat and coat from the chair and blew out the candle before leaving the room.

A certain something lingered in the air that night, something which he couldn't quite put his finger on. He attributed it to his frequent meditations on the element of Air as of late—certainly it must be affecting his thoughts. Or more importantly, the element itself pertained to his thoughts! James knew he needed to meditate on this further, as well as contemplate the cycles and patterns of thought which prevented him from clear thinking. After all, clear thinking was what marked the expert magician from the novice.

The wind suddenly picked up; this was a sign of his inner being reflected in the outer—the little world talking to the big world. He needed to calm and compose his thoughts. Meditate. Possess control over his thoughts and hence master himself as a magician. He held onto the hat on his head tightly, wondering if he would ever get the knack of this elemental grade. Inside his head, he slowly counted to four as he inhaled and exhaled and continued until the storm inside his mind had gone away.

But an oppressive feeling of darkness followed the sudden gusts of wind, and his Sight seized him and slammed images into his mind of terrifying demons and terrible temptations.

"Such a Fire existeth," he mumbled nervously, "extending through the rushing of Air. Or even a Fire formless, whence cometh the image of a voice."

A strange cackle sounded, as if some invisible being in the wind mocked him, and it made the hair on the back of his neck stand on end. This was most certainly not the voice he was trying to summon from within himself.

"Or even a fl-flashing light," he continued, "abounding, revolving, whirling forth, c-crying aloud."

The dark, terrible winds roaring around him coalesced into a familiar shape—that of a man—and as the shape grew more defined he made out the features of his face. Dark, intense eyes framed by a strong, angular face and long dark hair.

In his terror, James reached into his vest and yanked out the silver cross which he wore on a chain around his neck. Holding it out in front of his chest, he cried out, "In the name of the Lord of the Universe, who are you?"

The man gallantly bowed. "I am Vlad. Vlad Tepes. I have followed your magickal progress, James Sinclair, with great...interest." He spoke with a thick accent that James couldn't place.

The young adept blinked. *Dracula?* He had read of this man in a fictional novel recently released. But that was fiction! "How did you know my name? What manner of man are you?"

The man who called himself Tepes smiled, his distinctively sharp, pointed fangs prominent. James's eyes widened.

"You're no bloody man at all, are you?" He tried to master his thoughts. *Think, James, think! What do I do? Surely....*

He gripped his cross tighter and yelled at the man in front of him, "In the name of the Lord of the Universe, who works in Silence and whom naught but Silence can express...."

Vlad Tepes laughed, but James ignored him and continued, furious, "I command you to leave this place in the name of YHVH—"

"And here I remain!" Tepes, still laughing, raised his arms in the air. In response, the winds swirled around him, whistling in James's ears, mocking him with their insistence.

The young adept could do nothing but continue to stutter and try to repeat the magickal command. "I command you—in the name of

YHVH—"

"And you call yourself an Adept of the Golden Dawn?" Vlad asked him in a jeering tone. "My dear boy, you have much power within you, much potential—and you squander it painting tools and reciting scripture!"

"In the name of the Lord of the Universe, who works in Silence—"

"You be silent."

In that one statement, James's will and speech were completely squashed. He stared dumbfounded at the being before him, unable to move or utter a sound.

"I am here to act as initiator," Vlad stated solemnly. "There is no choice for you now but to join me and revolutionize the world."

James's eyes widened further.

"Your path has been carefully arranged for you. This is your destiny. You have no idea what I offer you—wisdom, knowledge, immortality!"

Faster than the gusts of wind blowing around him, Vlad Tepes was at his side. James swallowed. Was this the devil? Would he lose his soul?

"I am not the devil, James, nor your soul do I want. It is yours to have, to do with what you wish." His fangs shone in the moonlight.

The young adept eyed him warily, his breath coming in and out in quick spurts. Maybe this was all a dream, nothing but a sick nightmare.

"I come here to transform you to a god. As of this night...."

With one quick motion, Vlad clutched James's head in his hands. Inside his head, James continued to pray. If he was to die, let it be fast and painless, and may he join his family in Heaven.

"You will become Osiris."

Vlad's fangs sank into his neck, and James—Frater *Veritas Gladius Mea Est*—knew no more.

James awoke, the metallic taste of blood fresh in his mouth, and his ears and head rang. He Saw so much clearly, felt everything that had happened to him, and knew what it was that he was meant to do. Vlad Tepes had been very clear in his instruction, and while he knew that he was still Turning, there was much work to be done.

He was now an initiate of *Ordo Draconis et Rosae*, and he was to be the founder of the new Clan. All he had to do was choose a name for it and to initiate others as he had been initiated.

In honor of his past as an initiate of the Golden Dawn, he chose the name Clan Gladius—for truth would ever be as his sword.

* * * *

"Lynne, you're shitting me," Amanda blurted out. "Dracula, Golden Dawn, what? I don't even know what part of this story is more unbelievable. Come on, tell me the truth!"

The blonde vampire laughed. "I swear to you, I am telling you the complete truth! And just think of the funniest part of all!"

Amanda snorted. "What, that you think I'd actually believe it?"

Laughing loudly, Lynne replied, "No, silly—that the only existing lineage today that can be traced to the original Golden Dawn is an esoteric order of vampires. Just imagine how humans would react to that if they knew."

Thinking about it for a moment, Amanda chuckled. "Okay, you got me there. That is pretty funny."

With a light shrug, Lynne stated, "I will confess to you, Amanda, that I very much enjoy watching people's sacred cows get ripped into bloody pieces and eaten. But that could be my vampiric nature doing the talking." Abruptly, the elder vampire cleared her throat. "Anyway, about that assignment?"

"Yes?"

"I'm giving you a month. And, oh, don't you give me that look. I know you. You could finish it in less than a week, blindfolded."

Amanda shook her head. "I doubt it, but I'll take your confidence in me as a compliment. Thank you."

"Don't mention it. And please, next time you see Janius, feel free to ask him questions you have about anything regarding studies in ceremonial magick. He really is a great magician, honest—regardless of whether or not you believe what I told you is true."

With a wink, Lynne escorted her student out of her office, ignoring the fact that the young apprentice had rolled her eyes at her.

After all, she hadn't even met the Grandmagus yet.

Chapter Eighteen

"I have a present for you."

"Excuses, Turel. Excuses." The magister shook his head at him sternly. That magickal project he had assigned to him should've been done by now—at the very least, the research completed.

"I'm sorry, Magister." Jesse's words were hurried but no less sincere. "But I've been attending to my new Childe and I confess that it's been taking up a bit more of my energy than I had anticipated."

James sighed. *Busy shagging, you mean,* he thought, but dared not say it aloud. Inwardly he cringed, knowing that he was being unfair. After all, he could hardly blame Jesse for being so attentive towards the fledgling vampire. The Turning process was rocky for everyone, and Amanda needed special care.

Then a flash of insight struck him, so abrupt he almost jumped.

"Turel, you're right, and that's certainly important. In fact, why don't you have Lyrael assist you with your project? Maybe she has some insights on protection spell usage through her graduate studies in Greco-Roman magick."

Jesse's face looked as if he'd had a small object suddenly land on his head. "What? Magister—Janius—are you serious?" He frowned. "Sure, I'll do it. I'll ask her along. I just don't want to overwhelm her with such a task."

The magister waved his hand dismissingly. "I have no doubt in my mind that Lyrael can handle it and still turn in her first assignment. She got her Masters from NYU, didn't she?"

"True, true." Jesse smiled. "I don't doubt her skill or her intelligence. You know that."

"Turel, I'll tell you what. I know that for you these days, the sun, moon, and stars all shine on your beloved. But for what it's worth," the magister gave him a pointed look, "I don't doubt her skill, either."

"I'm glad."

"Or yours."

Jesse shoved his hands into his pockets and exhaled.

Watching him carefully, James continued, "You know that I think highly of you both, or I wouldn't have asked this of you. Now, go, tell your Bondmate what I think of her and about her new assignment. It'll give you both the chance to spend productive time together *and* get this assignment done. And Blood willing, you *will* finish it."

Jesse's jaw dropped a few millimeters before he quickly replaced it. He swore under his breath, but the magister heard him. "I figured you might've known. About the Bond. I'm sorry that I didn't tell you sooner, Janius."

The magister met Jesse's eyes calmly in response. "Don't apologize to *me*, Jesse. Apologize to that poor girl for not telling her what you got her into. Given how she's madly in love with you, she'll undoubtedly forgive you. But she has a right to know."

Jesse nodded. "I know, I know. I just—I've been waiting for the right time."

"No time like the present," the magister replied, brisk. But he paused, and his tone softened. "Jesse, I know it's been hard for you. I'm glad you finally found someone to love again after Minervia."

Tensing when he heard her name, Jesse only managed a curt nod.

"I just hope you Blood Bound her because you love her and not because you're looking to replace what you lost." Jesse's eyes suddenly got furiously dark and painful for James to look at. "Turel, don't you look at me that way. I know you love Amanda and I know you were hurt when Sarah died. And I want to see you both happy. But you were Blood Bound before. You know what it was like to be in such a strong connection with someone and you know what it was like to lose that someone. The breaking of a Blood Bond—Blood, I hope to never go through what you did. Frankly, I'm surprised you were so eager to embrace it again, and I can only hope it means that you've fully healed."

Jesse looked away from him, his face unreadable.

"Just get that assignment done, Jesse," he told him warily.

"I will." Quietly, he turned on his heel and left the magister's office.

James could only stare at his back as he walked out the door. *Blood help them both, and me, to be patient with him. And when he's done telling her what he needs to, so must I tell Lynne—and him.*

* * * *

Amanda was poring over her notes for her Apprentice assignment when Jesse walked into her room.

"Morning—evening, rather," she greeted him with a little laugh. Amanda embraced him warmly. Jesse smiled. At least she was in a good mood.

"Evening, Amanda." He pulled back to kiss her on the lips. "I trust you slept well?" She nodded. "Good. I have some things to tell you and I was hoping perhaps we can get the hell out of here and talk. Go to a nice restaurant or something."

Her brow furrowed. "Is there something wrong?"

"No, nothing...nothing at all. Just some pressing business to talk to you about. I just got word from Janius that he wants us both to work on the assignment I've been working on."

"Oh!" she exclaimed. "Another assignment? With you?" Amanda grinned. "That shouldn't be so bad. What's it about?"

"Let's talk about it over food and maybe some wine. I have a present for you."

"A present?"

He clasped her hand and inside of it he pressed a gold ring with a dark amethyst stone, not unlike the one which Lynne had given her. But this one was attached via a gold chain to a beautiful gold rope bracelet. At the connecting point was a gold ankh, and at its center a tiny pentacle.

"Jesse, I...." She stared at the piece of jewelry in amazement and confusion. "It's beautiful. How...why...?"

"Here, I'll put it on you."

Dazed, Amanda observed as he deftly slipped the ring over the second finger on her left hand and attached the bracelet to her wrist.

As the clasp closed, a sudden pulsing sensation coursed in her chest which spread to her whole being. She stared at him as he informed her with a smile, "This used to belong to someone very important to me, hence why I feel you are the perfect person to have it."

With a degree of caution, Amanda fingered it. In its links hummed an odd, unidentifiable type of energy, tightly woven into its very core. Whoever—or whatever—forged this had some magickal motive in mind.

"Thank you," she replied. "This—it's beautiful." Its weight seemed familiar to her in a way she couldn't place, but she shrugged it away to some corner in her mind. As he kissed her again, any doubt or confusion she had fled just as fast, replaced only by a feeling of rightness and contentment in her heart.

* * * *

He chose a small restaurant nearby, one which he had told her would serve her favorite foods.

"That bracelet will boost your ability to ingest human food," he said. "The amethyst ring alone would help with alcohol and most organic substances, provided they are light and easy to digest."

"What else can it do?" she asked him with great curiosity.

"Many things. I probably shouldn't be telling you most of them until you're of a higher degree. But some of them will be of use to you in the future. As for the rest," he paused and sipped his wine, "that's what I brought you here to discuss."

His eyes softened as he gazed upon her. "When I Turned you, I brought you over to a very strange, new world. I know that. Part of my having to do so meant you not knowing I would do it. Another part meant I would be letting you go eventually, to do as you wish as a fully formed vampire."

"Let me go?"

"Sires are around for the Turning process and for the training thereafter, but as time goes on, we have less of a say in the affairs of our...children, if you will. But in some cases, this isn't so."

Amanda sat back in her chair. "What sorts of cases?" She was glad for the wine swimming around in her bloodstream so soon; this conversation disturbed her a bit. The idea of him "letting her go" or not being a part of her life deeply bothered her.

"Cases where the Sire and his—or her—Childe are in love, which happens more often than you may think."

In love. "Jesse...," she breathed, afraid to ask to disturb the moment and yet knowing fully in her heart what he meant.

He squeezed her hand. "I have given you a gift upon your Turning. I consider it to be a gift. Not everyone would agree. It means you are more strongly connected to me and I to you. My only regret upon giving you this gift was not knowing if you were willing to receive it—had you been given the option."

Waiting to hear what he said next, she held her tongue and let him continue.

"Amanda, what I did I could only do when I Turned you—and unfortunately gave you no choice to accept either it or your Turning, to say yes or no. It's the...often difficult part of this whole process."

"What did you do?" she asked, an eerie sense of calm washing over her.

Jesse cleared his throat. "It's called a 'Blood Bond.' You are Bound to me by Blood, as Blood wills. It's like...how do I describe it?" He stared down at his hands.

"A marriage," Amanda filled in for him. Her head dropped into her hands, and her shoulders shook up and down. As her gaze lifted, she watched as his expression gave way to relief that she was laughing and not crying.

"Oh, Jesse.... Jesse, I knew something was odd between us, something that went past the usual connection between vampires and their kindred or whatever, but I had no idea what it was. And I thought that it was all in my precious little head. Thank you for telling me about what you did."

A long moment passed between them, during which Jesse gazed into her eyes. After a while, he spoke, and when he did, his voice sounded disturbingly grave.

"You have no idea what I did. You just don't."

Puzzled, she asked, "What do you mean by that?" But he continued to just look at her. Out of sheer nervousness, she downed the last of her wine. When she was done, he squeezed her hand again.

"I know you're too afraid to see it or acknowledge it. And you're shielding both yourself from it *and* me from you."

"What?" The question sounded stupid to her own ears.

Jesse smiled at her in response.

"Turel, you're driving me nuts. Just come out with it already."

"I would, if you were ready. Just meditate on it." She opened her mouth to speak, but he placed his finger over her lips. "Think about it. Think about what I've said. It'll come to you."

She sighed, irritated. "Fine. Bond me and don't tell me what it does. See if I care."

"Amanda." His voice was sharp, and it hurt. "Don't talk to me in that way. You know what I'm talking about—I know you do. *You* know that you do. And you're afraid of it. And as long as you're afraid, you won't be open to what I have to tell you—it'll only scare you further."

She paused. Was she afraid? Deep down in her core, she knew nothing he said to her was incorrect. It was most likely far more accurate than she wanted to admit to herself. Yes, she had an inkling of what that Bond entailed. She had sensed it on many an occasion, and the intimacy of the connection disturbed her. Was she willing to tell him that? Was she willing to face what the Bond meant? She had no idea, and in the end, she was forced to admit he was right.

As if he could read her thoughts—and most likely he could, she noted with chagrin—he squeezed her hand again.

"We still need to talk about that assignment," he told her. "Protection spells, purification rituals, invisibility spells—unload what you know of them on me. We need to work on this together."

* * * *

Hours later, they were still conversing and they had long since left the restaurant, as it had closed for the night. Instead, they had walked along the streets, chatting about the proposal to build a protection shield around the Sanctuary. Amanda had a number of good ideas and keen insights, which Jesse complimented her on and told her to make use of later when they'd managed to lock themselves in the Clan's library for further research.

It was sometime while Jesse had his arm lazily held around her waist with his other hand wrapped around hers when she noticed that the sky was an odd color and realized they had stayed up until nearly sunrise.

On cue, Jesse looked up at the sky and back at her with a grim look on his face. "Oh, this is not good. Come on, we have to hurry."

Amanda whipped her head around where they stood, not even knowing where they were. "But where are we? Are we near a subway stop or something?"

"No time. I think I know where we are. Time to run, and fast."

For the first time since her Turning, she was thankful for the lack of the need to breathe as they sped down the streets. Jesse stopped her and, closing his eyes, he quickly mumbled a few words.

He pointed off in a northeast direction from where they stood—and opened his eyes. "Sanctuary, that way. Come on."

A block away, they saw amber glimmerings off in the distance of what could only be the sun. What was once welcomed in her days as a mortal human now held a threat, and panic slammed into her with the force of a Mack truck. The echo passed through Jesse as he stood beside her.

Run.

Chapter Nineteen

"'But to love me is better than all things....'"

In her college years, Amanda had seen many sunrises while working on exam papers or studying. None of them, however, had so stealthily come upon her like this, leaving her in such dread.

Jesse clutched her hand and ran down with her towards the Sanctuary, which beckoned to them as an oasis in the distance.

"'Fear is failure and the forerunner of failure,'" he grumbled. "That's what Janius would be saying to us right now, were he here."

Fear is failure, thought Amanda absently. She recalled with great detail the speech in the Neophyte ceremony of the Golden Dawn, a text she had read ages ago. It was spoken by the Hiereus, who was the "Master of Darkness" and acted as a fierce protector of the candidate undergoing the initiation. He stood in the place of the West.

West, darkness.... Amanda's mind took a few seconds to process this. Perhaps if she used magick, called upon the forces of the West to bring darkness to protect them? In the form of clouds, even. Cloud cover would not be a perfect defense against the sun but it would allow them the most rudimentary of protection spells—one of which Lynne had taught her not long ago—and would allow them a chance to get inside the Sanctuary unscathed.

She halted, and in the ancient pagan gesture of prayer, she raised her hands in the air.

"Amanda, what are you *doing*?" hissed Jesse.

But magick, fueled by adrenaline, already coursed through her body.

"Guardians of the West in the place of the setting sun," she called out, "winds of the West, send us clouds between us and the rising sun."

After she spoke the words that flowed from her naturally, an awkwardness came over Amanda. It seemed so simple, these words. Would they work?

But the magick was true, and effortlessly the storm clouds rolled over and settled overhead. They hovered directly over the Sanctuary, vast enough to cover the distance between them and where safety lay.

* * * *

Jesse watched, completely stunned and unable to speak. His skin—which had previously started to itch—was perfectly fine. And he hadn't even done any sun protection spells yet! He looked at the clouds, then back at Amanda. Her face was serene, and her hair rippled in the winds. Her soft, dark eyes gazed off into the distance at something—he knew not what. Magick still clung to the air around them, igniting his senses and making the hairs on his arms stand on end. Something about the moment reminded him of another time in his life, but he couldn't quite place it. But he had the nagging sense of déjà vu.

* * * *

Haniel was on her way to bed when she spotted Theodotos looking out of a Sanctuary window, his gaze a mixture of concern and fear. He whirled around to see Haniel walking in his direction.

"Haniel, look out the window. Who is that woman walking towards us with Turel?" Theodotos ran his hand through his dirty blond hair and wore an odd expression of both frustration and confusion.

"Theodotos, what are you doing? It's almost sunrise!" But she looked anyway—albeit cautiously from the side—and frowned upon seeing the two figures heading their way. Mortal eyes couldn't have recognized them from that far, but they both could. "That's Lyrael, Turel's new Childe. And if they don't hurry they're both going to fry. What the Blood they're doing out so late, I don't know."

As Haniel spoke, Lyrael raised her arms in the air, palms outwards. They watched as the winds spun around her. While they couldn't hear her words, they saw shadows speedily settling over the Sanctuary and where the two vampires stood.

"Did you see what she just did?" he demanded.

Wow. "Yeah." She blinked. "Yeah, I did."

"I thought you said she was a new Childe? She shouldn't be past Apprentice at this point!"

Haniel shrugged. "I'm Second Degree. Wouldn't you know better than me?"

He shrugged at her in response.

"I guess she was really skilled in magick to begin with. Come on, we should probably tell the magister of what happened anyway."

He rolled his eyes. "I can't, he's still looking for me. I cut class with Asherael to practice my sword forms."

"You did *what*?" Clenching her teeth, she yelled, "How in the *Blood* are you going to pass your degree exam?"

Her angry blue eyes glared into his equally blue ones, but he stared her down. Giving up, she declared, "Fine, *I'll* go get the magister." She took off in the direction of his office.

"You're an angel, Haniel!" Theodotos called after her.

It was all she could do to prevent herself from laughing, as she knew he was deliberately punning on her Clan name. Damn him. She had to do the right thing, even if he couldn't. The magister had to know every detail of what just happened—especially if it meant that someone at Turel's level had gotten hurt. Not to mention his new Childe. Shouldn't he have been taking better care of his kin? And why was *she* the one running for the magister? If Theodotos had actually—but no, he was too busy getting into trouble. Again. She suspected that was why Asherael had taken him on as a student to begin with. He was brilliant, but his focus was in the wrong place. *Sword forms*?

The thought of Theodotos slacking and getting away with it forced a sigh from her lips. It was a nasty human habit, but at this point she didn't care. She struggled with her studies, but Theodotos zipped through like it was nothing. Was he really even dealing with his alchemy?

And why did she care so much, anyway?

* * * *

Jesse's mind drifted off as Amanda and James talked to each other animatedly over her magick spell. Yes, it could be used as a serious component to the protection spell they were researching, yes they had risked a great deal by not keeping track of the time—but at this point, he didn't care. They were both safe and sound, and Amanda with her quick thinking had saved their lives.

He kept seeing her with her arms in the air, her hair blowing in the wind. Something about it...ah, yes.

It had been a long time ago. But in vampire time, not much time at all.

* * * *

New York City, 1967

She wore black that day—unusual for her. A long, sweeping skirt with a peasant style blouse. The only item of jewelry she had on was the hand flower bracelet that Jesse had made for her, uniting both her religion and his in the form of the pentacle and the ankh at its center. When she walked, the skirt rippled.

He loved it, and he loved her.

Sarah had encouraged a few young vampires to go off and head to the rock concert that night—much to the dismay of James, who insisted that sort of music was "noise and nonsense." But she had laughed in his face.

"Music is good for the soul," she had told him, "regardless of whether or not that soul is in a human or vampire body."

Lynne had agreed with her—which only served to irritate Janius.

"James, Sarah's a free spirit—you know that. And that's why, deep down, you like her. I bet you even wish you could be more like her."

The magister only smiled at her. "I think you're projecting, Lynne." But it wasn't unlike the blonde vampire to stick up for her best friend. The two women were fairly inseparable—or would be if Minervia didn't spend so much time with her Childe, Turel.

She had even joined the young vampires—much to their surprise and delight—by the Arch that night, where they agreed to meet up before heading to the concert.

"Minervia is so *cool*," one of the apprentices had commented repeatedly to the magister afterwards. James had just rolled his eyes. He could never get used to the culture of living in the Village, and he vowed he never would. Greenwich Village was ideal for people like Sarah, perhaps, but not for him.

Jesse delighted in Sarah's whimsical nature, however. His Turning was just twelve years past—not very long for a vampire, but long enough to have gained a good measure of responsibility. At this time, he was in his second degree in the Order and making hints about entering into his third. All in due time, he was told. All in due time.

He was reminded of this with more than a degree of irony as he found himself dragged into a vicious magickal war between the *Ordo Draconis et Rosae* and another magickal order known as *Ordo Aureae Crucis*—the Order of the Golden Cross, an organization entirely devoted to the destruction of vampiric kind.

Wasn't soon enough, he had often thought bitterly.

Sarah was a high degree initiate, a first degree member of the Inner Circle of his order—a fourth degree member of the Clan. At the time, it was her, Janius, and Asherael who were among the prime movers. The lineage of Vlad Tepes and *Ordo Draconis et Rosae* was deeply respected and envied among various vampiric orders and their clans.

But Vlad Tepes had long made an enemy out of a particular Golden Dawn initiate, one who had known of his Turning of many a Golden Dawn adept in order to create a magickal order of his own. That initiate had advanced as far as the elemental grade of Spirit—the grade known as the Portal grade—before embarking on his own to form a new order, that of the Golden Cross.

That initiate's name was sadly struck from the record, but was known by his motto: *Lux e Tenebris*, Light out of Darkness.

* * * *

Jesse and Sarah had ventured out late that night in order to continue assisting her with a particular magickal project. The project contained something of minor importance, but he couldn't recall what now—something to do with some of the research ideas her students worked on, Jesse figured.

Even now, he remembered sitting at a table in the library with her when a sudden gust of wind moved *through* him. The wind hit through the Sanctuary like a sonic blast, causing everything around them to ripple and look distorted. And yet, all was still.

He looked up at her. Her eyes, usually tinted blue with magick, had settled back into their normal hazel. It meant she was troubled—and most likely afraid.

She reached out and grabbed his hand. "Come, we need to get moving."

"Where?"

"Outside. Someone's attempting to breach our magickal defenses.

Could be dangerous."

"Dangerous?" he echoed stupidly.

She didn't reply but merely half pushed, half pulled him to his feet and led him to the door. Somehow he found himself not much later standing at the door of the Clan's Sanctuary with Sarah in front of him. Then she opened the door.

A gust of wind billowed out, blowing her red hair behind her. An unsettling energy vibrated in that wind.

"Shouldn't we get the magister? And Asherael?" he asked.

Sarah's voice was quiet and measured. "I can summon them, but they went out for the evening."

"Out?" Why did he continually echo whatever she said to him? Turel had never before thought of himself as being so useless.

"Yeah, Asherael convinced him to go out with her and have fun. Told him it would be good for him. Get him to relax, or something."

Another psychic blast hit them, nearly knocking Jesse off of his feet.

"I guess that was bad timing of them, huh?" she said wryly.

Jesse stammered in return, "W-will they get here in time?"

"Probably not. Stay behind me, Jess. And don't do anything unless I tell you to." She shut her eyes, and he knew she focused her will towards her psychic senses. When her eyes flew open again, Turel knew without a doubt that they would not be blue.

"The Golden Cross," she whispered.

Another reverberation tore through them and into the building behind them.

"Sarah, if it's them—"

"They're out to kill us," she finished for him. Then she frowned. "You shouldn't be here. If anything were to happen to you, Jesse...."

"I would rather be here, by your side, than anywhere else," he insisted vehemently. "I'm not going to let anything happen to you, either."

Sarah smiled—a strange smile, filled with wistfulness. "Nothing can happen to *me*, Jess. Don't you worry."

He clasped her hand—the one that didn't wear the ring-bracelet—and drew close to her. Slowly, with his other hand, he brushed a strand of auburn hair away from her face.

"'O Nuit, continuous one of Heaven,'" Sarah smiled up at him, knowing the text he quoted, "'let it be ever thus; that men speak not of Thee as One but as None; and let them speak not of thee at all, since thou art continuous!'" It was from the *Book of the Law*, one of her favorite mystical texts.

With her bejeweled hand, she reached out for the hand that touched her face and gently squeezed it. In that moment, between them and in their Blood Bond existed a calm understanding.

"They're going to breach our shields any moment now, Jess. And I can't let that happen."

"What are you going to do?"

Sarah turned towards him, her eyes deep and luminous. "I am the only one here who can guard this place. If he and his helpers kill me, this Sanctuary will be no more."

"What about Janius? Asherael?"

"They're on their way physically. They would be present on the astral in order to help combat them, but much of their magickal energy is being used to actually get here in order to help protect the Clan. I'm busy fighting to make sure that they are not Seen, as right now they are quite vulnerable."

This time Jesse was knocked off his feet before the blast even hit him. Sarah steadied him.

"Do you remember," she asked him lightly, "when we first met?"

How could he forget! The short skirt, black leather jacket—he'd thought that she was a local college student, perhaps a beatnik.

"Yes," he responded, and on his voice was a broad grin.

"I said to you once that I would never leave you—and I promised you that. I even Bound you to me in rites of Blood to ensure that I would keep my promise."

He nodded. A sense of urgency underlined her calm, even voice, and a growing pit of fear stewed in his stomach.

"Listen to me, Jesse." She took his hands and clasped them to her breast. "In order to save this place, I need to abandon this body. Either way, they will kill me—or try to kill me. This way, they will not succeed in their attempt to harm this place."

The fear rose in his throat and made him ice cold.

"No," he insisted, moving his hands to grip hers tightly. "No, you can't. You can't do this. Sarah—"

"'But to love me is better than all things'," she told him, answering his previous verse. But her voice trembled as she continued, "'If under the night stars in the desert thou presently burnest mine incense before me, invoking me with a pure heart, and the Serpent flame therein, thou shalt come a little to lie in my bosom. For one kiss wilt thou then be willing to give all; but whoso gives one particle of dust shall lose all in that hour.'"

In one swift moment, she pushed him away from her and ran out in front of the building.

"*LUX E TENEBRIS*!" she shouted into shrieking winds. "You will not have me, nor the Clan!"

A burst of lightning bolts flew around her. Her long, crimson hair streamed behind her in the wind. The very image of Sarah burned.

A voice cried out from the shadows, "YIELD, denizen of darkness!" A strong, male voice. "It is over! By the will of God, it ends here!"

Her voice answered both clear and strong, "If that's what you want." Her face, amidst the flames, depicted a perfect picture of serenity.

In a single gesture, she raised her hands and called out a word. It sounded familiar to Jesse's ears, but he couldn't place it—nor could he clearly hear it over the rushing winds and strange lightning.

Then—in a single burst of light, as if from a tiny star exploding—she vanished.

Lynne and James arrived some moments later and found that the Sanctuary's defenses held firm—and the men who had attacked them were nowhere in sight. Later, they discovered several bodies around the Sanctuary dressed in the white robes of the Order of the Golden Cross. Each of the bodies looked as if it had been struck by lightning. While they knew the miracle that Sarah had caused, they knew it was at the expense of her own life. But in her sacrifice she had managed to take out more than half of the once flourishing magickal order of the Golden Cross.

James, from that day forward, took Jesse under his wing, both out of compassion and from obligation. Lynne, on the other hand, held him at arm's length. For whatever reason that Jesse couldn't fathom, she held him personally responsible for her friend's death.

The Clan survived, but it was never the same since. While the stars in the sky burned on, they knew that somewhere a black patch existed where a spark of light once shone—and that terrible absence haunted them.

Chapter Twenty

"Practice."

Perhaps it was due to his alchemy that Jesse was forced to revisit his past. He looked to his right, where Amanda sat, still talking with the magister. Watching her talk animatedly about magick and her studies in it, he couldn't help but smile in spite of his recent sorrowful recollection. While a part of him would always care about Sarah and mourn her death, his heart had opened anew for this Classical Studies student who loved Apollo—a sun god being worshipped by a vampire; how terribly amusing and almost tragic—and loved ancient Greece and Rome.

The two women he loved seemed to have much in common, regardless of their personality differences. Amanda held back much of herself from others (and perhaps, he realized, herself as well) and wasn't used to being open with people—the Blood Bond, in fact, made her very uncomfortable at times. Jesse knew that as intimately as he knew his own heart.

Sarah was a fiery woman, driven by her goals and passions like Amanda, but there was a lot more freedom in her spirit and much less caution in her self-expression. She hadn't been pinned back by academia for so long as Amanda had been, he reminded himself. Plus, Sarah had been very influenced by both Thelema and the 1960s social revolution—and neither influence had much of a part in Amanda's life.

But still, when he looked into Amanda's deep brown eyes, he saw a beautiful world filled with gods and magick. Jesse wanted to tuck himself away in that world and never return to his own. She made him feel as if he had a human pulse again and gave him back a piece of his soul that went missing once Sarah died—and another piece that was ripped away from him after he'd tortured and killed a few of the remaining *Ordo Aureae Crucis* members in revenge for her death. It was the one act of brutality he had partaken of in his whole life, and as satisfying as it had been to kill the murderers of his once beloved, it left a heavy mark on his soul.

If I were ever to die, I want my heart to be in equal weight to that feather in the Hall of Judgment. But after the way I ended their lives, I may have to do some compensation first.

He remembered how James had pulled him away from the place

where Sarah disappeared.

You can't stay here forever, Turel—the sun will be up soon.

The possibility that he would've taken his own life in the coming of the dawn now shook him. *I never would've gotten a chance to meet Amanda.* Her shining eyes gave him back his heart. Indeed, James had been correct—she was his sun, his moon, and his stars.

* * * *

As jolted as she had been by her brush with death, Amanda was further uprooted by the implications of the spell she had cast on the Sanctuary—not to mention the magister's reaction to it.

"Lyrael, this is remarkable," he declared, clearly astonished. "Do you realize what you've done?"

She shook her head. "Not really," she tried to say, but the words wouldn't come.

"Those clouds are currently holding in place right overhead—they haven't budged one bit, and we've had some rather heavy winds today. Local meteorologists on the telly—excuse me, television—are blaming it on pollution or chemicals or something. They don't know."

Squirming in her seat, she realized that this spell may be not so good after all.

"Don't worry about it. Lyrael—Amanda—this spell of yours, if modified, is absolutely perfect for us. If we were to cover the building we could stop boarding up the windows and reactivating spells every day. We actually have members of the Clan who work with the magick daily to make sure that we are completely safe from the sun. Thanks to your spell, we have the potential to no longer have to do all of that."

"How could it be modified?" Thinking for a moment, Amanda then added, "Perhaps if we made the clouds invisible?"

"And extended them not just overhead, but all over the Sanctuary. As much as I am understandably *furious* with you both for staying out so late and risking your lives," he emphasized his discontent in such a way as to make her cringe, "I am very happy you managed to come up with such a spell on such short notice and even happier that you are both all right. Apparently, whatever research you have been doing with Turel has been paying off. On behalf of the Clan—thank you."

"You-you're welcome."

"Don't be shy. Lyrael, your potential for magick is amazing. How long were you studying in the Golden Dawn?"

She gestured desperately, as if trying to grab the words in midair. "I was solitary—I never belonged to any order or organization—but I've been working on it since the beginning of my freshman year in undergrad. Before that was mostly just my own stuff. Nothing fancy, just homegrown witchery."

"Wicca?"

Amanda shrugged. "Sort of. A lot of Wicca influenced magick, definitely. I was working with the elementals before I found the Golden Dawn, and it's actually my research into them that led me to finding books on the subject."

"I see." He continued to probe her thoughts and philosophy on magick. She noticed out of the corner of her eyes that Jesse looked deep in thought, his expression unreadable. Was he happy with what she had done? Impressed? She had no idea.

At that thought, he turned towards her. She watched as a slow smile spread across his face, lighting up his eyes. Then he reached over and squeezed her hand.

"We'll be needing protection from other elements besides the sun," the magister went on, "but this is a major step in the right direction. I knew that I was doing the right thing in assigning you to this task, Lyrael. Thank you for proving me right. I'm quite, quite pleased with your progress in this Order."

"I'll do what I can—and I'll be sure to do my best."

"I have no doubt that you will." He turned towards Jesse. "Turel, your enthusiasm knows no bounds when it comes to your Childe, and sometimes you are not as clear-headed as I'd like you to be. Nonetheless, you made the right choice in bringing Lyrael over."

"Of course I did, Magister." His tone was neither snarky nor arrogant, but very matter-of-fact.

James smiled. "Keep up with your progress, both of you. Lyrael," he nodded at her, "good work. We'll be talking more in the days to come."

"You mean nights, right?" she asked, her voice half-shy, half-teasing.

The magister laughed. "You'll fit in here—not that you don't already." He waved towards the door. "Go, rest a bit, you've earned it. Just apply the same intuition to your Apprentice assignment,

Lyrael, and you'll be First Degree in no time. I can guarantee it."

Her eyebrows went up into her hair. "*Oi theoi*!" she exclaimed. "I'm just getting used to the Apprentice degree!"

"Always a sure sign you're almost ready to move on," he informed her with a wink.

Amanda shook her head at him, and with a quick smile, began to leave his office with Jesse close behind.

But Jesse paused and momentarily turned to face Janius. "Thank you for not penalizing me over our...transgressions last night."

The magister just gave him a pointed look. "The both of you have been frightened out of your wits enough to warrant what I hope to be an effective punishment. Just be more careful in the future—this is for *your* sake, mind you. And hers."

"Of course." Jesse grinned and with a curt nod he left the room.

* * * *

The two silently walked hand in hand down the corridor. After they were well on their way to Amanda's room, she turned towards Jesse to ask what had been on her mind during the conversation with the magister. "So...what do I do? How do I learn how to control these abilities? It seems so...simple. And I can't believe it's really that easy."

He laughed. "You thought that was easy? You're not even in the least bit tired?"

"No," Amanda laughed in return, "and all I had to do was say a few simple words and channel the energy. I just don't get it. I mean, I've done invocations, evocations, scrying...but nothing like this."

"You have a natural talent for magick, Amanda—one that has been augmented by your Turning. You were telekinetic to begin with, even. Of course this was easy for you." He held her hand with a gentle grip.

"But...how do I learn how to use all of this stuff?"

"Practice."

"Practice what? I'm not even completely certain that I know what I'm doing!"

Jesse smiled at her. "Oh, you will. You already do—you just don't realize it yet."

"But—"

He softly placed his fingers on her mouth. "Just trust yourself."

Removing his fingers from her lips, he replaced them with a kiss. The kiss quickly deepened and set them both on fire with its urgency. The stress of the early morning's events affected them both greatly, and they each needed the release of tension.

Shouldn't we go to sleep? It's morning already.

We can sleep after....

Turel cradled her head in his hands, kissing her lips, her cheeks, her face. He traveled downwards towards her neck, and she closed her eyes, wrapped in a state of bliss. His mouth met her skin, and she shuddered with pleasure.

Don't fight it, he whispered.

A moan escaped the back of her throat. Why would she want to? Not long ago, she was certain they would die a horrible, agonizing death. Now they were safe in her room, and she wanted nothing more than to touch and taste every part of him to assure herself that he was both alive and okay.

Her clothes were the first to go, her jeans once again tossed into a heap on her floor. Effortlessly, he picked her up to hold her closer to him, her legs straddling his waist, her hands and arms clinging to his neck and back.

Never leave me. Amanda didn't know why she wanted to utter such words, but something rose up inside of her, aching to be let out.

Of course I never will.

His hands stroked her back, neck, and arms with the lightest and silkiest of touches. Every caress set her insides on fire and made something deep within her stomach tighten. She ached to have his bare skin against hers, all of him pressed up against hers, and to dissolve into flames with him inside of her.

That can be arranged.

Jesse gently set her on the bed, and with a number of hasty jerks his jacket was off. Amanda's hands already touched his chest, unbuttoning his shirt with great speed. She helped him remove it, and it landed somewhere behind him on the floor.

Her hands fumbled at his buckle, but it wasn't coming off nearly easy or smooth enough. Frustrated and a little embarrassed, she exhaled in an imitation of a sigh and hovered her hands over the belt, attempting to will it to come undone.

See, I'm practicing.

Loud laughter echoed in the room, and she realized that it was

Turel. He grabbed both sides of her face and in an enthusiastic motion bent down and kissed her on the lips.

Let's practice other things right now.

She smiled, understanding his suggestion. He finished taking off his belt buckle and yanked down on his pants to remove them. She noted with slight amusement—and not without excitement—that he was apparently quite eager for her already.

He sat down on the bed, facing her, and pulled her on top of him. Amanda embraced him eagerly and was ready to move him inside but he stopped her.

No, wait.

She was about to impatiently ask him for what, but he slowly moved his hands down her back, stopping only to caress and massage her buttocks. A moan finally escaped her lips, and he bent down to lick her left nipple. Her hands clutched and scratched his back while he insistently played with the nipple in his mouth, alternating between pulling it carefully with his teeth and lapping at it with his tongue. By the time he moved to her right side to give her other nipple equal attention, her cries were incoherent.

His hands kept wandering all over her body, sensual strokes one moment and passionate grasping the next. It wasn't long before she trembled in his arms, her insides aching for release.

Not yet, he told her.

With his right thumb he circled her clit with deliberate slowness, applying soft pressure until Amanda thought she would lose her mind. Her last remaining self-control prevented her from lunging towards him and biting his throat. She wanted to taste him, for him to be inside of her, and she wanted that blissful explosive union, and she wanted it all right now.

Lift up your hips.

She complied. Jesse shifted slightly to get the angle just right, and with a quick stabbing motion, he plunged himself into her depths.

Amanda came hard and fast, screaming both in her head and aloud and clawing his back. But he wasn't finished with her. Moving his hand once again to massage the area on and around her sensitive folds and bud, he tormented her until he knew she was ready for another release. With his other hand, he grabbed her hips and pushed her closer to him as his right hand persisted its teasing motions. At this point, their hips were pressed together, separated only by his hand as he administered pleasure beyond comprehension.

It wasn't until her slick walls began clenching around him that he plunged his fangs into her shoulder, her sweet, coppery essence filling him. She Saw in her mind's eye his eyes rolling back and experienced through the Bond his pleasure of her taste. He began to increase the motion of his thumb, and Amanda climbed again to her peak and experienced it again and again in a crescendo until the pleasure was so great it turned to unbearable pain.

At long last he allowed himself to come inside of her, and the sensations went through her as if his ecstasy were her own, and the mingling waves of pleasure sent them both into orbit among the stars. The room went bright white, and all was still as the two clutched each other, drenched in blood-sweat.

* * * *

Lynne stormed into James's office in a blazing rage. "How *dare* he!"

"Wh-what?" stammered the rather confused magister. "How dare who what?"

"Turel! He nearly got his Childe killed! What is *with* that incompetent bastard? She's barely a few weeks Turned, and he's already almost exposed her to sunlight!"

"Lynne—"

"Don't you dare!" she roared, her hands slamming down on top of his desk as she leaned forward in her fury. "Let me finish! That man is trouble! I have always known he was trouble!"

"They're fine now, both of them. Lyrael cast a rather impressive spell and even managed to help the Sanctuary in the process. You shouldn't be so angry at Turel for what happened."

"BULLSHIT!" Her emerald eyes flared, and for a moment the magister thought that her pupils blazed red. "If Amanda had been killed—I swear—I'd kill him myself. I'd stake him on the spot."

"Lynne—"

"Don't you 'Lynne' me! Don't you see? Don't you get it? He can't handle having a Childe, and I doubt he ever will."

"Lynne, there's something you need to know." His voice sounded surprisingly steady to his ears, but he knew the time had come to finally tell her what had been troubling him these past few days.

"What? What more has he done? Please, tell me. I'm at my wit's end here and could really use further incentive to have his ass handed to him, or otherwise sent off into oblivion."

"Lynne, Lyrael is Minervia. She's Minervia reincarnated."

Chapter Twenty-One

"I never left you, you know."

James watched Lynne's anger dissipate as if it had been sucked out of her by a powerful vacuum. Her trembling hands slowly touched her face.

"I knew," she whispered. The magister shook as he listened to this proclamation. "Blood help me, I knew. I didn't want to see it but I knew."

The only thing he knew how to do at that moment was ramble. "Lynne, I'm sure in her own way she chose to come back for a reason. I can't deny that it's been hard without her. And I know that you've missed her. Just think of what she could do were she to remember...."

He abruptly came to a halt; red streaks marred her face. Lynne, *crying*. The magister didn't remember seeing tears from her even after Sarah's death—and he knew that she had been pierced very deeply by it.

"I, uh," he stammered. "Lynne, are you—"

She briskly wiped her eyes. "Yes, yes, I'm fine. I was going to argue with you every which way you could be wrong, and dammit, I can't. I know that you're right."

"I can show you the charts. They're right here." He picked up the papers and held them out to Lynne, who refused them with a shake of her hand.

"No, it's okay. I believe you. I wish that I didn't, really. I wish you were wrong. Rather strange of me, isn't it?" She laughed, but it sounded hollow.

"Lynne—"

"I need to sit down." The blonde vampire dropped into a nearby seat.

The two vampires stared at each other for a long moment, a heavy silence the magister broke when he stated the last of what he had been dying to mention to her for the past few days.

"We can't tell him. There's no way he can know about this."

Lynne burst into a peal of maniacal laughter. "Oh, no. Blood, no. He's obsessed now and chaining her to his side whenever he can. If he were to find out, he'd only get worse."

"Lynne...." In an uncharacteristically demonstrative gesture,

James stepped from behind his desk and took a hold of one of her hands. She stared at his hand on hers as if strange hieroglyphics decorated it. "Can you ever find it within yourself to forgive him and move on? I know you dislike him, perhaps even hate him—"

"I've never hated him," she replied automatically.

The magister blinked at her. This was not the response he had anticipated.

"After all, I wasn't even able to get there on time. At least," she choked, "he was there, right up until...."

Lynne jerked her hand away from his and leapt up out of her seat as if it had been on fire.

"Lynne," he called out, too late.

With a loud burst, she angrily thrust the door of his office open and bolted out into the hallway.

* * * *

"Hello, Lyrael!" a cheerful voice rang out. Amanda momentarily gazed up from her note taking at the sound. In front of her stood a short, peppy brunette who could've been anywhere between the age of twenty-five to perhaps forty-five when she was Turned. The woman looked strangely ageless. At the moment, she reminded Amanda of an elf. A short elf, but an elf nonetheless.

"Hi, Amaltheia." She knew Amaltheia to be the Clan's librarian but didn't know much about her beyond that. Jesse seemed to like her—she knew that much.

"What are you working on?"

Momentarily nonplussed, Amanda said, "Um, this protection spell thing. Turel's working on it too; Janius asked me to help him out as part of my Apprentice work."

The librarian's face brightened. "Ahhh! I had heard about that. You did a wonderful thing keeping out the sun, so I hear. Less apprentices wandering around and almost getting killed by that awful, awful sun. Thanks, hon."

She blinked at the "hon" but smiled. "You're welcome."

"Now you just have to keep out the other unwanted elements. Good luck to you on that one, hon. I keep telling Janius to just hang a sign on the door that says 'IRS' or 'Lawyers United' or some such, but he thinks that won't be enough." She shook her head and winked at Amanda, who giggled.

"Meanwhile, I don't mind a friendly new face around here. And ooh, would you look at this? One of the First Degrees gave me a jar of *mints*. Ooh. Would you like one?" Before Lyrael could reply, she quickly added, "Don't tell Janius. But I like mints."

"Sure, thank you—"

"Ooh, they're *chocolate* mints!" She frowned at them suddenly. "I wonder if they're vegan? I was vegan when I was mortal. They're probably not, I bet—probably dairy or gelatin in them, or something. Oh well, what's an unlife without chocolate mints?"

Amanda stared down at the notes on the table in front of her, trying to will herself not to laugh. She didn't succeed.

"Here, hon, have a couple." Merideth placed a few chocolate mint pieces beside the stack of books Amanda was reading. It was then that she noticed the bracelet on her wrist.

"Oh, a slave bracelet! How pretty!"

"'Slave bracelet'?" echoed Amanda, confused.

"Yes, that's one of the names of that type of bracelet, I think. The one where the ring is attached to the bracelet by a chain." The librarian peered at it more closely. "That looks strangely familiar too...." Her forehead creased into a semblance of a tiny frown.

"Turel gave it to me."

"Really?" Merideth looked her in the eye. "You don't say...."

A few moments of silence went by, and Amanda found herself drawn back into her notes again.

Then Merideth pointed finger at the ceiling with a loud "Ah!" that made Amanda nearly jump out of her seat. She resisted rubbing her rear, sore from the wooden chair upon which she sat. *Why oh why are library seats so often uncomfortable?*

"I remember now! That was Minervia's bracelet. Turel must really adore you to have given you that," the librarian commented with a soft smile. "It may be the only thing he still had of hers."

A strange feeling swept over Amanda. "Minervia?"

"His Sire. They were Blood Bound, in fact, as you two are. She died some years ago...back in the '60s, before you were born, no doubt. Really tragic too." She tsked a few times in what Amanda recognized as a sympathetic noise, tapping on the bracelet on her wrist briefly as she did so. As she did this, Amanda's thoughts swirled in her head. Blood Bound, Jesse's Sire and him? Had they been involved while she was alive? They must've been, to have been Blood Bound. Why didn't he tell her about Minervia? How exactly did she die? She decided not to ask the librarian the last question, as she figured it was too painful a subject to broach.

Merideth frowned again. “Wait a minute,” she mumbled.

Amanda fought back a degree of impatience—at this rate, she would never be able to finish today’s research. How in the world could a librarian be so distracting? Weren’t they supposed to be quiet and let you work?

It was when the librarian began chanting strange words as she touched the bracelet that the feeling of frustration gave way to alarm. Amanda recognized some of the chanting from the dream she had what seemed like forever ago, back when she was warned about “the dark moon”: *Ah-ay-lan-nar, ay-lay-oh-lan-dran-nah....* The librarian’s peculiarly light gray eyes glazed over for a few minutes.

Is this woman nuts or something that I should know about?

Suddenly, Merideth leaned over and grabbed a very startled Amanda in a bear hug. “Oh! Oh! I am so *happy* you are here! Come by any time, hon, you hear? Just let me know whatever you want, whatever books, whatever you need.”

Utterly baffled, Amanda stuttered, “I, um, thanks. I-I will. Thank you. Um—”

“No need to thank me!” She skipped off to the back of the room where her office was, waving vigorously in Amanda’s direction before shutting the door behind her.

“Oooookay...,” she muttered, now completely freaked out both by Amaltheia’s odd behavior and the similarity between the chanting she had done and what she had heard in the dream she’d had, the night before she had met Jesse. Amanda was only too eager to finish her research so she could leave the library—and fast.

On her way out, she nearly ran over a dark blond-haired man whom she didn’t recognize—but there were a lot of Clan members whom she hadn’t met yet. It made her feel awkward and young, as if she were once again a freshman on her college campus.

His light blue eyes sparkled with amusement as he saw who she was. “Oh, Lyrael! I hear you’re Turel’s new Childe. Nice to run into you. Meet you, I mean.” He chuckled.

What a strange day I’m having. “Hi! Um, how do you know me?”

“Word gets around. Besides, your fantastic little spell there with the sun didn’t go unnoticed—saw it from a nearby window, in fact. I’m Theodotos, by the way. I hear you’ve got Asherael as your new mentor. I had her as mine too, before I transferred to a new teacher. She's great, but man, she's tough. And don't piss her off either, no matter what you do."

Amanda smiled. "I'll do my best to remember that. And nice to meet you as well."

Stuffing his hands in his pockets, he produced a handful of dice and cheerfully proceeded to do what appeared to be an amateur juggling act. "If you need any help with Apprentice stuff or just want to hang out, give me a holler." He tossed the dice up into the air, caught them, and put them back into his pockets while Amanda watched, fascinated. "As strange as it sounds, some of us try to have lives outside of studying around here, and I try to help out with that whenever possible."

Theodotos cleared his throat as Amanda burst out laughing. "Take right now, for instance. I bet you just bailed from that library where you just did a *ton* of studying. I hear library dust kills brain cells and makes you go batty." He made a circling gesture by his head with his index finger.

That explains so very much, she thought ruefully, thinking of her amusing but also somewhat disturbing encounter with Merideth.

"Anyhow, just think about it. That's my advice, and I give it out to all of the new apprentices when they arrive here. Burnout is bad." He pivoted on his heels and began to continue walking. "Anyhow, I'll catch you later. Take care!"

"You too!" *Yup, definitely a strange day.* Then she remembered her earlier conversation with the magister.

"Hey, Theodotos?" she called out.

He turned around and yelled back, "Yes?"

"How...," she started to yell and thought better of it by running down to the hallway to where he was. "This is a strange question, but how would you recommend practicing magick?"

"Not so strange. It depends. What type of magick?"

"I don't know—anything. People want to see more things like what I did out there with the shielding of the sunlight and all, but that was spontaneous." She threw her hands up in the air in a gesture of helplessness. "I was wondering if you had any ideas?"

He paused, touching his hand to his mouth. "Yeah, I do."

"What?"

"Just *do* stuff."

She gave him a puzzled look.

"Anything that you would do on a regular basis, use magick in order to do it. Open doors, levitate books, give the magister a wedgie—or not," he added quickly. "Just think of stuff. Use your imagination and do what comes to you naturally. The point is to practice using it."

Frowning slightly, she wondered how she would go from being used to doing magick for spiritual purposes to doing magick that appeared to be everyday stuff she could do with her own bare hands. "But aren't those rather...I dunno...frivolous things?"

He laughed. "Nah, besides, you gotta start somewhere, right? Then there's that whole 'as above, so below' crap. Just enjoy yourself and practice doing what you do best. You'll get the hang of it eventually."

Amanda grinned at him. It made sense to her. "Thanks, I think I get it."

"You're welcome. Anytime! And don't forget to say 'hi' to Asherael for me!" He gave her a thumbs-up gesture as he walked away.

"I will!"

Once she was back in her room, she put her notes next to her computer on the desk and sat down to think about what Theodotos had advised her to do.

Then she stared down at the bracelet on her wrist—"slave bracelet", Merideth had referred to it as—and thought about the odd conversation she'd had with the librarian earlier.

"Hm." She fingered the bracelet, trying to remember the odd words Merideth had chanted. Then it hit her—a perfect opportunity to try and practice magick! Maybe she could use her skills to scry somehow into the bracelet and find out why Merideth had reacted so strangely to it.

But how to begin? She was used to praying to Apollo and she figured since this was a scrying exercise maybe that was a good place to begin—if nothing else it would put her into the mental state necessary to perform magick.

"*Khaire o Apollon,*" she began in Attic Greek. "Hail, Apollo." Then she realized she hadn't prayed to him formerly since she was Turned in English, let alone in Greek. She added in Latin, "*Ave, Apollo.*" *I just hailed him twice; will he care?*

Somehow she got the feeling that he was listening and she found the confidence to continue. "Far-shooter, Pythian, Delphic Apollo, please help me to see what it was that Amaltheia saw in this bracelet."

Amanda paused, beginning to feel the familiar spark stirring within her. When was the last time she gave him an offering? "As soon as I can find some around here, I will burn some frankincense in your name as a thank you for doing this for me. And...thank you. Thank you in advance. I greatly appreciate your help, Apollo." She bit her lip. After all, she was a vampire now. Would he still be with her in spite of what she had become?

I NEVER LEFT YOU, YOU KNOW.

The words flowed through her like a gentle river filled with light, a deep affection, and something ineffable. She opened her mouth to say something further, but her vision tunneled, and the room spun away.

* * * *

In her mind's eye, Amanda gazed into a mirror which beheld not her usual reflection, but that of a somewhat shorter, thinner young woman. She had pale skin, dark brown eyes, and long, shining red hair.

Startled, she reached up with her left hand—the one wearing the bracelet with the ring attached—and watched as the reflection made the same gesture. Her jaw dropped as she realized that the woman in the mirror was wearing the same bracelet!

This is me. It was, and yet it wasn't. She Saw something in the mirror, rather like the feeling she got looking at old photographs and walking through historical buildings and cemeteries—a certain fading around the edges and a weight that belied both time and age. This was a *past* reflection. Past, but not too much into the past.

The '60s. Didn't Amaltheia say that Minervia died in the '60s?

She blinked—hard. No, that was too pat of an answer. This woman couldn't be Minervia and couldn't have been *her*. Or rather, *she* couldn't have been Minervia.

"Apollo? Is this what the image is trying to tell me? Am I Minervia?"

Amanda heard a loud rumbling sound, as if made by distant thunder.

"Am I?"

The red-haired woman in the mirror that was her reflection spoke. "The wall will come down, should you choose this."

"*Apokalypsis*," Amanda whispered. She hesitated before asking,

"Choose what?"

"To know."

The thunder grew louder. Amanda clenched her jaw. "What if I don't want to know?"

"But you do. Otherwise, you wouldn't be here, now would you?"

In frustration, Amanda leaned over and pressed her hands against the mirror. She tried not to let the dreamscape's vividness terrify her in her desperation to uncover the truth. "Who *are* you?"

The mirror woman leaned in, touching her hands to Amanda's in a likeness of her gesture. "You," she whispered back.

In that instant, lightning struck the mirror, shattering it into a million pieces that turned into beams of light which pierced Amanda. These lights formed images which then formed emotions, thoughts, and memories long past. They flooded into her head with full hurricane strength, overwhelming her in their intensity and suddenness. She tried to cry out, but her vision in both worlds went black, and she hit the cold floor.

Chapter Twenty-Two

"I...I remember things. Things I shouldn't."

Amanda stood before James, engaged in a conversation with him. But no, it wasn't her, and she wasn't really there. It wasn't her voice that she heard either—it was Jesse's.

She kept blinking, attempting to will the image to go away. No matter what she did, it remained. Regardless of whether or not her eyes were open or shut, double vision assaulted her.

TUREL, I HOPE THAT YOU CAN GET RIGHT ON THIS. Amanda sensed him nodding in return, heard him speak—but saw everything happen out of his eyes. As intimately as she knew her own body, she knew he'd fed a few hours earlier, perhaps while she was in the library studying. As much as she tried to blink and rub her eyes, desperate to focus on something else—she saw both the inside of her room as she continued to lie on the floor and the world from Jesse's eyes. His rising anxiety was now as real to her as her own—too real and entirely too near.

Her arms instinctively hugged her knees to her chest, desperately seeking shelter from the lack of personal space.

"Jesse," she called out, her voice no more than a whisper, "help."

* * * *

While discussing the latest research on the protection spell project with James, something jolted Jesse's psychic awareness. Waves of Amanda's presence crashed forth into his mind far more so than usual. The scent of her perfume assaulted his nose, and her energy resonated with great power in his mind. For a moment, a part of their most intimate hearts—and even souls—had merged, beyond the typical light touch of their Blood Bond and into the realm of intense, intimate wonder he had experienced with Sarah so long ago. The experience of déjà vu startled him, and he fought to prevent a gasp from escaping his lips.

The magister continued talking, seemingly oblivious to what he had just experienced. "Lyrael's research has been extremely useful. I'm very pleased as to her progress. She'll be ready for her First soon, I'm sure."

As fast as the sensation passed over Jesse, so it had ended in an instant, and she was as a candle blown out. He frowned. Had she tried contacting him before falling asleep? A gentle nudge revealed Amanda to now be unconscious, but he couldn't explain what had just happened.

Jesse just nodded at James, thinking it would be a good idea to end this discussion as soon as possible and see what had happened to Amanda. A feeling of unease sat in his stomach, and he wanted to make sure it was just his paranoia and nothing else.

In mid-sentence, James stopped speaking and stared at Jesse, his eyes looking past him into the distance. *Oh no,* Jesse thought. *What does he see now?*

"Oh dear...*God*," James breathed. His words jolted Jesse. He hadn't seen the magister pray to anything but the Divine Spirit as Blood since...well, for as long as he had known him.

The sensation he experienced earlier hit him again with full force, almost knocking him off of his feet. If he could still breathe, the air would've been punched out of him. What was going on? Did the magister see what was happening? It wasn't until he saw the front of a desk and a chair by his head as real as James in front of him that he started to panic. *Amanda's room.*

"I'll be needing you for a special project, Turel," James stated briskly. "Both you and Lyrael."

"*Another* project?" he asked, incredulous, rapidly becoming disoriented. Trying his best to focus on what was in front of him in the material world, he clenched his hands into fists, all of his effort focused into willing him into the physical, the here and now. Not Amanda's thoughts which swarmed in his head, not the stark panic that came from her, but on his own thoughts, his own feelings—which were turning into the same fear which Amanda was also experiencing.

Jesse, help.

The words sounded so clear he could've sworn Amanda stood right next to him—but he knew she didn't, and oh Blood, he saw her room right in front of him....

"It's important. Turel, I hope that you can get right on this. Go fetch her as soon as you can and bring her to me. We need to talk."

It was with great caution that Jesse opened the door to Amanda's room—in part because he had difficulty seeing what was in front of him as his inner eyes were too focused on Amanda's surroundings.

What greeted his vision was Amanda curled up into a ball on the floor, unmoving. He knew she was conscious because he still saw out of her eyes, and the flickers of panic that kept hitting him in the chest were not his this time, but hers.

"Amanda?" He spoke with a soft voice, afraid he might frighten her further.

Whatever it was that I did, I'm so sorry...I don't know what happened. I honestly don't.

Given her current state, he wasn't at all surprised to hear her using telepathy instead. *It's the Blood Bond, not you. It's—it's been like this before. It's not unnatural.*

With Minervia, you mean?

Her words sent a tremor of shock through him. *"Who told you?"*

Amaltheia. Don't be angry at her. She's a little crazy but...she's very nice.

Jesse sighed. It was an annoying human habit that bothered James, but the magister wasn't in the room and he didn't care.

Jesse...Jesse, I need to tell you something....

But he brushed her off. *Tell me about it later.* He didn't mean to be curt with her, but at the moment he was more concerned for her sanity than anything else. *I need to teach you how to handle this... connection between us. I told you that you would be afraid of this and that you were blocking things out. I figured that this might happen someday, but gradually—not all at once! What were you doing before this happened?*

Scrying the bracelet.

There was a pregnant silence. *You did what?*

I prayed to Apollo and scryed the bracelet, and Jesse, there was this mirror and this other woman, and she was me, *Jesse....*

Something in him went cold, as if his last feeding had been days and not hours ago. *What did she look like?*

Why he had bothered to ask, he didn't know—he saw the image in her mind as she spoke to him.

Long red hair, shorter than me. A little thinner.

Kneeling down on the floor beside her, Jesse wrapped one arm around her while he used the other to lean on the floor in order to steady himself.

That was Minervia, wasn't it?

Yes, yes it was. He tried to collect his thoughts, think of what to tell her, how to say it.

I know how she died. I saw it through her eyes. Jesse, I'm sorry. I didn't know.

His lips came together in a thin line. *You probably picked up the resonance of her death when you scryed the bracelet. She was wearing it when she died.*

Turel sensed her struggle inside and experienced the turmoil as if it were his own.

Jesse...I don't know how to say this, but...I think it was more than that.

He held her closer to him, wishing he could do more to ease her obvious discomfort. *What do you mean?*

I...I remember things. Things I shouldn't.

Shrugging, he fought back the urge to pick her up off the floor and run out the door with her somewhere, anywhere. *Psychometry can sometimes do that.*

No, I've done psychometry. I get visions, flashes...but not memory. This is memory....

Amanda, listen to me. He gently brushed the hair away from her face. *I loved Minervia, and yes, it hurt me when she died. And a part of me still misses her. But you don't have to be her. I love you just as well, just as much—if not more.*

Hugging her knees closer to her chest, she whispered aloud, "I remember my First, Jesse. My First Degree. And my Second. I was in my Third when I met you."

She didn't need the Blood Bond to feel him becoming tense as he heard her words—his arms gripped her tighter. "Blood, don't tell Janius. Regardless of how or why you know these things, don't tell him. Okay?"

"I don't see...how I *can't*, Jesse. He would want me to tell him. I *know* this," she insisted.

Kissing her on the forehead, he knew that there was no way to convince her of the reality of what she had seen. Her powers had obviously grown in leaps and bounds, and for whatever reason, her encounter with Merideth and the knowledge of Sarah's existence had opened her up to receiving information about the life which his Sire had before she died. Amanda was an amazing psychic before, but he realized now that she was a force to be reckoned with—and now that their Blood Bond was stronger, he would have to try harder to shield her from him, or give away Fourth Degree secrets.

"I already know those secrets, Jesse."

He cringed. She was reading his thoughts already.

"I'm sorry, Jesse. I don't mean to do it, I just—do. And I wish I could help it, believe me."

"I know. I know that you do."

"It's just...too...overwhelming."

Aware that she was physically shaking, Turel held her more tightly. It was then that he realized how cold she was.

"Amanda, when was the last time you fed?" he inquired.

It brought a smile to his face to see her remember the rather... pleasurable circumstances under which she last had blood, but it quickly left once he realized her memory was of an occasion which was more than a day ago.

"Stand up. Now. You have to feed sometime soon."

With careful movements, she removed her knees from her chest and pushed herself up to a seated position. "But you go for more than a day. I've seen you."

"You're a new vampire. I am not, he pointed out. "You need to feed more often than me."

"Oh." After a pause she asked, "Can you come with me? Please?"

He looked at her for a long while, knowing it wasn't fear of taking blood that prompted her question, but an altogether different anxiety.

Grabbing one of her hands in his gentle grip, he pressed it to his lips as she smiled at him. "You are not losing your mind, I promise you."

Her smile faded. "I'm not so certain," she confessed.

At that moment, the stack of books on her shelf unceremoniously crashed to the floor beside them. The sound made Amanda jump.

Jesse let go of her hand and began to pick up the books—which he knew had been stacked all too neatly next to the computer as they were talking. "Oh, great," he muttered. And he had thought she was finally gaining some control over her powers too. He got up and placed the books on the desk—this time a much safer distance from the edge.

"I did that, didn't I?" she asked, her voice low and quiet.

"Yes, but you've had a lot of shock to handle tonight. I wouldn't worry about it." He watched out of the corner of his eye as she fidgeted nervously on the floor. "You might feel better if you sat on the bed or something."

"Yeah." She smiled at him quickly, but it didn't reach her eyes.

In his mind, he sensed her pushing away at something of which he only got shadowy glimpses.

"What's wrong?"

She bit her lip. "It's—"

"Don't tell me it's nothing. It's something."

Her voice shook. "I-I don't want to remember."

Jesse sat down on the bed beside her and put his arm around her waist. "Remember what?"

Amanda brushed his cheek with her hand before she replied. "What happened after...after I died." She swallowed.

His arm grew tight around her waist. "We need to get you to feed. We'll talk after that."

They got up off the bed and made their way to the door with Jesse hanging onto Amanda's arm, firm but gentle. As he opened the door for her, she turned to face him with an odd expression on her face.

"You don't believe me, do you?"

He gave no reply save a light kiss on her lips.

* * * *

Amanda's head still swam as they left the Sanctuary. There had been so many odd flashes which she'd had throughout the years, feelings of déjà vu upon her move to the NYU campus and strolling around the Village that she never could place, and now it was all finally coming together.

Still, she was at a loss to understand why Jesse refused to believe her and could only conclude he didn't want to know the full truth. At the time, he did his best to try and shield her from him, but flashes of his thoughts and feelings still kept peeking through, and she didn't know how to stop seeing and sensing them. It was bad enough having another lifetime crammed into the back of her mind without having to contend with another person's thoughts too.

What disturbed her most was the complete lack of conscious memory—all of it was unconscious. She would look at a painting in the hallway and remember when it was put up and who put it there, but none of it sprang from the usual location where her thoughts normally came from—they were just *there*, seeping out through the holes in the watery cracks of her innermost mind.

Despite their Bond, she did her best to hide her confusion. She didn't want Jesse being anxious about what had happened to her.

* * * *

They quickly found a bum in a back alley, and Jesse felt relief flood her. The bum proved to be more than easy to put to sleep with the magick Turel had taught her, and in his concern for Amanda's health he thought nothing of it.

The blood hit her system, and her senses swam—he experienced it all.

"Oh, great," she exclaimed. "I think he was drugged."

"WHAT?" Jesse ran over and sniffed at the blood. "Terrific. What kind of person living on the streets manages to get a hold of heroin?" Angry, he shook his head. "I should've smelled it on him."

"Will it hurt me?" She skipped around, obviously feeling much better. *Blood Bond, disturbing memories about life after death, who cares?*

"No, vampires can't get poisoned or have any physical ill effects from drugs—but we can still become addicted to them. Addiction is psychological."

"Coooool." She linked her arm with his, and he gazed on her with a mixture of resignation and amusement. "Well, not about the addiction but about the lack of damage. Yeah."

"You're in no condition to meet with the magister right now," he commented wryly. "We'll have to wait until the drug wears off."

"Meet with James?" she asked. "About what?"

Grim, Jesse watched Amanda twirl her hair in a strange but familiar gesture.

He grabbed her hand and pulled it away from her hair. "Come on, I think we'd better find a non-druggie bum."

"I dunno, Jesse, I feel okaaaayyy. Really."

"Amanda, you sound stoned." He knew he sounded disapproving, but underneath it all was amusement.

"I think we did that once, didn't we? Yes, we *did*! I remember. You got the munchies afterwards and begged me not to tell James that you went out and bought sour cream and onion flavored potato chips."

He groaned, but she rambled on.

"Can't we just sit somewhere for a while? Maybe watch people go by or something?"

"Amanda—"

"I liiiiike watching people. And it's nice out." She sniffed the air around her. "Think it'll rain?"

He sighed, and it made him think of James, who was bound to be furious with him for not bringing her to see him sooner than he had requested. "As soon as possible" meant "be in my office in less than an hour—or else." This recollection made him sigh again in frustration. Screw "human habits" anyway. They were out in public among them, right?

"Whee...."

He closed his eyes, not wanting to see what she was "wheeing" about. It was going to be a long night.

Chapter Twenty-Three

"Do what thou wilt."

Jesse knew he had little choice but to drag Amanda back to the Sanctuary to meet with James.

Or rather, it was the only choice which yielded a less pissed-off magister. He had little clue why the magister had summoned up the both of them for a project—let alone what the project was about—but he knew Janius well. The elder vampire wasn't someone who would summon people at random and with stern tones into his office for an "important project".

Still, Amanda's present condition made him hesitate. He knew everything was his fault. As her Sire, he should've checked the man to make sure he was clean—especially given how new she still was to the hunt. Had the man been high on pot it wouldn't have bothered Jesse, but he frowned upon heroin.

Observing the lazy smile on her face, he admitted to himself with a degree of reluctance that he was rather relieved for the intervention of drugs. The breaking down of the walls in her mind had put her into a very bad place, both in mind and in heart, and she needed a timeout, even if for a little while. But he also knew that her using drugs to diminish her discomfort—even if by accident—wasn't going to do her any good in the long term, either.

As they approached the magister's office, Jesse prayed Amanda would be in a mellow enough state that she wouldn't say much—if anything.

* * * *

Calm, James surveyed the scene in front of him. While he could've suspected that Jesse would've taken a bit more time to get back to him than he would've liked, he found that his reasons were sound. His new Childe did need to feed, and she didn't need to be running low on energy on top of her latest trauma.

Gazing at her aura, he frowned. She appeared to be both blurry and scattered, and he smelled something odd in her blood. *Drugs, probably from blood she ingested.* As she didn't seem like the type to use such things, he figured it might've been by accident—but having an idea of her current state of mind, he wasn't sure.

The psychic blast hit the magister earlier while he talked with Jesse, and a closer look at her aura showed a transparent image of a very familiar young woman—confirming his suspicions.

Ah, so she does know now. But he could tell that the two parts of her were not integrated, and she would need a lot of help to get back to herself—if she even knew at this point who that was. Her blurry aura was due to far more than a little heroin, a fact which only increased Janius's concern.

"Usually when I ask for students to arrive in my office for an important assignment, I don't typically expect them to be high on drugs when they show," he stated nonchalantly, but his voice was cold. "I wasn't aware that research into protection spells would require altered states of consciousness."

The magister tried not to smile as Jesse winced. "My apologies—it wasn't intentional. I didn't notice the drug in the man's blood until after she had fed from him."

With one quick motion, James reached out his hand and from where he was still seated, swept it over Amanda's body. Instantly her senses cleared, and although she wasn't at one hundred percent, most of the drug's effects—and probably the drug itself—had been removed from her system. Before she could thank him, he spoke. "I realize that you are both currently under a lot of...strain right now." The magister deliberately put on his blankest expression, revealing nothing of his thoughts.

"You mean the Blood Bond?" she asked hesitantly. Jesse gave her a little nudge, which she returned with a quizzical look.

James turned to her, feeling more than a degree of pity. "Actually, I was referring to something else entirely. Turel's intuition was dead-on in bringing you here; you would appear to have some past spiritual history with us."

"Now wait, Janius, I wouldn't speak so soon," Jesse blurted out.

But the magister only frowned and held up papers from his desk and waved them in the air at him. "I see you've found out. I wasn't going to tell you, Jesse, but I took the liberty not long ago of scrying Amanda's astrological chart. It's all there."

Jesse's hand on Amanda's arm tightened. "Jesse," she started to protest, but the look on his face prevented her from speaking further.

"In any event, Turel," he continued, seemingly oblivious to his reaction, "I have another project for you. I want Lyrael to take over for the protection spell project and for you to start work on something else."

Jesse blinked hard at the magister. "Okay, what is it?"

"I want you to pay a visit to Clan Corvus. They could use your expertise with Egyptian magick in regards to a project they are working on—namely your translation of the Egyptian Book of the Dead."

Jesse's mouth thinned into a straight line. "They're in New Orleans," he stated flatly. Amanda squeezed his hand.

"Yes, they are. You'd have to take a night flight out of JFK or La Guardia—direct is preferred."

"How long do you want me to be there for?" he asked quietly, his expression showing he feared the worst.

The magister straightened in his chair. "I figure about a month should do it. I wouldn't expect the project to last longer than that."

Amanda showed signs of going into shock, and the magister caught her thoughts: *Jesse, gone? For a month? This isn't happening.*

Jesse spluttered, "J-Janius, I can't leave Amanda for a month. Can't I at least take her with me? She could still do the research for the spell."

"She needs to be here for it," he insisted. "Besides, Turel, this project could help speed your progress in Fourth. I really could use your help with Fifth Degree work."

Abruptly, he let go of Amanda's arm and impatiently slammed his hands upon James's desk. Amanda jumped at the sound, but Janius didn't even blink at the violent gesture.

"Magister, with all due respect, I'm flattered that you think that I'm ready to take on Fifth, but I'm concerned about Amanda. She's—"

"First of all, settle down," the magister told him sternly. "Secondly, yes, she's under a lot of psychic strain, Jesse, and I think it would be best for her if you two were to spend some time apart from each other."

Turning his back to the magister, Jesse angrily thrust his hands into his pockets. "Have I not been doing a good enough job as her Sire, Janius?" His voice was deathly quiet, and Amanda visibly shivered. The psychic waves of rage coming off of him would've been unpalatable to anyone, Blood Bond or no.

James replied with reassuring tones, "Turel, you've been doing a good job. Better than good, even. This isn't about you, nor is it your fault," he added somewhat hastily.

Waiting for a reaction, the magister received nothing but stony silence in return. He went on, "Kalia is in charge of the project and she specifically asked for you. She remembers much of the work you've done in the past, particularly your last project in New Orleans."

"This is an odd question, Magister, but was I involved in that project?" Amanda asked.

Jesse shot her a look, but James responded mildly, "Yes, you were. I assume you may remember some of the details?"

"Only a little. The '*Vieux Carré*'?" She blinked as if surprised at what she'd said.

James slowly nodded. "Clan Corvus is located in the French Quarter, that's right."

Amanda turned to look at Jesse. "Jess, I'm sorry, I...."

Jesse's face paled, and the magister cringed. He knew full well that Sarah used to call him that.

The magister shook his head. "Lyrael, when's your birthday again?"

"June sixteenth," she replied automatically. When James raised his eyebrows at her, she corrected herself. "I mean, um, November seventeenth."

He gave Jesse a pointed look.

"One month, Jesse, that's all," he told him softly. "She needs some time to adjust, and you could use a vacation from worrying about her. I promise you that Asherael and I will keep a close eye on her for you, and with the Blood Bond you'll still be able to communicate with her at will."

Amanda walked over to Jesse and slipped her hand into his. He smiled at her gratefully.

"How long until I should leave?"

Rubbing his chin thoughtfully, James replied, "In a few days. That'll give us enough time to make the arrangements to send you down there and you enough time to do whatever it is you need to do to prepare."

Jesse nodded.

Looking the magister directly in the eye, Amanda inquired, "Is it possible I could take a break from working on the project to spend some time with Jesse before he goes?"

"I don't see why not. Have you adjusted the spell as it stands yet?"

Amanda paused. "No, I haven't. I was too busy collecting the rest of the data to improve it."

"Go do some work on that tonight and take the rest of the couple of days off before he leaves."

James watched as her face brightened.

"Thank you."

"You're welcome."

She nodded at him and left his office with Jesse following her. After they closed the door behind them, James whispered after her, "And thank *you*, Minervia."

* * * *

"Might as well get going on that spell," Jesse told her. "Do you know what improvements Janius wanted to have done to it?"

Amanda shrugged, not certain what the best approach was. Shouldn't he know more than she did? "Not sure. Let's go outside and take a look. I'm sure that we'll think of something."

Placing a hand on her arm, he asked quietly, "Not sure, or you don't remember?"

She was about to stammer out a reply when Jesse spotted Erik coming around the corner.

"Hey there, Theo," Turel called out. "How goes it?"

Theodotos nodded at them both and smiled. "It goes. I was just on my way to do some research with Haniel."

Grinning, Jesse replied, "Research, is that what they're calling it these days?" He was rewarded with a half-amused, half-disgusted look. Amanda smirked. This amused her highly.

"Look who's talking. And speaking of which," he turned to Amanda and asked, "Say, Lyrael, those clouds you got out there, you think you might be doing some work on that sometime soon? People will start to think the Munsters live here or something. Those clouds could really cause us trouble; we're not really talking much in the way of being inconspicuous, you know what I mean?"

Amanda blushed then laughed. "Oh, um, I had mentioned to James—Janius, I mean," she hurriedly corrected herself when Jesse mentally poked her, "that I uh, think that the clouds should be made invisible or something. That should fix it."

"Invisible. Hm." He fingered his chin and frowned in thought.

Then he nodded. "Yeah, that could work. Keep up the good work at any rate, and I'll catch you both later. Oh, and no making out outside of the Sanctuary in public view. Cops hate that."

"Will do," Amanda replied, cheerful.

Jesse rolled his eyes and nearly shoved her out the door.

She took a few steps out then turned around to look up at the sky. Sure enough, the clouds were still very visible, even against the night sky.

"Now...how do I do this?" she mused, looking at Jesse. "I was thinking of making them invisible, then sorta...I dunno...bending them around the place so that they covered the area."

"Like a dome, you mean?"

Amanda nodded with vigor. "Yeah, a magickal sun-proof dome."

He shrugged. "You're telekinetic. Bend them to your will, then make them invisible."

Reaching her hands up in the air, she paused for a moment. "How the hell do I make them invisible?"

"Do what thou wilt."

Glaring at him, she put down her arms and folded them across her chest. "Don't you go all Thelema on me. It can't be as easy as that."

Jesse only smiled at her. "Actually, I seem to recall being given that advice when I first started out as a young vampire in the Order, struggling with my magickal work."

She frowned. "By whom?"

Something in his eyes flickered, and she caught the thought before he said it out loud.

"Ah, I see. I guess I have to learn what I taught you all over again, then." She chuckled. "How stupid is that?"

Before he could reply she added, "I remember places I've never been to before but I can't remember how to do stupid spells. I also no longer remember what it's like to not have your constant presence in my head. Feeling, saying, and thinking things. I keep thinking that maybe I should call my parents so they don't think that I'm dead except I can't remember which parents I'm thinking about, nor can I remember if they're still alive." She stopped, realizing blood-tears welled up in her eyes.

Swallowing hard, she barely choked, "Shouldn't I remember whether or not my parents are still alive?"

Without a word, Jesse came from behind where she stood and gently enfolded her in his arms. In that embrace, she let go of what mental blocks she had been clutching onto for the sake of her sanity, and his love for her flooded her senses. It was the most comforting feeling she'd had in a long time, and she prayed that it might last. She wanted to forget about everything, how much she missed her family and worried about what they might think of what really happened to her, how much some of the memories made her ache inside, and how confused and disturbed she was at the strength of their Blood Bond, which prevented her from ever feeling as though she were at peace within herself.

Yet at the same time she knew that if the Bond were to be removed, she would ache even more at his absence. It was this knowledge which troubled her even further. She had never wanted to miss someone so much.

What would she do while he was gone?

Why don't we do this together? he suggested.

Sounds like a good idea.

They both looked up at the clouds and with their combined magickal skill, made them all invisible. It was as if the clouds had dispersed on their own—or so they made it appear.

"For the tourists," he told her with a smile. She smiled back. He was right; no one ever looked up while walking outside in New York.

To their minds' eyes, however, they still saw them as shining energy threads woven overhead. They watched together as the strands of energy that were once clouds were stretched overhead by their mental force, over and around the area.

"It's like an astral rainbow," she exclaimed.

He laughed. "It'll need some testing to make sure that it works, but I think it'll be fine. Come on, let's go somewhere."

"Where?"

Jesse smiled at her. "I was thinking maybe a nice coffeehouse or a bar. Whatever you're up for doing."

Amanda shook her head and laughed. "I keep hearing about this so-called 'vampire purity', but no one seems to really observe it around here."

He gave her an exasperated look. "Since when have you ever seen me eat human food or drink? It's an ideal, but not the standard. Like I said, I typically only do as part of a religious observance, but

I'll make an exception in this case."

"Okay, then." She smiled up at him as they walked down the street.

Wrapping his arm around her waist, he leaned in and whispered in her ear, "Just who have you seen eating food? I promise I won't tell anyone, especially not the magister."

"All right, I admit I was exaggerating when I said 'no one'," she confessed with a smile. "I was thinking of my trip with Asherael to the bar and Amaltheia's mints."

"Ah yes, Amaltheia's mints. She doesn't eat any other human food, nor does she care to. But those mints," he shook his head sadly, "are her downfall."

Putting her own arm around his waist, she asked, "I seem to remember you telling me that chai was good. Particularly vanilla chai."

Jesse chuckled. "I suppose for one night for a new vampire, vanilla chai may hit the spot."

"We'll worry about all of that vampiric purity later."

He squeezed her waist. "It becomes more of an issue in First, but you should practice now."

"Okay, after tonight then." She hesitated for a few moments, then added, "Think Amaltheia might like some chocolate mints?"

"A silly question. We'll get some on the way back."

She smiled. "Okay, then."

Chapter Twenty-Four

"I'm losing it."

The next couple of days went by in a blur as Amanda squeezed in as much time as she could being with Jesse before he left. They were unable to pass more than a few moments without each other's passionate embrace. They had made love perhaps thousands of times in the few short days, attempting to commemorate as much of it to memory as possible. Each time they tumbled from the heights of passion, they were both overwhelmed with the dread of separation—that it might be their last moment together. To Amanda, they had never been closer to each other—not just with the intensity of the Blood Bond, but with the ardor of their coupling. As they lay intertwined, tangled in blood-sweat-soaked bed sheets, she thought that maybe, just maybe, the magister might change his mind, or the day would never come when he would have to leave.

However, she didn't plan for actually having to leave him at the airport after traveling there with him on the subway.

They stood awkwardly side by side at the terminal, knowing that the painful time to part had finally come. Jesse wove his fingers in Amanda's hair and pulled her face towards his in fierce desperation. Several minutes went by until he reluctantly withdrew his lips from hers. As they separated, something in her chest involuntarily tightened.

"I'm really going to miss you," she whispered.

Jesse replied softly, "Me too." He kissed her forehead and gave her one last stroke on her cheek, then picked up his bag. "Don't you worry—the Bond will keep us close. Just don't block me out too much while I'm gone, okay?"

Blood tears sprang to her eyes. She knew she had to blot them immediately—even if she put her jacket's hood over her head, reddish liquid on her face might appear odd to others. With the heightened security at airports, she didn't want to look strange or suspicious.

"I never want to be away from you," she told him, tearful. "Ever. I mean that."

He gazed at her for a long while until he leaned in for one more fierce kiss on her lips. After he pulled away he answered her, "I know you won't. You never will. You didn't even leave me after death, damn you."

With a quick squeeze of her hand, he briskly walked towards the security gate, leaving her to stare after him. A hopeless, lost feeling filled her. Amanda stood there for a long time until finally leaving to catch the subway back to the Sanctuary.

* * * *

In the middle of correcting a student's paper, Lynne heard a knock at the door.

"Come in," she called.

In walked James, looking more than a little perturbed. He stood in front of her desk, fidgeting and wringing his hands.

She frowned. "What seems to be the trouble, Magister?"

"Lynne, this entire situation has been completely taken out of my hands, Blood help me," he declared, his voice and gestures frantic.

She tried not to appear exasperated. "What situation?"

"Don't ask me how, but Lyrael has been getting her memories back. Memories from her life as Sarah. Somehow, what she did was connected to her Blood Bond with Turel, and, oh hell...." He paced around the room.

"James, for Blood's sake, sit down," she told him impatiently. "And what happened? She *knows*?"

He brushed the papers off of the chair beside her desk and sank into it. "She not only knows, but the Blood Bond is completely out of control. I can barely even sense them separately, and I think the young apprentice is losing it. I'm really worried, Lynne."

Lynne swore profusely in several languages, most of them dead to the modern world. "Where's Turel?"

"New Orleans. I sent him there to work on a project with Clan Corvus. Amanda needs her space right now more than anything. He'll only be gone a month, but I figure that should give us—and her—enough time to get herself back together."

Fat chance, Lynne thought with worry. *She'll definitely lose it, if she hasn't already—you can't separate a Blood Bound pair like this and expect her to just cry about it for a few days and get over it!*

She held up the palms of her hands as if to ward away any further speech. "Wait, slow down...can I see her? What do you mean, 'back together'? Is she okay?"

"Her aura is blurry and...well, for the lack of a better term, fragmented." He rubbed his head as if it ached.

Great, a new apprentice who's now turning into a total basket case. Grimacing, she asked again, "Can I see her?" Then she frowned. "And who's working with Lyrael on the protection spell project?"

"No one, unless you think she really needs the help. Honestly, she has it almost wrapped up at this point," he added, his words picking up speed. "She just needs to put the final implementations in place, and if worse came to worse she has the Blood Bond and can ask Turel for his input."

She gritted her teeth. "James...."

"Oh, sorry." He waved his hands in the air. "Yes, of course you can see her. I'm not sure where she is right now, but feel free to track her down and have a talk with her. Maybe more than one, if you're up to it."

"Yeah, I think I will. Thank you, James."

"No problem."

He left her office and tried to shut the door, but she was right behind him. He laughed nervously. "Sorry, didn't see you."

Lynne smiled back. "It's okay. I'm just heading out to see her."

"Who? Oh, yes, yes, of course. If you need me, I'll be in my office." He scurried down the hallway with Asherael staring at his back, shaking her head.

Knowing her, I bet she's in the library. Studying and working her brains out. Again.

* * * *

Buried in books and notes, Amanda had confined herself to the library for much of the day—praying that her work would be a big enough distraction to keep her mind off the fact that Jesse was hundreds of miles away. Being kept busy with her work had always helped her focus on the important things in the past; why should it be so different now?

I was never separated from him more than a day. When she was Sarah or in this lifetime? *Both.* They had been a tight magickal team. A partnership. Everything they did, they did together.

Back when I was Sarah, rather, she corrected herself.

Instinctively, she reached out to him with her mind. Feeling his presence still there, she was comforted. It didn't totally fill the void within her but it was never the same, just feeling that awful physical distance between them. She sensed him in her mind, but he kept the contact light. Much of the work he did with Clan Corvus was above her degree level, and in spite of her mental protests, he had insisted she was overburdened enough as it was.

He's probably right, she thought wistfully.

Staring at her notes, she remembered some of Jesse's theories and ideas, which he had spoken to her about earlier. An Anubis of the East on the inside of their Sanctuary and an Anubis of the West guarding its outside, rather like the Hall of the Neophyte in the Golden Dawn. People were concerned about the scope of such things, and if their invoked forces were banished, whether the whole system would be destroyed.

They should install one of those fancy security systems. The kind that contact police departments and all that if disrupted.

Then she had it. Why not rig the system so that some sort of "alarm" would go off if someone tried to either enter without permission or disrupt the spell? Amanda tapped her pen on the desk. Now, what would define "permission"...? Instantly, she thought of what Jesse had given her "permission" to do while he was away, and her cheeks grew warm. Then she remembered other occasions, what he had said to her when he first gave her the slave bracelet and the time they had spent together afterwards.

I'm supposed to focus on this how? I can't even figure out which memories are mine anymore. Her dreams last night were foreign to her, but they contained within them recollections of strong emotions she had experienced as Sarah—including some memories she had of her own death and what it been like. She tossed her pen on the other side of the table and folded her arms. Leaning back in her chair, she forced a breath into her lungs and sighed. As Sarah, she could barely remember having been human, but as Amanda, she could still vividly remember, having been human all that long ago. The sensation of sighing brought her back to herself, but couldn't dispel all of the strangeness that filled her inside.

"Don't let Janius ever catch you doing that—he hates it."

Startled, Amanda turned around. Lynne stood behind her with a pensive expression on her face.

* * * *

"Oh, hi, Lynne."

She nodded curtly. "Busy at work, I see."

"Yeah. I think I've made some progress on this, but I'll have to run it by the magister—and maybe you too." Amanda began rifling through her notes. "I was thinking—people are concerned about the spell being tampered with, right? So why not rig the spell so that if it's tampered with without a particular "code" or password, if you will, it sets off some sort of alarm? Kinda like the magickal equivalent of those systems they set up in homes these days?"

Lynne smiled. "Hey, Amanda?"

"Yes?"

The blonde vampire walked over to another chair at Amanda's table. Gesturing to it, she asked, "Mind if I sit down?"

She nodded. "Sure, sure, go right ahead."

"Thanks." With a degree of grace which she wasn't feeling at the moment, Lynne sat herself down on the chair and gazed at Amanda intently. "Do you do this often?" she asked the young vampire.

Amanda blinked. "Do what often?"

Gesturing at the papers and books, she replied, "That. Every time I see you you're either with Turel or buried in your work. Theodotos tells me that you're a workaholic—and I believe it. But I think it's more than that."

Amanda shrugged. "I enjoy it. And besides, isn't this project supposed to get done sometime soon? It's just me now working on it, after all." Her tone of voice was light, but bitter.

Not knowing what to say for a few moments, Lynne settled for gazing at the young vampire thoughtfully. It was so hard to believe that the woman who sat before her was a carefree "wild child" in her last lifetime and had never once appeared to get stressed. When certainty of approach finally hit her, she cleared her throat.

"Amanda, I'll be frank. Between the Blood Bond being as strong as it is now and with the added burden of your new memories, I'm a little worried about you." She went on, albeit cautiously, "I want you to think about taking a break every now and again, get some fresh night air or something. Let's hang out—we can go to that club again, enjoy some jazz music. What do you say?"

She paused to observe Amanda's reaction and to see if her words had sunk in or not. Her expression was unreadable, a mixture of emotions which Lynne could only describe as confused. She watched as she picked up her pen—again—and began jotting down notes.

"I can't."

Lynne's brow furrowed. "Can't what?"

"I can't. I can't stop doing this. If I stop, I-I don't know what I'll do. And I'm afraid to know at this point."

"Amanda—"

"Lynne, this is the only thing right now standing between me and insanity. I can't—I don't know—what to do. I don't know what to think. And I look at you now, and I think, and I remember...." She suddenly choked. "Oh, gods, Lynne, I remember. And I'm so sorry. I keep...I keep seeing you on the ground and Jess crying and I'm so sorry, Lynne. I keep seeing everything in my head and I never meant it to be that way. I never did." The pen flew out of her hand across the room as Lynne's hand flew to her own face in alarm.

"I remember now, what I was thinking when I was out of my body. I remember thinking that I wanted to come back, set things right—and here I am, with all of this shit in my head, and Jesse in New Orleans, and I can't think straight with him gone, and I just, don't know...."

The books on the table lifted and fell to the floor, and somewhere in the back of the room Lynne heard a loud crash. *Oh no.*

"Amanda, it's okay. Yes, it hurt when Sarah died, but it's not your fault. You saved us." Lynne fought back her own blood tears as she watched them streak down the young vampire's face. "You saved us. You saved us all. And dammit, I'm *proud* of you."

Wiping the tears on her sleeve, Amanda could only answer, "No... no, you're proud of who I was. And I'm not...I'm not that person anymore."

"Then who are you?"

Amanda looked directly at Lynne, and the look in her eyes saddened her to the bone. "I don't know. It's so stupid, I know. Devotee of a god who tells you to 'know yourself' and...fuck...I don't know who I am. And I've barely talked with him since I've been here, and he says he's never left me, but I just don't *know* anything anymore...."

Another crash in the room, but Lynne ignored it. *I'll help Merideth straighten up later*. Instead, she leaned over and put her hand on Amanda's shoulder. "You won't know who you are if you continue to bury yourself in work. You'll never know." She bit her lip, then continued, "Janius—James—he wanted you to learn. His sending away Turel wasn't supposed to be a punishment for you or for him."

Amanda smiled, but it didn't match her eyes. "I never would've known that, as it sure feels like it to me."

Blood, I don't agree with him either.... "I'm not going to deny this is hard for you—I know that it is. I can't even imagine how hard."

The two women stared at each other in silence, not knowing what to say to the other.

* * * *

Amanda finally broke the silence. "No...." She shook her head. "You can't, Lynne. I know you can't. And I...I don't hold it against you. I never did." She frowned. "And I don't even know where that came from...."

"Don't worry about it," Lynne told her. "Just focus on *you* right now. Is there anything I can do for you?"

Gazing sadly at a mess of papers—which had once been a neat pile but had somehow slid all over the table—she could only reply, "I don't know. I really don't know. What do you normally do when your head's a mess and you have no idea where your real thoughts and emotions are when they're tangled up in someone else's—who happens to be hundreds of miles away from you, no less—and a bunch of others from someone who you used to be before you were born and is you but isn't you?" She stopped and stared off into space.

"I'm losing it," whispered Amanda.

Nearby where they sat, a book-filled cart tipped over with a loud thud.

"Come on, let's get you out of here," urged Lynne. "Before you completely wreck the place."

Amanda barely noticed the comment about the mess. She was far more concerned about their destination than where she currently sat. "Where?" she asked listlessly. "Where would we go?"

Lynne threw her heads up in the air in frustration. "I don't know, anywhere."

Suddenly, Amanda brightened. "New Orleans?"

The blonde vampire gritted her teeth. "No. James would be furious with me."

"Oh."

"How about this: where do you feel the most 'you'?" suggested Lynne.

The idea made blood tears spring to the young vampire's eyes again. "I…hm." She thought about it long and hard. Places, things, people…in the end, she managed to draw a conclusion so evident it physically jolted her.

"Lynne, I know just the thing." She ran up and hugged her. "Thank you. You've always been such a good friend to me." Practically running, Amanda headed for the door.

"Wait, where are you going?"

"To the closet, where we store the incense and herbs. Then to my room, where I can do a ritual to Apollo."

Lynne's dazed expression met her words. "Your room is where you feel the most you?"

"No, I feel the most me when I'm…when I'm with Apollo." Amanda gestured with her hands helplessly. "With the gods. I can't explain it and I can't describe it, and it's the one thing I haven't done enough of since my Turning."

Lynne shrugged and smiled. "Come talk to me when you're done, okay?"

"Okay."

With a little frown, she demanded, "Promise?"

"Promise. I will. And thanks again."

Chapter Twenty-Five

"Unfinished business."

The storage closet of ritual items was filled with all sorts of materials: candles, incense, charcoals, incense holders, candle holders, herbs, matches, lighters, and resins—it was a mess. However, Amanda knew inside her that the closet contained frankincense. Or normally did, rather. Thankfully, when she got there, she wasn't disappointed.

Yay, frankincense for Apollo! It was a standard offering for a Greek deity—especially for Apollo—and while she didn't maintain all of the ancient customs, it was one she kept in her personal practice. While she was there, she found charcoal and an incense burner on which to burn the frankincense. *Excellent.*

Once in her room, she realized she had very few flat spaces to put ritual items on. *Note to self, ask Janius for a small table or something.* She settled for clearing off the small dresser of papers and books and laid the incense burner, matches, and frankincense on top. Thinking it through, she decided to place the small bust of Apollo next to the items.

Amanda's next impulse was to perform the banishing ritual she did often during her self-study in the Golden Dawn. Afterwards, her mood shifted to become calm and more balanced. The feelings she had been experiencing earlier—the obsessive desperation to keep mentally checking on Jesse, the disconnect between her memories and those of her past life, and the usual discomfort she had with the intensity of the Blood Bond were greatly reduced. *Note to self,* she echoed with chagrin, *until I can get a handle on my situation, do this daily.*

A similar ritual popped into her head; it involved moving counterclockwise and a lot of Greek—along with chanting the names of various deities whom she vaguely recalled from the times she had read Crowley's *The Book of the Law.* Somehow, she recalled it as a practice she had performed time and time again after her usual banishing ritual. Afterwards, she would meet with James and Lynne and discuss the progress of their students.... Then she remembered who and where she was.

Okay then, twice daily.

Grabbing the package of matches, she stared at it for a few

seconds. *Wait...I'm supposed to be practicing magick, right?* Amanda envisioned a flame on the charcoal—which promptly went up in flames like a small candle.

"Ow, fuck!" she cried out, quickly dropping it into the incense burner. *That worked a little* too *well.* Frowning, she ran into the bathroom to run her hand under cold water. Could she even get hurt by a little burn as a vampire? How would injuries affect her, and how would she heal? Not really knowing for sure, she figured better be safe than sorry.

As she rinsed off her hand, she puzzled over how fast and to what extent the charcoal had gotten lit. She found it a little disconcerting that magick was so easy to perform—shouldn't there be *some* amount of effort involved? It seemed the only effort she needed these days was to prevent herself from either burning down the place or destroying the library. Wincing in shame, she realized she had a long way to go before she would get a handle on her magick—or much of anything, for that matter.

Returning to her room, Amanda began what she considered a quick invocation to Apollo and placed some frankincense on the charcoal as an offering. Its sweet scent filled the air, instantly bringing back recollections of rituals past. It wasn't long before she perceived Apollo's presence and knew she would have to do some additional steps if she wanted to hear what he had to say.

Now...let's see if I can still do this. After moving the chair to the middle of the room, Amanda sat down on it and closed her eyes. In this position, she willed herself into a deep meditative state. Being as receptive as she could make herself was the only way she knew how to deliberately receive any sort of message or communication with the god.

On the astral plane, Amanda had always perceived Apollo as a distant, golden light. Sometimes he looked like an ordinary man with golden hair and dark, intense eyes she couldn't bear to look into. At other times he was just a disembodied voice, strong but sure in her mind. She was never certain whether or not she spoke directly to him or through her guardian spirit, her Agathos Daimon—and she certainly didn't care. Badly in need of a divine guide and reassuring voice, direct or indirect, she would accept it.

In a matter of moments, she was enveloped in a golden rush of energy, and a sonorous voice filled her mind: ***YOU CANNOT MASTER YOUR MAGICK IF YOU CANNOT FIRST MASTER YOURSELF.***

Thrilled that Apollo was still around to give her advice, she fought back the impatience which made her want to demand, *"How?"* But the god, perhaps in a desire to be merciful, had more to say.

Meditate and you will find it. Spend some quiet time alone.

This time she couldn't bite her tongue. *"But how do I get my work done?"*

Amusement flashed in her mind. ***Everything in moderation.*** There was a long, quiet moment before he added, ***You are not without help.***

"What do you mean?"

A gentle wind floated through and lifted the weight of his presence from her.

"Figure it out for yourself," she stated ruefully. "Got it."

Another blast of amusement surged through her senses as she tried to determine if amusing him was either a good or a bad thing. *Oh, this is going to be interesting....* She slowly opened her eyes. The pieces of frankincense had already burnt down with no more smoke dispersing into the air. Fishing into the bag, she added a few more pieces of resin.

"*Eucharisto, Apollon.*"

Not knowing what else to do, she supposed it would be a good time to go out for a walk. No sooner than having set foot a few paces outside her door, Erik arrived.

"Ah, Lyrael, just the person I wanted to see. I need to show you something important. Do you have a minute or two?"

She stared at him for a few seconds before saying, "Sure, Theodotos, I think I do. What's up?"

"Just follow me. You'll see."

Curious, she went with him to a nearby room. Small but cozy, it had a few elegant padded chairs, a loveseat, and a small desk with a lamp beside it. She figured it was a study room for small groups of people—or least, it was supposed to have been. Dimly, she remembered some of the younger students getting together in that room to smoke a bowl or two and having joined them on more than one occasion.

I must've gotten the "World's Coolest Teacher" award, she thought with amusement. What kind of life had she lived then, and why was it so different from the one she had in this lifetime? Aside from an occasional glass of wine and the odd cup of coffee, she'd never once tried drugs.

He turned on the lamp, put his hands between it and the wall, and began forming shapes with his fingers. Amanda made out the distinct shape on the wall behind it of what appeared to be a shadow bunny.

"Know what this is?" he asked her, his eyes wide with anticipation.

She fought back giggles and replied, "Um, a shadow...bunny?"

Erik pointed his finger at her. "Right! And do you know why this is important?"

Shaking her head, she could only imagine what had possibly inspired this bout of silliness, her giggles finally escaping.

"This...is what you cannot do outside anymore!"

Amanda blinked. "Um...okay...."

"Do you know why?"

Again she shook her head, utterly baffled.

"It's because when you adjusted the shield, you blocked out *all* of the light."

Her eyebrows went up into her hair. "Oh," she stated meekly.

"I suppose we could get a few Thirds together, maybe a few Seconds, and run around with some flashlights. Lots of flashlights. With lots of batteries. But it wouldn't really help."

At this point she could barely choke out the words, she was cackling so hard. "But...I thought...isn't-isn't sunlight...bad?"

"*Sun*light, yes. But...take a look around you. There's light in this room, yes?" She nodded. "And yet...you're not turning into a little pile of ashes! And thank Blood and all that, neither am I! But yet, if either you or I go out during the day, we will."

It finally hit her. "Oh! So it's the radiation from the sun, then? That's what harms us?"

"Bingo!" he exclaimed happily. "Never go into a tanning booth. You might as well commit suicide. Besides, we'd miss you, and Turel would be climbing the walls. Probably, knowing him, that might be a literal statement."

She laughed. "I wouldn't dare do that to him again."

He shook his head vigorously as if to clear the confusion. "Huh? *Again*? What did you do to the poor guy?"

Amanda's mouth dropped open. Should she tell him? It wasn't like he was around back then, she reasoned, and hence, her revelation wouldn't be very meaningful. She surmised his Turning was probably in the seventies or eighties as he didn't feature in her memories. Sometime, when she thought of it, she would have to ask him precisely when he joined the Order. "Um...it's a long story."

Laughing while holding up his hands in protest, Erik replied, "It's okay, you don't have to tell me. But between you and me, please don't make that crazy bastard—and I *really* call him that with the greatest of fraternal affection, really—climb the walls. It's bad enough his entire life revolves around you. Why bother making it worse?"

In between giggles, she nodded. "Yeah, I understand."

"So, my suggestion to you, filter out the UV and all of that crap. As much of it as possible. I hear you're a devotee of a sun god?"

"Well...a god of the sun," she amended, "he's associated with light. Helios I tend to define more strictly as a sun god."

"Hey, whatever. We like you to learn how to do magick on your own around here—and I'm sure the gods do too, being that they tend to only help those who help themselves and all that—but it might be a good idea to invite his help for it. We could certainly use it. Other than that, filtering it out through some sort of specifically worded spell could do the trick. If you need any help, just come get me," he offered. "I'm always around."

Amanda grinned. "Thanks, I really appreciate that."

"You're welcome. Now, go take care of that shield so we can do a shadow puppet theatre someday—if we really wanted to, that is."

Laughing so hard she almost snorted, she managed to get out a "Sure" in response before leaving the room. *Well, now I know what to do on my walk outside....*

The air outside was pleasant, albeit a little muggy. Amanda liked it just fine that way; she hated the cold and could already feel the chill of autumn in the air. Knowing intellectually that as a vampire she should prefer the winter so she would be able to spend more time outdoors didn't really help. Her favorite season had always been summer, followed by spring.

Using her inner eyes, she studied the energy strands that had once been magickally created clouds, which now stretched over the Sanctuary as a cover from the sun. Carefully, she reached out her hands and started to perform a simple spell, calling upon the forces of nature to make the shield into that of protection from the sun's radiation and not its light.

She wasn't much more than halfway done before the winds picked up and her hair blew in the breeze as she stood out there with her arms outstretched beneath the dimly lit night sky and streetlights all around. Suddenly, a powerful feeling of déjà vu swept over her.

"But to love me is better than all things...."

Visions of her final moments as Sarah flooded her head, and she crashed onto her knees, unable to bear their heaviness. Jesse sobbing—gods, not Jess!—Lynne utterly distraught, and the peace of the afterlife she remembered completely disrupted by the chaos and despair she had left in her wake.

Weeping, she rested her head between her knees, unable to withstand any more of the images and memories in her mind. With Jesse in New Orleans, it seemed like an echo of that long ago forced separation, and with it, pain clenched like a fist inside her chest.

Gods, I wish you'd take these memories away from me, she begged. *No one should have to remember this...any of this....* Wrapping her arms around herself, she wished desperately for the pain to go away, all of it to go away....

IDIOT.

Amanda became utterly still. Where had that come from? It certainly didn't come from Jesse, nor did it feel like it had a corporeal origin. Was she truly losing it?

YOU SAVED THE ENTIRE CLAN FROM BEING DESTROYED. YOU WOULD'VE BEEN KILLED, JESSE WOULD'VE BEEN KILLED—EVERYONE WOULD'VE BEEN DEAD IF IT HADN'T BEEN FOR WHAT YOU HAD DONE. NOT JUST YOU, BUT EVERYONE.

Dumbfounded, she could only ask in her head, *"Who is this?"*

IT'S ONLY A FEW HOURS BEFORE DAWN. FINISH YOUR SPELL AND GET SOME REST.

"Okay, but...shouldn't I know who you are?"

YOU WILL.

She shook her head. This was nuts. All in all, she probably should finish the spell, and truth rang in what the voice had told her—everyone would've been dead. Yes, the memories were painful, but what she did, she did for a greater good.

And she was back now, wasn't she? In a different body, living a different life, but she was back. Maybe there was some sense to that, some rhyme or reason. She hadn't wanted to leave her family and friends behind, but something had dragged her back here.

Unfinished business, she figured. On the astral plane, she did a quick banishing ritual. Once she came to, she wiped the blood tears from her face and continued working her spell. She finished, and the energy strands flared and sparkled. As she regarded her work, she couldn't help but think it was somewhat ironic that even after her death, she did protection magick for the Sanctuary and the Clan.

Somehow, there was a certain sense of poetic justice in that.

* * * *

"Lynne, where have you been this whole time? It's an hour before dawn!"

The blonde vampire merely lifted her shoulder in a half-hearted shrug. "I had to help Merideth clean up the library. I figured it was only fair."

The magister's brows knitted together as he saw Lynne attempting not to laugh.

"Clean the library? Why?"

"Lyrael had one of her poltergeist fits when I went to talk with her earlier. Ordinarily I'd make someone do their own cleaning up after that, but given what she's going through right now," her forehead creased as she frowned, "I figured I'd be merciful."

Leaning back in his office chair, James contemplated what to say next. This was an ugly situation with a lot of variables—and some of those variables were not to his liking. How often would Lynne have to clean up after Amanda before things were resolved? "I'm glad you spoke with her, but I'm concerned about the fact that she still isn't able to control her abilities. Do you think there's any hope of her learning any amount of control?"

Her green eyes flashed. "You have no idea, James, what that girl has been through over the past couple of days. I'm amazed the Sanctuary is still standing, frankly. Under the circumstances, I'd say she was pretty damned restrained."

"Lynne...."

But she appeared past the point of hearing or caring what he had to say next. "*You* were the one who chose to send Turel away, and now she has the backlash of the Blood Bond to deal with on top of it all. Honestly, what did you expect? For her to cry on her pillow for a few hours and then get back to work like nothing happened?"

A long pause occurred before the magister spoke quietly. "Lynne, I know you think I did a terrible thing and I don't blame you. A part of me is still at odds with what I did as well—make no mistake about it. But I really do think she will be better off for having spent this month on her own. Well, as much on her own as possible, given the

Blood Bond," he added.

Her fists clenched and unclenched at her sides. "James, with all due respect, you don't know what's going on with her—not the full story. She remembers way more than you think. She remembers her own death. She even remembers what happened *after* she died."

A queasiness filled James's gut. "I see," he replied neutrally. Then his voice softened. "Please don't get the impression that I'm trying to be unnecessarily hard on her. I'm worried about her too—that's why I'm asking you if you think she'll get past all of this. Eventually."

Lynne pursed her lips together before nodding thoughtfully. "She will. I've given her some stuff to think about and actually got a genuine smile out of her before she left. She's certainly not a lost cause—that's for certain—but I am worried about her in the short term. The things she said to me, Blood...." She leaned against a nearby wall for support.

"Keep talking to her and keep working on her. And truly, I'm sorry." With his eyes looking directly into hers, he continued, "I had no idea of the extent of the situation. I know her current memories are confused with her other memories as Sarah, but I had no idea how traumatic some of those memories were. I remember her life as a good one, a fun one—she was always happy." Distraught, he put his head in his hand and gazed down at his shoe. "I didn't think it'd be such a problem to remember what a good life she had," he added helplessly, looking up at Lynne.

The corners of Lynne's mouth turned up in a mockery of a smile. "Well, right now she remembers a whole lot of death and lots of people crying over it. I'm sure there's more, but for the moment, she can't get past that."

"Lynne, you were her best friend, weren't you? Sarah's, I mean?" She gave a short nod. "I think that you of all people are the best person to remind Amanda of who she was—and help her to come to terms with who that makes her now. In a good way, I mean."

She folded her arms and gazed at the floor. "There's a lot she'll have to come to terms with on her own, but I certainly don't mind helping out with the rest." Swallowing, she jerked her head back up to meet the magister's gaze. "And...I can't say I'm not glad to have her back. Well, sorta back."

"Good. And thank you. I know I can count on you, Lynne."

This time, she gave him a genuine smile. "Thanks, I appreciate that."

"Now, are you done helping out Amaltheia? Because if you're going to be seeing her sometime soon, I have something to give her." He produced a small jar from his desk.

He watched as Lynne peered closer to see the chocolate mints inside. Her eyebrows flew up. "James, I didn't know you knew about that! Who told you?"

He laughed. "I'm the magister of this Clan; I know these things. Just don't tell her I know—let it be our secret, okay?"

Shaking her head Lynne told him, "You're incorrigible. I'll deliver them to her and I'll be sure not to tell. Honest."

Chapter Twenty-Six

"Desperately seeking serenity."

Amanda had been trying to buy cloaks at a dime store. Frustration ate away at her because she possessed all of five dollars to spend, and the only cloaks they sold were orange and pink. By the time she finally found one in a suitable shade of blue, she tried haggling with the store owner, who insisted upon speaking to her in Chinese.

It wasn't until a man walked into the store that she went lucid and knew she was dreaming.

His long, dark hair spilled over his torso, and his black leather pants left very little to the imagination. A distinctive scent followed him in. Something musky and sweet, strange and familiar, all at the same time. Amanda made out an earthy fragrance with an undertone of patchouli that reminded her of fields and trees covered with dew.

Her instinct prompted her to say to him, "I don't think you're allowed to go topless in this store." Instead, she froze; his energy hit her square in the gut. It struck her as primal, dark, and sexual. An image of a black panther ran through her head.

Who was this man?

Swallowing hard, she tried to fight her next instinct: to run somewhere, anywhere—and fast. This man obviously wasn't Jesse, and she had an inkling that he was interested in her. This reaction of hers didn't make any sense; after all, she had never seen him before in her life. But his intense energy struck her deep within the core of her being and made her feel nervous and naked.

Then he turned to look directly at her, and for a brief moment she saw his darkly bright eyes. It hit her hard, and she was thrust backwards. The next thing she knew, she lay on her back in a very vivid dreamscape with a strange, bright-eyed man with long dark hair bending over her. He reached out his hand to hers, and, unthinking, she took it. His hand pulsed with the sensual rhythm of life, and on her tongue was the taste of something deliciously intoxicating. In that space she was completely free, all of her burdens flying away on the breeze as she truly remembered herself and knew who she was.

"I'm Dionysus," he said, his voice low and melodious and oddly familiar. It was as if she had grown up listening to it telling her bedtime stories and later in life it whispered sweet nothings into her ear as she slept.

She gulped, and he gently released her hand. Amanda had read many things about the god in her Classical Studies classes and in her many books on ancient Greece, and how he had been cast in the modern day world as a "party god." This didn't annoy her, but rather filled her with a good deal of pity. No one who had read *The Bacchae* could ever think of Dionysus as a "party god."

"Lord of initiation," she stated matter-of-factly. Maybe this was some sort of allegory as to her experience thus far, a message from her unconscious.

"Amanda, *agapi mou*, I am not Apollo."

She blinked. His love? He called her his love?

"You think too much."

"I...what?"

"I've come here to claim you as my own."

Her eyes grew wide at this proclamation. "I—what about Apollo?"

"You belong to both of us. You always have. I'm here to remind you of that."

Irrational panic struck her. What was going on? Was this real? Her urge to run away grew stronger.

He continued speaking, his voice wistful and heavy with sadness. "You've always run away from me. Buried yourself in your books. Apollo tells you to be moderate, but you don't listen."

It made Amanda feel horrible. "What do you want me to do?"

"Listen. Listen to me." He gave her a warm smile.

Flustered, she continued to question him. "Is there something I should stop doing, or things that I should be doing, or—"

He hushed her with a look. "Burdens and boundaries aren't my way."

"Then what?"

Dionysus merely smiled. "Just be you. Be the wonderful, real you whom I both love and adore. That's all I ask."

Wheels began turning in her head. "So...Apollo wants me to know myself, and you want me to be myself?"

The god shook his head at her. "You're still thinking too much."

"But—"

Amanda's words were halted by a gentle kiss, and shortly afterwards, she awoke.

Once her shaky legs allowed her to stand, she spent a long time in the shower thinking about the dream. She always experienced a sort of peace in being with Apollo, but the peace she sensed while with Dionysus was a very different sort of peace. It left her unsettled and wondering what she could do to bring that sort of peace into her every day life.

But peace wasn't the right word. As the water cascaded down her back, she finally pinned it down: serenity. Yes, serenity was the term for it. She was desperately seeking serenity.

Once done and dried off, she surveyed her closet. She didn't know why—in fact, she typically didn't spend too much time on her appearance. Except, of course, when she was going out with Jesse.

Rifling through her clothes, she reached the conclusion that she had three pairs of jeans, one black and two blue. She also owned five skirts, three dresses, and a couple of blouses and some tank tops. Her shoes consisted of one pair of sandals, one pair of sneakers, and two pairs of boots, one dress and one for winter. Her sweaters were still back in her apartment along with a couple of jackets. Frowning, she remembered why her wardrobe was so sparse: she spent most of her time buried in her papers and books, not to mention she had been deeply broke as a graduate student, with little to no time for a job to supplement her income. She made up for it by doing paid internships and selling her possessions—including some of her clothing—on the Internet. With her goals intently set towards her spiritual life, she'd figured clothing was an unnecessary thing with which to be concerned. Besides, given the tiny studio she lived in, she had no choice. It was the closest place she could find near her college campus that was affordable.

Which reminded her of her days at NYU and all of the times she'd turned down going to social events. Parties. Times when she could've hung out with her friends more often, as opposed to slavishly studying on a weekend. She realized that the only friends she had were people in her classes, as they were the only ones who had actually seen her on a regular basis—if at all. And when she wasn't busy with her studies at school, she was preoccupied with her magickal work, studying and practicing everything she could get her hands on and mixing it with her spiritual practice as she continued to honor the gods in her life. When it came down to it, she had allowed herself to not have much interaction with the outside world beyond professional contacts—and isolated herself as a result.

Meeting Jesse was probably the best thing that ever happened to me.

Would she have ever realized there was a world outside of her books, magick, and spirituality otherwise? The answer was a firm and definite no.

Amanda put her hands on her hips and contemplated matters for a few moments. She vaguely remembered having money to spend when she was Sarah, but didn't recall where it came from or what the proper procedure was for obtaining permission to have any of it. Did anyone in the Order get jobs, either within the Order or in the mundane world? She knew the Clan was independently wealthy and money was of little object to them, but the details of how those finances were managed and who had access to it was beyond her memory.

She concluded that when she was Sarah, she just plain didn't care—or had no reason to be worried. Either way, it wasn't a part of what she could pull from the 'new' memories that now occupied her head. Perhaps it would come to her later, but right now, she knew of only one course of action, and that was to ask someone else.

* * * *

Lynne wrinkled her nose as she surveyed Amanda's wardrobe.

"As far as I'm concerned, you have my permission." Amanda squealed with delight, which made Lynne add cautiously, "But go ask Janius. You typically get things by doing projects and favors around here, or through barter arrangements. Some of the other Clans allow a few vampires to pass in the mundane world and work night jobs."

Amanda's face brightened. Maybe she had a chance of contacting her parents eventually after all.

"Usually, once you reach a certain degree, you gain a corresponding amount of trust," the elder vampire continued. "You're still new here, but you have a lot of...well, odd circumstances in your favor."

"I wouldn't even need that much," insisted Amanda. "I just...I don't know. I look at everything I own and it's not even that it's not me; it doesn't even feel like anything. I know it seems like a frivolous request, but...." She shrugged, not knowing what else to say.

"Personally, I don't think it's all that frivolous. We do go amongst the public—even if just to feed—and if we don't keep up with clothing trends, we stand out like a sore thumb. Therefore we have to buy new clothing every so often. Imagine me walking out in some of my clothing from the twenties?" She shook her head. "I'd look like a walking relic."

"But...I don't have that excuse. My clothes are still current—well, relatively speaking. I just feel...well, I feel odd asking for this sort of thing. It seems so shallow—"

Lynne cut her short. "Amanda, you're a woman, and you didn't stop being a woman when you entered into this building. You're not asking for $500 Gucci shoes; you're asking for a little money so you can start caring about your appearance." What she thought and nearly bit her tongue off to prevent herself from saying was, *Just the fact that you even care gives me hope you're on the mend, for crying out loud.*

Amanda nodded vigorously, and Lynne took that as a sign of encouragement to continue. "Tell you what, if Janius doesn't approve, I'll give you some of my own money."

Amanda beamed. "Oh, Lynne, thank you. I really appreciate it, and if I can pay you back somehow, I will."

The elder vampire raised a blonde eyebrow at her. "Amanda, I may have only known you a short while in this life, but I knew you for a long time in your other life. This is what friends do. Consider it a gift. And I'm good for it even if Janius is okay with giving you some money," she added.

Blood-tears welled up in Amanda's eyes. "I-I really appreciate it. You really don't know how much."

Lynne smiled. "You're welcome. But I can tell you one thing which I may like in return."

"What?"

With a wicked grin, Lynne replied gleefully, "I want to go shopping with you. I haven't gone in ages and I think it'd be fun."

The young vampire grinned back. "You bet." Then she paused, momentarily appearing lost in thought. "I seem to remember there were a few times that we visited this boutique; I think it was somewhere in the East Village."

Oh, for Blood's sake. "Amanda, if the last time you remember shopping was almost forty years ago and in a previous life, you're in more trouble than I thought. Come on, let's go."

"But, um," she stammered, "shouldn't I be asking Janius for, I mean—"

"Screw asking Janius. You'll ask him for your own funds next time."

A stupid grin slid onto Amanda's face, one which didn't leave her face even after they had finally left the Sanctuary. Lynne considered making fun of her for it, but wisely held her tongue. She didn't know what had caused Amanda to start thinking of things such as clothing and socializing, but she considered it to be a welcome and unexpectedly fast improvement. Hoping furiously for continuing breakthroughs, Lynne looked forward to the opportunity to hang out with Amanda and help get her thinking about matters other than Jesse's absence and the burden of another lifetime's memories being squashed into her head.

Lynne also considered the reality of the scenario at hand; she had truly no idea how Amanda was adjusting to her new life as a vampire. Given how she had spent most of the time after her Turning being caught up in her Sire, what would she do now and how would she react to her new life?

Guess the only thing there is to do is to wait and see what happens, she thought ruefully.

* * * *

Her new clothes covered her bed, and Amanda surveyed them with delight. Finding items to wear which she liked had proved to be troublesome; the fact was she had no idea what she liked. She never really possessed a "style" she was comfortable with, save what was practical and comfortable. The whole shopping trip helped her to understand the "try as you go" process, with Amanda trying on so many different styles of clothing her head still spun. Some of the items were outlandish, ridiculous, and even funny—and she had a blast trying them on just to make Lynne laugh. The others she tried on because she remembered wearing the style when she was Sarah, and she was pleased to discover that she still liked similar things as back then. And yet at the same time, much of what she liked as Sarah still took on a new twist from the person whom she was now.

But most of all, she had enjoyed spending the time with Lynne. It made her feel more composed and had helped her to process much of what was going through her head. Her nature didn't lend itself to opening up to people easily, but she had the memories available to her about what Lynne was like when she had last known her. She knew she could trust Lynne and remembered her as being a very close and dear friend, almost a sister.

She fingered one item of clothing she had surprised herself by getting—and stunned Lynne even more, perhaps. It was a pair of soft, black leather pants. Dressing up in the different outfits was fun, and she was delighted to find out through trying them on, as well as other items of clothing, that she wore a size smaller than she had originally thought. The leather pants were a size four and fit her very well. They were also reasonably stretchy and comfortable. However, she knew the pants were also completely impractical; she had no idea when she would wear them next. But she decided it would be a good idea to try something new.

Besides, they reminded her of Dionysus, and she figured buying an item of clothing in his honor wouldn't be so terrible.

Thinking of the god, she smiled. Maybe belonging to two gods wasn't such an overwhelming thing after all. She remembered Apollo's words about having help and wondered if Dionysus was indeed that help.

A knock came at the door. She quickly got off her bed and answered it.

"Ah, Lynne, what's up?"

Lynne smiled at her. "I was wondering if you were hungry? Maybe you wanted to get a bite to eat?" After Amanda groaned she added, "Horrible overused pun intended?"

Amanda chuckled. "I suppose that wouldn't be such a bad idea. The only thing I have on my plate is figuring out some way to test the adjustments I had made to the protection shields."

"I'm game for that. I may be able to come up with some ideas that could help you."

Awesome, Amanda thought. *I may actually get this part of the project working so I can focus on the rest of it.* "Okay then, I'm ready to go whenever you are."

"I'm all set. Just one thing, though."

Oh boy.... "What?"

Lynne poked her in the arm. "No feeding off of druggies." At this, Amanda blushed. "If you want we can head to the *Blue Moon* afterwards, though. Their wine was more than decent, as was their music."

Wine and music. Hm.... "I should put on my leather pants then, if we'll be heading straight there afterwards. Don't want to miss out on an opportunity to wear them."

Just watching Lynne's face light up was entertainment for Amanda.

"Oh! Yes! You should definitely wear them. And if any drunken jerk hits on you," she added gleefully, "we can practice our 'Go away you dirty little man' magicks. I'm filled with them. I can teach you everything I know."

"Ah, I think I remember some of them," she remarked, her voice slipping into a dreamy, nostalgic tone. "Or at least one. There was this one where I gave one of them a migraine and convinced him to go home and sleep off his hangover before it got even worse."

"I was also thinking of the 'kicking them in the crotch' spell, but that works too."

"Got it."

Chapter Twenty-Seven

"Now."

Muscles Amanda didn't remember possessing ached with every movement as she and Lynne stumbled back to the Sanctuary. They had wound up going to more than one club, dancing in so many places, seeing many interesting people—it was an amazingly busy night, and she had a surprising amount of fun.

Her sides and shoulders, however, didn't agree with her. Amanda rubbed them with a touch of ruefulness. *I guess vampires aren't automatically in good shape like in the movies.* Perhaps it would be a good idea to take up an exercise program or something. She had never had the time for it in college—maybe now was a good time to start getting into shape.

Although if I keep going out dancing, that could be all the exercise I need. How long had she been on the dance floor, anyway? She couldn't recall, and her head still swam in wine.

After a hot shower, she slumped into bed and soon sank into a heavy sleep.

Fragile, soft light and piercing shadows filled her vision. In her dream, something warm pressed against her thigh and moved its way across her stomach.

Amanda stirred but didn't wake. A feeling washed over her, the dim knowledge of firm, silky-smooth hands caressing her body, stroking her skin. As the hands moved over her, so did a cool, mild breeze. Her nipples hardened.

Sounds emerged from deep within her throat, though she was barely cognizant of them. She desperately wanted to be touched, missed the feel of Jesse's hands and his presence beside her as she slept. As if in response to her desires, the pressure from the invisible hands roaming over her sensitive parts grew stronger. The sensations that had been so slight she could have imagined them became a firm, concrete reality.

Awareness crept stealthily over her. She knew she was dreaming and yet she was wide awake—trapped in the border between the dreamworld and the real world. A part of her consciousness still sensed her body on the bed, and yet she also felt herself being touched by unseen hands. The light, gentle fingertip-like sensation made sparks fly all over her legs as they traveled along the insides of her terribly sensitive thighs and stroked her aching stomach. The caresses traveled downwards and softly brushed over her pubic hair. Deep in her belly something primal clenched.

A warm blanket of energy hovered over her skin. It solidified and held her in place, immobile. Invisible hands held her wrists and ankles down, and fingers slipped between the sensitive folds of her skin and swiftly plunged into her wet entrance. Amanda moaned. Did she cry aloud? In her head? She couldn't tell and she was beyond caring as the hand pumped fiercely inside of her, sparking one wave of intense delight after another.

Fingernails raked over her skin, mingling delicious pleasure with pain. A mouth over her nipple, teeth grazing over her skin, biting in places, sucking in others.... She threw her head back, her eyes involuntarily closed, and she experienced an eerily familiar sensation of something sharp sinking into the flesh where her shoulder met her neck. Her hips bucked; powerful surges of feeling overcame her.

You always will be mine, Amanda....

A forceful wave of energy reached inside her chest and squeezed. It was possessive and commanding, and in the sensation lingered an undercurrent of a dark and strange emotion. Alarmed, Amanda tried to struggle out of its grip, but the fingers moved in and out of her slick walls in a way that was blissfully irresistible. Pressure from a thumb rubbed at the throbbing, sensitive bud between her legs. She came hard and fast, the ecstasy gripping both body and mind and rendering her utterly thoughtless and mad. Her surrender to the feverish burst of delight forced her in turn to surrender to the energy possessing her. Even as its waves lapped against her raw insides, it left her helpless.

It wasn't until she awoke the following evening that she knew the voice had been Jesse's. She saw and felt the marks on her skin from where he had apparently marked her with his teeth and nails. But it had been just a dream. Jesse wasn't to be found anywhere in the room. And yet, she sensed his presence as if he were right beside her, following her every move. Amanda felt his piercing gaze, knew somehow he could see her. She sensed his awareness of her, her thoughts and feelings.

She touched her neck, and, sure enough, bumps like a large bite on her skin met her fingertips.

The memory of the energy and hands holding her down came

crashing into her mind with startling clarity. Amanda closed her eyes, not knowing whether she was terrified—or worse yet, turned on. And she wasn't certain which disturbed her most.

Hurriedly, she got dressed, throwing on a pair of black, low-cut, hip-hugging slacks and a red baby doll top. With every article of clothing she put on she tried to banish the thoughts from her mind, the energy from her sphere of sensation—but to no avail. The harder she tried the more it clung to her. The very act of moving against it only tightened its grip around her.

Absently, she fingered the bracelet Jesse had given her. As if she had turned a key inside of the piece of jewelry, the energy she had felt in the dream sprang forth inside her chest. Coursing through her core along with the energy was the very strong presence of Jesse. *No,* she thought, correcting herself, *Turel.* For some reason it was hard to think of him as Jesse while she was experiencing these strange sensations.

What in the world was affecting him so that he had sent her such a dream, and what was happening to her? To them both? Was it something he had been working on in New Orleans? The pain of missing her? What?

Racking her brain, Amanda tried to remember what her relationship with Jesse had been like when she was Sarah, but she remembered very little. The knowledge of how they had met and some of the moments they shared were there, but there were a startling number of blank spots where he was concerned. She frowned. Memories of her family both then and now were mingled to the point of being nearly indistinguishable, but she couldn't recall much of her past relationship with him. Did she block out the memories from herself on purpose, or had he messed with her head at some point?

Something just isn't right about this. She shuddered. Deep down, Amanda knew that Jesse had nothing to do with how messed up her head was, but these holes in what were otherwise crystal clear past memories distressed her greatly.

She practically bolted out of the room, but it didn't matter. It wasn't as if running could help her to get away; the situation was futile. His eyes were still on her, his mind still touched hers, and worse yet, she wasn't even sure that her discomfort over their intimate psychic connection bothered him in the slightest.

In fact, she began to wonder if it excited him.

Amanda gritted her teeth. Maybe it was time to have a chat with Dionysus. Or Apollo. Perhaps arrange a joint conference.

Not like it'd help, came the unbidden thought. She sighed. A part of her, she knew, was painfully aware of the fact that she had gotten herself into this mess—unwittingly, to be certain. Looking back, she couldn't help but wonder that if she had been more aware, she would've sensed something about him which would've made her pause.

But she knew better. She had been attracted to him precisely for that reason. Amanda fell deeply in lust with the passion and the distant sense of danger he had brought into her world. Maybe deep down, she mused, she had wanted an escape from her life and a reason to be someone other than who she had been, and he had provided her with that very excuse.

Or maybe, she thought reluctantly, *the excuse itself had been an excuse all along.*

As the night went on, Amanda was left with the impression of being both small and chained. It was as if she could sense psychic spy cameras on her at all times. Everywhere she went, everyone she spoke to, she both sensed and heard Jesse's reactions to the world around her. She knew he was thrilled to be so close to her and feel everything she did, and other emotions were present too, ones she couldn't quite pin down with words.

It was when she started to intuit him glaring at her disapprovingly that she wondered what precisely was wrong with him.

Nervously, she thought at him, *Do you have a problem or something? Don't you have things to do in New Orleans?* Silence. *How can you do this and focus on your project at the same time?*

She was treated to a vivid and almost satirical mental image of her dancing provocatively on the dance floor from the night before, and saw visions of the men around her eyeing her as if she were candy and they were starving.

I don't approve, he said calmly and simply, as if he were informing the waiter at the restaurant that no, he would not like grated parmesan on his pasta, thank you.

What? she stupidly thought back. Underneath the electricity of the connection between them she perceived static that contained an almost sinister energy from Turel, filled with emotions she could only ascertain as being composed of a dark rage, something which she recognized as being jealousy and...lust? It made no sense.

Don't go out with Asherael to those clubs again. A pause while his words slowly sunk into her mind as something approaching being understandable. Was he seriously ordering her to—*I mean it.*

Amanda froze. She was in a hallway filled with other initiates running to various lectures scheduled for that day and not exactly in a position to be able to make a scene. Nonetheless, she began sputtering, *What the hell do you think you're—*

Just please do what I say.

It was all she could do to keep herself from swearing aloud and alarming several of the people around her. *Why? And if I don't?* she shot back, pissed. What the hell was his problem, and who did he think he was, anyway?

*You'll find out just why, right about...*now.

The moment he uttered the word "now", Amanda's knees nearly buckled as her body gave way to a piercing orgasm which nearly made her pass out. As the last of the white-hot lightning crashed through her, she leaned against a nearby wall and prayed no one around her was empathic or observant enough to notice what had just happened.

Gritting her teeth, she figured tonight would be a good night to spend some time on her shielding project. Surrounded by distracting, overly academic books, she could immerse herself and forget for a while that she was psychically welded to Jesse—who apparently had more tricks up his sleeve than she had originally given him credit for.

It was just beginning to dawn on her just why she might not have remembered too much about her relationship with him in her past life....

* * * *

Lynne frowned at Amanda's back after she left her office. It wasn't that she was displeased with her; she still saw a good deal of the real Amanda coming out of her shell at long last in spite of her obvious stress. But she had the nagging feeling that something deeply troubled the young vampire. Her usual openness had vanished, and she remained surprisingly quiet on a good number of topics about which she had previously babbled freely to her.

Maybe she feels she's changing too fast and it's overwhelming her, she guessed. However, judging from the outfit she had claimed to only "throw on" this evening, her alchemy certainly wasn't harming her any. The young vampire was just…quieter than usual, quiet in a way which made Lynne nervous.

Nonetheless, Amanda had a number of good ideas for her magickal "alert system" for the shield and spoke about them at great length. It was obvious she was planning on spending time in the library versus going out later, and Lynne decided not to press her on the issue.

It could be Amanda is just concerned about letting her work and responsibilities slip due to her social outings, she reasoned with herself, but the nagging feeling persisted. She would have to talk to James, who was fairly skilled at intuiting people either through visions or divination. Maybe he would have some insight.

Or maybe she was just paranoid. It certainly wouldn't be the first time, and she had to admit she possessed a good deal of a big sisterly protectiveness towards Amanda—especially once she had learned the truth of her identity.

With my luck, I'll just wind up smothering the poor girl, she thought ruefully, *and she could use a healthy dose of independence right now, with that stupid Bond with Turel and all. The last thing she needs is me bugging her.*

She sighed. She had to learn to relax and let the poor woman be. Rubbing her head wearily, Lynne wondered if there was ever a moment where she didn't foresee a crisis at every turn because she herself was too damned frazzled to see anything else.

Blood help her, she was turning into James.

Throwing her pencil across the room, she stomped out the door, both frustrated and annoyed with herself.

Chapter Twenty-Eight

"I am so fucking done."

"Y'know, Lyrael, this isn't supposed to be all that difficult," Erik chided her.

Amanda brushed her hair away from her face impatiently. He was right. This was, as far as she could tell, elementary telekinesis. She'd succeeded in doing far more difficult things on previous occasions—after all, weren't the shields currently over the Sanctuary among her best work?

And if anything, this particular activity should be something she'd love—darts. Erik was showing her how to control her skills by having her levitate the darts and aiming them at the dart board before her. Just a little bit of a hover, then a "shove" of the dart. Being a devotee of a god who specialized in projectile weapons should've made this a snap for her, and she was greatly irritated at her inability to focus.

Memories of the dream she'd had the night before kept floating back into her mind, images flickering in at inopportune moments.

The dart hovered in front of her with little effort but shook a bit.

In the dream she was Sarah, like she was in so many of her dreams of late. This time she found herself seated on a bed while Jesse was behind her. He gently brushed her hair. With each stroke of the brush, she lost herself in the sensuality of the contact. It was strangely comforting, and she remembered many times when he had taken care of her in this manner before.

Gritting her teeth, she readied the dart to be aimed at the board. Again.

After he had groomed her long, red hair—*Black,* she insisted, my *hair is black*—she had risen from her seat on the bed, sat on the floor by Jesse's feet, and placed her head on his knee. In response to the gesture, he softly placed his hand on the back of her head. As Sarah she delighted in his gentle but firm touch. It was an intoxicating combination of affection and possession which satisfied some deep longing in the core of her being; at the same time it made parts of her ache. Moisture trickled between her legs as she sat there, warmed by his presence. The ring and chain bracelet on her left hand gleamed, and contentment filled her. However, this disturbed the part of her who identified as Amanda. The intimacy and strangeness of the situation had eventually startled her awake, where she sat for hours gazing at the ceiling. Something about it greatly bothered her, and she wasn't entirely certain why. Nor could she understand why she had experienced the feelings she had when she sat before him as she had in the dream.

The dart dove from her hand into the air and shot itself into the corner of the room like a bird attacking an unsuspecting prey.

Amanda's hand flew to the side of her head as if to prevent it from falling. This wasn't her day.

Erik threw his hands up in the air. "I think you're working too hard. Why don't you take a break, go out with Lynne tonight? Maybe to a jazz club or something," he suggested.

She grimaced. "I wish I could, Theodotos, but...."

"But?" he asked expectantly.

"I, um, don't think Turel likes it when I go to those places," she told him. "I drink too much, I don't know."

He shook his head. "Oh, c'mon. He's not even here, Lyrael. Besides," he added, "it's not like he owns you or anything."

An electric current shot up her spine. *Owns*. Theodotos kept talking to her, but she couldn't hear a word he said.

That was it. That was what had been bothering her this entire time. Her discomfort with the energy between them, the Blood Bond, the way Jesse acted towards her—he acted as if he owned her. To her chagrin, Amanda felt his touch deep inside and realized that in essence, Theodotos was right.

Jesse owned her. And as Amanda, she hated it, as much as she loved it being Sarah.

The emotions warred within her, and she truly couldn't tell which belonged to which. It wasn't as simple as being split into two people; she was still as much Sarah as she was also Amanda. But the details—oh, the details as she added them up in her head made her nearly groan aloud. How had she not realized? Had she been blind? The bracelet he had given her—wasn't it usually called a slave bracelet? She winced, realizing that the innocence she'd had about it from the beginning wasn't due to genuine innocence but willful ignorance. She *knew* deep down where she had such knowledge and had hidden it from herself. As Sarah, she knew just what it had meant to him—to them both: a sign that she belonged to him, always.

Familiar words echoed in her head: *You always will be mine,*

AMANDA....

She wasn't certain what disturbed her more: the realization of how truly strange their relationship was—and is—or how much a part of her yearned for it. Craved it, even, as if he truly satisfied some deep longing within her to belong to him as much as he wanted.

But what did *she* want?

"So what do you think, Lyrael?"

"Hm?" She came to with a start, blinking at Theodotos.

He smiled at her. "Don't play dumb. I know that you miss him and it's hard and all. Do you want to take a break maybe, spend some time alone? Do whatever it is that makes you happy. I just don't want you to get stressed out. I only want to help."

It was safest perhaps, to just nod slowly. "Yeah, I do miss him," she admitted.

"Do you know when he's getting back?"

She shrugged. "Supposedly in a few weeks. Dunno."

Theodotos gave her a sympathetic look. "I'm sorry."

Managing to smile back, she replied, "It's okay. I think I'm going to get a coffee and go meditate or whatever. I-I'll think about the jazz club."

"Good, good." He gestured at the room around him. "Feel free to come in here and practice any time. Besides, it's fun. Really," he added.

"I believe you," she told him. With a wave, she left the room and headed down the long, narrow stairs.

Maybe, if I do an invocation to Apollo...or even Dionysus...and ask them for advice, I could get a clearer head on this.

Once back in her room, she lit some frankincense resin on her charcoal burner and settled into a deep trance.

Jesse's face floated into her mind, but she brushed it away. She had to focus on the presence of her god and get some sense into her before it was too late. As it happened to her all too often these days, she wished that she didn't remember nearly half as much as she did of her lifetime as Sarah.

But, she thought ruefully, *at least it helps me to better understand him and what's going on.*

She focused her energy towards first praying to Apollo. Then she wondered if maybe Dionysus might be the better choice. She didn't know.

Damn it, I'm too scattered. She couldn't focus, let alone be able to perceive any sort of contact from either of her gods. Images both exotic and erotic kept filling her mind.

Amanda shook her head, desperately trying to clear it. Twenty, maybe thirty minutes went by.

What if all of this...madness...takes away my ability to talk to the gods?

Something cold and icy gripped her heart, and she buried her face in her hands.

She pondered what to do next and settled for a more formal invocation of Apollo. She started with a Homeric hymn she had memorized in honor of him and added more incense to the charcoal.

Suddenly, she sensed a presence, but it wasn't that of Apollo but of Jesse. Apparently, whatever she did at the moment had attracted his attention.

Clenching her jaw, Amanda continued with the invocation, trying not to feel his mental eyes upon her.

I MISS YOU. His voice echoed in her mind.

She closed her eyes. Gods help her, why did she love him so damned much? *I MISS YOU TOO.* But she knew she couldn't help it; she'd certainly cared for him before she had two lifetimes of memories crammed into her head of how much she deeply loved and why.

Gods help me, all the same....

HM?

NOTHING, she replied.

* * * *

"Greetings and salutations, Clan Corvus."

Lynne screwed up her face at the cell phone in her hand before placing it back at her ear. "Oh, please, don't pretend to be formal with me, Kalia. You have that caller ID thing, don't you?"

Laughter tinkled on the other end. "Yes, but I couldn't help myself. You almost never call here. What can I do for you, Asherael?"

"Put Turel on the phone for me, please? I need to talk to him."

"One moment." A hollow sound ensued as the phone was placed on a solid surface...and talking in the background. Lynne's keen vampiric ears picked up Kalia's request to someone named Tana to go "fetch" him. *Tana,* she thought absently, *must be new. An Apprentice or a First, maybe.*

"Asherael." Jesse's tone of voice was clear and noncommittal, but she detected a faint note of impatience underlying it. "What's up?"

"Turel, hi. I need a favor from you."

A pause. "What sort of favor?"

"I need you to back off your Childe. She's completely strung out, and you know how good she is at getting to that point."

She sensed him bristling on the other end. "Excuse me?"

"Did you tell her she couldn't go to the clubs with me anymore?" She didn't let him answer as she continued, "Turel, for Blood's sake, she's with *me*. And I promise you the moment a guy even as much as tries to speak to her I'll have him flung out of there with his head first, balls second."

A faint chuckle at the other end. "I just don't like the thought of her dancing like that when I can't be there to watch." He sounded wistful, and Lynne found herself almost feeling sorry for him. Almost.

"Dancing like what? Turel, were you spying on her?"

"No! I mean...come on. You know...it's hard. I can't help but watch sometimes. I miss her, Asherael." His tone grew hard. "You should understand that."

"I guess I do," she admitted. "But you gotta go easier on her. Turel, she's barely stable. She's not at all like Sarah; maybe she never will be."

"I love her anyway."

"I know that you do. And I know how you used to...I dunno...you had your games," she fumbled, searching for the words, "with Sarah, and you two were happy with them. I can't pretend to understand them myself, but whatever. I just want to make sure that she doesn't go over the edge, because believe me, she's been on the verge a few times."

"I know."

"And I'm worried about her."

"As am I. And I don't want to lose her again. I wish that you would trust me. I know what I'm doing."

She fought the urge to exhale in a way that only vampires could. "Do you? Honestly?"

"Asherael, you have never been Blood Bonded. You have no idea what she's up against. She needs to stop fighting the bond and to start trusting me. The more she fights, the harder it becomes for her."

Lynne shook her head, not caring that he couldn't see her. "She's a fighter, Turel. That's her nature."

"I'll keep an eye on her and will try not to make any sudden movements, okay?"

She rolled her eyes. "Just don't make me call you on this stupid phone again, you hear? I can't stand these things, and you know it."

"You know, Asherael," he stated nonchalantly, "you can be a real pain in the ass."

"And you're real swell too, Turel." She hung up on him before he could retort.

* * * *

An hour had passed, and Amanda was still no closer to being able to focus on performing an effective invocation. She stared at the nearby wall pissed off, frustrated, and wishing she had a few darts to start throwing at random objects.

She had tried doing a divination using tarot cards. Nothing. Pendulums. Nada.

"I am *not* performing an animal sacrifice," she grumbled under her breath. But she suspected it was nothing that she wasn't doing for the gods—she just couldn't feel Apollo's presence effectively enough to commune with him, or any of the other gods she tried, either.

Her emotional and mental energy was entirely too focused on bizarre dreams, the Blood Bond, and the turmoil of feelings inside of her.

I can't let this come between me and the gods.

Suddenly, something inside of her snapped, and she stood in the middle of the room with her fists clenched.

"I can't fucking take this anymore," she hissed.

With a quick motion of her arm, she leveled a stack of books on her desk—which crashed rather satisfactorily on the floor.

"I am so fucking *done*."

She took a few steps over to her closet and grabbed her leather pants and a black tank top which barely covered her midriff. In a few minutes, she managed to wiggle out of her clothing and put them on along with a pair of ankle-length black leather boots.

Her outfit garnered a few whistles out of Erik as she walked past him. “Hey, looking good, Lyrael! You going to a club?”

“Hey, Theodotos. You bet,” she replied briskly.

“Great! Have a good time, you hear? Shall I tell Asherael you’re going out?”

She stopped and shrugged. “Sure, why not?” In the back of her mind, she suspected Jesse would be furious since he had asked her not to go anymore, but she was too angry to care.

“Okay, will do! I’ll have her meet you there.”

“Sure thing.” As she walked towards the small, winding stairs to the front door, a smile slowly spread across her face.

Chapter Twenty-Nine

"'Know thyself,' indeed."

Jesse hung up the phone and glanced at the doorway where Kalia stood.

"Well," she stated slowly, her Southern drawl beginning to thicken, "shall I take a quick guess? You've been summoned back to Gladius, haven't you?"

He shook his head. "No, Kalia, just—just needed to talk."

"Ah." She stared down at her necklace and played with it. It was an odd piece made up of jet and snake vertebrae, and Turel couldn't help but stare at it also.

"How's Lyrael?" she asked, not looking up from the necklace.

He thrust his hands into his pockets. Now was a good time for a cigarette, he figured. Shortly before he met Amanda, he had succeeded in kicking the habit—mostly at the urging of Janius, who insisted it was better for his spiritual progress within the Clan—but between the stress of being separated from his lover and the culture of Clan Corvus he found himself lighting up every now and again. Well, more than every now and again, but who was counting them, honestly?

"She's all right, but Asherael is worried about her."

"How come?"

"She's had a rather difficult Turning, and well, I don't know. She has a lot going on. Alchemy, I guess."

Kalia finally glanced up from her necklace and looked directly into Turel's eyes. "Don't you think it might be a good idea to go up there and see her?"

"I, um," stammered Jesse, surprised by this unusual turn of conversation, "I want to, but I'm not done here. You know that."

She arched an eyebrow at him. "Yeah, well," Kalia shrugged, "you *are* her Sire, right? That's a huge responsibility, and she's rather new to this world. I would think that you should be running right up there versus staying down here."

Jesse gazed down at the little coffee table where he had put the phone down. He wanted nothing more than to run back to the city and hold her, take care of her. The sound of her voice would be welcome music after nearly a month spent without her.

Kalia blurted out, "You know, I'm surprised Janius let you come here. Your Childe's in trouble; go to her. We can take care of our own. It's not a big deal, honest."

"Janius...Janius wanted us separated for a time," he admitted with a degree of reluctance. Then the thought hit him, *I wonder if Kalia'd be sympathetic enough to help send me back....*

Blinking at him, she let her necklace fall back onto her chest. "Just what in the Blood are you talking about?"

He winced. This wasn't a conversation he wanted to have as he didn't know her feelings about Blood Bonds, especially to the newly Turned. "She's my bondmate," he replied, his voice low and quiet.

Her eyes widened. "Blood Bonded? You two are *Blood Bonded*? For Blood's sake, you get your ass back up there to New York. What the *hell* was Janius thinking?" she asked the ceiling.

Turel, much to his amusement, almost expected it to reply to her. The Order had its share of unusual people, and the Magistra of Clan Corvus was certainly no exception.

Attempting to protest—or at least appear that he was—he stated, "But, Magistra, I can't leave without the Magister's permiss—"

"Oh, *go* already. I'll handle Janius. If you want to fly back after a few weeks up there, be my guest, but I'm not going to be held responsible for your sanity *or* hers if you don't, y'hear?"

Jesse smiled. This was almost too easy.

"I'll have someone arrange for a flight out tonight if possible. If not, you'll be on the next plane to New York tomorrow night. In the meantime," she lowered her voice, "I think you could use a drink." She grabbed him by the arm and led him to the next room—a tiny kitchen filled mostly with wine and liquor bottles.

"It's—it's really not necessary," he insisted. "Maybe just a cigarette."

Kalia laughed, a deep, mischievous belly laugh. "Now you stop it with your 'vampire purity' crap. I never did understand Janius's crazy theories," she stated with an eye-roll, waving her hand behind her as if to ward herself off from Clan Gladius's Magister.

She grabbed a bottle of Southern Comfort and another one of what appeared to be amaretto liqueur.

"I think it comes from that Golden Dawn background of his," he theorized.

"What-the-fuck-ever. Here, have a drink." She handed it to him, and he took a cautious sip, thankful he had done some magick earlier to allow him to digest food and drink more easily. It tasted good, but it was pretty strong—rather like Southern Comfort with a hint of almond, and he was more accustomed to drinking wine and beer than he was hard liquor.

"You don't have any soda to go into this, do you?"

She smacked her hand to her forehead. "I knew I forgot something. Go in the fridge, it should be on the top shelf."

"Thanks." As he rummaged through the fridge to find something else to put in his drink—club soda, Sprite, anything—Kalia continued talking.

"So, when are you going to tell me about how you met this woman and why the hell you Blood Bonded to her so damned quickly?"

He smirked and poured some soda into his cup. Now the reason for the offering of alcohol became apparent. "I met her almost by accident. I stumbled across a reference to her research online—she was a grad student at NYU," he explained, "doing a paper on Ancient Greek and Roman magick. And she's gorgeous and a fellow mage besides. How could I not love her?" He sipped his drink. Much better, but could use something else to balance it out. *Maybe orange or cranberry juice. Eh, screw it.* He wasn't about to protest—after all, he had his pride. Taking another healthy swallow of the drink, he figured it might be nice to get a little more buzzed than he'd originally planned on, anyhow.

"Greek and Roman magick? Cool," commented the magistra. "I see now why Janius actually agreed to this little arrangement between you two. Does she happen to know about Minervia, or what?"

Choking on his drink, he barely managed to get out, "Funny you should ask that...."

* * * *

Late that night, Amanda left the club and walked back to the Sanctuary, deep in thought.

She had sensed Jesse's presence once, perhaps twice, while she was intoxicated and on the dance floor, but there was no reaction. Not a word or a gesture. It puzzled her greatly and left her feeling curiously mixed.

It occurred to her maybe she was, of all things, disappointed. Perhaps she wanted him to react in some way to her going to the club against his wishes.

Blank, just blank?

Lynne hadn't been able to come out that evening due to meetings and work, but Amanda had a good time regardless of her friend's absence. She stopped to reflect for a moment. Friend. She had a friend here, one whom she remembered as having been a friend to her in her past memories—one who had even been a friend before either of them knew about her past. Maybe this friend was someone whom she could talk to, if only she could come out of her shell as Amanda for a few moments by means other than dancing or drinking.

And could she even talk to Jesse? The part of her who was Sarah longed to run up to him, apologize for not listening to his request to stay away from the clubs, and explain that she badly needed something, anything, to take some time away from being trapped inside the walls of her mind. Being at the club gave her a sense of ecstasy, in that classical *ex-stasis* or out-of-body experience she craved. Amanda was no longer comfortable living in her own skin, but knew she wouldn't be happy being Sarah again, either.

Who was she really, anyway? She rapidly concluded that knowing herself was impossible and that the only ones who did were blissfully dull and ignorant. *"Know thyself," indeed,* she thought ruefully. Did Apollo mean for people to figure this out for themselves, or let them think that they could truly ever know themselves?

As she strolled down the street, she walked past a blonde girl in her late teens talking on her cell phone. "Oh, God, I'm sooooo drunk, it's sooooo late, my mom is gonna *kill* me...."

Amanda's heart ached. She hadn't even allowed herself to think much about her family these days. What did they think of her absence? Had they tried to reach her? They must think she had been abducted or was dead by now.

Out of the corner of her eye she saw a payphone and, like a marionette, she was suddenly compelled to twist around and walk towards it. Before she knew it, she gripped the phone in her hand.

I shouldn't be doing this....

She swallowed and with a trembling hand put in a quarter into the slot of the payphone and dialed her parents' number.

Ring, ring....

"Hello?" Her mother's voice sounded groggy, as to be expected given she had just been woken up at what she knew her mother would consider to be an absurd hour of the morning. Her parents always had gone to bed earlier than her, and she figured it must be around four.

There was so much she wanted to tell her mother. She was in love, she did well in her classes, everything was great but everything was also hell at the same time. So much was changing around her, inside of her, and she didn't know who she was anymore or what she wanted. All she desired so desperately was to hear a familiar, comforting voice telling her it was okay, she was okay, and everything would get better soon. She thought of all of the times she had gone to her mom in her teenage years and cried about classes or social drama in high school. And her father, the one who had supported her in earnest the entire time she was in college and had even bought her the statue of Apollo.

"Hello?" she heard again, this time louder and more insistent. Amanda bit her lip, the phone almost vibrating by her ear as she failed to hold it steady. What could she possibly tell her mother now? *Hi, Mom, I fell in love with a vampire, and he turned me into one too. How are you? How is Dad*? Blood-tears stung her eyes, and she was never more distant from herself as she was then.

Mom, I'm so sorry....

Squeezing her eyes shut, she hung up the phone and ran back to the Sanctuary.

* * * *

Lynne frowned as she stared at the little bit of annoying metal that was her cell phone. One voice mail message. It couldn't have been James because she'd just seen him a few minutes ago, and he was far more likely to pay her a visit in her office or relay a message via someone else than he was to call her while they were both in town.

Checking the caller ID, her frown grew more pronounced. It was the number at Clan Corvus.

Egads, what now?

She pressed a few keys on the cell phone pad and listened to the message:

"Asherael, I'm headed on the next flight out to New York. By the time you get this message I'll probably already be there. I had to act quickly due to the time zones, as I don't want to get caught by sunrise. Kalia talked me into this, so you can blame her. She said

that I can come back in a few weeks if they need me. And you'll be happy to know that I gave Amanda no grief tonight and she seemed like she was having a good time.

"Oh, and by the way—please don't tell her about this until tomorrow. I'd like to surprise her. Just tell her tomorrow evening that I'm back in town and looking forward to seeing her again. Ciao."

Lynne growled and nearly threw her cell phone across the room. Great, just what she needed. Just what everyone needed right now, in fact. What in the Blood was he thinking? The timing couldn't have been worse.

"Turel, you—you fucking idiot," she spat. Not only would the magister be less than happy, but the likelihood of Amanda getting any breathing room after his return would probably be minimal. The young vampire had undergone a lot of changes in just under a month, but was it enough?

* * * *

In the dream, Amanda kept taking off and removing the slave bracelet. It seemed that each time she did so, the strange energy that gripped her heart only increased in intensity.

Frustrated, she burst into the next room, startling a surprised looking Jesse.

"I can't take this anymore, Jesse," she told him furiously. "I can't. I want this resolved, now. Or you to get out of my head. Once and for all. I mean it."

Like a dam had burst, she continued to ramble, her words running into each other. "I can't make any sense out of these memories, and they disturb me. This bracelet disturbs me. You disturb me. I love you but you disturb me. I don't know what to make of you, or what you want from me. I mean, I do," she added, "but I don't. Not really. And I miss my parents. I tried calling them tonight but I didn't speak. All my mom kept saying was 'Hello', and I couldn't reply back. I didn't know what to say. I'll probably get into trouble. Am I even supposed to talk to them again? I know that I'm supposed to keep my life here secret and all, but does that mean I can't even talk to my own mother again?

"Jesse, I love you and love being with you, but I miss my mom. And these thoughts and feelings and memories I have disturb me, and I don't know what to do with either you or them."

Jesse stared at her for a long time, during which she realized she was dreaming. Without a word, he reached out and gave her a comforting hug. Before she had a chance to react, she woke up.

Chapter Thirty

"Now I'm free."

Amanda leaned back into the chair and continued to chat with Lynne. It was rapidly approaching four o'clock in the morning, judging by both her sense of time and the growing sensation that light was about to arrive to the outside world within the next few hours.

That and her exhaustion.

She had spent the better part of the time rambling to a sympathetic Lynne, who was still in the midst of working on grading various papers from her other students.

"Frankly, Amanda, I haven't always gotten along with your Sire," Lynne stated in a matter-of-fact way. "But still," she added with caution, jotting down notes in her book as she was speaking to her friend on the opposite end of the couch in the back of the room. The young vampire was amused that Lynne had brought her work with her to the coffeehouse, but it was better than working back at the Sanctuary.

She froze. "But still what?"

Lynne shrugged. "I suppose that no one told you, but I hear that he's in town. I haven't had confirmation of it, though."

Something icy gripped Amanda's heart, and for once it wasn't some odd effect from her Blood Bond with Jesse. He was back in the city? And he hadn't contacted her?

And worse yet, did she even want him to?

Lynne fiddled with the binding of her notebook and began tapping her pen on it. She seemed a little distracted.

Tap, tap.

Well, maybe that was a small understatement. Lynne looked a bit more distracted than usual. Even for her.

"Anything else?" Amanda asked impatiently. She tilted her head down to look at her. "Lynne?"

Lynne shook her head, as if waking up from a dream.

Amanda regarded her with a frown. "Lynne, what's going on?"

The blonde vampire drew in breath, then let it out slowly. "Sorry, I was thinking of something else."

"What?"

"Well, your meditations with Dionysus. Have they told you

anything?"

Dionysus, god of life, death, and rebirth. Ecstasy. Unrestrained passion and freedom. The vine. The wine. The blood. All of these images floated into Amanda's head. "Yes, I'm learning quite a bit... and quite a lot of it is very relevant for me. I...," she paused, then smiled, "Honestly, I don't know how I got along without him. Even towards Apollo, I've had a Dionysian streak. I think I was just afraid...."

The freedom, the joy of living. The life. The unlife. The ecstatic energy searing through Amanda's veins and gripping her heart. And yet at the same time, the pain of loss and separation from her family, her old life, and everything she had to leave behind—not to mention the intensity of her feelings towards Jesse and not knowing what to do about them.

"Of letting go?" Lynne finished for her.

She's unusually perceptive.

Amanda nodded slowly. Lynne smiled at her.

"Well, you might enjoy this. This," she gestured around her, "this life more. Get to know it better."

"Even so, I...."

Lynne's eyes narrowed, and she leaned forward.

"Lynne?"

"Amanda, I think that you should confront Turel and deal with him. Once and for all. I think that Dionysus would appreciate it, and you've certainly grown since he left."

She bit her lip and folded her arms. "I...really don't know."

"No, I mean it. Do it. Seriously. He deserves a lesson. And you need to free yourself from holding back your feelings. Do it. Be free. I know that you're upset with him. Maybe you just need to be honest with him about how you feel. You two are going to be together for the rest of your unlives, after all."

Amanda stared at her for a moment. Then with a swiftness she didn't know she possessed, she went into her purse and grabbed her knife—a beautifully ornate, ivory handled knife with gold etched designs in the ivory. Originally she had procured it as a ceremonial dagger but she thought her rapidly evolving ideas for it would be just as suitable if not the same thing. She gripped it at her side, the gesture hardly noticed by the humans around her.

With a grin, Lynne poked her. "That's a little extreme, don't you think? I wasn't advising killing him."

Amanda pursed her lips. "No, wasn't thinking of that," she replied seriously to her friend's jest. "But scare him a little...that could be fun."

The elder vampire couldn't reply, she was laughing too hard.

Amanda rose, grabbed her purse, and walked out the door, leaving Lynne smiling after her.

The nearly full moon hung over the clear sky, the air blowing through the streets like a memory haunting the alleyways. Amanda walked briskly; her shoes made very little sound as she made her way through the streets. She went down the streets with great speed and grace, though she took care not to move much faster than the average human. Quiet and subtle.

Then, with a quick prayer to Dionysus, she did what she had never done before—she opened up her mind to the psychic bond, the Blood Bond that had bound both of their minds together since she was Turned.

Lynne was right. He was here, right in the city—not much more than a few blocks away from her. She sensed him. And she knew he could sense her as she moved through the streets.

I should have a bite to eat before I find him, she thought to herself, trying not to giggle at her unintentional pun. She found a bum asleep on the streets and, with a practiced grace, took a long drink from his wrist before letting him go. The wrist fell back upon his chest like only so much weight, and she stood there, satisfied, her senses heightened. She wiped her mouth and nonchalantly kept going. As she strolled through the city, she became more a part of the night and the shadows. Night, after all, held its sacredness—she knew that from her studies of Dionysus and her experiences with the god. And that sacredness beckoned to her, and she opened up to it, surrendering completely to the night and its embrace.

It was *good.* Most importantly, it was right.

Amanda had no idea where her courage came from. Maybe it was from Lynne's support or her advice. Maybe she finally realized that running from him just wasn't the answer.

Or maybe she really had fucking had it.

She made her way quickly in the other direction, her dark hair sailing behind her. These days, she wore it loose. Tonight she was dressed in a black jacket, a burgundy lace top, and her now usual pair of black leather pants and boots. He probably wouldn't recognize her, she realized, but knew that the thought was silly. He'd know her anywhere.

He won't know what hit him. The thought entered her mind like a breeze blowing in, then blowing out again, leaving her feeling touched by it even as it left.

Amanda gripped onto the blade with her full strength, her ethereally white skin growing whiter around the knuckles. Having seen a shadow, her dark eyes twitched to the right. She knew too well that it wasn't whom she was looking for, but she knew that he was close by.

On the street, he stood holding nothing but a cigarette, looking as if he was waiting for someone to arrive. There he stood in his usual black leather jacket, black dress pants, and boots—something of an odd mixture of goth and prep. Amanda remembered with a smile what she had thought when she'd first met him: "business goth." She had no idea what shirt he was wearing under the jacket, but she figured black or some other dark color. She smelled him from where she stood. Leather, cigarette smoke, light cologne, and the faintest trace of blood coated the scent, and the rest was him and the particular trace of scent that she always detected from other vampires. She stopped abruptly, her lips curving into a smile.

Looking at him, she realized that as much as she was frustrated with him and their Bond, she also deeply loved him. Not just because she had been Sarah, but because she was Amanda. The thought was a light shining in her.

The wind blew, but otherwise the night was almost deathly quiet. She heard the trees shaking, the leaves rubbing together in a symphony of sounds that could only be made at night, deep in the heart of the night. Images, bright and piercing, went through her head. She remembered how they met, back when she was human and didn't know vampires really existed, nor cared. The night they met he'd looked pretty much the way he did now: calm, collected, as if somehow he were a part of the night as he moved through it. She felt it in him even as he stood still. Like nature, like he was a part of nature. Amanda didn't have the words for it then, but she did now. At last she understood. Dionysus had sent him to her all along, sent him long before she could possibly be ready for it.

Did she insult the god by being afraid, by running away from him? By blocking him out of their Bond and telling him to stay away from her?

She shook her head, and her whole body trembled, but she knew it had to be done regardless of the consequences. She had to confront him. Why did he act the way he did around her? Couldn't he see she was confused enough inside without him adding to it? Why did he order her to stay away from the clubs? Why did he make her feel the things she did?

"You can't tell me what to do anymore; now I'm free," she whispered. "Now I'm free, now I'm free...." The words fell from her lips but they failed to calm the savage emotions in her breast and the whirlwind of thoughts in her mind.

She continued to watch him smoke his cigarette across the street. Her eyes burned, and her head was light. Giddiness filled her, and her insides were sinking as if she were drunk. Drunk on the spiritual wine in her soul, burning into her.

She licked her lips.

Then she made her way out of the shadows and across the street to where he stood.

He took a long drag from his cigarette and released the smoke slowly from his lips, all the while staring at her. Jesse had seen her coming, long before she came. This she knew too.

"I was wondering when you'd get here," he said to her calmly.

"Since when did you smoke?" she inquired with equal tranquility. But if her heart could still beat, it would've been racing.

Jesse shrugged. "I picked up the habit again when I was in New Orleans. Stress, I guess."

He seemed very calm, very much at ease, very sure of himself. She wondered briefly how much of it was a mask and how much of it was the calm inside of him. But she knew him too well for that. Already she felt the emotions swelling up inside of him into a huge tangle, a volcanic mess of passion that threatened to erupt to the surface.

He was very much excited to see her...and something else—another emotion that welled up inside of him—that she couldn't quite place.

Then she realized what it was.

Fear. For whatever reason, he was afraid of finally confronting her. After all of the time he spent teaching her, making love to her, lecturing her, fucking her, talking to her, touching her, uniting with her psychically, mentally, spiritually, physically, and emotionally... the half images floated into her mind, most of them not her own memories but Sarah's. The more she invoked the night and Dionysus, the more her previous life came into memory. Blood-sweat, knives, teeth, hands, bodies clinging, the sounds, the sensations, being tied to the bed, half fearful out of her mind and somewhere on the brink of ecstasy in the literal Greek sense of the word, *extasis*, outside of herself. And *he* was afraid.

Of her. It didn't make sense. Shouldn't she be the one to be afraid?

And of course, she realized, with a nod from Dionysus, that she was indeed afraid. Afraid, and.... She braced herself, then spoke. "So. Jesse."

He looked at her, his dark brown eyes meeting hers. She tried not to blink or look away, but stared him down.

"Yes."

Her knife was already carefully pocketed where she could get at it quickly, and she was pretty certain that he didn't see it. "We need to talk."

Still he gazed upon her with eyes as dark as hers and slowly nodded. "Yeah." He finished his cigarette, ground it beneath his boot, and walked towards her.

The night seemed to shift and shimmer around them as they walked down the street. It was like it took on an electricity of its own, moving as they moved, and they blended with it. They and the night were one.

"I didn't expect to see you back...so soon."

"Or at all," he interrupted her, his voice rising in volume. "I would've thought that you knew me better than that."

She sighed.

"I missed you, you know."

Smiling slightly, she replied, "I missed you too."

"So, tell me...why did you go to the club after all?" His cold voice annoyed her. She didn't like it. By his tone she could tell that this conversation was going to end in a fight if she wasn't careful. It occurred to her that Jesse was terribly good at pushing all of her buttons, like he'd been doing it his whole life. And longer. She was loath to admit it, but some of those buttons she didn't mind him pushing. Not at all.

"Well...tell me this much," Amanda demanded. "Do you plan on staying, or what? Do you have to go back or are you done?"

Jesse shrugged. "Does it matter? You seem to be doing better since I left. Maybe if I left again, you'd do even better." He sounded cold, detached. It set her off.

She hissed at him, baring her teeth. He barely even blinked at her reaction. “Do you really think that I, for a second—”

Jesse grabbed her by her wrist. She had forgotten how fast he was at doing it. One second her hand was by her side and the next it was in his grip. Amanda cursed under her breath, for when he touched her skin the electricity in the air leaped from him to her, and something in her lower stomach tightened. She gritted her teeth and tried to pull back. But she knew once he got a hold of her hand that she wouldn’t be able to get away from him, so she settled for glaring at him instead. Thankfully, at this point she had enough control over her abilities that objects weren’t randomly flying through the air, around them and at them, but she wondered how long that control would last.

“What is it?” she asked irritably. But her voice barely registered above a whisper.

He said nothing to her, but continued walking, his pace increasing with every step. In spite of his speed, she managed to keep up with him. The moon raced above them, and the air in the night picked up its howling. The night and the air moved with them, and the buildings went by her blindingly fast. Shadows and buildings and street corners raced past them in a blur as he dragged her along.

They turned a corner, and he forced her into an abandoned warehouse. Her night vision observed broken beams in the ceiling, wooden crates everywhere, rats running around the room, and broken windows. The windows let in moonlight, but not much. Darkness enveloped them, and aside from the occasional scratching of rats, Amanda heard nothing.

They both stood in the shadows glaring at each other.

After a long, charged silence, he spoke. “So, what did she tell you?”

“Who?” she asked.

His eyes flashed in the darkness. “Don’t give me ‘who.’ You know who. Asherael. What shit is she feeding you now?”

Amanda blew air out of her mouth in an imitation of a sigh. “Nothing, Jess. Only that you were back.”

“Don’t give me that. I—”

Hissing again, she took a step towards him. “That’s all she said. I don’t know what the hell you want to know, but that’s all she’s said about you or anything regarding you.”

"Oh, really."

"Really."

He leaned up against a crate behind him and watched her. It seemed like a fire lit his face, but no light flared, no flame. His dark eyes suddenly lit up from within, and she was held there for a moment, staring into them.

Then he reached for her side where she kept her knife. But she was quicker. The knife was in her right hand, blade pointed at the floor. Her grip kept it by her side, and her feet separated to support herself on the floor in a defensive pose.

Jesse, no longer leaning against the crate, stood and stared at her. "Okay, then," he spoke quietly. "If you want to kill me, then—"

She lunged at him, but not with the knife. Her body had moved from a defensive to an offensive position in less time than it took for him to blink.

* * * *

She reminded him of a leopard, and the imagery made him pause. *Where's Apollo?* he thought. He was so used to her controlled, almost restricted movements. This was more fluid, more free—uninhibited. She was in another god's grip, and it startled him. This was something that he hadn't expected to find after he had returned. She was a wild woman, with her dark hair flowing around her, loose and free. Something about it thrilled him, but he couldn't help but feel a degree of anxiety. And he had no clue what to do, nor what to make of this new but...eerily familiar Amanda.

He stopped and stared at her, realizing what it was in her that he recognized. Gods, she looked just like Sarah. But Sarah was lighthearted and carefree—Amanda seemed to have a darker, fiercer streak that he couldn't recall seeing in Sarah.

What happened to her? he thought numbly, not knowing if he liked the changes he saw in her or not.

He knew that it was still her, minus a lot of baggage that he thought that she'd never lose. It shook him. Then he realized that what shook him wasn't just the idea, but that he was literally shaken off of his feet from her knocking him to the ground. One moment he spoke to her calmly, and the next she was on top of him, both of them on the floor, with her holding his hand—the same hand that had previously gripped her wrist—down on the ground with her left hand and gripping the knife with her other.

He laughed. "What, you're going to drag this out? Just do it already. Stab me. Kill me. That's what you're here for, right? What Asherael wants and what you want, I'm sure."

* * * *

She realized that she had been right—he really had no idea what hit him. "Shut up," she hissed.

He turned his head towards her wrist and brushed his lips against it. The sensation of his mouth on her skin caused the tightening sensation in her lower stomach to return, and the electricity flowed through her again, that electricity that consumed the night around them and now threatened to consume them both as well. His actions and her reaction to them sent a stream of white-hot, searing rage down through the center of her, and she held his hand tighter, her nails digging into his flesh.

In response, he sank his fangs into her wrist. The sudden sharpness of them coupled with the joining of their energies with the mingling of her blood in his mouth opened up whatever shields she had put up between them, and the Blood Bond returned with full force. They were in each other's minds now, and the ecstasy of the blood-sharing that she experienced was impossible to hide from him. At the same time, the pleasure that he had from taking her blood, his lips on her wrist, was something that she could no longer ignore either.

Amanda ceased to care. She had separated from the rest of her already, the madness of the pleasure taking over her. On top of all of the sensations, she rode it like a wild beast. All around her and inside of her was aflame.

I knew that you couldn't get away from me, she heard.

Amanda glared at him and brought the knife down to his throat, then the center of his chest. For a moment, they remained in that position, the two of them made flesh and blood and blood-sweat, the emotions bouncing back and forth between them and increasing tenfold with each reflection. The anger, the ecstasy, the passion, the rage, the hurt, the fear—it all melded into one, and they became a statue dedicated to the fires lit within them, frozen at that instant.

He looked into her eyes, and she lightly brought down the knife. It nicked the center of his chest, and she drew a line with the blade, piercing the skin enough to make him bleed. The fires between them grew larger, and it seemed that his eyes were a dark, never ending abyss.

Chapter Thirty-One

"I want you to admit it."

In that stillness Amanda smelled his blood, the blood that came to the surface of the cut that she had made. Still gripping his wrist with her left hand, she stabbed the knife into the floor beside them. Supporting her body by both of her hands, she swiftly brought her head down, her tongue slowly licking up the blood on his chest.

The overwhelming silence between the two of them drove her insane, and all she heard was his thoughts, emotions, and energy in her head, and in that moment, realized that the madness was mutual. Of all of the crazy things that she had never thought of, the madness that drove her to blood-tears due to the Blood Bond, this suffocating madness and intimacy, was mutual. Amanda wasn't alone in the sharing, wasn't the only one ripped open in the deepest part of her—Jesse was with her, echoing everything she experienced as his own. A sudden, swift burst of intimacy unlike any of the smoldering, almost suffocating closeness that she had uncomfortably sensed before assaulted her, and she knew at once after all that they had gone through that they shared it. A moment in which they both stood on level ground, and she had done it. It was in her hands, the control was all hers.

Or was it? For even as she licked the blood off of his chest, feeling and tasting the blood and the skin underneath, she knew that she wanted more and probably wouldn't be able to control herself. Then an appealing idea hit her. With a quick jerk, she yanked the blade out of the floor. She was losing it, losing herself even as she hovered over him, teasing him with her tongue and her blade. She completely had him, and he completely had her. And the god beckoned her forth, and she knew in her heart that she was free. This was her freedom. But it was an unexpected freedom, and a freedom that she hadn't wanted.

Even that she wasn't so sure of—did she really not want this? Her mouth parted, and she raised her head from his chest. He released his fangs from her wrist, then they looked at each other again.

I was supposed to win, to get back at him, she thought dumbly, somewhere in the back of her mind where she was uncertain if even Jesse could reach. He licked at her wrist, and she became extremely conscious of the wetness between her legs.

He stared at her, and his eyes narrowed with amusement. Something hard pressed into her stomach.

I can smell you, he said, the words accompanied by a strong blast of too familiar, passionate lust that she sensed empathically from him.

Her eyes widened, and she brought herself up to a standing position, releasing his wrist, her grip on the blade in her right hand growing tighter. Amanda glared down at him, and he raised himself on one foot, then another, very slowly, and stood up to look at her.

Jesse's eyes drifted from hers down to her chest, her hips.... "I love your outfit." It was almost a purr, the words loud in the large room, the only sound that either of them had heard or uttered for what had at this point seemed like ages.

She inhaled and heard it echo in his head. She understood about inhaling now. It was more like a habit, a vampire imitating a human, wanting to look alive. Be alive. As the sound echoed, she heard another voice in her head and knew at once it wasn't Jesse's.

This game that you two are playing won't last long...it'll last forever.

She began circling around Jesse slowly. She knew the voice to be that of Dionysus, but didn't know what exactly he was trying to tell her. It occurred to Amanda briefly that Jesse may be able to hear the voice as well, but if he did, it didn't register on his face. The words were genuinely for her and her alone. In buying time, she hoped to hear the rest of the message before Jesse could act next.

Not because you two are both too stubborn to admit to each other that you care, but because neither of you are able to handle being so close to each other.

This angered her. It was true. She lunged at Jesse again and backed him into the crate. He grabbed onto both of her wrists as she shoved him into the crate.

You especially are bad at it, and it is you being bad at it that is causing you to push his buttons.

She snarled, but she wasn't sure who she snarled at, at this point: Jesse, Dionysus...or herself. Somehow in the process of reacting to the comments in her head, she violently leaned towards Jesse, and in what seemed like something out of a dream, her tongue and mouth found his, and she kissed him.

When their lips touched, a surge of heat flared in the center of her chest, burning her all the way into the pit of her stomach. The electricity danced like flames in the air as their tongues danced feverishly in their mouths, playing with each other and tasting what each had to offer. The kiss became quite heated, and the Bond between them fueled the fire, adding a rich intensity. During the kiss they merged, and she lost what control she had left of herself. Amanda didn't know exactly what transpired in between, but somehow she leaned on him up against the crate and the next they were on the floor with Jesse on top of her, still kissing her, and his jacket underneath them. He had one leg firmly pressed between her legs, one hand holding down both of her wrists—the knife had fallen somewhere, she didn't know where—and his other hand did amazing things to her under her lace shirt.

Amanda, when are you going to admit to yourself how you feel about him and how he makes you feel?

She couldn't take it anymore and snarled back to Dionysus, *Now is not the time to be having this conversation.*

Oh, yes it is.

Jesse's lips closed around the skin between her shoulder and neck. Fangs pierced her skin, and she no longer had any thoughts left in her head. They were lost somewhere between the union of flesh, blood, teeth, and ecstasy. She started kicking at the ground, unable to keep her body still, the intensely pleasurable sensations filling her body and mind. But he gripped her wrists tighter. What remained of the shields that she had so carefully created between them shattered like fragile glass. Amanda felt everything that he experienced as her own emotions and sensations, experienced both the sweet bliss of his lips on her skin and the taste of her own blood. What always unnerved her most about the contact between them was the feeling of him sensing her. There was no space between them, nothing left unshared.

All of that was gone now, and there was nothing but the release, the passion, and the intense rapture of it all.

Jesse removed his mouth from her shoulder, and while still gripping her wrists with one hand, he used the other to remove her blouse. The bra underneath came off with a slice of the knife—he had found her blade, then—and he tied her wrists together over her head with the bra.

Bras are useful after all….

Amanda wasn't certain if that comment was meant for her to hear, spoken to her, or just something he happened to have thought.

Then she realized that he had both of his hands free and she had none, and those hands of his gently massaged her breasts while he nibbled on her shoulders, her neck, occasionally biting her but only lightly. He was teasing her, and she knew it—and he knew that she knew it.

He ran his tongue down her neck and paused at her breast. Then he licked her nipple, slowly. His tongue flicked over it several times, until suddenly his teeth closed around it. A scream echoed in the room, and she realized it was her own. A surge of lust and passion coursed through her being, and she couldn't tell anymore if it was her own or his. It no longer mattered; their emotions were united as they bounced off each other, increasing each other's passion and pleasure.

And the Blood Bond pumped between them at full force.

Jesse sucked at her nipple hard, his fangs digging into her breast. He licked up the blood that sprang to the surface, and the sounds at the back of her throat grew louder. His hands caressed her body, over her skin, sometimes feather-like and silky and other times rough and passionate, and she couldn't keep track of where and what he touched. Before she knew it, he'd unbuckled and unzipped her leather pants. A cool brush of air swirled on her stomach. While one of his hands played with one of her nipples, he bit the other nipple as his other hand made his way down her pants. She wore no underwear, and she knew this pleased him. His fingers played and teased the folds between her legs, and one of his fingers made its way inside of her. She cried out and arched underneath him. He moved his leg slightly to separate her legs and continued to probe inside her and bite her.

He grew impatient and tugged at the sides of her pants until they came down her hips and over her knees. He tore them off and threw them to the side. She now lay naked on top of his jacket on the floor, her hands still bound by her bra over her head.

Amanda looked at him, and he stared back at her. Then he lunged towards her, kissing her fiercely, his fangs pressing into her lips. At one point he drew blood, and they both tasted it. His tongue played with the blood on her lips and licked them as he brought his hand to her shoulder, then traveled down her chest to her breast again to tease and pull at her nipple. His other hand slid up and down her inner thigh, his touch both slow and light. She became aware that the voices in her throat were rather loud at this point, and she hoped that anyone passing by the abandoned warehouse wouldn't hear them, even at this hour.

Fuck it. Did Jesse smile back at her for that thought?

His fingers that had been caressing her thigh a moment ago made it to the sensitive folds between her legs and began stroking them—sometimes rubbing them roughly, other times feeling like so much silk touching her bare skin. He moved his head down over her chest. He held the knife in his hand, and as it was and had always been between them, she knew the thoughts that passed in his head and what he was about to do to her.

Fast. He was so fast. The knife had cut her chest with the barest of scratches before she had a chance to blink, but it was enough to bring the blood to the surface. He plunged his fingers into her and licked the blood that trickled down her chest and her breasts. She gave in to the human urge to gasp, too many sensations swimming around her, and she was ready to climax.

Jesse knew it and with great speed pulled his fingers out. With a few, quick motions, he removed his top; then the zipper came down. His pants and his shirt fell to the floor, one after the other. He too wasn't wearing any underwear, she noticed with a slight smirk. The odd thought crossed her mind that he had anticipated this... encounter. It wasn't impossible.

He nodded. She smiled back.

He came down on his knees in front of her and parted her legs with them. Leaning forward, he licked off the remaining blood on her chest, and with his hands, raised her hips towards him and plunged deep inside of her. She growled in the back of her throat as the two rocked back and forth violently on the floor—a floor hard and painful against her sensitive back, but she didn't care. She arched her back to meet his thrusts, and his arms held her sides.

Amanda felt herself losing it, slipping away off into someplace sharp but distant and ecstatically surreal. His head came down again, and he bit into her shoulder. She screamed, overwhelmed by the intensity of the sensations wrapping around her and within her. She felt him inside of her both physically and in her head. Again, as it was before, the energy circled around her heart, pulling her towards him, deep into the center of her being. The spiritual connection between them grew into a white hot fire, and when she came, she was ripped apart into a million pieces and scattered across the room. He cried out, feeling her come, and thrust into her again. She experienced his climax when he did, and she came again, screaming, and he whispered in her mind.

"What?" she asked, drowsy. Her insides still begged for release, to ride that huge wave of body bliss as it dragged her under.

I want you to admit that I am your Sire and your Master.

"*What*?" she sputtered. Somehow, in her excitement she'd managed to get part of her body unpinned from his. As she sat up, he grabbed her wrists. She couldn't stop herself from looking into his eyes—and nearly drowned in their dark depths.

Please. I want you to admit it.

"Admit to what?" The afterbliss rapidly faded into panic, but between her legs she was both sore and throbbing—and not due to the physical activity, either.

"Amanda...." He gripped her wrists tighter, and she struggled to get free.

Her eyes narrowed as her irritation level rose. "Jesse, if this is some fetish of yours, I'll understand, but—"

He silenced her with his mouth, and she sunk into a vast, sensuous abyss.

Just say it. His words caressed her mind. They swarmed over her skin, slipped themselves into her most intimate places, and ultimately drove her to the brink of madness. Where was Dionysus now? Most likely he was as much of a force in all of this as was Jesse. Or maybe he'd snuck out the back door to leave her with the consequences of her handiwork.

With his mouth still on hers and his tongue teasing the wetness of her mouth, she could only mentally reply, *I shouldn't have come here like this.*

He chuckled. *Oh, you* came, *all right.*

Amanda bristled and with a great effort removed her lips from his. "I mean it, Jesse."

She sensed him withdrawing from her, and where he was inside of her became an icy void.

"I see," he replied, his voice calm...but she felt the silent accusations.

"That's not what I mean, and you know it," she hissed.

Jesse gazed at her, and with that one glance a weight pressed into her chest. "I ask you for one thing, and you want to run screaming out of here. Why is this so difficult for you?"

"Because I—" She stopped. The words for what she experienced right now just weren't there. He had tormented her in her dreams, suffocated her with the strength of the Blood Bond, and overwhelmed her with the insanity and intensity of her own desires and love for him. And still, all in all, none of it was enough to declare him winner of it all and give him a victory she didn't want to grant. Jesse had her heart, her mind—wasn't that enough?

As he softly stroked the side of her face, the walls closed in on her. A part of her wanted to run to him and give him everything he wanted from her—and more. Another part wanted to grab her clothes and dash out of the building and forget that this entire incident ever happened.

In that moment, she noticed her freed wrists. Her mind whirled.

"If I give you the opportunity to get your clothes so you don't run out of here naked and get arrested," he inquired, his tone slightly teasing but still intense, "will you promise me that you'll think about it, at least?"

She swallowed, the sound loud to her ears. "Think about what?"

Swiftly, he handed her the blouse she had been wearing. "The bra's gone, and I think I killed the buttons, but you could tie the top in front or something."

She took the clothing from him and stared at it, confused. "Jesse...."

"Don't make me change my mind, or you won't leave here until I get the answer from you that I want."

His energy swirled around her, dark and chaotic and heavily laden with desire and other emotions too remote for her to name.

She managed to put on her clothing, fighting the urge to run once she left the building. A part of her shrieked—and it pierced her to the core—to leave him standing there with unanswered questions on his lips and a piece of her still in his hands, but another part of her wanted her to save herself from the rising dark waters. It tempted her to be consumed; she wanted no part of it.

Jesse didn't have to say it, and she didn't have to admit to it—she was afraid, desperately afraid.

Chapter Thirty-Two

Hiding in plain sight.

James listened to the young vampire's proposal, a gleam in his eye the sole indicator of how greatly intrigued he was. Amanda had proposed some ideas for the protection magick over their Sanctuary which he claimed to be nothing short of brilliant, but remarkably ambitious. She could almost hear him add, "Just like you" and tried not to beam. Amanda had intuited a while ago that receiving compliments from the magister was rare and to regard them as being quite high.

"With your permission, Magister," she concluded with a small hand gesture, "I'd like to get started tonight."

The magister pursed his lips together. "Lyrael, what you are proposing will take a lot of work and effort from those of the Inner Circle of this Clan. I have no doubt that you got much of your idea from your life as Sarah and at times I don't doubt you think of yourself as being more her than you."

"She *is* me," she insisted. "Or at least is a part of me. I get that now, Janius. I honestly do. Or at least, I'm starting to. And I can't deny that much of what I knew when I was her is extremely helpful to me—and could be to you and this Clan too."

Amanda was rewarded for her speech with a raised eyebrow. "Amanda, I don't doubt that you've been doing an awful lot of introspection as of late and are in better shape these days than you were to start with. However," he held his hand up to prevent her from speaking, "this spell you are proposing to do really should be done by someone of the First Degree."

The young vampire gritted her teeth. "With all due respect, Magister, I believe that I can handle this. I honestly can."

Nodding thoughtfully, he replied, "I believe you. Which is why, Lyrael, I have decided to schedule your First Degree initiation two weeks from now. Have you turned in your Apprentice project to Asherael yet?"

Sputtering, she protested, "Janius, I'm—I'm not ready! Not even remotely! There is still so much more I need to do, and I just...."

To her surprise, he laughed. "Oh, you're ready all right. Don't worry—it's two weeks from now."

"I, um, I'm almost done. I was going to turn it in tonight. I've made a lot of headway in the past few days."

The magister looked at her strangely. "Yes, I see that. And I don't mean just the project either."

She suddenly became very aware of her choice of clothing, which consisted of a red crop top that showed off her increasingly toned midriff and a pair of black, low cut, hip-hugger jeans. Her face warmed, and she wondered if vampires could blush—or if she could blush.

"There's something else that I would like you to do before you reach your First, however," he added. He produced a phone from his pocket and tossed it onto the desk in front of him. Curious, Amanda gazed at it.

"Yes?" she asked, her voice cautious.

"Before I allow you to do this, please know that this is a privilege normally reserved for Firsts and those of higher degree. But you...," he paused, "you have special circumstances surrounding you and have undergone far more than most apprentices who come into unlife here."

He stood up from his seat and paced around the room. Amanda watched with growing concern. The magister seemed anxious about something, and she wished that he would just get on with it and tell her what it was, already.

"Some of us have lives on the 'dayside', as we call it. Sometimes, we are forced to interact with humans for one reason or another. We are not entirely unknown to the outside world; in fact, we have small groups of supporters who are human and are sworn through various oaths to keep silent about us and aid us from time to time. We also interact with other vampires from other Orders, but apply a similar discretion in dealing with them in regards to our oaths.

"Naturally, this sort of...secrecy...typically means that we are very cautious about our dealings with those who are not initiated into our Order, let alone those who are not vampires. In fact, all of them must be approved first by the Grandmagus before we can even think to have any interaction with them that would give away our true natures."

Amanda nodded. "I see." She waited for him to continue.

"Lyrael, we would like you to eventually be able to take on a special role in the 'dayside', if you will, but to prepare you for that, there's one thing that you need to do."

She frowned. "What?"

"Lyrael, before I have you do this, I have to apologize to you. Most of us here are too old to have any personal connections to the dayside in our lives from before we became vampires. Some of us barely even think about it anymore. You've been here, what?" Now it was his turn to frown. "Two months, three? I don't even know." Managing a small shrug, he simply remarked, "Time doesn't matter for us after a while. We don't even pay attention to it, as you probably still do. And in time...no pun intended...you'll understand that."

"Janius, what are you saying?"

He cleared his throat. "I want you to contact your family. You can make up something, some excuse for your absence. If you can't think of anything, we'll help you. I'm sure your relationship with Turel alone may be enough to convince them that your absence wasn't malicious or caused by foul play."

Blood-tears sprang to her eyes. Her family. Mom. Dad. Being allowed to talk to them again, to let them know she was okay. She thought it would truly and honestly be forbidden. She couldn't even remember the last conversation she'd had with them and she missed them terribly.

James wrung his hands, clearly embarrassed. "I should've thought to do this sooner. Secrecy is one thing, but...we didn't want to be cruel to you, Lyrael. I am sorry. I should've said something sooner. I was thoughtless. It was thoughtless of me. Amanda—"

Before he could finish speaking, he was almost thrown off balance as a very grateful young vampire launched herself into his space faster than he could blink and hugged him. He stood there looking awkward before giving her a gentle pat on the back. When she could finally speak, it was barely above a whisper.

"Thank you, James."

He blinked at being addressed by his personal name. She didn't know if she spoke as Sarah or Amanda, and could only conclude that she spoke as herself.

The conversation went easier than expected. She blamed her silence on starting a whirlwind romance and told her mom she was now engaged. The reason she gave them for not having been able to contact them sooner was due to not knowing how to tell them that she was dropping out of the Ph.D. program in order to get married, and figured that they would be disappointed in her.

It was probably the best acting job she had ever done in her whole life, woven with bits of truth. True enough, she had started a whirlwind romance with Jesse, which was the closest thing to being married to him because of the Blood Bond, and due to what had happened during him Turning her, she knew that she had no choice but to inform NYU that she was dropping out of their Classics program.

After she hung up, James gazed at her with a slight smile on his face.

"Let me guess, they now want to meet him, right?"

She gave him a rueful grin. "How did you guess?"

He shrugged. "I remember how parents are. It was a fairly easy assumption to make." He folded his arms across his chest. "This is, of course, where things get complicated, and why yes, we typically choose to try and cut ties if we can. Not everyone can, and we respect that. Some of us came here with no families, or weren't on speaking terms with them at all. That made the job much easier.

"But," he added, "this approach is best—actually resuming some contact with your folks, I mean—especially for interacting smoothly with the dayside if we have to. Hiding in plain sight is often the best approach, but also not without its risks."

She smiled. "So, you have a job for me?"

"You bet."

"And what is this job?"

"I'll tell you when you're First Degree."

Amanda made a face at him. The magister saw it and gave her a pointed look. "Just who do you think you are, anyway? Sarah?" he asked her sternly. But his eyes twinkled, and she knew that he wasn't genuinely upset with her.

"Nah, I'm just me."

He nodded curtly at her. "Good. Be you. Please. And if you have any problems, call me. Or you can call Asherael. Remember, we are here for you—and not just to give you assignments or initiations, either."

Chuckling, she replied, "I know. And I will." Amanda thanked him again and left for her room to finish her paper.

On her way there, she bumped into Lynne and Jesse, who were engaged in what appeared to be a tense discussion. The mere sight of him made her ache inside in various ways—some of which were pleasant and some of which were not. Moisture seeped into the crotch of her pants at just seeing his face and hearing his voice as a nervous twinge gnawed her stomach.

She swallowed.

"Turel, how many times am I going to have to tell you—" Abruptly, Lynne turned and saw Amanda standing there, blinking.

All at once, Amanda felt Jesse's eyes on her, burning their way into her. She fought to keep her face serene and her insides composed.

"Oh, Amanda, um...good to see you. Did you just get back from the magister's office?"

The young vampire nodded. "Yes, he scheduled a date with me for my First Degree initiation."

Lynne's eyes lit up. "Wonderful! But your assignment," she looked at the apprentice pointedly, "is it finished yet?"

Amanda did her best to avoid Jesse's heated gaze as she replied to the blonde vampire. "Almost. The paper just needs some tweaking, and I'll bring it over to you tonight."

"Excellent. Great work, Lyrael. And Turel, I'll be talking to you later." Without another word, she turned and walked down the hallway.

Jesse looked at Amanda, who simply looked back at him in the awkward silence.

When he finally spoke, his voice was quiet—and if she wasn't mistaken, a bit uncertain. "Amanda, are you avoiding me for some reason?"

She folded her arms in front of her chest and gazed down at the floor before replying, "Not exactly, I just need some downtime. I have a lot on my mind."

Clenching his jaw, he could barely get out the words, "Are you angry with me for something?"

Amanda blinked at him. "Angry? No. And besides," she continued, puzzled, "haven't you been able to tell?"

He responded with less calm tones and as he did, she noted the strange expression on his face. "Usually I can, yes. But these days...I don't feel as close to you as I normally do, even with the Bond we have."

"Jesse," she blurted out, "you know that I love you, right?"

"Did you block me out?"

She blinked again, frozen to the spot.

"Amanda? Did you block me? Did you do it on purpose?"

Biting her lip, she repeated, "I need some downtime, Jesse. Too much has happened to me over the past few weeks." She tried to keep her voice from shaking.

He touched her face. The touch was gentle, but she sensed the all-too-familiar gut-wrenching hunger for him sear through her. Amanda fought to keep herself from reaching up with her hand to hold his, and it rapidly turned into a losing battle.

"Then why don't you let me help you?"

Conceding in a desire to give him comfort, she reached out with the hand that still wore the slave bracelet and placed it on his. With the contact, sharp electricity went down her spine.

"Because I need to do this alone," she whispered. Gods, she wanted him badly, but she also knew she needed to keep sane—not to mention figure out where their relationship was headed. She still didn't understand what he wanted from her.

Or so she told herself. The real question was, was she at all capable of giving it to him? And did she even want to give him such power in her life? Didn't he have enough power over her already?

She released her trembling hand from his, which lingered on her face before he finally lowered it slowly to his side.

"So you aren't at all angry with me?"

She smiled, and as she did, her skin stretched strangely on her face. "No, I'm not."

"Do you think this 'downtime' of yours," he asked, "will last long?"

The smile faded from her face. "Gods, I hope not."

"Same here, Amanda. Same here." He glanced down momentarily before lifting his gaze to hers, holding her spellbound for a few moments before he walked away.

Chapter Thirty-Three

"I'm not all that sure I've been myself ever."

"So, are you done with that protection spell thing yet or what?"

Amanda fought back the inclination to sigh. James was right; it was a nasty habit. "Not yet. The last touches that I wanted to add to it, the magister feels I shouldn't add until I'm First Degree."

Erik nodded. "Okay, then, and what were they?"

Rapidly she went into the description of the psychic alarm system—anyone in the Inner Circle at any time would know based upon the spell she would be placing on the area if someone or something had entered the Sanctuary uninvited. There would be guards placed both on the inside and outside that would signal the alert, and she went into detail about the idea she had with Anubis of the East guarding the inside and Anubis of the West guarding the outside of the Sanctuary.

The other vampire laughed. "Oh, Janius must've loved that one. It's so obviously Golden Dawn. Did you do it to kiss his ass, or what?"

Now it was her turn to chuckle. "Nah, I've been involved in the system solely based on my own studies for a while now. But I have to admit," she added, "it didn't hurt to use an idea he could understand."

"Now...you have an alarm system, but do you have anything that would actively prevent the intruder from getting very far into the place?"

She thought for a moment before replying, "I had a number of ideas, but thought it best that such measures be done by the Inner Circle—and let them handle it according to the occasion."

Shrugging, Erik commented, "All right, not a bad solution; better to not have the spell automatically assume the intruder has malicious intent, just in case. I mean, I guess magickal swords coming out of thin air to decapitate the person probably would be a bad idea if it were someone's blood family just dropping by."

In her mirth, Amanda managed to both cackle and snort at the same time. "Yeah, definitely not a good idea."

"So when's your First? Not that long away I would think, right?"

"Just a bit over a week. I've already turned in my assignment to Asherael, and she said it received high marks and I'll be fine to go through with it."

"Excellent! I look forward to it. I still remember my First," he declared with nostalgia. "It was such a transformative experience. If you thought your Apprentice initiation was interesting, wait until you undergo your First Degree. Don't worry," he added hastily, "I won't spoil it for you."

Amanda fought to hide a grin. Somewhere in the back of her mind she remembered bits and pieces of the ceremony back from when she was Sarah, better known to the rest of *Ordo Draconis et Rosae* as Minervia, but had no desire to make that knowledge public.

He looked at her with curiosity. "You know, I heard a rumor recently that you're the reincarnation of one of the dead Inner Circle members. Is it true or just speculation?"

The corner of her mouth turned up, and she felt sheepish. "I had wondered how many people knew about that. I figured it would just be Janius, Asherael, and Turel."

With a wave of dismissal, he told her, "Oh, you'd be amazed at what gets around here. Trust me. I figured there may be something to it but what really mattered was what *you* thought of it."

She folded her arms in front of her chest. "I...I have her memories. Some of them are pretty detailed. I'm convinced it's true."

There was a long silence, during which Amanda heard sounds of footsteps going up the narrow, winding staircase down the hallway.

"So...what now?"

Amanda shrugged. "What now is that I live out my life how I should live it. I mean, I admit...for the first few weeks after I started to really remember shit, I was a little out of it."

"A little?" His tone was skeptical.

She internally squirmed. The carpet pattern beneath her feet looked very interesting. "Okay, a lot. But I couldn't remember things like...which day was my birthday or which set of parents were mine for a bit. I have things mostly sorted out now."

Erik's eyes widened. "Holy shit. Are you okay?"

"Yeah, yeah, I'm fine." She nodded, deep in thought. "I went through a lot, but I'm fine. Or at least, I'm getting there. It's...it's a lot to integrate. That's all." She thought about Jesse and her last conversation with him. Integrating him into her life had been so easy, yet so terribly complicated. She was starting to wonder if she was saner with him or without him—and it was so hard to tell.

"Hey, Lyrael? Did you hear what I just said?" Clearly Erik had been in the process of saying something to her, and she had briefly tuned him out. *Dammit I'm such a space cadet,* she thought, embarrassed.

"Sorry, Theodotos, mind wandered. It's been a long night."

"It's okay. I was just wondering if you had seen or spoken to Asherael lately. She's acting a little odd, and I know that you two are on good terms."

Amanda blinked. Lynne, acting odd? "No, I haven't seen anything strange, but to tell you the truth, I haven't been paying attention. I'll see what I can dig up next time I see her."

"Cool, cool, not a problem. Not trying to raise the alarms or anything, just noticed she seemed a bit out of sorts."

"Okay, I'll keep that in mind—thanks."

"No problem. Give my best to Turel. Later!"

He left Amanda standing there deep in thought. Come to think of it, she had found Lynne yelling at Jesse in the hallway the other day, but hadn't given it much attention. She knew the two of them didn't always get along and she had been so terribly...distracted...by Jesse's presence.

Amanda frowned. Lynne had been a good friend to her since her arrival, long before she had realized Amanda was Sarah. The blonde vampire had gone above and beyond helping her, even when she was too preoccupied to realize it, let alone return the favor.

Memories of her past life and present floated through her mind with all of the times she had spent with Lynne. Shopping in East Village. The time when they'd looked at each other and declared simultaneously, "Fuck vampire purity!" and went out to the new ice cream shop around the corner. The early morning talks before they each went to their rooms and crashed, exhausted. The "field trips" they had taken some of their students on to the local blues clubs. Their strange experiments with magick that had caused Janius to shake his head at the two of them and declare that neither of them ever took magick seriously in all of their lives—and his reaction to discovering their experiments had yielded real knowledge, used later to help out the Order.

Lynne hadn't been just a friend to Sarah, she had been a sister.

Friendships like that don't come often in any lifetime....

Vividly, she saw in her mind's eye Lynne's reaction to her death, mingled with other strange images that had greeted her "eyes" after she was but a spirit in the otherworld.

Guilt overwhelmed her. She had gotten so caught up in her own troubles, her relationship with Jesse, and everything else inside of her that she hadn't let herself get too deeply into friendships during her time here. Where was her usual radar for when her friends were troubled? Where had her awareness of the world around her, and those within it, gone?

Gods, I've seriously become self-absorbed, she thought, cringing. And it wasn't the person whom she wanted to become, regardless of whether she was either Sarah or Amanda.

This wouldn't—and couldn't—do.

Not surprisingly, she walked down a familiar corridor and knocked on a certain blonde vampire's door.

"Come in," Lynne cried out from inside of her office.

Amanda smiled and opened the door. Greeting her sight was Lynne surrounded by a mound of papers on her desk and looking incredibly frazzled.

"Um, hi...am I catching you at a bad time?"

Lynne laughed. "No, I could use a few minutes of distraction. How are things?"

Lyrael thought for a moment. "Good, pretty good, actually. How about you?"

"Stressed. A bunch of students have applied for their next degree, and hence I have a million of their assignments to grade." She grimaced. "I'll never be able to get through these in the next few days."

Amanda nearly opened her mouth to say, "I can help," but then remembered she was no longer Sarah. As Sarah, she had helped Lynne countless times with work, and vice versa. But now she was but an apprentice and certainly not qualified to act as a teacher at the moment, let alone grade papers for students.

The young vampire settled for, "I'd help, but...." She shrugged and chuckled.

"Oh, Amanda, there's time enough to be a teacher. Just focus on your own studies for now. If you like, however," she added, "you could form study groups with others of your degree. Something to think about when you're a First."

"Okay." After a few moments, she spoke up again. "Hey, Lynne?"

"Hm?" Her head had dipped once more to one of the papers on

her desk.

"What are you doing later? Would you like to do something, even if for just a few hours?"

Lynne smiled. "Blood, Amanda, I have so much to do—"

"Didn't you accuse me earlier of being a workaholic?" Not waiting for an answer, she continued, "Well, you were right. Now I'm paying back the favor. Wanna head to the *Blue Moon* or something? It'll help you unwind, and besides...you might find it easier to work on your students' assignments afterwards."

Dead silence ruled as Lynne paused for a moment. Then she put down her grading pen and looked up at Amanda as if she had witnessed something altogether remarkable.

"Amanda?"

"Yes?"

"It's good to have you back." With a grin, she stated, "And I'm looking forward to being there for your First."

The young vampire grinned back. "Thanks, Lynne."

Lynne shook her head at her. "No, really...I mean it. I...you had me worried for a while there, regardless of whether or not you were Sarah. And I can't say I'm not still worried."

Amanda nodded.

"You've come a long damned way since you first got here, do you know that?"

She thought back to when she'd first met Jesse. It seemed like a lifetime ago. With a laugh, she realized in essence, it was. She had been "reborn" when she was Turned and additionally changed when she took on much of her past memories as Sarah. She was no longer the woman she was, but she also wasn't much different from who she *really* was.

"Yeah," she replied absently. "I really have."

"I'll tell you what...let me finish this last one, and I'll meet you at the *Blue Moon* in about an hour. I think you and I could use a drink or two and some good music."

Smiling, Amanda said, "Sounds like we got ourselves a plan."

"And that plan will be executed in an hour. See you then."

"Will do."

On her way back to her room, she ran into Erik, who was with another female vampire she didn't recognize off the bat. She had short, dark hair, light brown eyes, and wore a simple pair of jeans and a black t-shirt with an unrecognizable cartoon character on it. Her eyes grabbed Amanda's attention, and she liked her immediately.

"Oh, hi, Lyrael. Lyrael," he gestured towards his companion, "this is Haniel. She's a Second Degree student of the Clan."

"Hi, Haniel. Nice to meet you."

"Nice to meet you too, Lyrael. Theo here has told me an awful lot about you. Didn't you just get Turned a few months ago? I hear you're up for First."

Amanda nodded. "Yes, in a little over a week."

"Nervous?" Haniel asked, her voice sympathetic.

"Actually...I feel I can handle it. I'll be okay."

"Good. You'll love the degree. If you have any questions about the work you're doing, just come see me, and I'm sure Theo here wouldn't mind helping you out either."

"I will, thanks." Amanda turned towards Erik. "I-I just wanted to thank you for the help you've given me lately."

"Eh, don't sweat it."

"No, really," she insisted. "I can't say I've been myself in the past month or so, and to be honest...." She paused and realized for the first time the truth of what she was about to say, "I'm not all that sure I've been myself *ever*." She laughed nervously.

"That's the First Degree alchemy kicking in. Got to go with Haniel to a meeting, but I just want to say you're doing fine and don't worry about it." He winked at her. "We should hang out sometime when you have less work to do."

"Will do. And thanks again." She grinned at Haniel. "Good meeting you. I'll catch you both later."

Once back in her room, she changed to a dark burgundy top, left her black jeans on, and put on a pair of black boots with thick high heels. She studied her reflection in the mirror.

It wasn't the first time she reflected upon her past, and these days she did so as seldom as possible—the sensation of vertigo upon realizing how much had changed in her life had been overwhelming. Now she needed to look back, collect the pieces, and figure out who she really was and what she wanted to do.

And for the first time in a long while, she thought that everything was good in her life and with herself.

Chapter Thirty-Four

"Blue Moon *specialty*."

The *Blue Moon* was unusually crowded, and it took an inquiry or two with the bartender to find out precisely why—undergrad students visiting the NYU campus. Amanda hadn't even thought of it, and it seemed to be the most obvious explanation, what with all the young people there and all. She had finished her work already, and naturally those graduating or looking to attend were out celebrating their good fortune. Well, good for them. Undergrad seemed light-years away to Amanda.

She ordered a glass of shiraz for herself, and Lynne had some raspberry-pomegranate alcoholic concoction which she tried and agreed was quite delightful. The bartender was only too happy to give Amanda a sample of the drink for herself, which made her even happier.

"Give the guy an extra tip, why don't you?" whispered Amanda to Lynne.

"But of course," she whispered back. "Just what do you take me for, anyway?"

The television broadcasted the current baseball game. Amanda couldn't make head nor tail of it, but Lynne watched and made strange clucking sounds with her tongue.

"Lynne, what's going on with the game?" she asked. "Who's winning or losing?"

A guy next to them answered, "The Yankees are losing to the Mets."

Amanda blinked. This could've been in Chinese to her. "Okay, um...but they're both from New York, right? How could one be losing to the other?"

"Oh, yeah, Mets are totally winning over the Yankees."

"Kicking their ass, I see," commented Lynne nonchalantly.

"Bright spanking red, their asses are, yes," he answered, sipping his drink.

Amanda almost inhaled hers. This was downright hilarious.

"The Yankees have handed their asses to the Mets on a silver platter. Just what the fuck, I gotta ask." The man, still nameless, shook his head and pounded his drink.

"What the fuck, indeed," Lynne remarked.

Amanda just shook her head. She never had been a sports fan and didn't get any of this. Yet the two seemed enthralled with the television set and the various numbers printed at the top of the screen.

"What the *fuck*, Jeter?" the guy hollered at the screen. "Fuck, just...*fuck*."

Lynne sighed, and Amanda fought the urge to tell her that it was a bad, bad human habit. They still had to blend in with these people, right?

"I think it was the umpire's fault," offered Amanda.

The man seemed vaguely consoled by this. "Yeah, the umpire's a total vampire," he stated with confidence. He chugged the rest of his drink down. "Man, I wanna be a vampire," he declared.

Lynne's eyebrows shot up into her hair as Amanda descended into a giggle fit.

"Um, why?" asked Lynne, her voice neutral and polite. Amanda let out a very unlady-like snort.

"Dude, I wanna be a vampire," he repeated. "Then I could have crazy, kinky sex with all of the chicks. Just look at me. I could be like Blade without the daywalker crap."

Amanda looked at him studiously. He was African-American, clearly built in a more than pleasing way, and clean-shaven. Not quite Terminator-man built, but he definitely looked like he worked out on a regular basis.

Lynne nodded, her face a perfect mask of serenity. "Yes, you could seduce all of the women and bite their necks."

Amanda choked on her shiraz. *I need to stop drinking while they're talking*.

"Yes, of course! But I could get one of them to follow me around and shit, and then she could help me do crazy stuff to the chicks."

"That's the best part," remarked Amanda.

Now it was Lynne's turn to almost inhale her drink.

"What's your name?" he asked.

"Amanda."

"Amanda. I'm Clay. Good to meet you." They shook hands. "I dig your style. These Yankees are losing, but at least you have style."

She settled for nodding her head. This was turning out to be a more interesting night than usual at the *Blue Moon*.

"I like Mandy here. I'm gonna call you Mandy. You're definitely a Mandy." Amanda fought back the giggles again. Only one of her professors and her parents had gotten away with calling her that, but somehow from this man it seemed all right.

"Hey, Jimmy, I think Mandy needs another drink or something."

"You're right. She's barely touched her glass. You come here often?"

"Um...sometimes. I've been busy with work lately."

Lynne barely swallowed her drink as she gazed down at the counter. "Yeah, she's a total workaholic. I brought her out here to relax."

"Me?" asked Amanda, indignant. "You were busy with those papers and shit. I practically had to drag you out here."

"Says who?" Lynne shot back. "Besides, you're practically toast on that one glass of shiraz, Ms. Lightweight. Mr. Bartender, sir—Jimmy, is that your name?—I'd love another one of these raspberry-pomegranate-I-don't-know-what-the-fuck-these-are. But they're great."

"Thanks," he replied. "*Blue Moon* specialty. Hey Clay," he called out to the man beside them, "want another?"

"Please. These Mets are seriously pounding it to the Yankees. Fuck." He shook his head and graciously accepted another alcoholic beverage. "Crazy vampire sex. Yes," he stated, deep in thought as he gazed upon his drink. "I could totally go for that."

"I'm a little bit kinky myself, I have to admit," stated Jimmy, who dispensed a drink to another customer at the bar.

"Who isn't?" Clay commented. He turned his attention back to the monitor above them. "What the fuck, these Mets...I dunno, man. This shouldn't be happening to the Yankees. Damned embarrassing."

Amanda smiled and shrugged. She still didn't get it. Who honestly cared?

Lynne merely gave her a look, which Amanda deciphered in less than a second. Yes, she shouldn't comment. This was New York, where their sports teams mattered. Amanda needed to keep her mouth shut and nod like she comprehended what the hell was going on.

Before she knew it, Amanda had pounded down two glasses of shiraz and seriously felt it coursing through her system. The amethyst ring allowed her to ingest alcohol, but certainly didn't prevent her from getting drunk in the least.

"These *damned* Yankees," Clay yelled, almost throwing his drink on the counter. "Waitamin...wasn't that a movie title or something? Fuck. I don't care. Stupid Yankees. What the fuck?"

Lynne shook her head, looking sympathetic. "Maybe it's the weather or something?" she offered.

"I don't fucking know." He sighed. "Whatever. At least these drinks are good."

Jimmy the bartender nodded. "Yeah, and if you were a vampire, you could have your pick of the women here."

"Oh, *yeah*, man." He chugged down more of his drink. "I'd bite their necks and everything. It'd be great."

Amanda hiccupped. Then she blinked. When was the last time she'd hiccupped?

Clay laughed. "Cut this girl off, man," he told the bartender, laughing. "I think she's done."

"I just...inhaled too quickly, that's all," explained Amanda, her words rushed.

Lynne's eyebrows shot up into her hair again, and Amanda almost heard her thinking: Inhaled, yeah right. Vampires don't inhale. They *couldn't* inhale.

But they had to blend, right?

"Mandy's drunk," laughed Clay.

Obviously, she was the entertainment for the evening, but surely anything was better than watching the latest Yankees versus Mets game on television. She tried to swallow, but only hiccupped once more.

"It's okay—I'll get her some water," offered Jimmy, who poured some ice and water into a glass and handed it to a grateful Amanda, who was still trying to recover from her repeated giggle fits. She drank the water but hiccupped in the middle. Lynne giggled at the sight. This wasn't her evening.

"What the hell, girl, don't inhale the water," Clay ordered. "Siiiiip it. It's water, not air."

She drank the water, but hiccupped again afterwards. Lynne attempted to suppress a giggle fit of her own and failed.

"It's okay," Lynne offered, "I'm escorting her home."

"Good," replied Jimmy. "I don't want her doing anything stupid on the way there. You a friend of hers?"

Lynne nodded. "Yeah, we live nearby each other."

"Great, good to hear. What do you two do?"

"I, um," choked Amanda, "I'm a grad student at NYU."

"And I do independent archaeological research," stated Lynne.

Both Jimmy and Clay looked impressed.

"Wow, do you two have any free time ordinarily?" asked Jimmy.

"Not usually," Lynne replied, "so we're out here to make the best of it."

"Go you," Clay declared and raised his glass. "Good luck to you two."

They all clinked glasses and afterwards drank their beverages.

Sometime during the night, they got lost in the music from the band that played. Amanda couldn't remember the name by that point, but remembered a song they were playing before they left. Something about boundaries and limits and living life the only way you can, and somehow…it just seemed appropriate. And that was what really mattered.

Amanda was still hiccupping when she walked back to the Sanctuary with Lynne very late in the night.

"I thought *hic* vampires didn't breathe *hic*. How come *hic* I still have these *hic* hiccups?"

Lynne looked at her and shrugged. "It's psychological."

"Really? *Hic*."

"Really. You may have been breathing at one point out of habit or an unconscious desire to fit in. Either way, usually it's the diaphragm spasming that causes the hiccups to occur."

"So mine *hic* spasmed because I was thinking too much about being human?"

"I guess," offered Lynne.

"I *hic* wish I knew how to stop them *hic*," Amanda stated, feeling hopeless.

"Ordinarily I'd tell you to inhale slowly then breathe out slowly, but you're, well, a vampire. But maybe you should give it a try anyway."

"Okay." She tried, and it seemed to work. "I think they've stopped," she informed Lynne.

"Good."

"Now I can sleep, I think."

"Great, we could use that."

Amanda didn't remember getting to back to the Sanctuary and to her room, but somehow, she got there. Somewhere in between drifting off and being awake, she remembered Clay's declarations of his intent to become a vampire and have kinky sex and wound up giggling all over again.

If only he knew.

* * * *

Sometime before dawn, she awoke with a start, but the dream played on in her head. She laid back into her pillow, staring at the ceiling as the images danced before her eyes.

Thirty years ago, and in unknown space. She saw herself watching the people around her again for the millionth time. Jess in hysterics, Lynne inconsolable. James beside himself with grief. All because of her and her sacrifice that their lives may be spared from the attack by the Order of the Golden Cross.

She watched the events unfold, the symbols displaying themselves before her. And suddenly she remembered.

At some point, she spoke to someone/something. She realized the nature of the reality around her, and wished/asked/demanded the following: to be reborn again, to undo what she had done, to finish what she had started, to right the wrongs she had committed by ending her life so soon, so early.

So damned violently.

She floated. In time and space, she floated calmly amongst the fabric of reality, and the serenity and love of the gods was with her. Any sane person would've stayed.

But she never courted the seductive play-toy that was sanity.

In her head, it all seemed right. And she remembered. And then it hit her, all at once. And it punched her in the gut hard enough to physically hurt.

She chose this lifetime. She chose to become a vampire again.

And...*oh my gods, oh my gods, oh my gods....*

The choice. That very choice she had thought denied to her, from day one—the denial was an illusion, a falsehood. She chose the face she wore before she emerged from her mother's womb, this very incarnation, picked out the pattern and danced herself right into it.

Amanda could've laughed. She was *free.*

The very choice she thought Jesse had removed from her had been hers to begin with.

The burden of the cage fell away. Time fell away. All at once, she saw things as they were.

Deep down, she had resented Jesse for placing her into this position, was angry at him for taking her away from her previous life, didn't trust him for what he had done to her.

And in reality...she never genuinely lacked for a choice.

Jess...gods. She didn't realize genuinely how angry she had been inside at him until this moment, and a great sorrow filled her heart.

If I had never realized...never gotten back these memories...I never would've known. I would've hated him forever.

And she saw the pattern weave itself, and indeed, she saw the mess that was made of their relationship, had she not realized her being here as a vampire was never really his fault to begin with—that in reality, there was nothing given to her which wasn't of her own choice.

The knowledge of this, cascading down upon her like a waterfall, set her free, amazingly free. She knew in an instant she could do and be anything and anyone she'd ever wanted to be.

All she had to do—and desired to do—right now, was to find Jesse and apologize to him somehow. Let him know that at last, she understood.

So deep in thought she was that she barely noticed the ripple that went through her into the walls of her room.

A ripple that tore through her once about thirty years ago. A ripple which had altered the course of her life forever.

A cold fear chilled her core.

Fuck. They're back.

Ordo Aureae Crucis. She could Feel them—and she sensed somehow they had returned.

The shockwave pounded through the shields of the Sanctuary, and she knew at once that she had come back to pick up where she'd left off, to right the horrible wrongs she had committed upon leaving this life so soon—and to try and save the Clan once more from a mass extinction.

Oh gods. What do I do? What the fuck do I do?

After all, she wasn't Sarah—she was a drunken Amanda, an apprentice and barely made vampire who had spent most of her life with her nose buried in books. How could she begin to do what she had arranged to do before her very birth?

The ripple went through again, and at once she was terrified.

"Fear is failure and the forerunner of failure," she whispered before jumping out of bed to get out of her room.

Her time had come.

Chapter Thirty-Five

"It can't end this way."

There weren't many Clan members who were still awake who had been hit psychically by the blast. The Inner Circle members, at least, were up and about, and Amanda sensed their panic.

Jess, are you okay? she asked, reaching out to him wherever he was.

Amanda, stay in your room, came the curt reply. *That's an order.*

She bristled. Was he crazy?

Jesse, don't give me that. Are you okay? What the hell is going on?

Stay in your room. His tone was harsh and firm. *Don't you dare make me tell you again.*

You aren't the boss of me, sir, she thought before she bolted out of her room, scowling. How in the world did he manage to push so many of her buttons in a single sentence? Jesse was entirely too adept at it, and she had too much to do and worry about at this moment to deal with him and his issues.

She needed to get to the entrance of the Sanctuary.

As she ran, strange images floated into her head, carried on such a gentle breeze that she hardly noticed it. An event, a newsletter, a vision of a commentary: *Asherael met the dawn at 4:55 a.m.* People distraught, history repeated all over again.

Amanda halted in her tracks.

No. Fuck, no. Gods, please no.

Lynne.

Somehow, that woman—that crazy woman, Amanda internally ranted—got it in her head to make a similar sacrifice that Amanda had made thirty years ago in her previous incarnation. And Apollo was delivering her the message of this potential future.

Not if I can fucking help it. Determined, Amanda felt her jaw setting into place. Lynne wasn't going to die. No way, no how.

She fought to keep the blood-tears from springing to her eyes. *Gods, Lynne, this isn't the answer....* Trying in vain not to remember how Lynne had reacted to her own death, she ran faster.

When she got to the entrance, Erik, Jesse, and James were all there. Erik's face looked pale, paler than even a vampire should be.

"Lyrael, you shouldn't be here," he said, his face grim. "Haniel—

Stacy, they have Stacy...."

Amanda cursed under her breath in several languages. She didn't know Haniel personally, but this wasn't good news.

"She's Asherael's student," he continued listlessly. "Asherael just went to go—"

Amanda didn't stay to listen; that was all she needed to hear. She mumbled something under her breath and attempted to run outside the protective barrier. Something—someone—grabbed her.

Jesse.

"Let—go!" she yelled, trying to get her arm out of his grip.

"I ordered you to stay inside," he hissed at her, his eyes flashing. "And you deliberately disobeyed me."

She had no patience for this. "Jess, fucking cut it out. This is crazy."

"Amanda, what is wrong with you?" He looked at her, pain and anger clear in his eyes. "When will you listen to me? When will you learn how to trust me?"

Everything in her exploded into fragments of brilliant light. The part of her who was simultaneously Sarah and Amanda responded.

"No, you dolt," she snapped, "the question is, when the hell will you trust *me*?"

"Amanda—"

"Don't you 'Amanda' me." She held out her left hand, the slave bracelet he'd given her still on her wrist. "Do you remember what you said to me when you put this on me? Do you?"

He gave no reply. Given she spoke from her memories as Sarah and not Amanda, she shouldn't have expected one.

"In perfect love, and in perfect trust. Jesse, I love you, but you need to fucking trust me. If you want anything from me—any type of relationship—you need to trust me. And you clearly don't."

His face grew dark with anger, but she continued.

"And it's my fault. I know that. I wrecked that trust thirty years ago, and I'm sorry. I can't pay for it enough. I can't apologize for it enough. But Jess," she continued, "I need to make up for it now. I need to apologize for it now by doing what I'm about to do."

"But Amanda—"

"Jesse, I need to do what I fucking came back here to do. And that's precisely what I'm going to do."

She didn't even have a clue what that was, but that didn't stop her from managing to work her way out of his grip and running out of the protective shield around the Sanctuary to where the numbers of those in the Order of the Golden Cross stood. All déjà vu in a distinctively macabre way. The events playing out now were how she had met her last death.

Lynne. She remembered Lynne and the strange vision she'd had earlier. She had to prevent that future from happening at all.

Fear is failure and the forerunner of failure.

There she was, surrounded by a crowd of people in white robes wearing golden crosses around their necks. How all of this played out in the middle of Washington Square in the early hours of the morning with no one noticing, she had no clue. And she didn't particularly care. After all, it was New York—who the hell bothered to notice this shit, anyhow? All she knew was that Haniel had gone missing—presumably captured by these people—and that Lynne was planning to sacrifice herself so that Haniel may be saved.

Amanda, however, had other plans.

"*Lynne*!" she shouted.

The people in white robes turned and saw her. Asherael froze.

Fucking get back inside, Amanda, she heard inside her head. It was the first time, perhaps, that she had perceived a telepathic voice besides Jesse's and her gods'.

Fucking make me, she retorted.

A bolt of energy hit her—she recognized it dimly as some magick spell from one of the *Ordo Aureae Crucis* initiates—and she fell to the ground, dazed and unable to move.

* * * *

The man who had hit her with the energy bolt fingered his golden cross, thankful that God had allowed him to strike out against the vampire.

Soon this will all be over, he reasoned, *and our world will be free from this menace.*

Some said that their founder had abandoned them and their cause, dismissing them in his famous work as "God's madmen." But he knew better. The founder of their beloved order, *Ordo Aureae Crucis*, had written about Vlad Tepes and his unholy minions in order to warn the world. Save them from the evils which preyed upon mankind.

He had a holy duty. As much as he pitied the young woman

whom he had struck down, he also believed that his actions would save her.

God, he prayed, *help me to set this young woman and the others like her free from their cursed paths.*

As he readied himself to cast another blow, his cheeks grew wet with tears. How had it come to this, that he and others like him had to kill in order to save?

* * * *

It can't end this way, came her thought through the mental haze. She knew she was losing consciousness, slipping away into some cold yet comforting corner where she didn't have to worry about all of this anymore, none of it. She could just rest peacefully, undisturbed.

But she was determined not to succumb.

Apollo, I need you, she begged desperately. But she felt nothing.

Dionysus, I need you. Gods, I need you.

The quiet within her was deafening, but she continued.

I need to help Lynne, help this Clan, PLEASE.

Silence.

All of her will, the last of her energy, and her hope focused on one thought: Please*, dear gods, please help me to help them!*

All at once, the fog lifted from her eyes, and she saw within myriad strands connecting everything and everyone. All of the buildings, the people, the streetlights, everything—strands, strands everywhere. Light, sound, and energy. It was everything. It was in everything.

It flowed through her and through the world.

She was Arachne, caught in the web she had woven. She was Ariadne, holding the thread to Theseus that he may escape. Clotho guided her, teaching her how to spin the thread.

The web was everywhere, a brilliant, blinding tapestry.

She saw the individual strands that ran through each of the members of the Order of the Golden Cross. The strands ran through Lynne, Jesse—everyone who was outside, inside—everywhere.

Beautiful, stunningly so. But what could she possibly do with this knowledge?

Amanda fought to stand up, her head still spinning.

Someone laughed. "Look at the vampire—she doesn't give up," a voice said, pitiless and mocking.

"It's time for you all to sleep an endless sleep," someone else declared imperiously, but his voice cracked with something that sounded like...pain? "The time for darkness has ended."

Sleep. The word jolted Amanda. They wanted the Clan to sleep forever, in a daze of dimly lit strands forever.

No.

As she stood up, she saw in her mind each of the threads that connected the members of the Order of the Golden Cross together. She could touch and feel every single one in their uniqueness, their energy, their strength.

She held them in the palm of her hand.

Before she knew it, she stood in the middle of the circle of people, her arms outstretched, the wind running through her hair—all of it as it had been so long ago.

Ring around the rosy, pocket full of posies....

Everything was so familiar, so right. The pattern was so easy to slip into if one wasn't awake enough, not paying attention. There it was, waiting to be grasped with bare hands. She could just go to sleep and end it all.

"Amanda!" she vaguely heard Jesse cry.

In that cry, she remembered. She remembered that she had remembered. In that recollection came a realization: she needed to be here. She needed to realize something. She needed to set things right.

"Amanda, what the fuck are you doing?" Lynne, and the last voice to jolt her back into consciousness.

With that awareness came the sensation of each of the threads that bound the members of the Order that threatened her Clan. She mentally tagged each and every one, savoring the feeling, gathering them as she would a basket of flowers.

Ashes, ashes, we all fall down....

She held out her arms, as she had so long ago, and gave herself to the brilliant, blinding light of the tapestry. But unlike that time, she had other intentions. She could both sense and See the fabric that bound each and every one of the people who threatened the Clan and *tugged.*

As she tugged, one word emerged from her lips and mind:

"SLEEP."

Ashes, ashes....

The members of the Order of the Golden Cross, who had surrounded them with both physical and magickal weapons, suddenly collapsed to the ground, unconscious. A figure she made out to be Haniel ran out from amongst them towards the door of the Sanctuary.

We all fall down....

She cried out something she could hardly hear, let alone understand, and her world faded to black.

* * * *

"Fucking idiot," sobbed Lynne, watching her fall.

Jesse shoved her aside to get to Amanda, who now lay limp and unmoving on the ground.

"She's fine, Asherael." He brushed the hair away from her face. "I can feel her."

Lynne wiped the blood-tears on her sleeve. "You better not be shitting me, or you'll pay for it, Turel."

Jesse just looked at her as Erik walked over with Stacy close behind him.

"In my view," he informed her, "these people should all be turned into food for what they have done to us tonight."

James nodded, unable to speak or do much else. It was vampire law, and no one could possibly argue with it. To leave these people alive would only endanger the Clan and even the Order itself.

"No," stated Lynne. Stacy's eyes widened as James whirled around to fix his stern gaze upon her. "At least, not all of them," she added. "Save one of them for questioning. The rest...yes, feel free. They are as good as food at this point."

Erik nodded. "So be it. That one." He pointed towards one of the crumpled figures on the ground. "I'll restrain him myself."

"I'll help," volunteered Stacy. She gazed down at Amanda's unconscious form, now resting in Jesse's arms. "Will Lyrael be okay?"

"She's fine," answered Jesse, cradling her body. "Once again, it appears she's saved us."

Stacy's brow creased. "Again?" she queried, confused. "She's saved us before?"

"Come on, Stacy," urged Erik, pulling her into the Sanctuary. "I'll explain later."

James stood motionless while Lynne staggered into the doorway. It was only then that he spoke.

"Once again...I couldn't do anything but stand there."

Lynne sighed. Human habit be damned after they'd just stood on the brink of death. "It's okay, Janius."

"No...no, it's not." She could see the blood-tears in his eyes as he struggled to speak. "I stood there then...and I stand here now. And an apprentice—a mere apprentice—saves us all."

She wanted to argue: *That was no mere apprentice, that was Sarah reincarnated,* but could only get out, "James, that was—"

"I'm the magister of this Clan and I'm useless to everyone, save for research and scrying. I couldn't even defend us against The Golden Cross."

"James. Look at me." The sound of his personal name startled him, and he turned to look at Lynne, his face blank.

"James, you were calm. You were cool. While the rest of us panicked, you were the eye of the storm. In essence, you are our anchor. You underestimate your importance to this Clan again, and I'll have no qualms about beating the snot out of you. Understood?"

He blinked at her violent words. "Um...yes. I think I get it."

"Good. I'm out of practice with swordplay and I really don't relish kicking your ass with my bare hands. Now, let's get inside and bring some of these bodies with us while we're at it."

James smiled at her. "Lynne, what would I do without you?"

"Convince yourself of the delusion that you don't matter when in fact you do, no doubt," she answered him, her tone brisk. "Now, help me to move these bodies before the police get here, okay?"

"We were fortunate. They could've wiped us all out. All of us. How did we escape?"

"Let's worry about it later. Right now, we have bodies to dispose of and a prisoner to question."

He nodded. "You're right. Let's get moving, and we'll assess the damage later."

"Good thinking."

Chapter Thirty-Six

"I believe it was my true will that brought me back."

Amanda stood awkwardly in the magister's office. Lynne, Jesse, Merideth, and James were all there, looking very serious. James sat at his desk, his hands in front of him, fingers interlaced.

She had been called into the room only moments before and as she stood there silently, she wondered if she'd been called in because something had gone wrong.

The magister predictably broke the silence in his usual direct fashion. "Lyrael, good to see you. I suppose you are wondering why we called you in here."

The young vampire nodded. She could almost feel her fangs start to emerge in her nervousness and she did her best to keep them in.

"What you did out there was reckless and stupid. I understand that your Sire, Turel, had ordered you to stay inside with the rest of the students in order to stay safe. I also understand that you directly disobeyed him and went outside, where you endangered yourself, and possibly your life, in order to help us fight *Ordo Aureae Crucis*."

Inwardly Amanda winced. This wasn't sounding too good.

"What can I say, Lyrael? What you did was undeniably foolish, and I have full right to postpone your First Degree initiation as a result of your actions. At the same time," he went on, "you acted bravely and saved us all. I've thought a good deal about what happened over the past few days, trying to make sense of everything and pondered on what would be the right course of action in this instance. And this is my conclusion."

He paused, and while he did so she braced herself for the outcome.

"I was an idiot to have not let you finish your task to complete the protection spell over this Sanctuary, Lyrael. I treated you as an apprentice, when in reality you have full knowledge and skills of a Fifth."

Amanda blinked at this, but said nothing.

"We nearly paid for my mistake with that attack. Amaltheia here," he gestured to the elfish-looking vampire to his right, "wisely commented that you must've reincarnated here in order to work on the shield and finish the job you started thirty years ago. And I can't help but see the logic in that.

"It may interest you to know that the members of *Ordo Aureae Crucis* did indeed attack on the thirtieth anniversary of when they were dealt a losing blow and lost many of their key members. It was, in essence, a retaliation prompted by their younger and more inexperienced current members. That day, I must note, was also the anniversary of Minervia's death, and I cannot deny that her light has not been missed here in the Clan."

"Her light is still here," Amanda blurted out, "in *me*. I may be a wholly different person in many respects, but I still have a lot of her memories. That must count for something."

James nodded in agreement. "It does—more so than I've been willing in the past to acknowledge. And that lack of acknowledgement ends now. I would like you to finish the work you began on your spell tonight. We have been interrogating the prisoner we captured from that attack on our Sanctuary, and he claims there are others who will come to try and finish the work they started. And we can't let them."

Amanda shook her head. "When do they *stop*? We've done nothing to them."

The magister twisted his mouth into a grimace. "Lyrael, these people believe we are all evil due to the simple, plain fact that we are vampires. It's truly that simple. They are on what they believe to be a holy crusade to get rid of us all."

"They're dangerous fanatics," added Lynne, "and can be quite scary. We liked them better when they were taken up with getting their stories printed on that Interweb thing and got treated as kooks by reasonably sane people."

Amanda fought back a smirk. Internet. She meant to say Internet.

"Interweb, Internet, whatever—the point is that they're crazy," Lynne declared. "They have altars to Van Helsing and Bram Stoker in their temple, and they think that they're doing God's work, appointed by God himself to rid the Earth of the evil vampires."

Jesse rolled his eyes at her last statement. "The point is that we were lucky," he stated grimly. "These were essentially a bunch of kids trying to do the work only their fathers and mothers could have done. They were also too stupid to think of attacking us in broad daylight when we were all asleep—I'm guessing for the joy of being able to confront us and to try to literally pound us with stakes and garlic and crap. If they try to attack us again and bring with them their more experienced members, we could be in trouble."

The magister spoke up. "Lyrael, I know your spell originally called for tying the members of the Inner Circle together in a 'psychic protection network', if you will, which would notify each of us if an intruder had broken in or was attempting a break-in. We are thinking of expanding upon that idea to include radar against all initiates of the Order of the Golden Cross. If they are anywhere within one thousand feet of this place, we want to know.

"We also," he added, "would like you to be hooked up to that network."

"But...but...," spluttered Amanda. "Why me?"

"Two reasons. Number one, we would not be alive if you had not done what you did that night. Number two, you *are* Minervia. If you didn't have her memories, this would not have been as significant. But we need you here. You acted admirably—foolishly, I cannot deny, but you acted with great courage.

"Your First Degree initiation will go on as scheduled, and you will continue to undergo the degrees, their work, and their alchemy. But from now on, you will be treated as an honorary member of the Inner Circle—specifically that of the Fifth Degree, which Minervia held at her death—which we have no doubt will someday become a real degree bestowed upon you at a later date."

Amanda nearly collapsed with relief. Her initiation wouldn't be postponed—nor would she be overwhelmed with work she didn't feel she was ready to handle just yet. At the same time, the idea of being treated as an honorary Inner Circle member made her giddy.

"This means that you'll be present at all of our meetings and be privy to everything we know in regards to the Clan—which you may or may not remember anyway." The magister smiled. "But at least we can keep you posted of the latest and hope that we can help each other in the future."

"I—gods—thank you, Magister," gasped out Amanda. "I don't even know what else to say at this point other than...thank you."

Lynne laughed. "No, thank *you*, silly. All of us are still alive due to your crazy reincarnation trick."

"I can't help but wonder," Merideth piped up, "if somehow you consciously chose this life on purpose. I have no idea if you know or not, Lyrael, or if you'd even remember such a thing. But we believe that somehow you did, even if it was just your Higher Genius guiding you to do so."

Amanda thought back to her dream the other night and the realization she'd had afterwards. "Meri...." Merideth's eyes widened at Sarah's old nickname for her, issued with calm from Amanda's lips. "I do remember some stuff and I really do believe I chose this lifetime somehow on purpose. I remember it being my wish before and after my death. I think—I think my Agathos Daimon helped me to honor that wish."

Her gaze caught Jesse's, and they smiled at each other.

James studied Amanda, deep in thought. "I would imagine that knowing this makes you feel differently about how you originally came here, Amanda."

She noted the use of her personal name. "Yes...yes it does."

"Have you thought about it much since?"

"Yes, quite a bit, actually," she answered him with honesty. "I believe it was my true will that brought me back."

The magister grinned at her. "That sounds like something Sarah would say. In any case...I'm glad that you're here, regardless of whether or not you're Sarah. I just want to set the record straight on that one. You're truly a credit to this Clan. Never forget it. Just one thing," he added.

"Yes?"

"Typically we look to our Sires to dispense wisdom, and there's an unspoken hierarchy there. We look to them as our mentors and guides. Regardless of your relationship with yours, he's still your Sire. When he orders you to do something, listen next time—or that next time may be your last."

Amanda looked at him, feeling sheepish. "I guess I hadn't thought of that."

"No, nor would I otherwise have expected you to. Just a small piece of advice from your magister."

She nodded. "Okay."

Lynne snorted. James gave her a look. "Do you have anything to add for yourself, Asherael?" She shook her head in response. "Good. All right, Lyrael, let's get moving on that spell, shall we?"

* * * *

The spell, complete with minor adjustments, surprised her with its easiness to put into place—but Amanda had at this point the assistance of the members of the Inner Circle of Clan Gladius to help her out. And for that, she was rather grateful. This was a very complicated spell, and since it affected them all, there was no way to perform it without either their consent or their assistance.

After the rest had gone back inside the Sanctuary, Jesse remained outside with Amanda, who admired their handiwork. The combination of the shielding from the sun during the day with the protection against their enemies was nothing short of sheer genius, and she hoped it would genuinely work and help protect the Clan.

Amanda thought of Stacy, who had minor injuries after the incident with the Golden Cross and she was thankful that she had recovered fast from them. Merideth demonstrated talents beyond bookkeeping and served as an excellent healer using nothing but her own magick. She wondered what else the librarian had up her sleeve—besides numerous chocolate mints, that is.

"Penny for your thoughts," offered Jesse.

Amanda just smiled at him. "I was just thinking that I'm glad everything went so well."

He smiled. "Me too."

An awkward silence lingered between them. The wind blew, and she smelled his skin combined with the aroma of his leather jacket. Her stomach tightened with lust. She had missed him a great deal and wasn't about to deny it.

No time like the present, perhaps, to let him know about her realization.

"Jesse?" she queried. She felt as she did when she had first met him—innocent, quiet, and uncertain.

He glanced at her. "Yeah?"

"There's something I need to tell you."

He inhaled with great deliberateness and let it out. The magister wasn't around to see him anyhow, so who cared?

"Amanda, when a woman says that to a man, it usually means he's about to receive the shaft." He sounded wary, and underneath it all she detected a good deal of pain. "I really hope that's not your intention."

"No—gods no," she protested. "If anything, I need to apologize to you."

Jesse blinked hard. "Apologize for what?"

"I didn't realize it for a while, but...I think I've been resenting you this whole time for dragging me into this world. And that wasn't fair of me, for many reasons." She went on in a hurry, "It wasn't just that I had chosen it before I was born. I really do like it here. The people here are wonderful, and I have opportunities here that I never would've had if I'd stayed by my lonesome in NYU—opportunities to be who I really am.

"And...I don't think I've ever expressed any gratitude to you for that and I think I did you a big disservice as a result."

Before Amanda knew it, he enveloped her in a passionate hug.

"Amanda, what you went through, absolutely everyone here did before you—including myself." His voice was husky, and she could barely hear him. "Most people don't even get over resenting their Sires until maybe Third Degree. And some never do."

She put her arms around him and clung to him, not knowing what else to say.

"Our relationship isn't perfect, and I don't ever expect it to be—but one thing I never wanted was to lose you—ever. I already had to go through that once, and...it was hell."

Amanda blinked away blood-tears as it suddenly hit her—Jesse had been a pain in the ass to her upon her arrival out of fear, fear of her getting hurt or worse. Even his attempts to control her life were all a part of that. She grimaced. It wasn't that she could entirely excuse him or his behavior—after all, he hadn't been the best at communicating to her a great many things. But she wasn't entirely blameless, either.

"So...what you're saying is that this relationship needs work," she stated, her voice sounding hollow to her ears.

She heard him laugh against her shoulder. "All relationships do. And for the record," he added, pulling away from her just enough so he could look her in the eye, "I think you enjoyed going after me with that knife a liiiiittle too much."

Her face warmed. *Guess vampires can blush after all,* she thought with amusement.

"I also want to say that Janius is right. You need to think about the advice he gave you." He let go of her and shoved his hands into his pockets. "You need to learn how to trust me more. But you were right," he amended, "I need to trust you too. You're right about that."

"We suck at this, don't we?" Realizing what she'd just said, she half snorted, half giggled. "Um, well, in a manner of speaking."

He gazed at her for a long while, his face serious. "Having a relationship with your Sire isn't frowned upon, exactly, but it typically is discouraged—and I'm starting to see why."

She blinked at him. "But you had one with me before, when I was Sarah—what's so different now?"

"You, for starters. And me." He kicked a pebble on the ground.

"Well, I'm—I'm willing to work at this if you are."

He smiled at her. "I'm glad to hear that."

"And I promise not to go after you with a knife again," she offered.

He chuckled, a pleasant, rich sound that filled her ears and made her think of all sorts of delightful and sensual things to do with him when they were back inside.

"I don't know—I found it kinda hot, actually," he admitted, giving her a sidelong glance. The look in his eyes told her everything she needed to know at that moment...and then some.

She licked her dry lips. "We should um, probably go inside. It's getting late, after all."

"Not a bad idea," he agreed.

"I mean, we could talk more in there—"

"I have a better idea," he interrupted, and with great agility, had her up against the door of the building, silencing her with a kiss that shattered her remaining resistance to him. As the kiss deepened, she grew wet, and her insides ached with desire.

I think it's been too long, she stated matter-of-factly, choosing the telepathic route as her mouth was otherwise occupied.

I would agree.

Chapter Thirty-Seven

To Bear the Double-Edged Sword

As she lay in bed, savoring the feel of Jesse's hands as they moved their way slowly along the insides of her thighs, Amanda had lost all memory of why she had been upset with him to begin with. Everything prior to that moment seemed absurd, and in the sweet intoxication of his fingers, nothing else mattered.

With a flick of his tongue on her clit and the insertion of his fingers, her body spasmed as a powerful orgasm ripped away her ability to think.

It also ripped away her shields, the precious shields she had cultivated in order to not deal with the full effects of the Blood Bond she shared with Jesse. His energy slammed into her full force. Had she been human, the breath would've been knocked from out of her.

"Jesse, you did that on purpose."

He didn't answer, but continued to flex his fingers inside of her, producing myriad intense sensations. It wasn't long before the room had gone white; her head jerked back as the second wave of euphoria hit her.

I often find the Bond is actually...helpful in bed. His voice in her mind was a sensual delight, and she found herself getting lost in the sound.

Yes, in bed, she retorted, trying desperately to bring her mind back to awareness and not succeeding. *But what do I do after this?*

Enjoy it. His tongue did deliciously evil things to the sensitive folds between her legs and to the tiny, swollen bud which now ached for release.

Amanda could barely think in return, *But I...I like my space....*

Space is overrated.

And I like...having my thoughts to myself....

Suddenly a crescendo of ecstasy swallowed up the rest of her speech, and she was relentlessly hit with wave after wave of unbearable pleasure.

And you like being stubborn.

Her hands gripped the sheets on her bed, and she finally let go and allowed the sensations to wash over her. She was still floating somewhere in some nameless space when Jesse's lips kissed hers.

I love you too, were his only words, uttered gently and affectionately before she drifted off to sleep.

* * * *

Through the darkness of the blindfold, Amanda could see nothing—only the sounds of faint footsteps were her indication that anyone was nearby. Following her prior instructions, she knocked on the door, relieved that the rapping of her knuckles was loud and sure in spite of her hands shaking.

"Who wishes to enter the hall of the Mysteries?"

The young vampire recognized the voice as belonging to James. Clearing her throat, she replied, "I do."

Silence.

"Your name, if you will, Apprentice."

"Lyrael."

She heard the door creak open and shortly afterwards someone took her hand and carefully led her into the room. The hand was small but the grip was strong.

"Follow me," a female voice said. Lynne.

Amanda slowly moved forward, wondering who was present for her First Degree initiation. She knew only the Firsts and above could attend, obviously, but who was available and willing was another question entirely. A familiar energy brushed across her consciousness, and her barely conscious question had been answered—Jesse was indeed present in the room.

She smiled. Knowing he was there was one thing, but being able to feel it was another level of knowing that she could admit to enjoying.

Maybe he was right about some things, after all.

Taking a deep breath, she continued walking forward until a slight pressure on her hand and a whispered command told her to stop.

"Lyrael," James's voice boomed, "do you come here of your own free will?"

"Yes, I do." Her voice sprang from her lips, sounding both calm and sure in her ears.

"And do you solemnly swear to keep silent and sacred whatever you partake of in this room, as you did in your prior initiation?"

"Yes, yes I do."

"Very well," the magister responded. "Before we begin, I must ask of you one question."

Amanda fought to keep from biting her lip. "Yes?"

"What does it mean to you to be a bearer of the double-edged sword?"

She racked her brain, the pain of the quiet in the room bearing down on her as she thought.

Perhaps sensing her anxiousness, James stated firmly, "Take your time. We have all night if need be."

Double-edged sword. Concepts she had meditated on previously floated into her mind. "It means...it means balance, balance between mercy and severity. To temper one's nature between two extremes and use them both as a spiritual guide and to ride the middle road."

His nod was almost audible. "Go on," he encouraged her.

"It means to be both a part of order and chaos, peace and passion, freedom and restriction. Or more accurately," she added as an afterthought, "freedom and discipline."

"Freedom and discipline." A questioning note edged his voice, and Lyrael found herself answering it.

"Freedom cannot exist without discipline in order to focus one's will. Nor can one have discipline without the freedom to perform one's will."

"Right you are, Apprentice. And very insightful. I see that you have truly grasped what it means to wield the double-edged sword."

A slight pause before he continued with, "On behalf of Clan Gladius, I welcome you as a First Degree in *Ordo Draconis et Rosae*. Asherael, please remove the new First's blindfold."

Abruptly, many candles, faces, and people in robes assaulted Amanda's eyes.

"Hold out your left hand, please."

Without thinking, she did so. A sudden, sharp pain pricked the center of her palm. She glanced down. Blood trickled over the lines on her hand. Amanda blinked. She hadn't even seen James move, let alone put any sharp objects near her skin.

"Quicker than the eye, the sword can cut." James produced a small, shiny dagger, its tip marred with her blood.

The young vampire watched silently as he placed a few drops of her blood with the dagger onto a petite, black glass mirror on the altar in the center of the room.

"Amaltheia, if you please, I would like for you to scry for us."

"Certainly, Magister."

Amanda watched the elfish vampire bounce into the center of the room towards the altar and fix her gaze upon the mirror. The magister's eyes seemed to gleam with amusement, and he handed her a pad and pen. She took it eagerly, although the mirror continued to hold her eyes firmly in place. Furiously scribbling, a few moments, or perhaps minutes, went by until she lifted her head with a nod and a grin.

"Magister, I see a First with much potential," beamed Merideth.

James smiled slightly. "More information, if you will, Amaltheia?"

"Certainly, Magister. I see roses, red roses everywhere. She is a red rose. She came here as a bud and she has blossomed and continues to grow. I also see...," she glanced through her notes hurriedly, "a shining light in the center of the rose, almost like a cross. An equal-armed cross," she added.

James laughed. "A Rosicrucian vampire. Well, we've certainly had worse. Interesting that the cross is inside the rose and not the other way around," he remarked thoughtfully.

In the time it took Amanda to blink, the magister was beside her, pinning something to her ceremonial robe. Once again, she hadn't even seen him move. It was the first time she had observed such odd behavior from him and knew he had to be using some special powers. Why hadn't she noticed him use such abilities before?

As if in response to her thoughts, he informed her, "As a First, you will be privy to information and teachings which you haven't before. Some of the legends about vampires are true, some are only symbolically true, and some are downright rubbish. As a First in our Clan and in this Order, you will learn to separate fact from fiction and also learn how to use these powers for yourself for the betterment of yourself and this Order."

She glanced down. On her robe was a pin in the form of a sword pointed upwards. Between the hilt and the blade was a red gem.

"This is the symbol of our Clan. Wear it well and proudly."

* * * *

Hours later, Amanda spent a good deal of time talking to the other Clan members, drinking blood-wine, and pondering the teachings she had been given during the rest of her initiation into the first degree. She had no idea how the blood managed to not congeal in the wine and figured it was another occult secret. Maybe the magister would tell her once the after-party was over.

Lynne had just left to get some more blood-wine, leaving her lost to her thoughts, when a warm hand was placed on her shoulder. She didn't have to turn around in order to know who it was.

"After this party is over, do you think we can get together?" Jesse asked her quietly.

She turned to face him. Her eyes met his, and at once she was assaulted with a million intense emotions, all of them frenzying inside of her chest. "I'm glad you were here," she told him gratefully.

He just gave her a look. "I never would've missed your initiation, Amanda. Even if I were still trapped in New Orleans, I would've flown up for it. Honest."

She smiled at him, wondering if she would ever get rid of the feeling that her chest would either explode or implode from being around his energy, or if it was just a natural side effect of the force of the Blood Bond. "Regardless, I wanted to thank you. It means a lot to me for you to be here."

Jesse picked up her hands and pressed them together in a gentle but firm grip. He stated, "I wouldn't ask of you what you cannot give. Or do not want to give." He gestured to her slave-bracelet, which she wore even for her initiation.

Her teeth clenched together, and it took her a great deal of effort to force out the next words from her mouth. "I don't know what you want from me—"

"Yes, you do," he replied softly.

Her insides involuntarily twitched at his tone, and she was certain it was not a negative reaction. Amanda was about to sigh in frustration when Jesse put a finger over her lips.

"The magister hates that," he reminded her, his voice still gentle. "You're a First now. You've long gone past the human realm."

Amanda would've preferred it if he were yelling at her. "Jesse," she began, but it was a mistake. Her lips brushed against his finger as she spoke, sending little earthquakes up and down her spine. When he withdrew his hand, she wasn't ungrateful.

"Jesse, I love you. You love me. Why do you have to make things more complicated?" She couldn't keep the exasperated tone out of her voice, which struggled to get past the tightness in her throat and chest. Just standing in front of him drove her crazy.

He pressed his lips against her forehead before leaning forward to rest his head on hers. "You haven't had a chance to meditate on things yet, have you?"

His breathy whisper reminded her of ocean winds. She could only shake her head in response.

"You will soon, I hope?"

She nodded.

"Good." He bent his head to brush her lips with the silkiest of touches with his own. "Go have fun. I don't want to spoil your evening."

Before she completely withdrew from his embrace, Amanda brushed his face with her slave-bracelet-clad hand. "You haven't," she informed him with a smile.

* * * *

After finishing her blood-wine, Amanda decided to go outside of the Sanctuary for some fresh air and found herself wandering into the nearby park, staring up at the sky.

The moon was full that night, and its silver light beckoned to her. With it she felt the promise of the end of autumn and the beginnings of winter; the air was cool but she had upped the temperature of the surrounding layer of air over her skin to compensate. Her magick grew stronger daily, and for that she was thankful.

Something about the silver of the moon as she stood there continued to catch her eye, and she fell deep into thought, remembering her words to the magister earlier. Beneath this moon was a sense of freedom which struck her. She could do anything, be anything, have anything she wanted. This life—this unlife, as the rest of the Clan referred to it—offered her so much, and she had shunned it due to so little. She looked forward to rejoining the dayside world and continuing her college degree at night.

The blackness of the night sky stood against what stars she could make out with the streetlights, and the light of the moon shone down on her in promise. She realized then with a calm but startling clarity that she loved her new life, loved who she was—and nothing and no one could possibly take what she was from her. Who she was had nothing to do with her memories, her name, her abilities, or the people around her—it was what she chose to do with them. She didn't have to be Sarah again, or Lyrael, or "Jesse's girl"—she was entirely her own person.

Under that moonlit night sky and in the presence of her gods, she was home.

Epilogue

A few hours before dawn, the initiate of the Order of the Golden Cross awoke. Blinking wearily at his surroundings, he concluded that his final prayers to God had indeed been answered.

He was alive.

Going over the last events in his mind, he realized that the young woman whom he had struck down with his spell had cast one of her own, knocking him and his brethren unconscious in the process.

Not dead, he thought. *Just unconscious.* Perhaps the intent had been to keep them all for food. All that he knew was he was tied in a rather clumsy fashion to a chair in the middle of a room.

Come on, Custos Morum, he thought, addressing himself by his initiatory motto: "Guardian of morals." *Think. What can you do to get out of here alive?*

It was clear he was being held, most likely in order to gain information. His life may or may not be spared, but he certainly wasn't planning on telling them the truth—that the people who came in to attack the Sanctuary were testing their defenses and had gone in with full knowledge that it meant their death. He was supposed to use a special device to escape from the battle undetected and report on his findings.

Guess that didn't go according to plan, he thought with wry amusement. Now what? He was trapped in the unholy one's headquarters, by the grace of God...and perhaps a token of mercy, of all things, from a female vampire.

When I get out of here, I will have to make mention of her, he mused. *Her end should be painless and merciful, unless we can find a way to reverse her condition.*

If they could capture her and obtain blood samples, it was possible for their scientists to research ways of controlling her vampirism—maybe even bringing her back to God as a result. Tom Harker, better known to *Ordo Aurae Crucis* as Brother Custos Morum, had long argued in favor of such research. If they could be turned back versus killed, wouldn't that be a better service for the greater glory of Adonai?

But he knew in his heart of hearts that their evil condition was most likely irreversible—as did his brothers and sisters of the Order—and their best and only option was to send them back to the Lord for redemption.

With his hands still tied to the chair, he moved his fingers over a special ring he wore. *This is a most dangerous idea, but I must do this. I must report on my findings and succeed in my mission.*

A few quick prayers were made, and he placed his focus on the ring, willing it to obey his commands. The enchantments still held, and within a matter of moments he grew lighter, his vision fuzzier.

* * * *

When Merideth came to the room later to check up on the prisoner, she saw that he had vanished without a trace.

Adrianne Brennan

Adrianne Brennan stumbled into her love of writing by accident at the tender age of ten when she was given a creative writing assignment for her science class. The end result was her writing a brief science fiction comedy featuring numerous puns regarding vegetables. Once the writing bug bit, it bit pretty hard, and from the age of fourteen onwards she worked on a lengthy fantasy novel.

At this time, this fantasy novel is still a work in progress as she continues to focus on her other works. In addition, she is a member of the Romance Writer's of America , EPIC, Infinite Worlds of Fantasy Authors, the Midnight Seductions Authors group, and is an alumnus member of Kappa Gamma Psi, a co-ed national professional performing arts fraternity.

An avid reader, Adrianne has been most influenced by various science fiction and fantasy authors including Madeleine L'Engle, Roger Zelazny, Laurell K. Hamilton, LA Banks, Yasmine Galenorn, Michael Ende, Neil Gaiman, and Alan Moore. Like her main character from *Blood of the Dark Moon*, she professes a love for Iamblichus and Greek philosophy.

The author resides in Boston, Massachusetts with two cats and a car she has aptly named "the TARDIS." She assures her readers that people tell her it looks bigger on the inside.

Excerpt from

Blood and Mint Chocolates

by

Adrianne Brennan

A rather generous gift from one of her students sat on Merideth's desk in her office within the Sanctuary's library, begging to be enjoyed in many different and most sinful ways. She sampled it eagerly: rich, dark heaven with echoes of mint in just the right places.

Oh, how she loved chocolate mints. And these Godiva dark chocolate ones embodied the definition of "exquisite."

Closing her eyes in ecstasy, she sank back into her chair and savored the taste. How fresh the taste of mint, and how decadent the chocolate. For a moment, she let her mind wander back to the days of her mortal youth. Merideth never had the privilege to have such indulgences in those days, and she refused to allow herself to be any less deprived as a vampire.

Why should immortality restrict one from such delights?

A knock came at the door. "Amaltheia? Are you there?"

Oh, shit. Janius. With great haste, Merideth stashed the rest of the sweets in the desk drawer. She didn't want to let the magister know about her addiction to mint chocolates and be forced to submit to his stern lectures on "maintaining vampiric purity" and the necessity of alchemical transformation through transcending physical needs typically ascribed to humans.

Blah blah, no longer human, we're above that nonsense, blah blah blah.... "Sure—come in, Magister."

The door opened, and the magister briskly walked in and closed it behind him. Merideth gazed warily upon Clan Gladius's leader. Janius earned his magister title on numerous occasions with his stern, albeit gentle guidance. Being the founder and head of the Clan, a fairly prestigious reputation within the magickal order of *Ordo Draconis et Rosae*—also known as the Order of the Dragon of the Rose—preceded him. She respected Janius a great deal and thought well of him. However, in spite of the fact that the two of them shared a strong friendship and had worked together as fellow magicians for decades—Janius often called her "the Clan's favorite librarian"—Merideth thought little of his stuffy and pretentious demeanor, but she kept her opinion to herself. Sometimes she wished she belonged to another Clan within the Order. Perhaps Clan Corvus in New Orleans, or even Clan Diamhair Aingeal in Boston. Both lacked the taciturn nature which embodied the character of Clan Gladius.

And neither, as far as she knew, upheld the ideas of vampiric purity by the letter of the law as much as its spirit.

"Hello, Merideth," he greeted her, addressing her by her real name versus Amaltheia, the one given to her by Clan Gladius as her Order name. Dropping the formality relieved her of any notion that the magister sought her out for any negative reason, and she was thankful for it. Only those who knew her well called her Merideth, and her closest friends called her Meri for short. "I hope that I have not caught you at a bad moment?"

The elfish vampire was all sweetness with her smile, all the while praying that bits of chocolate didn't show on her teeth. "Of course not, James," she replied, dropping the customary Order tradition in return. They were behind closed doors, after all.

"Excellent. Merideth, you've been working hard keeping the Sanctuary's library the way it is, and I notice you haven't taken any time off recently."

She blinked at him. "Time off, James?"

"Well," he shuffled his feet, "I notice you go on occasion with Theodotos to play darts in the common room, but you could use some time away from the library. As much as we know you like it here."

Blood have mercy. "James, I love it here—you know that. Do you have the impression that I'm unhappy or something?"

The magister laughed. "Meri, don't be silly. You're a workaholic like the rest of us, and while some of us have our ways of managing time off, I thought that you alone could use a special...respite."

She fought down a smirk. Workaholic, indeed—James was certainly one to talk! When did he ever take a vacation? *Had* he ever taken a vacation? But she bit her tongue in her customary fashion.

"Me, James?"

"Yes, you." He placed an envelope face down on the desk in front of her, and she stared at it curiously as if it might leap up and bite her. She hesitated and raised an eyebrow at him.

"Plane tickets to Hotel Paradisio on Crystal Island. The flight will arrive at the airport near the resort, and an escort will be there to take you to your hotel well before sunrise."

Merideth began to sputter. Never in her wildest dreams did she ever imagine that the magister would ever present her with such a gift. She would've been grateful just for the license to take the night off and attend an event at a nearby blues club with Asharael and Lyrael. "James, this is so...," she fought for a word adequate enough to describe how she felt, "frivolous. I just can't—"

He raised an eyebrow at her in an echo of her previous gesture. "You're allowed to indulge yourself every now and again, Meri. Moderation and all that, you know. Oh, and by the way," he added, "remember not to overindulge too much. You're among humans but not of them. Enjoy some alcohol, but stay away from those silly confections."

Grateful blood-tears filled her eyes. "I...I don't know what to say, James."

Her head swam. A hotel resort on a beautiful island. Granted, it'd take more than a few light spells to allow her even an hour's comfort in the sun, but surely the nightlife must be sultry, grand—exquisite like her dark chocolate mints.

"Say 'Thank you, James'. Then get on that flight and have a good time."

"Thank you, James," she mumbled, her voice not much louder than a whisper. What would she wear? What should she take? What would she do while she stayed at this hotel? But above all of her concerns she felt an enormous sense of gratitude. This generous time off touched her more than she could possibly express to James.

"You're welcome. Consider it a thank you from the rest of the Inner Circle for all of your hard work well done. Have fun!" With a big, almost goofy grin, he left her office.

Merideth stared at the door in disbelief, a blood-tear finally coursing down her cheek.

LaVergne, TN USA
15 August 2010
193366LV00009B/33/P

9 781936 222070